Carpathian Starscape

Maria L. L. DeWillow

Psy Fantasy Crusades

Book 2

DEDICATION

For my military sisters and brothers. Thanks for your support over my twenty-one years of service, and may the wild adventures continue.
'Til Valhalla.

&

To the Top-Secret Squirrel Society of Successful Authors, who consistently write the phrase, "He/she released a breath he/she didn't know he'd/she'd been holding," in their best-selling novels. This one is for you. I have hidden the sacred phrase somewhere within these pages. Please accept the offering, welcome me as your sister, and bless this story with many readers.

CONTENTS

AUTHOR'S NOTE

My writing may contain triggers. This book is for mature readers. Read responsibly.

Playlist

☙

"Space Queen" - 10Speed

"Fancy" - Reba McEntire

"Toxicity" - System of a Down

"Bullet with Butterfly Wings" - The Smashing Pumpkins

"Faerie Raide" - Grim Faeries

"Separate Ways" - Journey

"Last Kiss" - Pearl Jam

"Love You Madly" - Cake

"Moon Trance" - Lindsey Stirling

"Lose Control" - Teddy Swims

"Amor Prohibido" - Selena

"Magic Dance" - David Bowie

"Possum Kingdom" - Toadies

"The Stranger" - Billy Joel

"Come To My Window" - Melissa Etheridge

"So Far Away" - Avenged Sevenfold

"Get It While You Can" - Janis Joplin

"If You Could Read My Mind" - Gordon Lightfoot

"Dreams" - The Cranberries

"Kiss Me Deadly" - Lita Ford

"Purple" - Pop Evil

"How It Feels to Be Lost" - Sleeping With Sirens

"Try" - Pink

"Ray of Light" - Madonna

"Battle Without Honor or Humanity" - Tomoyasu Hotei

"Take Me to Church" - Hozier

"Magic Man" - Heart

☙

PROLOGUE: CONSTELLATION EDEN

On a high rocky overhang, Robin perched with his bare toes gripping the cold, jagged edge. The fae king watched Adam emerge from a tunnel and into the main cave with his battle-weary tribe. He didn't need to wonder about Eve's fate. The stench of her death surrounded them, and Robin sensed her residual power lingering as their auras absorbed it.

His gaze followed their somber procession through rays of moonlight that beamed past the entrance, the dim light cutting irregular holes through the cave's shroud of darkness. His growing heartbreak for his lost lover smoldered within his heart and his mind before it burst into incendiary hatred for the Children of Eden.

Adam, Duncan, Trent, Hayden, and Ty halted just within the cave's entrance. They hurled their torches onto the ground and huddled around to wait while Hayden burned them into ashes. Their eyes remained focused on the flames, but their minds were still stuck in the holy place.

"That was Gaia? We saw Gaia's light?" Ty asked. "All I know is I woke up, and it was there, and I couldn't look away. It was . . ."

Ty never found words to describe it, and his last word lingered on an echo through the stone walls.

"Yes," Adam stated.

"I saw Adonai's light as he left the Green Earth as well," said Trent. "I never thought—I didn't know—we could see their spirits like that."

Nobody responded to Trent's statement. He shifted on his

1

feet and looked up from the fire, glancing around at each man standing with him. After a moment, Adam raised his head to meet Trent's gaze. As the flames flashed in Adam's eyes, it reminded Trent of Adonai's golden glow, and he shivered.

Still looking down, Duncan said, "Our old legends said seeing the gods' spirits is a step forward on the road to enlightenment."

Adam turned away from the fire and the circle of witches, and breathing into the dark, he whispered, "Indeed. And now they're gone. Perhaps for another five millennia."

Robin remained above the witches, savoring the fragrant smoke as it swirled around him and saturated his cloak. He'd always had the power to see the gods' spirits and didn't like hearing his enemies had gained that power. He wondered what else had changed for them and waited to hear more.

As the fire turned to subtle red embers, Trent and Ty started absent-mindedly kicking dirt over the dimming ashes.

Instead of using his power to cool the ashes quickly, Hayden watched them. His shock from witnessing divinity and bloodshed waned as his distrust for Adam reemerged into the forefront of his mind.

"Mr. Godwine," Hayden stated and waited for Adam to turn and acknowledge him.

Adam faced his descendants and asked, "What is it, Mr. Rosemont?"

Hayden's tone was loud and defiant as he asked, "What's next for us? Can my family go back to our lives?"

Adam patiently explained, "We must find the tapestry, but for the most part, you can go back to your life, of course."

"Why do we have to find it?" Hayden asked. "The Edenians

obviously know their way around without it."

Duncan interjected, "It's a priceless relic with immeasurable primal magical power, Hayden! It maps out far more paths than the Edenians regularly travel or know by heart. Of course we must find it . . . before someone else does."

"And what if Eve left it in the fae realm?" Trent asked.

Far above them in the shadows, Robin's breathing intensified. He glared at the top of Trent's head, willing himself not to growl or do anything to give himself away. Leaning closer in anticipation of Adam's answer, Robin almost slipped over the edge of his perch when Adam began walking past the cave's threshold to stand under the open sky.

"Then we'll find the fae realm," Adam replied. "Nothing stays hidden forever."

Once clear of the stone dome and supernatural interference, the witches stopped and checked their communication devices, and Lilith's sleek spacecraft approached on the horizon. Knowing the Edenians would sense his presence once they were close enough, Robin disappeared with a snap.

— — —

The Emerald Keep quaked when Robin appeared on his throne, already screaming and cursing into the empty throne room. Grinding his teeth with each forced word, spit flew from his mouth and glistened on his lips. He paced and raged until he was red in the face and tears rimmed his bloodshot eyes. Tremors continued to roll through the keep with each step he took.

When his guards flooded into the room, he blasted them with magic. His subjects fell and were paralyzed on their backs all around him while glass shattered from every window lining the great, long chamber.

His wits deserted him so completely that he dashed around

the castle on foot instead of snapping directly into different rooms. His movements were erratic and clumsy. Stumbling into his study, he clutched the tapestry with both hands and raised it high in front of him.

Lifting his voice in passionate prayer, he shouted, "Mighty Gaia! Hear me! Do not let your exquisite tapestry fall into Adam Godwine's inferior hands! Let me protect and shelter it here in my vault of treasures! I promise I dare not wield your awesome power, but I seek to keep it from my enemies! Bless me in this purpose! May you see fit to make it so, Supreme Mother!"

He hastily folded the soft relic into Eve's wool and leather satchel and hugged it to his chest. The satchel still smelled like her, so Robin took a deep breath and savored her scent. He then thought about how far it was from his private rooms to the sub dungeon and finally remembered to snap himself directly there.

Appearing in front of his vault, Robin dismissed the guards there with a wave of his hand before making a series of traces with his fingers against the door. The antique titanium door rumbled as it swung open to reveal priceless treasures long lost from the Blue Earth, the Green Earth, and the Red Earth.

WITCH TRIAL

Phoebe's face remained stoic as she sat in front of the other voting members of the Faithful Watchtower Cabal. Her pride and her guile kept her composed amid embarrassment and potential ruin at the hands of her own people. She was on trial for murdering her disgusting great-aunt, and the worst part about the whole situation was that she didn't kill the old hag. She'd always dreamed of looking her childhood abuser in the eyes while slitting her rotten throat, but someone had robbed her of that dream.

Although her facial expression showed little emotion, her body language betrayed an impatience with the proceedings and hinted at the anger stewing beneath a cool façade. Her index finger tapped against her chair's wooden arm at an even, medium tempo, telling everyone they were wasting her time. Although she sat with a serene posture, she crossed her legs and angled her body away from the voting jury as much as possible.

"Now that we've heard facts from the crime scene," Ty stated, "I'll ask you to make a statement in your defense . . . Chloe Phoebe Rosemont Astor, explain your involvement in the murder of Scarlet Rose Reilly. Explain using your magical gift against her."

"I didn't kill Aunty Rose," Phoebe said in a growling whisper, "but if I had killed her, everyone here knows she had it coming, so—"

"Cut the bullshit flippant act, Phoebe," Trent interrupted. "This is your life on the line."

As quick as a flash, Phoebe uncrossed her legs, slammed her heels down on the stone floor, and faced the jury directly. She dug her nails into the armrests and took only a short moment to breathe before spewing a vehement response at her former lover. She knew she'd cracked but didn't care.

"Just because you've fucked me doesn't mean you know my life!" Phoebe spat as she pointed at Trent.

The room remained quiet. Phoebe had the floor, and none of the witches wanted to be there. Danielle's eyes were a bit too shiny, holding back tears. Trent wished he could disappear. Leilani kept her head lowered to her glass tablet, perusing the evidence repeatedly. Jeremy sat in the jury, but his focus was across the room with a sobbing Giselle. None of them wanted to put their fellow witch through a trial, but they had made rules and agreed to them. Procedures had to be followed if they were to grow into an established society of their own.

"You don't know what it is to be me. Killing her would have been an answered prayer. It would have quenched the nightmares I have of her locking me in a brothel as girl—just a girl! While nobody—not even Adam—could have her prosecuted for it. And now you put me on trial because a monster is dead? How dare you? All of you!"

"That's enough," Adam said sternly. "Everyone in this room loves you, Phoebe."

"Then why are you humiliating me with this farce of a trial?" Phoebe retorted. "She was garbage and she's dead, so what?"

"Because we agreed to a system," Ty said. "Lawlessness among our kind didn't work. It wasn't right or fair. It needed to stop, so here we are."

Phoebe laughed. "And this is fair?"

"She was killed with magic. You're the only witch with a motive, and nobody can say where you were last night," Ty explained. "Everyone else with the power to kill with magic has an alibi. Really, that's the only reason we all agreed to have this meeting. We didn't come to the decision lightly."

"Then my only crime is a lonely night," Phoebe replied,

waxing faux dramatic. "Empty nest. Partner out of town. Lover visiting her son. What's a lady to do?"

Phoebe rubbed her temples, willing herself to calm down and reason her way out of the situation. She knew the rules, but they weren't supposed to protect the guilty like the normie laws did. She could hear Giselle whimpering somewhere in the small audience area behind her and tried to concentrate on a way to prove her innocence.

Danielle said, "Everyone's not convinced of your guilt. We want to work this out for the best. There's no city or private surveillance footage of you in Astoria last night. You went into the city—okay, sure. However, there's no evidence to suggest you left Manhattan after arriving in the afternoon. I, for one, would vote in your favor based on that alone."

Scrolling through his tablet, Adam added, "I don't see anything here that convinces me beyond a reasonable doubt either, but we need your testimony, we need to hear the evidence, and we need everyone's input and vote."

"But who else could have done it?" Leilani asked.

From the back of the room, a calm voice said, "It wasn't a witch."

The jury looked past Phoebe as she turned to look behind her at the person speaking.

It was Sylvia.

Ruby and Duncan flanked Sylvia as they approached Phoebe's chair, and all three of them stood firmly behind the accused. The jury held their peace and stared at Sylvia.

"I listened to the residual magic radiating from the body," Sylvia said, "and it was a strange frequency. I think I've heard it before, but I can't remember where. I can say for certain it wasn't

Phoebe's magic or any witch's magic I've ever heard."

When Danielle hadn't been able to get answers by reading the objects that were on or near Scarlet Rose when she died, Ruby had called Sylvia and explained the dire circumstances unfolding in New York, convincing her to travel quickly from Central Europe. Ruby had then taken her to Scarlet Rose's home before continuing to the private mortuary where they'd had the body transferred earlier in the day. She'd been able to identify an obscure magical frequency within seconds of entering the cold room.

"We could all sense the magical damage, especially the way her internal organs were all destroyed," Adam explained. "It's consistent with an attack from one of us."

"It is similar, yet it is absolutely not the same," Sylvia replied.

Phoebe stood and asked, "Are we done here, Adam?"

Giselle ran into Phoebe's arms and embraced her dramatically. Phoebe swayed a bit but quickly caught her balance and returned the embrace. The mother loved her daughter and would endure anything for her, including Giselle's propensity for lamentation under any uncomfortable circumstances. Phoebe knew her growing headache was preferable to a murder charge, so she closed her eyes and took a deep breath.

Ruby saw Phoebe trying hard to mask her distaste for Giselle's prissy shrieking, so she threw her arms around both women and attempted to calm her best friend with reassuring whispers.

Adam gave them their moment before answering, "We need to finish discussing this properly. Phoebe's involvement may be ruled out, but we still need to piece together what we know and plan how to proceed with investigating what happened."

"Yes," Ty added. "We have other issues on the agenda as well."

Trent slammed his tablet on the table and looked at Danielle in hopes of gaining her as an ally for his objection, stating, "We can't expect Phoebe, or even Jeremy, to have their wits about them after this. Phoebe's ready to punch us all in the face, and Giselle is beside herself."

Danielle listened to Trent in earnest. When he mentioned Jeremy, she looked over his shoulder at the young man who was staring blankly at his distressed partner whimpering into his sister's ear.

"I agree," Danielle stated, and turned to Leilani. "We need to adjourn and give everyone the rest of the day to decompress . . . Leilani?"

"Yeah," Leilani said softly. "The moods in here are completely wrong. Even Adam and Ty aren't putting out healthy vibes right now. Adam is trying hard to hide it from me though."

Adam ignored Leilani's comment about him, but Ty replied, "If we're all feeling like shit right now, why don't you change it? Use your gift to lighten the mood in here so that we can move on with our important work."

"That's not a good idea," she answered. "I'm also affected by this situation, and with all of us needing a magical mood adjustment, it could go very wrong for me, or us."

With Leilani's input and Jeremy's silence, Adam knew they were done. He hadn't done anything wrong, but he still wanted to apologize to Phoebe. However, when she saw him looking at her and starting to speak, she shook her head as if warning him to keep quiet.

Adam nodded, turned to Ty, and said, "Get everything wrapped up here for the day. You and I will meet in my office before dinner. I'll get an update from the technicians now."

Ty and Adam were working with a team of their best

technicians, inventors, and scientists to develop a way to block the vampires from reading witches' thoughts. They'd been stalling the alliance negotiations for months in hopes of achieving a way to disable the one power vampires held that could really cripple the witches if negotiations failed.

The implant Joe had placed inside Eve was a sleek and safe design that he'd easily inserted into her spine, so Adam's think-tank had started with the idea of placing a similar device inside each witch closer to the brain. The basic idea was to repurpose the device as a signal jammer of sorts. It already contained a highly sophisticated transmitter and receiver, which was how Joe had been able to disable her remotely. However, what they needed the implant to do was much more complex, especially since the desired results would need to be continuous, meaning they needed to significantly adjust how it operated, and then ensure it operated consistently enough to keep the vampires out of their heads all the time.

Adam glanced at Sylvia as he left the room, thinking how much easier their path to success would be if he could leverage her power to recognize different magical frequencies. He couldn't risk Sylvia exposing their plans to Sorina, but perhaps he could find a way for her to help under the pretense of contributing to a different project.

Ruby and Giselle were flat on their backs and holding hands on a bed in Phoebe's hotel suite a few blocks down the street from Dust. Queen Mab, Phoebe's sleek gray cat, was kneading Ruby's chest with her claws. Because Ruby wore a thick sweatshirt, the cat's claws only poked through to sensitive skin sporadically. Both women watched the dainty paws lift and fall, waiting to see if Ruby could use Giselle's gift to persuade Queen Mab to sit down.

Ruby was finally beginning to test her syphoning power. She had felt safer suppressing that part of her magic from the night she discovered it until her world felt stable again following Eve's fall.

Borrowing Giselle's ability to communicate with animals, as a tool to train and control her magic, seemed to be a low-risk route that could yield a high reward.

"Ouch!" Ruby howled as her body twitched.

Giselle laughed, and Queen Mab stared at Ruby for a second before continuing to knead.

Ruby was surprised her yell didn't scare the cat into jumping to the floor or at least moving.

Ruby looked sideways at Giselle and asked, "You're telling her to keep doing this, aren't you?"

Giselle laughed again, but didn't answer the question.

"Oh, my stars, please tell her to stop," Ruby said while laughing.

"I'm not doing anything!" Giselle shouted. "Do it yourself!"

"Yes, you are!"

"No, I'm not!"

"You're making her not listen to me!"

"Ruby, you're failing all by yourself! You can't be perfect all the time."

"Fuck you!" Ruby laughed. "I know I'm not perfect. That's why I'm trying to talk to a cat."

"She's a good cat," Giselle explained, "but she can't tell you how to be perfect."

Ruby giggled, then squeezed Giselle's hand and took a deep breath. Queen Mab arched her back, stretching thoroughly. The cat walked across to Giselle's chest and turned around.

"I did it!" Ruby shouted.

"Oh, how impressive," Giselle said sarcastically, turning her face away from the furry tail swishing across her cheek. "She would have eventually put her asshole in my face anyway."

"Okay, let me try something else then," Ruby whispered.

"If she shits on me," Giselle whispered back, "there will be consequences."

Queen Mab jumped from the bed and dashed through the door to the sitting room. Ruby listened closely and heard Phoebe in the other room speaking softly to the cat. She let go of Giselle's hand and faced her, rolling onto her side and smiling.

"I think it worked," Ruby whispered.

Giselle lifted her head and looked towards the other room. "What did you do?" she asked.

"I compelled her go give Phoebe kisses," Ruby said. "I thought your mother could use some extra love tonight. Especially with your father still in Albany . . . with my mother."

Giselle noted Ruby's tone turned sour when she mentioned her mother and said, "You know Father and Faustina don't belong here in the middle of witches' business."

Faustina and Jameson didn't come with Phoebe on meeting days unless they had business or appointments in the city as well. The cabal had voted that only witches could attend meetings, so Phoebe always asked them to stay behind rather than having them stay in a small suite or apartment all day. Camilla Rosemont House was a much more comfortable place from which to work and live.

"She shouldn't be there," Ruby said.

Giselle asked, "Who are you to question what makes her happy or what's best for her when you won't see her or spend time with the family?"

"You know I'm taking time to unpack what happened, Giselle."

"You've had your time," Giselle argued. "Now it's time to heal with your family. I mean, you're living with the man who holds most of the blame for literally everything, so why is it still difficult to spend time with Faustina and Jeremy?"

"I need a few more weeks."

Ruby couldn't admit what they both knew. The difference between living in Adam's house and seeing her family was that she felt her father's absence deeply around her family. There were three of them instead of four; it was like a visible, gaping hole in the family tree.

"No, you don't," Giselle insisted. "You've been comfortable with your new life out at Sands Point, so you're avoiding home and family because you know those things will never be the same as they were before."

"You make it sound so cinematically tragic," Ruby said in a dull mumble.

Giselle shrugged. "I know you all think I'm dramatic, but you must admit it's appropriate right now, Ru. Or do you expect me to downplay your family trauma, like you do?"

"What do you expect me to do, Giselle?"

"You can start by coming by the loft tonight to see your brother," Giselle answered, and then paused to grapple with another thought before adding, "I was also hoping . . . you'd help me bring mine home."

"Hayden hates me."

"Hayden loves you."

"No, Hayden used to love me."

"No, Hayden still loves you, or he wouldn't be so hard on you."

"I'd rather go after your brother than face mine alone right now," Ruby admitted. "Maybe I'll talk to Trent and Adam about taking some time to travel alone. I can track down Hayden."

"Ru . . ." Giselle said, her voice trailing off with a sigh.

Giselle crossed her arms and put on a disappointed face. Queen Mab reappeared and seemed to be judging Ruby, too. The cat sat still and upright next to Giselle. They both kept looking at Ruby.

Ruby started to reply. "If Hayden comes back with me—"

"When! When he comes back with you," Giselle interrupted.

"Fine," Ruby said. "When he comes back with me, I'll talk to Mother and Jeremy. We'll all move on as family."

Giselle looked at Queen Mab, and the cat got up and rubbed against her best friend. She nodded and slid across the edge of the bed to sit closer to Ruby, hugging her before falling back onto the mattress with a loud sigh.

Giselle stated, "That's an acceptable compromise."

Leilani walked around the table, placing tablets in front of each cabal member in attendance. Along with asking their non-witch family members to stay at home, it was part of the security measures they'd voted into their covenants to have separate tablets that never left the headquarters and stayed on Adam's private network to protect their secrets. She hesitated when she reached Duncan and pulled a tablet from the bottom of the stack, flushing when she noticed he saw her give him a different tablet than the one everyone else received.

Duncan smiled and said, "It's okay. We understand."

Leilani looked around and asked, "Is Sylvia here?"

Duncan nodded. "She's with Adam and Ty. She's helping them experiment with cataloguing different magical frequencies."

Across the table, Phoebe looked skeptical and asked, "Why would she help them do that? It sounds like they're trying to artificially duplicate her gift."

Duncan shrugged. "So, what if they are?" he asked. "She's the only witch alive with her gift. If she dies, the gift dies with her."

"Maybe it should die with her," Phoebe argued. "She's a tracking device for all of us. It's a serious privacy issue."

"Agreed," Danielle interjected as she approached the table. "I love this new table, by the way. It's like we're knights in archaic European mythology."

A new table had arrived for their meeting room while they were adjourned the evening before. Adam had it commissioned to make each witch feel like their input was equally important while sitting at the round table and contributing to business such as meetings, votes, and elections. It was also practical, helping them all see each other easier.

Phoebe said, "I think that was the point, Dani. Adam wants us to forget he thinks he's better than us, but about tracking us—"

"That's not the purpose of what they're doing," Danielle interrupted, "but I think we should discuss specifically banning its use for tracking people."

"What's the primary purpose then?" Phoebe asked.

Leilani finished placing tablets around the table and took a seat next to Phoebe. She activated her tablet and swiped her finger up and around it a few times before showing Phoebe a file containing descriptions of all known magical objects across the universe.

Phoebe recognized the object Adam had used to call Lilith, and she recognized other objects by legend only. Descriptions of powerful jewelry and weapons filled the screen among other things. There was an entry for the missing tapestry map as well.

"If we can understand Sylvia's gift better, then we might be able to keep track of objects like these," Leilani explained.

Realizing something, Phoebe gasped and asked, "Can't Sylvia listen for the tapestry instead of us sending Ty all over the world looking for fae legends?"

Duncan answered, "No, that's not possible yet."

He and the ladies discussed Sylvia's gift. Her magical hearing not only depended on knowing what to listen for, but it also depended on active magic. She knew she could hear witches while they were using their powers, and she knew she could hear magic propagating through an object when it was being used for magic. Sometimes she couldn't hear anything if she was out of range of weaker magic. Adam was always easy for her to hear, but gifts that didn't require pushing out large amounts of raw energy were more difficult to hear over a distance. Giselle, Youngae, Bastion, and Danielle were especially difficult for Sylvia to hear from afar.

"Sometimes she hears things but can't recognize the sounds," Duncan explained. "When the Edenians arrived, she didn't know what she was hearing, but it was so loud."

"So, what if she listened for something like the Edenians?" Phoebe asked.

Duncan shook his head slightly. "The tapestry wasn't made in Eden, remember? But she does try to listen to and identify anything she can."

"Too bad she wasn't in the cave with us," Phoebe said. "If Gaia made the tapestry, she'd know what it sounds like."

Jeremy and Giselle entered the room as Phoebe was speaking and sat down next to each other. They'd recently made their partnership official, and they were preoccupied with the nameplate placed in front of Giselle's place at the table. The nameplate read, "Camilla Giselle Cohen Rosemont."

As he picked up his tablet and sorted through information, Jeremy asked, "Starting the meeting without us?"

Danielle adjusted her gloves. "Just having friendly conversation and getting caught up."

Sylvia appeared, smiling when her gaze found Duncan. She made her way to him as Ruby, Adam, Ty, and Trent walked in together right behind her.

The four of them were quietly discussing something as they took their seats next to each other. The others sensed tension between them. Ruby and Trent seemed to be arguing in whispers while she tried to ignore him in favor of setting up her tablet to record the meeting notes. Ty's look was solemn, but Adam's expression betrayed nothing.

"Good morning, brothers and sisters," said Ty. "I see everyone present at Dust is here at the table, so I declare the meeting officially open. In the matter of Scarlet Rose Reilly's murder, there is only one witch acquainted with her who is not in attendance—"

Phoebe and Giselle both interrupted Ty at the same time, Phoebe shouting about the cabal trying to frame another member of her family in his absence. Giselle was pleading Hayden's innocence, saying he was somewhere in the Mediterranean and couldn't have been involved.

Ty glanced to Leilani, and she smiled at Phoebe and Giselle.

They both calmed and held their peace for long enough for Ty to continue.

"Carolus Hayden Rosemont is not suspected of murder, but it is imperative we bring him here for questioning," Ty said. "As I said before, he's the only family member of the deceased who isn't here and has knowledge of magic. As we have no other leads, he must be asked if he knows anything. The investigation will remain open, but with no other leads, we will move to the next order of business pending a vote . . . All in favor?"

Phoebe watched as everyone in the voting jury raised their hands except for her and Trent. She figured that must have been what Ruby and Trent were arguing about. He looked like he wanted to say something.

"The vote passes majority, five to two," said Ty. "Dissenters, statements for the record?"

"I think we all know my thoughts," said Phoebe, "but I'd love to hear what Trent has to say."

Trent cleared his throat and stated, "Ruby asked me and Adam if we'd be comfortable with her going to find Hayden. I was. She asked for herself as a concerned friend and believes he'll feel overwhelmed if we send escorts with her. When Ty and Adam decided to use it as an opportunity to officially bring Hayden before the jury, I changed my mind. It could be dangerous." He looked to Adam.

Adam patiently explained, "I understand your concerns. Before she leaves, I'll spend a week training with her to improve her syphoning powers, so she has a strong self-defense option."

Ty paused a moment before continuing with the meeting. "If there are no other statements from the voting jury, do we have anyone else wishing to make a statement on the matter of Ms. Reilly's murder and bringing in Mr. Rosemont for questioning?"

Giselle glanced at her mother and then at Ruby before slowly raising her hand. Jeremy put his arm around her for encouragement.

"Yes, Ms. Rosemont?" asked Ty.

Giselle simply said, "My brother wouldn't hurt anyone here. He fought Eve for us, as did my mother. Thank you. That is all."

With that, the meeting moved on to discuss the matter of the tapestry. Since Ruby would be preparing to travel, Giselle and Danielle volunteered to help continue her research into Eve's past. Their best plan was still to trace her travels in hopes it would lead them to the fae. Ty's direct research into fae legends hadn't turned up any leads. Even though they couldn't be sure, the prevailing belief among them was the tapestry occupied the fae realm and needed to be reclaimed for Eden.

SECOND DARK AGES

Seville, Spain, Blue Earth, 2321 A.D.

Verity Paz, a seventeen-month-old baby girl, snoozed peacefully in her hand-carved maple wood crib. Excited to finally have a daughter in a family full of sons, her father and her grandfather had crafted the crib together during the three months leading up to her birth. It swayed smoothly and without the slightest sound as a warm Sevillian breeze swept through the open window, gently caressing Verity's skin and fine black hair.

The hand that rocked the cradle belonged to a Dust Companion. Several of the adult humanoid models were gaining popularity over smaller humanoid robots as consumers throughout the world needed nannies and housekeepers more than they needed the entertainment of watching artificial children grow. Even though all growing Companion models had unlimited storage and multiple household and office organizational applications, kittens were the bestsellers. Puppies ranked second best, followed by sloths. Consumers wanted pets more than they wanted to pay for extra humans in their houses who were too short to put away the dishes.

The Paz family had one such pet. A Companion puppy ran in the courtyard below the window with Verity's brothers. The little beagle kept the boys occupied while their mother tended the family garden. Their father wouldn't be back from the market for another hour, and Verity was expected to sleep until then. The Companion nanny started singing a soft lullaby to drown out the faint sounds of boys playing outside. Baby Verity's head moved slightly to the side, but she stayed asleep.

Then, the Companion's hand stilled. The crib came to a halt along with the singing. Verity stirred when familiar hands wrapped around her, and she yawned and made a few weak crying sounds before looking into the face lingering above hers. Verity wasn't used to her nanny's face wearing such a strange expression, so she stared mesmerized as the trusted being picked her up and walked to the window. When the Companion held its arms out straight, placing Verity as far away from its chest as possible, the child thought her nanny was playing a game with her and released a joyous, squealing laugh.

Outside, the smiling mother ran her fingers over the smooth skin of a perfectly ripe tomato before plucking it from the stem and placing it in her basket filled with similar treasures. A skirmish across the courtyard intruded upon her serenity, so she started gathering her gardening tools. Soon she'd need to turn her attention to the children.

Hearing sudden, loud noises, her expression went blank while her head snapped up to look at her sons. One boy kept screaming while their Companion puppy's teeth remained latched onto the calf of his leg. The other boy was helping to remove the puppy. Moderately concerned, she started to walk to them, but then she froze. Her vegetables spilled all over the ground as she dropped the basket and her bag of tools. She was temporarily struck mute while trying to make sense of what she saw in the window above the boys.

Then she cried out for the boys to catch their sister while she sprinted to join them under the window. She heard Verity begin to cry and shouted for the nanny to put her back inside.

"Mama," her oldest son interrupted while kicking the unresponsive puppy. "Nana is dead just like Lobo."

The mother looked closer at the unmoving robot holding her baby and said, "Stay here and catch Verity if she falls."

She dashed through the house and up the stairs, moving so frantically that she fell in the corridor and crawled the rest of the way to Verity's nursery door. Using the doorknob to pull herself back up, she ran to the window.

Verity's amusement at the nanny's mystery game went away when the robot's face became blank, and its body went stiff. It didn't look like her nanny anymore, and she didn't feel safe. The hands holding her began to hurt, and she squirmed and cried for Mama. Her little fists banged away at the robot's arms while her own wild screams filled her ears.

Verity quieted when Mama appeared and reached for her. She clung to Mama and took comfort in her heartbeat and the warm hand stroking her back.

New York City.

Ruby floated just below the chandelier in Dust's formal event room. When she started to sink, Adam flew up to her and offered her his hand. Taking more of his power, she ascended until she was almost to the ceiling again. Adam let go of her hand and sank back down to the floor to join Giselle.

Giselle was seated with her chin rested on her knees on the bare hardwood floor. The room wasn't set up since there weren't any upcoming events. The dining tables, the rugs, and other furniture were in storage. Only a piano remained in a dark corner, and Trent sat at the piano bench to watch Ruby's training.

A Companion entered the room with a tray of water and served Adam and Giselle.

Ruby thought about her thirst and began slipping from the air. On instinct, she reached for the chandelier.

The sound of large crystal shards clanking together in conjunction with Trent's laughter prompted Giselle and Adam to look up from their glasses of water. Adam smiled and Giselle spit water across the floor before the sound of her belly laughs echoed around the empty room.

"I'm glad you think this is so funny, Elle," Ruby shouted. "You, too, Trent."

Giselle kept laughing. "It's just been too long since I've seen you really let loose and swing from the chandeliers."

"Well, you still party enough for both of us," Ruby replied. "Are you going to just stand there and let me fall, Adam?"

Adam began levitating to her and said, "I was waiting to see if you'd save yourself before I do it for you."

Trent continued to chuckle softly at the scene until he saw Ruby wrap her legs around Adam's waist before letting go of the light fixture and throwing her arms around his neck. He inhaled a large breath and then let it go slowly to keep calm while watching his lover cling to another man in a way he thought was both overly familiar and unnecessary.

As Trent left the room, he heard Giselle's voice confirming his own thoughts as she asked, "Why didn't you just syphon more of his flight power and float yourself down?"

"I'm just a bit tired and spooked," Ruby replied while lifting her head from Adam's chest.

Ruby's head bumped the chandelier, and a few loose pieces of it fell. Giselle stepped back when crystals came crashing to the floor. As she watched them shatter across the hard wood, another crystal fell into a glass of water still sitting on the Companion's serving tray.

When Adam's feet hit the floor, he and Ruby turned to Giselle just in time to see the Companion stab Giselle in the chest with a long crystal shard. The machine then just stood there motionless. It was still, and its arm was outstretched as if frozen in time. Its dead hand gripped the shard that was embedded inside Giselle.

Before Giselle knew what had happened, she was coughing up blood and struggling to breathe. Her trembling hands came up to her skewered chest. She tried to brace herself against the robotic arm that was stuck against her body. Every little tremble and movement she made hurt her even more.

Adam and Ruby rushed to Giselle. Ruby struggled to hold her best friend upright and still to reduce further injury while Adam pried the robot's hand from the crystal. Once he was done, Adam kicked the Companion to the floor. Laying Giselle down gently, he called for help on his bracelet and tried to begin healing her.

With his hands over her wound, he said, "It's not working. I think the crystal is absorbing the magic."

Ruby asked, "Can we pull it out?"

"It could injure her faster than I can heal her with magic alone. It's best if I use my magic to keep her breathing and stable temporarily," Adam explained. "The medical team is on the way."

Adam's personal team of doctors and nurses flooded the room seconds later, followed closely by Jeremy, who was brandishing his Companion control tablet and shouting about an aggressive virus invading the network.

Jeremy's eyes widened at the site of Giselle on the floor, and he used his power to skip the distance between them in a blink.

Holding her hand while in shock, he managed to ask, "What happened?"

One of the nurses gently moved him away as the medical team prepared to move Giselle. Jeremy watched helplessly as Adam spoke with his doctors, and a decision was made. For the first time, he noticed his sister was in the room, too. She was sitting on the floor covered in blood, and he went to her.

"Are you hurt?" Jeremy asked.

Ruby shook her head slowly while still looking at Giselle as they carried her away. "It's her blood . . . It attacked her. The Companion."

Jeremy approached Adam aggressively. "Where are they taking her? What is happening?"

Helping Ruby up from the floor, Adam explained, "She needs to have a lung replaced. They're rushing her to Liberty General. The three of us will go right now."

It had been two hundred years since the last organs were transplanted from human donors. After the unequivocal discovery that deceased donors' consciousnesses were partially transplanted along with their organs, which affected organ recipients' personalities, the medical field had scrambled to find a better way. Some believed it had been an unnecessary setback to medical science, but after years of trials and improvements, the result had been saving lives at a much higher rate for almost a century.

Most people received temporary emergency organs, which were replaced as soon as possible with organs made specifically for each recipient. However, Giselle was not most people. Adam had all his tribe's replacement organs synthesized as soon as they reached adulthood. When Dust's headquarters moved to Hell's Kitchen, he'd ordered their organs moved to Liberty General Hospital a few blocks away.

Jeremy was frantic and becoming frustrated with Adam. "Why didn't you just heal her?"

"The weapon's material was reacting with my magic in an odd way, and with the way it was lodged inside her . . ." Adam said and struggled for words. "I think this is the best way."

As they made their way through the building and headed to Adam's private car, Ty, Danielle, and Trent joined them.

"We have a problem—" Ty started to explain.

25

But Danielle interrupted, arguing, "No, we have a catastrophe."

"Alright, everyone," Adam stated. "Just keep walking. We're all going in the car. I'm assuming what happened to Giselle wasn't an isolated incident?"

"What happened to Giselle?" Trent blurted. "Is she alive?"

Adam and Ruby nodded.

At the same time, Ty asked, "Is that why the medical staff was deployed? Shit. Trent's already directing the security staff in conducting a full security sweep across all offices worldwide. The breach lasted less than a minute, and there are no other casualties reported within the company so far, but our consumers . . ."

As they all got inside the car and Trent closed the door, Adam said, "Wait, who is on the executive floor right now?"

"Leilani is handling the office," Ty said. "I thought her power would be used best upstairs to keep the staff sane, especially the public relations team."

"And where is Phoebe?"

Ruby answered, "I've just been communicating with her. She's on her way to Liberty General as well."

Adam nodded, ordered the car to begin driving, and then said, "Jeremy?"

Jeremy was in a trance, but Ruby had picked up his tablet before they'd left the event room. She placed it on his lap and nudged him.

"Jeremy," Adam repeated.

Adam's distrust of artificial intelligence drove him to add an additional fail-safe to the Companion network. Jeremy was that fail-safe. He had his father's talent for innovation and developed a hair-trigger alert system for critical threats detected in the Companions.

"It was some kind of aggressive remote access Trojan," Jeremy said. "I shut it down as fast as possible. The entire Companion system is dead. My team is working to trace the attack, and I was coming to tell you, but then Giselle."

"Adam," Danielle interjected. "I've just received word from Sylvia. She heard the attacks. She heard all of them at once, and said she's heard magic like it before. She's on her way back to New York."

"When before?" Adam asked with a hint of suspicion in his tone.

· · ·

Prague, Bohemia, Blue Earth, 2125 A.D.

Robin needed a diversion. With Eve confined and under the influence of a mysterious husband he'd never seen, many fae secrets could be in peril. She'd simply disappeared, taking crucial fae knowledge with her.

It had taken him years to begin fearing she'd never come back to visit the fae, then one day he'd calculated at least a hundred years must have passed. The only mention of her he could find had been from the lips of a witch he'd spied near Athens, but she'd only conveyed rumors to her friends about their leader, Adam, punishing his treacherous wife. All witches and every other powerful earthbound being needed to be distracted while fae nobility relocated the universe's most valuable magical objects to new hiding places.

He perched above a tower clock and watched people filling the cobblestone streets of the Blue Earth's cultural center. He'd been watching them all week. It had been hundreds of years since he'd paid any mind to the modern world, so he watched closely for a weakness to exploit.

Their lives seemed especially mundane as days passed by during which most of them never looked up from strange objects. They always kept the objects with them. He knew about cameras, films, and telegraphs, but he quickly understood he was far behind on his knowledge about human inventions. It looked like they had thin square tiles with moving pictures in them attached to the palms of their hands. The tiles had a star symbol on the back of them with the word "Magus" written beneath the star in sparkling script.

It was then he realized the tile was feeding them every direction and piece of information they used to live. The object told them where to go, it told them what to eat, and it even told them how to vote for community leaders. Best of all, their money was tied to it somehow.

Robin smiled. Once he sorted out how to get inside those objects and corrupt them, the human world would descend into anarchy.

⚊ ⚊ ⚊

Jeremy, Phoebe, and Ruby had been inside the hospital for hours, but Adam, Ty, Danielle, and Trent remained in Adam's car and used it as an emergency makeshift command post. Ty made the decision to stay in place and work when they realized all transportation routes everywhere in the city were slowed significantly because of the Companion crash. The hospital was experiencing emergencies at a higher volume as well, but Trent was able to determine serious injuries related to the crash were far lower than any catastrophe in recent history. It was still best not to change their location until they could get a better handle on the situation. The vehicle was large and equipped with everything they needed due to Adam's vigilance and experience with thousands of years' worth of catastrophes, both natural and man-made.

The door closest to Adam opened, and Sylvia climbed inside the vehicle and sat across from him. She somehow looked younger than the last time he saw her, but her hair was just as white as ever.

She got straight to the point and said, "It's the same magic that caused the Second Dark Ages. And perhaps just as importantly, I've realized that's also the frequency I heard faint traces of when I stood near Scarlet Rose Reilly's body."

Adam said nothing, but it was apparent to everyone in the car that he was thinking about Sylvia's words. He leaned back and looked at the ceiling while practicing deep, even breathing.

"What are the Second Dark Ages?" Trent asked.

Ty laughed despite himself. He put down his tablet and silenced his bracelet. Leaning back next to Adam, he closed his eyes.

Watching Ty, Danielle whispered, "This was a deliberate attack from a very old magical enemy."

"Yeah," Ty agreed, "but the worst part is our great-grandparents never knew where it came from."

"At this point, common sense tells me it's likely the fae," Adam said.

Trent was busy researching the Second Dark Ages. He browsed through headlines that all mentioned the gross negligence and brutal fall of a company called Magus Dynamics. The company's generative artificial intelligence had been the backbone of a world economy for decades before its mass AI hallucinations crumbled twenty-second century society in less than forty-eight hours. It had taken fifty-one years for the world to fully recover.

"Magus Dynamics was our people's company?" Trent asked.

"Yes," said Danielle. "Of course, witches didn't know Adam's true identity as our people's patriarch at that time, but they knew he was powerful. They followed him into building Magus. My great-grandfather ran it. Well, we all know Adam really ran it, but since he had stepped down by then, the world saw Julian Cheshire at the helm when the ship went down."

"I guess you shouldn't have shown your face at the Companion announcement last year," Ty said to Adam.

"Doesn't matter," Danielle told Ty. "The world thinks you run the company."

"We need to focus," Adam stated. "Do we have a security and damage report yet?"

Trent answered, "All our offices are closed, and our people are staying secluded for their safety. There are only around twenty deaths worldwide, which although low, that's still a large moral and financial liability—"

"Move on, Trent," Adam interrupted. "The legal team will determine liability, cost, and the like."

Trent looked like he wanted to vomit.

Ty added, "We didn't kill those people, Trent. The fae killed them."

"We're not sure it was fae magic," Danielle whispered.

Sylvia started to argue, but Adam held up his hand for silence. "Let Trent speak."

Trent swallowed hard and continued, "Injuries, property damage, and financial losses are estimated at twenty percent of Companion network users, but no active threats remain. It's confirmed: Jeremy killed them all in under a minute."

Adam asked, "Ty?"

"The impact is far smaller than we initially feared," Ty stated. "Our caution and preparation served us well today. Considering also that Companions were still relatively new luxury items and not yet integrated into the fabric of society, this issue is going to be a drop in the ocean compared to the global tsunami Magus Dynamics' generative AI failure turned out to be . . . Basically, assuming this is it, our enemy hasn't fully succeeded this time."

Ty handed his tablet to Adam, letting him read Dust's initial public statement for himself. Adam also perused the message traffic concerning media queries about Ty's credentials and competence, or whether he was qualified to replace Joe.

They'd discuss Ty's position later when they would also decide if Dust would successfully continue, or if they'd set up a new company to front their cabal, or if they even needed a company anymore. Adam didn't want to deal with long-term decisions until the metaphorical fires were extinguished. He'd also prefer to focus on squashing the enemy once and for all.

"I don't think our enemy realizes their true failure yet," Sylvia said, "because we do know it was the fae, and now that I can track their magic, they've lost an advantage."

"How do you . . ." Adam started to ask Sylvia the question before understanding struck him, and he stated, "Sorina."

The last thing Adam needed was another top priority, but since the first thing he needed was more allies, he had to prioritize finishing the tech to block his people's minds from the vampires. He knew most of the team would work around the clock until the task was complete if he offered them double salaries, so it was done with a few taps of his finger on his bracelet.

Ruby rejoined the group, embracing and kissing Trent as soon as she sat down.

He looked uncomfortable, so she explained, "I just needed to be close to you for a moment. Watching Jeremy fret over Giselle for hours got to me a bit. The other injuries from the Companions were hard to see, too."

Trent went back to working and asked, "How is Giselle?"

"She's recovering well," Ruby answered and moved to sit between Adam and Ty. "I've already arranged for a bus to come for her, Jeremy, and Phoebe. Our medical team is setting up a special room for her at headquarters. They said she'll need a few days of monitoring while she rests. I figured we'll all be there sorting out this mess anyway, so . . ."

Ruby's speech trailed off while everyone else in the car seemed occupied with work. The silence around her persisted as the car started driving back to headquarters. She went into the mini bar and pulled out two euphoric candies.

Ty looked up from his tablet to see Ruby stuff two candies into her mouth at the same time, so he said, "You're doing well, Ruby."

With her family estranged, Ruby spent most of her time with either Trent or Giselle. She wondered if her new life was about to fall apart as fast as her last one did. She smiled weakly as the feeling of euphoria dulled the loneliness eating at her heart.

Trent watched Ruby patiently fold perfect creases into clothing and separate accessories and sundries into color-coded containers while packing a suitcase. He admired that she tried her best at every task no matter how small. Even though he enjoyed laughing at her little failures, especially because she was cute when frustrated, he was attracted to her intelligence and her drive for perfection.

He loathed the idea of her going to visit Hayden, but he was relatively new to their intimate group. He'd already voiced his objections, so he knew persisting in his objections would only sow resentment between them. His rational mind told him she was justified in not considering his opinion more important because they were not in an official partnership yet, but his heart thought of her as something else, or someone else. It was difficult and painful for him to remember his old life and a wife who had died in another universe on the Green Earth.

"Ruby, do you ever think of partnership?"

Ruby paused what she was doing a looked up at Trent. "Of course, I do."

When she went back to packing, he added, "And?"

"With our knowledge of the universes, my thoughts about the future have changed," she said as she zipped the suitcase. "I know motherhood isn't in my future, and I feel like some other great purpose is."

"That doesn't mean you can't have a partner," Trent snapped back and then cleared his throat nervously. "I didn't mean for that to sound harsh."

Ruby understood, as she usually did, so she went to him, held his hands, and said, "I know. I just don't feel the need to rush. I love you, but partnership hasn't been the first thing on my mind . . . You're used to her being your wife, but I'm not her."

Trent gently pulled his hands away from hers and said, "Maybe this time apart will be for the best after all. We'll have time to think, yeah?"

"Yeah," Ruby agreed. "Kiss me?"

He leaned into her and placed a soft kiss on her mouth.

She stood still and kept looking up at his face. "No, kiss me like you mean it."

Trent looked away. He wanted her badly, but he also wanted her to stay and had no immediate outlet for those negative emotions building inside of him while she stood there with her suitcase.

Ruby put her hand on his cheek and forcefully turned his head back to face her. "Make it angry if you have to but kiss me like you mean it before I leave."

Then she slid her hand gently down his cheek before lifting her palm a few inches away from his face and slapping it down hard on his cheek again as a smirk appeared on her face.

He went for her, placing one hand behind her head and one at her back. He had a fistful of her hair as he pressed her body against his. His lips came crashing down over hers like he was ravenous from not tasting her for days.

Titillation claimed her body and heightened her senses when he bit her lip. As the taste of her own blood filled her mouth, she threw her arms around his neck. She jumped up and wrapped her legs around him, so he moved his hands down to keep her pressed against him by gripping her ass tightly and turning to pin her against the wall.

Trent relinquished his control over her lips and panted against her neck. He wanted to catch his breath and disengage before he did something he'd regret, so he also slid his hands up to her waist. When he realized the hot breath against her skin was only making her grind harder against his jeans, he changed his method to regain his wits and dowse the desire building between them.

Ruby knew the moment was over when Trent placed his palms on the wall on either side of her head and pushed himself away from her. She let her legs fall, but not without a heavy groan of disapproval. Once her feet were steady on the floor, she dropped her arms from his neck. She gifted him a reserved, somber smile when he lifted his eyes to her face and studied it. She knew he was having his last look, and she wanted it to be honest but pleasant.

"You are a treasure, Trent Pinkerton."

"I love you, Ruby Cohen," he said, barely able to whisper the words before turning from her.

34

Ruby didn't follow him. She knew he was grappling with negative emotions about her and the journey she needed to make. Their last words to each other were beautiful, and there was no reason to risk ruining them with a fight and insults they'd regret.

It was time for her to look forward to the journey. She was surprised when Hayden had replied to her messages and told her to meet him in Valletta, Malta. Hopefully getting him home would be as easy as finding him. Her success was essential. Giselle was in recovery and needed her brother. Dust was in turmoil and needed a complete team. The cabal had another enemy to face.

VAMPIRE ALLIANCE

Sorina and Vlad did not wish to meet the witches in Manhattan and politely declined Adam's first invitation, suggesting safety concerns. They'd requested a quiet property with plenty of space, so preparations were almost complete for the cabal to meet the vampires at Sands Point instead. Not everyone was comfortable having vampires in their patriarch's home. Several members of the voting jury preferred the meeting to take place on Adam's private island in the Caribbean, but everyone eventually agreed they needed to stay close enough to the city to keep cleaning up the mess at Dust.

While the rest of the cabal received their tech implants to block the vampires from reading thoughts, Adam arrived at his home a day early to play host. He'd already received his implant, knowing it was the right thing to do for him to be the experimental guinea pig before letting his people have new, untested tech placed inside them.

Adam gave Vlad and Sorina the best guest rooms on the property and made sure they had dedicated household staff to make them comfortable. He invited them to dinner and had a smaller table set for the three of them in the formal dining room. He wanted to give them the respect of his best dinner accommodations, but he also wanted dinner to be intimate enough for them to break the ice, so to speak.

The vampires brought water from their home and told Adam they'd drink while he ate dinner. He thought they seemed grateful for the invitation to his dinner table, but he wondered at their dietary choices. He'd assumed blood and wine would be involved.

"Since we're not speaking of business tonight, I hope we can chat about other things that will help us understand each other better," Adam said. "I've been curious to ask if you were aware of your souls being split upon leaving Eden . . . I have no memories of it happening to me."

"We suspected," said Sorina.

Vlad added, "Because we knew it had been done to you."

"The Edenians told us stories about you as if your life was a fiction," Sorina explained.

"More like a cautionary tale," Vlad clarified.

"Yes," Sorina agreed. "We knew what happened after you were punished, and we knew about the three Earths."

"You have me at a disadvantage then." Adam smiled.

Vlad nodded. "Our story isn't very different than yours when it comes to our fall. We disobeyed."

Sorina told the story. "We were made to be a warrior race with a military rank structure. Lilith chose Vlad to lead us, but eventually one of our brothers, Cyrus, gained support and wanted to challenge Vlad's leadership. Lilith saw it as a betrayal against her and ordered us to execute Cyrus and his supporters. When we refused, she executed them and exiled the rest of us."

Adam watched Sorina with unveiled interest. Her appearance was striking, and he found her infinitely alluring in that moment. Her voice carried a unique accent that was doubtless developed from centuries of change across Central Europe. She had a somewhat deep voice. Its timbre was dark, yet the sound was feminine and smooth. He found himself wondering what his dark hands would look like against her porcelain skin if he were to peel the catsuit from her body.

Vlad watched Adam and knew what he was thinking even though reading his thoughts was proving impossible. He and Sorina would need to discuss Adam's new power to block his thoughts. He wondered if Sorina could still read Adam. If she could, Vlad was sure those thoughts were indecent at that moment.

Vlad leaned closer to Adam and said, "Your lustful thoughts are misplaced. She has become asexual over the years."

Choosing not to engage in talk of his thoughts, Adam changed the subject, asking, "Before your fall, did you drink blood in Eden? You're made in their image the same as I, but you're otherwise so different."

"Our thirst is a mystery to us as well," Vlad said. "I think it's also partially unknown to Lilith. Of course, she clearly made us with more advanced materials and techniques, but she never intended for us to become blood-drinkers."

Sorina explained, "Lilith's intent was to punish us by making the mountains our prison. Only the water from the lake under the mountains nourishes us, or so she believed—we all believed—at first."

"But we were young and angry at our mother." Vlad's face held a reserved frown as he spoke. "Finding any way to defy the Edenians was our only purpose back then, so we left the mountains intending to starve if we couldn't find nourishment elsewhere."

"It was an accident," Sorina stated in a sorrowful tone.

"Yes," Vlad agreed. "The magic of Eden's lifeforce smelled delicious as it flowed with the blood that spilled from an injured witch along the banks of the Danube. We feasted on blood for the first time that night, and we kept going."

"We settled anywhere we could hunt witches," Sorina whispered, ashamed. "We thought your kind were simply primates of the land that could provide us nourishment. Our sharp teeth and strength made it easy."

"The magical abilities didn't raise questions?" Adam asked.

Vlad finished the grotesque tale. "Most of them couldn't wield magic strong enough to affect us, but eventually some did. Then questions were raised, but you must understand our desire for survival and freedom. Even when we discovered witches were born from the original Children of Eden, it took years for us to reorganize our coven, embrace peace, and make emends when appropriate."

"When was it not appropriate?" Adam asked, trying to keep the agitation out of his tone. "You never came to me."

"Eve could not be tolerated, and you would not let her go," Vlad said confidently. "I witnessed her slaughter her own kind more than once."

Adam simply nodded. He was too proud to voice it, but he clearly understood. He observed them imbibe their water and understood other things, too. He knew where some of the vampire legends came from. It was true they needed their homeland, but they needed the water to drink rather than the dirt in which to sleep. They likely preferred to be in public at night, so humans didn't see the light make their eyes gleam unnaturally silver.

Adam had one more question and asked it as gently as possible. "Can you reproduce?"

"Maybe it is universal balance at work," Sorina said, "that we cannot produce children, yet we never grow old."

Watching Sorina and Vlad interact and react to personal questioning, Adam realized something else. They were not partners. It surprised him. Two attractive beings had ruled a race together for almost two thousand years without bonding beyond friendship.

Vlad stated plainly, "We cannot create more vampires by biting humans. That is a fiction. We've lost numbers over the years but never gained."

Adam knew, because how could he not, that Sorina kept Sylvia and Duncan alive and young. That seemed to be a secret process they were not ready to share. Perhaps if the alliance turned favorable for all parties, both sides could share secrets to power and longevity and use them together. That was Adam's hope for his people's future.

With no days off since the fae attack on Dust, Trent decided to use his downtime between shifts to play guitar and have a drink before getting a few hours of sleep. He'd been working at the house for the last few days, getting it ready for the alliance meetings. The guest wing's recreation room was adjacent to the suite he shared with Ruby. It had great acoustics and a shelf of good liquor, so he preferred to play music in there.

While Trent played, Duncan entered the room and sat in a dark corner. Trent wasn't in the mood to socialize, so he continued playing until the song was done. He paused to take a sip of whiskey before playing another song. He could tell Duncan wasn't doing anything except watching him and wondered if he and Sylvia had arrived with the vampires during the night. Trent still didn't trust Sorina and couldn't wait to get his mindreading blocker implanted the next morning. He'd been actively avoiding Adam's guests all day.

Almost an hour passed without a word between them. Trent put his guitar in its case and slid it behind a shelf. He finished his drink and left the empty glass on a serving tray for the household staff to take to the kitchen later.

Just as Trent approached the door, Duncan said, "I'm ashamed I didn't notice how much you look like him at first."

Trent stopped. Duncan finally had his attention. From their first meeting, Trent knew Duncan and Sylvia knew the Trent Pinkerton from the Blue Earth, and he'd been looking forward to learning more. He shut the door, took a seat next to Duncan, and maintained his poker face.

"Since you went to the trouble of getting me alone," Trent said, "and you're here without Sylvia, I'm assuming this conversation isn't happening as far as the others are concerned."

"Right you are," Duncan agreed, speaking in a pleasant tone.

Trent smirked slightly. "So, why feel ashamed you didn't recognize me? I'm sure you've forgotten thousands of people in your long life."

"Yes, ashamed and curious as to why you don't know your ancestry . . . I'm your soulmate's great-great-great-great-grandfather."

Trent leaned back in his chair and looked into Duncan's eyes for a moment before answering, "Well, Duncan. My fourth great-grandparents likely died around a century ago. The Green Earth is a somewhat tumultuous world. Most families don't know their histories. If my Adam and Eve knew my ancestry, which they likely did, they never told me . . . I don't remember having relatives with the surname Cavendish."

Duncan leaned closer to Trent and spoke softly. "Sylvia and I had a daughter, Mina. Even though she never gained magical gifts, Sorina helped us keep her and our subsequent bloodline hidden from Adam. We didn't want any of them to become obligated to him like we were . . . It was Mina's daughter, Diana Keleti, who had a son named Pinkerton. None of them ever received magical gifts until now."

"So, you knew Trent's parents on this Earth?" Trent asked.

"Jack Pinkerton and Claudia Devereux," Duncan said. "They're living in Chicago."

Trent closed his eyes. "I never saw my parents again after my gift manifested. At eighteen I joined Adam and Eve and left my old life behind. It would have been dangerous for them to know me."

"My Trent Pinkerton won't be able to avoid Adam much longer, not with the alliance and new cabal. Sylvia and I want to report our deception, but it's his choice to come forward when ready," Duncan explained. "Adam will want to document his parents, too."

"My understanding of this situation is me and my soulmate know about each other, but we're pretending we don't, and you never told us."

"Exactly.

Trent asked, "Does he look very different than me?"

"His appearance changes often."

"Should I know what you mean by that?"

"You will."

"So, that's it?"

"For now," Duncan said as he stood and put his hand on Trent's shoulder. "I know you don't trust Sorina, but I hope I've proven you can trust me."

Trent watched Duncan leave and continued staring at the empty doorway while deep in thought. He didn't think he would ever like Sorina, but keeping Duncan's secret wouldn't be difficult. He'd kept his own secret from Adam and the others for almost two years. Knowing himself, he deduced the other Trent changed appearances because he was somehow involved in spycraft, which intrigued him. More than anything, his thoughts lingered on hope. He hoped they'd be able to live on the same Earth together, he hoped to see his parents again, and he hoped to learn more from Duncan one day.

Malta's hypogeum, a labyrinthine underground temple, pulsed with primal magic. A soothing low-frequency hum composed of a multitude of ancient Maltese spirits flowed from the Oracle Room, creeping through every chamber like whispered secrets from the distant past.

Bastion Roth emerged from the hypogeum through a secret passage, looking for the hired car he'd arranged to take him to Malta International Airport. He needed to catch the first available flight to New York, or Adam wouldn't be happy. He'd already missed one appointment with the medical team.

As he opened the car door, a warm breeze blew across his face, and he paused. The scent of magic was in the air. It smelled like smoke, and he recognized it as the byproduct of Hayden's fire gift.

"Shit!" he whispered to himself. "I guess I'm not going to the airport yet."

The wind was blowing from the direction of Valletta, so he gave the car new directions, hopped into the back seat, and lowered the windows. As he approached the waterfront, he directed the car to park. The moment his feet hit the pavement, he felt the winds die, and he lost the scent.

Once Bastion started tracking, he didn't want to stop. His new challenge to himself was to find Hayden and then make it back to the airport before lunchtime. If he kept walking north toward the ancient battery, he felt sure he'd be able to encounter more breezes rolling across the island and recapture the scent. Sumptuous, manicured gardens lined his path. The sweet flowers' fragrances mixed with salty air would make the smoky magical residue even more noticeable. Anticipating his success, Bastion picked up his pace.

Outside the cathedral ruins he saw charred marks against a pile of stones from a crumbling buttress. The smell was strong, like a smoldering campfire but with the added spice of witchcraft. Placing his hand over one of the stones, he noted it was still hot.

He leaned closer to the stones and inhaled. He knew a different, older magical being had been there, too.

Pivoting west, he continued to track his kinsman to a nearby hotel. The concierge noted him as soon as he entered the lobby, so it was time to use his handsome features and charming interpersonal skills.

Bastion smiled at the older gentleman in a black suit with silver crossed keys on the lapels, and not seeing a nametag, he approached the desk and said, "Good morning, sir. My name is Bastion, and you are?"

"Azure, at your service, sir." The concierge smiled politely.

Bastion took the pleasantries as an opportunity to subtly lean over the desk a little more, ensuring he could see the flat glass panel the hotel used to communicate with all the rooms. He saw numbers glowing across the glass from his peripheral vision as he pretended to check his bracelet for information.

"I seem to have lost my friend's room number. I would greatly appreciate it if you could let Carolus Rosemont know I'm waiting in the lobby," he said, giving Hayden's first and last names.

"It would be my pleasure, sir," Azure said while touching number 306 on the glass. "He's not available at the moment, perhaps you should contact him directly."

Bastion held up his wrist and pointed to his bracelet. "He's not responded for hours, but perhaps he's resting. I'll try another time, thank you."

Bastion's full blonde hair and seafoam green eyes were conspicuous, but they looked pleasant and comforted people. Azure was very keen to make Bastion feel welcomed at the hotel. He pulled a glass coin from his pocket and handed it to Bastion.

"Please have a discount token for our lounge or restaurant

and enjoy an early lunch while you wait," Azure said.

"Your hospitality is appreciated," Bastion replied as he turned toward the lounge.

Knowing the coin would be tracked, he gifted it to an attractive woman at the bar and then waited for a good time to join a group in the nearby elevator. As luck would have it, the woman from the bar approached the elevator with a large party in the mood to chat with their new friends, to include him. He smirked when a man in the party called the elevator to the third floor.

Bastion approached Hayden's room and knocked softly. The door opened quickly, and a hand impatiently beckoned him to enter.

Closing the door behind Bastion, Hayden said, "Mr. Roth, this isn't a good time."

Hayden didn't even ask how Bastion had found him. He knew the older man could smell nearby magic and sporadically sense events minutes before they happened. It was likely easy for him to get past the hotel staff.

"I agree, Hayden. It isn't a good time for you to be in Malta . . . He doesn't know you're here yet, but he will know soon."

"Obviously. You'll tell him if Ruby didn't already," Hayden scoffed while neatly placing things into a bag. "Or did he send you here to bring me home instead of her?"

"I'm not talking about Adam," Bastion said while approaching a latticed wooden box and looking inside. "I'm talking about the owner of this, and he'll come for you himself. He likely already knows you killed at least one of his people to get it. I smelled it at the church ruins."

Hayden snatched the box away, pulling a sheet over it and placing it next to his bag. "I wasn't aware you were acquainted with him."

Bastion's face was expressionless. "It may only take him seconds to get from his realm to the hypogeum, and when you're not there, and it's not there," he said, pointing at the box, "and his steward here is dead, he'll hunt you much faster than I did."

"You see me packing, don't you?" Hayden returned to his task. "You'll tell Adam, too, I suppose."

"I've got a car arriving in a minute," Bastion said. "I'll give you a ride, but after that, we never saw each other here, right?"

Hayden had his bag in one hand and the wooden box tucked under the opposite arm. "Agreed."

***

Jeremy was relieved. Giselle was well enough to attend the vampire alliance meeting. He worried about her lung transplant recovery in conjunction with the new device implanted in the back of her head, but he knew she was stronger than most people gave her credit for, including him most days. They were seated together at Adam's great round table he'd moved from Dust just for the meeting. Their early arrival was a mutually agreeable decision since both were fascinated with Sorina and Vlad.

Cabal members gradually trickled into the room, each congratulating Giselle on her recovery before finding seats and socializing.

Seeing the Cavendishes together at the table, Trent sat on Duncan's other side but kept his peace. He spent time going over the updates Leilani had pushed to his tablet.

Bastion took the seat on Trent's other side and said, "How's your eye? Looks normal to me."

Trent laughed. "What the fuck are you talking about, Roth?"

"When I saw you two days ago, you had an eye patch. Lost your ability to read up close a bit early, huh?" Bastion joked.

"I didn't—" Trent started to say, shaking his head.

Duncan interrupted Trent, clearing his throat loudly and kicking him under the table.

"I mean, I didn't remember seeing you," Trent continued explaining. "Yeah, I just had to get my reading vision corrected a bit. Getting old early. Good as new now."

"Lost your memory and your sight then." Bastion slapped Trent on the back. "Hang in there. It doesn't get better but hang in there anyway."

Trent turned to Duncan and looked past him at Sylvia. She was engrossed in conversation with Youngae and didn't seem to hear anything he'd said to Bastion.

"An eye patch?" Trent mouthed the question at Duncan.

Duncan shrugged his shoulders and laughed. "It'll make sense one day," he whispered.

Trent mumbled, "Unless he's an ancient pirate, I doubt it."

"It's interesting you make that comparison—" Duncan started to say, but Sorina and Vlad arrived with Adam and distracted them.

Adam walked around the table with the vampires and made introductions. Phoebe noticed his hand hovering close to the small of Sorina's back and leaned closer to Danielle to gossip about it. As Adam passed by Phoebe, he placed his hands on her shoulders and leaned to whisper his disapproval into her ear. She and Danielle chuckled together but dropped the subject. The Lee sisters seemed excited to meet the vampires, while Leilani was visibly nervous. Adam asked Bastion to sit next to Leilani and help put her nerves at ease lest it affect her magic.

Giselle squeezed Jeremy's hand in anticipation as Sorina and Vlad approached and sat next to them. Her face told the vampires she thought they were beautiful.

"It's a pleasure to see you again," Giselle said to Sorina. "We didn't get to be properly acquainted on the spaceship."

"We are pleased at the opportunity to meet you properly now," Sorina replied.

Giselle smiled. "Jeremy and I look forward to a strong alliance with your people."

"We hope you'll still feel that way after you've heard what we have to say," Vlad interjected.

Jeremy and Giselle were taken off guard by his tone, but Jeremy said, "I hope so as well. Eden's progeny should stand together for the Blue Earth's protection and betterment."

Ty called the meeting to order, and when he asked if the vampires had opening remarks to share, Vlad stood and looked around the table.

As the vampires' high priest and leader, Vlad announced, "Gaia chose to reveal her light to witches and vampires together on the same night. This is a sign. A time for unity between Eden's creations on the Blue Earth is upon us. Sorina and I are honored to be among you and represent our people in Adam's home among his people. We hope this congregation will keep an open mind for the knowledge we must share with you today, and thank you all for welcoming us."

As the meeting began, it was apparent to everyone the fae conflict was the paramount issue to both parties, so it was agreed the alliance would start there. If the collaboration against the fae proved a successful endeavor, they could continue to build together.

The vampires offered their strength as an army. In return,

they needed Adam and his people to provide the technology and magical gifts necessary to invade the fae realm.

"Are you expecting to take fae blood and eyes?" Trent asked.

Sorina quickly responded, "It is our right in battle to take what we want of our enemies, and we would have their blood."

"But you all can have the eyes," Vlad added.

Ty cleared his throat and looked to Adam as the witches passed some moments of silent discomfort, and then he said, "Okay, let's put a pin in that. We've jumped ahead a bit."

"We'd like to hear about the information you have regarding the fae attack on my company," Adam said.

"The fairy king, Robin, committed the murder of Scarlet Rose Reilly to gain the trust of Carolus Hayden Rosemont in exchange for access to your network," Vlad explained. "The access was initially achieved through a high-security company computer system from your finance department. Rosemont uses it to perform his company work remotely."

The table was again quiet while the cabal processed the information about one of their own committing such a betrayal. Giselle had closed her eyes and buried her face in Jeremy's chest.

Then Phoebe spoke while trying to maintain her cool. "Is this organization going to keep coming for my family, Adam? What proof do the vampires offer?"

Adam looked to Sorina for Phoebe's answer.

Sorina's voice sounded genuinely sad. "Our spies are reliable. In point of fact, you sent Ruby Cohen to recover Rosemont. He's already wanted for questioning in the murder. When he appears before your court, you will have proof."

Trent was getting fed up with the ongoing murder investigation. "Ty, put me on record as being tired of hearing about the infamous Scarlet Rose Reilly while twenty innocent Dust customers were killed last week. Can we at least acknowledge Adam would have killed Reilly years ago if she wasn't connected to more powerful people than he is, and now we need to focus on the fae?"

Phoebe stretched her arms out toward Trent. "Thank you! Finally, someone said it!"

"If Robin did the crime, we could move on, Trent," Ty said with an attitude. "However, Hayden still faces questioning to corroborate the vampires' statements and to answer for the network breach, and that is more than fair, Phoebe."

"Sure thing, Ty," Phoebe announced. "By all means, let's get back to the completely legal and morally sound discussion of drinking blood and eating eyes."

Bastion and Trent laughed openly while the other witches tried to keep neutral, professional expressions.

Giselle lifted her face from Jeremy's chest, her voice trembling as she asked, "Mother, isn't it practical in a magical battle to do those things to gain the strength to keep fighting and survive?"

"I don't think that was her point," Jeremy gently told Giselle.

Phoebe sighed. "Thanks, Jeremy."

Ty regained control of the meeting. "Right. Clearly, we have more to discuss, but we're making progress. We'll adjourn now for an informal luncheon together in the conservatory."

Phoebe wanted to take a candy and nap in the rec room, but Giselle and Jeremy encouraged her to go with them to the conservatory. Trent embraced Phoebe before following Duncan and Sylvia from the room. Sorina smiled at Giselle as Adam escorted the vampires to lunch alongside the witches.

Ruby entered an opulent Maltese hotel and climbed the marble staircase to approach a sharply dressed concierge. The piano man was positioned at a baby grand under the main skylight, and she recognized the song as one of her favorites and hoped it was a good omen for her stay in the island paradise.

"Azure?" Ruby asked.

"Yes, madam."

"Good morning. We spoke yesterday. I'm Ruby Cohen."

The man looked down and checked his information. "Of course. I'll check your room is ready." He slid a small tile of glass across the desk to her. "In the meantime, you have a private message you can retrieve from this. The sender asks that you wipe it clean after reading."

Ruby snatched up the message, hoping Hayden hadn't ditched her. She was disappointed, but not surprised, to discover he had indeed left Malta. So much for good omens, she thought. Wiping her hand across the glass, she watched the message dissolve before sliding it back onto the desk. At least he'd left her his new address.

Ignoring messages from New York, she hastily noted the new destination on her tablet, and said, "My apologies, Azure. I'll not be staying after all. Please charge the account for tonight's stay and cancel the rest of the reservation."

"As you wish." Azure remained as pleasant as ever. "We hope for the opportunity to provide you quality hospitality for your future visits."

Although Ruby was feeling restless, she tried to look patient while waiting for Azure to call her a car and have her luggage reloaded. Her lips curved into a slight frown as she made her way back outside. The thought of having to travel even farther before she could relax was putting her in a bad mood. As soon as she was situated in the car and riding back to the airport, she booked the fastest flight she could find to Skopje.

FAIRY RAID

The ride from Skopje to Lake Ohrid was breathtaking. The mountains reached so high into the sky that Ruby mistook the snow-capped summits for clouds more than once as she admired the cloudy, mountainous landscape. She lowered the window to feel the outside air, noting it was much brisker than Valletta but still pleasant. As the elevation declined, she noticed an abundance of green farmlands and lush vineyards. She'd never visited that part of the Balkan Peninsula before, but the ride to her destination was quickly convincing her she'd discovered a new place she wanted to experience in detail.

As the car approached Hayden's lakeside bungalow, peacocks scattered from the dirt driveway and roamed the hillside. Everything about the scenery put Ruby at ease. The vast blue surface of the lake was a calm backdrop to the quaint, charming home. Not expecting a welcoming committee, she got out of the car promptly and dragged her bag with her to the front door. It opened before she had a chance to knock, so she stepped inside.

Hayden stood there in his perfectly tailored clothing and neatly combed hair. He embraced Ruby. His posture was stiff due to his nature rather than awkwardness, and Ruby could tell his hug was genuine.

She melted into his arms and whispered, "I wasn't sure if you'd missed me. We've all missed you so much."

He pulled back and looked her in the eyes. "I'm sorry for the things I said to you, Ru. I never was good with change. I had so much misplaced anger."

"I know, but it's okay." She pulled him close again and rested her head on his shoulder.

"But it's not okay."

"It will be. Giselle was hurt, but she's recovering and wants her brother. Your mother needs her son. Jeremy and I need you, too. We've known you our whole lives, Hayden. We love you."

Hayden squeezed her tightly and sobbed loudly.

Ruby's empathic nature was on overdrive as Hayden's body shuddered around her. His emotions were in more turmoil than she'd realized. Hayden never showed emotion in abundance. She'd only seen him cry once in their lives, and that had been when Jeremy had accidentally hit him in the jaw with a golf club. Even then, it was more like his eyes leaked water instead of complete bawling. She held him and rubbed his back until he quieted.

Leaning back to face him, she said, "We're still standing here by the door." She laughed.

Wiping his eyes, Hayden replied, "Yeah, sorry. Let's sit down. I have a lot to tell you."

He guided her to the sofa. She removed her shoes and then kneeled in front of him and removed his shoes, too. As she began massaging his foot, he leaned back into the cushions and moaned. For about five minutes, she didn't say anything, and Hayden kept his eyes closed and let her finish one foot and move to the next one.

Finally, she asked, "Do you feel better?"

"Honestly, no," he said, opening his eyes and looking down at her. "I feel worse."

Without stopping, she said, "Tell me about it."

"I appreciate what you're trying to do. I know you feel my pain and want to ease it, but . . . but you don't realize my romantic feelings for you are still alive and clawing away at my resolve to respect your relationship with Trent."

She moved her hands up to his shin and kept rubbing. Her lover back home didn't want to touch her, but the man sitting in front of her did. Her loneliness dared her to prolong the intimate moment, but she was also scared of going too far. Touching began to make her feel better and better, so she rocked forward on her knees, placed herself between his legs, and started rubbing his thighs.

Hayden sensed her nervousness. He knew her better than anyone other than Giselle, and he knew she wouldn't go with him to his bed. He could see she needed attention, and he could tell she genuinely enjoyed touching him, but he also saw the hesitation and fear in her eyes as she looked straight at him and grazed his groin with her thumb.

"Ruby, stop. If you don't, I'm going to fuck you."

She dropped her hands and sucked in a deep breath. "I can't believe you said it like that."

"I'm not exactly the same young man you left last year," he said while pulling her up to sit next to him. "I'm also a traitor to the cabal, and I need to tell you about it."

"Oh, my stars," she moaned, looking at him with concern. "You. You did kill your Aunty Rose!"

"Firstly, never refer to her as my aunt. Secondly, I did something far worse."

When he hesitated, she encouraged him. "I'm with you. Tell me."

"Somehow, he knew things. He must have had me followed. Foolishly, I've found the bottom of a few liquor bottles over the past months and voiced some sorrows to the bartenders and whores who would listen."

As if recounting the story reminded him that he needed a drink, he went to the kitchen and came back with a bottle of scotch and two glasses. He poured one for himself but left the second glass and the bottle on the table next to Ruby. She poured a sip and knocked it back. Then she poured a second sip and held it while he continued his story.

"Mother's abusive childhood has always weighed heavily on my mind. He appeared in my room one day and said he'd kill Rose if I let him use my computer. I asked why, and he said he was going to ruin Adam. Well, that sounded good to me, too."

"Who?"

"Robin, the king of the fae."

"What? You cannot be serious!" Ruby shot to her feet and stood over him. "No!"

"Ruby, I handle company money. I thought he'd use my files to bankrupt Adam or something. It's no secret I don't like Adam . . . I didn't know how his magic works—I didn't know he could worm his way so deep into the company and hurt people."

"He almost killed Giselle!" Ruby was crying, and her expression was pure horror.

Hayden reached for her, but she jerked away. She drank her sip of scotch and slammed the glass on the table. Then she went to the door, picked up her bag, and turned the doorknob. An agonizing scream roared from her throat, and she collapsed onto the floor. The doorknob was smoking as Hayden cooled it with his power. He rushed to Ruby and soothed her hand with his cooling power as well, immediately regretting his trick with the knob. It looked painful, and he couldn't heal her.

"You burned me!" Ruby cried.

She hit him. Then she hit him again. After a pause, her hurt erupted. She continued to repeatedly land blows against his chest and his face while he sat on the floor taking the beating calmly and holding her.

When she was spent, he said, "I can fix it. I took something from Robin. We can use it against him. I want to go back and face the cabal, but I wanted your understanding and support before I walk into Dust."

"They'll exile you," she whispered, her voice broken. "Take everything from you."

"Maybe," he said. "But I risked my life defeating Eve. I didn't know Robin's plan was to kill those people. He manipulated me. Yes, I was a traitor to Adam, but I have a gift for him that I'm hoping will barter me a pardon. If not, I'll accept my fate."

Ruby went limp against him. She was tired from traveling and tired from mental distress. Hayden picked her up and took her to his bed.

He went to the washroom and gathered supplies to clean and bandage her wound. When he came back to the bedroom, she was on her bracelet, and he knew she was checking in with Trent.

"I'm not telling Adam I'm here with you because someone told him everything, and they'll start looking for you soon, but I'm telling Trent where I am."

"Then Adam will soon discover me anyway." He took her hand and started doctoring it. "Robin will take a bit longer. He has no influence in this country, but I'll eventually be caught. It's best if we only take another day to rest and then prepare for New York."

"Will you take me down to the lake in the morning?"

He finished wrapping her hand and kissed it. "I'll make you a delicious breakfast and take you out in a boat. You'll love it. I promise."

She smiled weakly and closed her eyes. He kissed her hand again and placed it by her side. He then leaned over her and kissed her forehead before covering her with a blanket and leaving the bedroom. He prepared to sleep on the sofa, leaning against the cushions with a pillow, a sheet, and the rest of the scotch.

Phoebe walked along the beach with Snoopie. Even though the vampires had returned to Romania until the alliance's next meeting about the fae problem, most of the witches were still sequestered at Sands Point when they weren't handling business at the Hell's Kitchen office.

Jameson and Faustina had dropped off the pets with Phoebe on their way out of state. Jameson was attending a governors' meeting in Houston, and Faustina decided to accompany him instead of staying alone in Albany. Phoebe was content to have animal companionship since all the people in the house seemed to be hellbent on labeling her son a traitor.

Moonrise looked beautiful over the water, so she found a place to sit and watch it while playing fetch with Snoopie. She picked up a skinny piece of sun-bleached wood and thew it down the beach. When he brought it back, she threw it again and turned her attention back to the glowing horizon.

She felt the stick poking her arm, so she reached for it and tugged. That's when she realized there was a hand holding it, and someone was sitting next to her. It was a small man in a cloak with the hood pulled over his head, but Phoebe could see he wore a crown beneath the hood. It wasn't the first time she'd attracted a weirdo while out for a walk, so she wasn't worried if Snoopie was okay with the stranger. She leaned forward to look around the man and saw Snoopie sitting on the other side of him.

Snoopie was usually good at protecting her, so she assumed the man wasn't dangerous, but she wondered how he got there. All the land around them was private, and the next estate was quite far down the beach.

"You get lost playing D and D with your friends?"

"I'm not familiar with that game, Ms. Astor," said Robin. "Is it a human game?"

Phoebe became much more interested in their exchange. The man was there on purpose and wanted something from her. It annoyed her he was playing with her and had the advantage of knowing her name.

"Yes, and fetch is a dog's game, yet you stole my dog's stick and played anyway."

"Oh, I like you," he drawled.

"I like me, too. In fact, I was enjoying my own company until you showed up. Mind telling me who the fuck you are?"

Robin lowered his hood and said, "You may call me Robin. Unless you'd prefer to call me lover?"

Phoebe failed to hold back a laugh even though she knew instantly she was in danger after all. She noted his ears, his eyes, and his crown that she realized was real emerald.

"Am I going to die tonight, lover?" Phoebe whispered.

"No, not unless you want to die a little death," Robin replied with a mischievous smile.

"You're nothing like I expected," said Phoebe, "but I know you're a killer."

Robin sighed and crossed his arms. "If you insist on the unpleasantries, I promise I won't kill you tonight. There are too many witches afoot, and you have some who can sense my magic when I use it. It's been a long, boring day waiting to get you alone without using too much magic or approaching others at that ridiculous house."

"Can't you order your subjects to come here and help you?" she asked.

"Everyone knows only fae nobility may leave the fae realm, and your son already killed one of my favorite cousins, so maybe another time, lovely witch."

Phoebe didn't know if she was smart enough to keep up with whatever game Robin was playing with her. If there were fae casualties in their new war already, she couldn't imagine the night passing without some tragedy.

"Would you like to come with me to my room, Robin?"

Robin laughed. "You know how to play, and I find that incredibly erotic, but no."

Phoebe thought he was a fascinating creature. His eyes looked like real liquid gold, and she wondered how many universes they'd seen. She wondered how many souls he'd killed in his long life.

Robin asked, "Would you be my ally, Phoebe?"

"No," she answered firmly. "Is that why you've come to me?"

"Your son has betrayed your tribe. Perhaps you'd do it to protect him. Is it not smart for me to approach you? Especially after I slew your own personal monster for you."

"My son isn't my only concern. I have other children to protect. Furthermore, you robbed me of my dream to kill that monster myself."

"No matter," Robin turned to her and placed his mouth against her ear, barely whispering, "I have another ally. I'll do you another favor and warn you to keep your young lover from following him. Next time, I might kill that cocky spy."

She felt his lips touching her ear when he spoke. As she

turned her head, they grazed her skin all the way from her ear to her own lips.

She didn't pull away when she spoke almost into his mouth. "If one of my lovers is a spy, I'm not aware of which one it is."

"The one who moves through spacetime. He reminds me of you with his hair and eyes, but he annoys me. He will die if I catch him."

They were still speaking with their lips almost touching as if daring each other to make the next move.

Phoebe had no idea what Robin was talking about. He seemed to be describing Trent, but Trent's powers were inert, and she didn't think he was a spy. He was usually in the house or with Adam and Ruby.

"I consider myself warned, thank you," Phoebe said, finally pulling away from him but keeping intense eye contact.

"You have the same look about you my Evita had," Robin said, "but I suppose she *was* your matriarch. None could ever replace her in my bed, but I think you'd come close."

"I'd outperform her." Phoebe smirked.

Sometimes Phoebe didn't know the limit of her own sexual deviance until it was staring her in the face. In that moment, it turned her on that he'd been with Eve, but it turned her on even more to know she'd kill him as soon as she had a chance.

Nobody answered the door, so Trent picked the lock and entered. Looking around, he didn't notice signs of distress or foul play. Ruby's overnight bag sat on the dresser in the bedroom, so he knew she'd been there. He felt somewhat at ease and thought he'd wait for her on the porch, but then he noticed another bag. It was sitting on a nightstand in the corner. Men's clothes were folded and stacked next to it. When he approached it, he saw Hayden's full name embroidered across the top by the zipper. Trent noted the one bedroom and clenched his fists. He went into the main room and rested against the sofa's arm.

He listened to his breathing, staying calm and unthinking until he heard a man and a woman chattering outside. When the woman laughed, he knew it was Ruby. Trent moved to the center of the room and faced the door to confront his lover as she entered the house holding another man's hand.

As the door shut behind Ruby and Hayden, they saw Trent and stood still.

"Good afternoon, Pinkerton."

Trent raised an eyebrow but acknowledged Hayden. "Rosemont."

Hayden looked at Ruby and said, "I'll go to my bedroom and give you two some privacy."

As Hayden walked past him, Trent asked, "Your bedroom, or Ruby's bedroom?"

"We're not sleeping together," Hayden said as he kept walking. "She's sleeping alone, just like when she's at home."

The bedroom door slammed, and Ruby was alone with Trent.

"You're making this easy for me, Ruby."

"Oh, so you came all the way to the Balkans to end our relationship? Couldn't wait for me to get home?"

She was holding a picnic basket and an empty wine bottle, so she went to the kitchen to place them on the counter. Trent followed. When she turned to face him, he reached for her bandaged hand and held it carefully. After he looked under the cloth wrapping, anger flashed in his eyes. He pulled her closer to him and examined her carefully.

"It's okay. I'm not hurt."

"He burned you."

There was no excuse for the burn, so she didn't even try to justify it or say anything about it at all. "He's coming with me to New York tomorrow and facing the jury. He has something that could help us find the fae realm."

"Come back with me now."

"Did you already move out of our suite?" Ruby asked.

"Yes."

Their voices crescendoed, reflecting the incendiary emotions behind their words.

"Then I think I'm better off staying here until tomorrow!"

"Ruby, I moved out and came here to tell you because I wanted a clean break. We can start our separate lives when you get back, and our separation won't be messy in Adam's house. It's for the best!"

"I see. It's going to be messy here, and then we can go about our lives when we get back there," Ruby stated dully. "Your offer to take me home today makes even less sense through that lens."

"I still love you and want you safe. You're burned for fuck's sake!"

"And I love you, but somehow that isn't enough for you!"

"She was more to me than you're ready to be, and I can't adjust," Trent admitted, lowering his voice. "And sometimes, when it's apparent you're not her, I feel guilty."

Ruby tried hard to hold back tears. She'd already shed too many recently, and she was tired of feeling like she needed to cry. Breathing in and out, she fanned her face with her hands. When she was ready, she faced Trent again.

She cleared her throat and asked calmly, "Where did you move?"

"I'm still on Adam's property, but I moved from the house. I'm in the little house behind the pool now."

"That's two bedrooms though."

"I'm using one as a music room."

"Are you sure that's enough space between us?"

"I don't want to leave Adam's service right now, so it's the best solution."

"Look," Ruby said. "There's nothing we can say now that will make this less awkward tomorrow. Let's have a pleasant goodbye and then try our best to move forward."

Trent took her hand in his. "Are you sure you're good here?"

Ruby smiled. "Yes. I'll see you when we get to New York."

He gave her a warm embrace and kissed her forehead. "I'll worry for you until then. Message if you need anything."

"I love you," she whispered, "but I won't message you. Not for a long time."

Trent nodded. "One day it will be better, and you will."

Ruby watched Trent leave the kitchen, then she leaned around the corner and watched him leave the house. She kept staring at the front door and thinking of their time together. Resting her head on the kitchen doorframe, she closed her eyes and willed herself to stay strong and own her emotions.

SEPARATE WAYS

Ruby's clairvoyant vision hit like a lightning bolt, coming with no warning and without mercy. She slid down the doorframe and collapsed onto the kitchen floor. It felt like she kept falling through the floor, and she couldn't claw her way back to the surface. Light from the kitchen got smaller and smaller above her as she sank, and blackness enveloped her. When she gasped and tried to inhale, it felt like water rushed into her mouth and nose. She panicked, not understanding how she became submerged in water. Her throat and lungs were burning, but she kept taking in more water as she fought to find the surface or an escape.

Her terror melted into tranquility. Her limbs ceased thrashing, released their tension, and stilled. Her body was peacefully floating. Thoughts of her soulmate lingered on her mind's edge, and she was vaguely aware of losing consciousness.

Ruby's back hit something hard, which nudged her awake. She could breathe again, but she knew she was still deep under an ocean because she could also see. Luminescent sea life danced around her in the gentle underwater current, and she remained on her back while observing their ethereal beauty.

When she regained enough presence of mind to realize she was having a magical vision, she sat up and looked around. There was only strange flora close by, but she ascertained the outlines of man-made wreckage in the distance and wondered if she needed to explore it. She stood, and that's when she looked down to observe the hard object that had broken her fall.

It was a marble sarcophagus covered in symbols that looked like runes. Since it was the only thing there, she knew the object of the game was to discover the box's contents. She was scared at the thought of a zombie or a mummy crawling out of it and attacking her. She reminded herself the surroundings were only a vision and

65

pushed against the stone lid. When it didn't budge, she told herself again that it wasn't real. With another push, the lid slid away and tumbled to the ocean floor.

A body rested inside, but it wasn't a macabre sight. It was a woman, and she looked asleep rather than dead. Ruby then noticed her pointed ears, so it wasn't a woman. It was a sleeping fairy, and she was gorgeous. Ruby admired the little female's tawny skin and silver hair. A red crown rested on the fairy's head. It looked like it was carved entirely from a gemstone, like garnet or ruby. A clear orb was clutched in her hands and rested on her abdomen.

Ruby recoiled when the fairy's eyes popped open, but her fright subsided when the body didn't move. Leaning back over the sarcophagus, she saw golden eyes staring back at her. Even in the low light, Ruby thought the irises looked like shining gold rings.

"Find me," the fairy whispered.

From far away, someone shouted, "Ruby!"

Ruby looked around, but there was nobody out there.

"Find me," the fairy whispered again.

"Ruby!"

She recognized the muffled voice calling her name and fought to stay with the fairy a bit longer.

"Who are you?" Ruby asked her.

The fairy's lips didn't move again, but Ruby heard her voice's echo rippling through the water. "Una."

"RUBY!"

Hayden held Ruby's limp body on the floor. He leaned against the kitchen cabinets, pulled her onto his lap, and cradled her head with his elbow. Her eyelids fluttered and closed repeatedly between periods of rapid eye movement, and he watched her face intently while stroking her forehead and calling her name.

"Ruby!" he shouted. "Wake up!"

He thought it possible she was having a magical vision but could tell she was too far gone, and it scared him. Fear told him it might be a medical emergency. Her lips were blue, and she was pale. He carefully used his magic to warm her and gently rocked her like a child in his arms.

He started to call for a doctor, but then her lips began moving. She repeated a phrase he couldn't hear, so he propped her head on his shoulder and leaned his head against hers. With their cheeks pressed together, and his ear a breath away from her mouth, he listened.

"Who are you?" Ruby mumbled.

Hayden then understood. She was communing on a different spiritual plane, like she'd done with Adonai and others in the past. He knew there was always a reason for her visions. He wanted to be patient and let her complete the journey, but she convulsed. He held her tighter and felt her skin grow clammy.

His decision was made. "Ruby, come back! Ruby!"

He felt her body stiffen, and she gasped for air. Her coughing felt wet against his neck, and he leaned her forward to see her eyes open and looking around as if trying to remember where she was. Finally, she rested her gaze on Hayden and calmed her breathing.

"Welcome back," Hayden said. "How do you feel?"

"I don't know. I thought I'd drowned. I was underwater."

She embraced Hayden and pulled herself tighter against him for warmth.

"You looked almost dead," he said. "You're starting to look much better now though."

"Is that why you woke me?" she asked while slipping her cold hands under his shirt.

"Cold!" he exclaimed with a start, and they both laughed.

"I needed a little more time," she said.

"What did you see?"

"A fairy. She was buried alive in a watery grave. I don't know where or why, so . . ."

Hayden's reply was stern. "Good. You shouldn't get involved with the fae."

"I know," she agreed, "and it was so violent. Drowning really hurt. I've never been hurt in a vision before."

Hayden rubbed her back and kissed her forehead. Ruby held onto him tighter and rested her eyes. They stayed on the floor in a cuddle puddle, living in the intimate moment.

"Pinkerton didn't leave you on the floor, did he?"

"No, the magic took me after he left," Ruby whispered and sighed. "Trent already moved out of our home. We've separated."

Hayden carefully asked, "How do you feel about it?"

Ruby gently kissed Hayden's neck, first pressing her tongue against his skin before following through with a soft brush from her lips. She searched her mind for the right words.

He tilted his head back and moaned quietly. He wanted her to do it again and thought about initiating more intimacy, but he waited. Her breakup didn't matter to him, but he knew it mattered to her.

"I feel needy—hungry," she whispered. "I've not been satisfied in a long time."

Hayden slid his hands into her hair, gripping it and lifting her face to meet his. "Do you want me, Ru?"

Ruby nodded.

"Tell me," Hayden demanded, pressing his forehead against hers.

She exhaled. "I want you."

He pulled her lips to his and kissed her with a vengeance. He felt a pull of magical energy leave his body, and then it surged back into him. It was like the ebb and flow of a magical tide, overwhelming and dangerous but also the pinnacle of rapture. He lost control of his senses and thought he was going to climax before even getting his jeans off, but the feeling slightly subsided. His body was still on the verge of orgasm but held perfectly on a delicious precipice.

Ruby gradually calmed the magical current between her and Hayden. Her lips and tongue continued to massage his until she had his fiery remnants under control. She pulled away and locked her fingers behind his neck, leaning back. She arched her back and turned her face towards the ceiling before breathing a small gust of flames.

"My stars, Ruby," Hayden blurted while catching his breath. "How did you learn to do that?"

A coy smile crept across her lips. "You really don't want to know."

He thought about it for a second and said, "Ah. I guess I understand why you ditched me for Adam now."

"I'm glad you liked it that much." She laughed.

"Liked it? I almost finished before getting inside you," he said, "and the insane part is I wouldn't have cared. It felt . . . I don't have words."

"Just wait until you *do* get inside me while we're exchanging magic," she said while grinding against him.

He moaned. "Do I have to wait?"

He grabbed her hips and guided her pace as she rocked back and forth against him. They played with each other, nibbling and touching.

"You don't have to wait if you're ready and comfortable with me syphoning your power again."

Hayden asked, "It won't give me your clairvoyancy power, will it? I don't think I could handle that."

"That's never happened before," she explained, "but back when he showed me how to do this, I wasn't using my syphoning gift for anything else. I'm stronger now. I don't know if that increases or decreases the chances of something like that, but I'll be careful."

Hayden pulled her completely against him. "If it's even better than what just happened, I'll risk it."

"Want to go to the bed or do it on the floor right here?" she asked.

Hayden felt Ruby's attempt to move and stopped her, pulling her back to him by the hips. Keeping her straddled over his lap, he pushed up her skirt and grabbed her cotton panties. He had handfuls of fabric from each side, and he smiled when Ruby gasped at feeling his hands warm up against her skin. When he opened his hands, the pieces of cloth he'd been clutching were burned away. What was left of her underwear fell between them, and he tossed them across the floor. He then lifted her until she was standing above him.

With his back still against the cabinets, he looked up

between her legs and said, "Lean over the counter and spread your legs a bit more."

As she carefully lowered her thirsty quim onto this impatient mouth, he grabbed her ass with both hands and pulled. Feeling herself slip down, she braced her arms hard against the counter and whimpered at the feel of his hands on her backside followed by his tongue inside her.

He used his powers to enhance her pleasure, sending both cold and hot sensations from the tip of his tongue. The magic tingled along her sensitive folds of skin before flowing up to join his tongue to push her button and give her the release she'd been desperate to experience for weeks.

She cried out and rested her face on the countertop, breathing heavily. The feeling of his hands rubbing up and down her trembling legs accompanied the last flutters through her core. When she felt him planting soft kisses down her inner thigh, she reached one hand down to his hair and combed through it with her fingers.

"Hayden?" she whispered sweetly.

He kept his mouth against her skin. "Mmm?"

"Undo your jeans. I'm ready to come down."

While continuing to lazily nibble and lick her, he dropped his hands to his belt. Despite his anticipation, he steadily removed his belt and worked on his buttons and zipper. He wanted to savor every moment. The woman he truly wanted was standing above him playing with his hair. Her scent was on his face and all around him. He inhaled it deeply while pushing down his jeans.

"Come down. I've got you," he said, reaching for her waist.

Putting her hands on his shoulders, she dropped to her knees before sliding herself onto his cock. She was slowly riding him while unbuttoning his shirt and pushing it open. Then she threw off her shirt and pressed her bare chest against his.

He felt her magic moving, shaping, and transforming his magic into an erotic art experience. Their hearts were beating together, and he loved the sensation and the knowledge that she was making it happen. Each time she rocked her hips forward to drive him deeper into her, the pleasure building between every heartbeat intensified. He marveled at her ability to work her magic through his chest as she'd done before through his mouth, and then he lost his will to think about it. All he could do was feel.

Ruby's face was pressed against his neck while she embraced him tightly and clawed at his back with every thrust of her hips. Reaching into his heart with her magic, she took a long sip of his cooling magic. Her breathing became erratic. She exhaled cold air before directing magic back to Hayden.

Hayden's chest around his heart felt pleasantly cold in contrast to the body heat he and Ruby were generating between them, and the feeling propagated throughout his body, like cool saline in his veins. He felt a wave of warmth chase the cold away, moaning when Ruby exhaled hot air into his ear while biting his earlobe. The fire and ice sensations, the heartbeats, the shifting magical tides between them, and the passionate sex reached a fever pitch.

Riding him harder and faster, she gave a last magical push against his chest, returning all the magic she took from him. Her body pulsated, and she moaned into his ear and felt him come undone with her.

She leaned against him in his arms and closed her eyes. "Thank you."

He chucked quietly. "No, I should thank you."

"I want to stay here with you," said Ruby. "I'm scared of what will happen."

"As long as I have your support, I feel I can face anything," Hayden stated.

She sat up and touched his face. "I am with you . . . My love for you hasn't always been of the same nature as your love for me, but it has always been there. And in this moment, I feel closer to you than anyone. I only wish we could hold onto it a bit longer."

"What if I make a promise to bring you back here one day?" he asked.

Her smile was tinged with sadness. "That would be perfect, Hay."

"You haven't called me that since we were children." He laughed.

"You stopped letting anyone call you that! It went against your perfectly professional and exceedingly boring image!" Ruby squealed with a peel of laughter.

Hayden calmly argued, "You're also a perfectionist in your own way. It annoys all of us how frustrated you get at failing. Although, I admit you rarely fail."

"Yeah," she agreed. "We probably belong together after all."

"It took you living without me to discover that?" he asked, teasing her.

"To be fair, that's a tale as old as time. You shouldn't blame me too much for human nature."

"Let's move this conversation to the bed and get some rest, Ru."

"That sounds like a perfect plan, Hay."

They helped each other up and stumbled together into the bedroom. The pillows and blankets felt like clouds after being on the floor for so long. Bending his rules, he let her bring snacks into the bed in exchange for another foot massage. They had the rest of the evening to ignore the obligations dragging them back to New York. For a few more hours, they were old friends and new lovers existing in a lakeside paradise.

PRODIGAL SON

The fae realm, the day before Eve's Death:

Robin gently touched Eve's back. A puffy blister surrounded by wounds that looked like black spider veins marred her fair skin. As his hand moved down her spine, the electronic device rose to the surface from within her body and fell to the floor. It sounded like a pin dropping, and Robin reached for it before it rolled under his bed.

"It's a lump of hard unnatural material," Robin said, holding it between his thumb and index finger and looking at it closely in the light.

"It was a weapon," Eve said and turned to look at it. "I must have thoroughly melted it. Can you do anything with it?"

After Joe paralyzed her in Albany, she'd realized something was in her body that didn't belong there. Lilith had disabled the device but hadn't bothered to remove it. Later, when she'd eaten the Edenians' eyes and escaped, the extra surge of energy she'd experienced had made it possible for her to feel the foreign object inside her and fry it to a crisp.

"No, but I can heal those nasty wounds you gave yourself," he said.

Placing both hands against her skin, Robin gently rubbed. A bit of damage wiped away with every careful pass of his hands. When her back once again looked healthy and perfect, he remained on his knees behind her and placed kisses down her spine. He then threw himself onto the bed before pulling her down beside him.

"Did they read your thoughts?" Robin asked.

"Most of them can't read thoughts."

"But the creators can. The vampires can."

"I didn't see the vampires."

"Evita?" Robin's tone communicated annoyance.

"I didn't think of you in the creators' presence. I didn't betray your secrets," Eve said, returning an annoyed tone of her own.

He pulled her against his body and wrapped his arm around her. "Good. I'd rather stay here and worship you than go collect the keys."

She laughed. "Other than us, the Daughters of Selene are the only souls with knowledge of the keys, and they're certainly not talking."

Robin responded with a low chuckle that turned into an excited growl when she suddenly rolled over and pinned him against the mattress. He would never tell her, but he loved Eve in his own way. His desire for her was immeasurable, and he held none of it back from her in that moment. He thought if he unleashed his lust hard enough, it would devour his fear of losing her imminently.

——— ——— ———

Ruby and Hayden arrived at Dust hand in hand with their luggage. They'd come directly from the airport and contacted the cabal along the way.

Adam, Ty, and Danielle met them in the building's main foyer where Ty placed an electronic belt around Hayden's waist as a means of arrest. Hayden was restricted to the Dust building until his trial, and Ty made sure a room was furnished for him to use.

Danielle removed her glove and shook hands with Hayden and then with Ruby. She touched Ruby's bag and then the lapel of Hayden's jacket. Noticing Ruby's bandaged hand, she touched it. Although there was a trace of surprise in Danielle's expression, she simply nodded at Adam and Ty and then excused herself to go work on research with Leilani.

"Was that really necessary?" Ruby asked Adam in response to Danielle using her magic.

"I can't give you special treatment," Adam said. "We have to verify nothing is amiss."

"We're at war, Ruby," Ty added as they escorted Hayden to his room.

When they arrived in Hayden's room, Adam watched Ruby take her luggage inside and sit with Hayden. As Ty left them, Adam stood by and studied the two young people.

"I see," he said.

Ruby smiled. "Yes."

Adam approached Ruby and held up his hands. She understood he wanted to connect with her, so she stood and let him hold her head between his hands. Likewise, she reached up and took his head in her hands and pulled his forehead against hers. She used her gift to push visions of things she wanted him to understand. They stayed connected with their eyes closed for several minutes while Hayden observed them with a solemn expression and a still, proper posture.

When they finally opened their eyes, Adam took Ruby's injured hand in his and carefully unwrapped the bandage. The burn was red and swollen, and Adam briefly cut his eyes to Hayden but said nothing. He'd understood enough when Ruby arrived and stayed with Hayden. He cupped her hand in his and closed his eyes. His heavy breathing was like a tempest in the quiet room. A slight glow of healing magic appeared between their hands.

"Thank you," Ruby said. "I'll come to you tonight about my premonition."

Adam kissed Ruby's healed palm and left the room without

another word. His footsteps down the corridor became mixed with another sound. Someone else was in the corridor.

Ruby realized it was more than one person, and their steps grew louder as Adam's grew faint. They were approaching quickly, so Ruby sat with Hayden. Both watched the doorway, believing angry witches would arrive to call him a traitor. She threw an arm around him and placed her other hand in his lap where he covered it with his hands. She was ready to protect Hayden, and he was ready to face his accusers with her support.

When Phoebe and Giselle appeared, Ruby and Hayden breathed sighs of relief. Giselle ran squealing at her brother while Phoebe walked casually behind her. Sitting at Hayden's other side, Giselle plopped her head onto his shoulder and hugged his arm.

"I'm so happy to see you, brother," she cried.

"It's good to see you, too," he replied. "I love you. No matter what happens."

"And what, exactly, is going to happen, Hayden?" Phoebe asked in a reproachful tone.

Phoebe observed her children. She noted her lover's daughter clinging to Hayden. She loved all three of them. She'd even grown to love Jeremy, and her son had put them all at risk.

"Ruby, will you please leave us?" Phoebe asked.

"No," Ruby and Hayden stated in unison.

Giselle raised her head to look at them, and understanding soon followed. "Oh. My. Stars! You're lovers! I'm not sure if I want to vomit or celebrate."

"Trent is fine with that?" Phoebe asked.

"Trent left me, so it's none of his business," Ruby replied.

Phoebe rubbed her forehead as if to soothe a headache. "So, your second—no, your third? Your third choice is good enough now?"

"We belong together, Mother. Let it go," Hayden said.

Phoebe nodded and shrugged with a bit of attitude. "Sure. We have more important things to discuss anyway, don't we? Because you're a traitor." She pointed an accusing finger at her son.

Giselle shouted, "Mother!"

"She's right," Hayden stated.

Observing her daughter cling to her son, Phoebe said, "I know I'm right. Not only did you almost cause your sister's death, but Robin could have killed me, too. He came to me last night on the beach—"

Again, Giselle snapped up her head. "You didn't tell us!"

Ignoring Giselle, Phoebe continued, "And tried to get me on his side in exchange for your life."

"What did you say?" Giselle asked.

"She wouldn't be alive if she told him no," Hayden said.

Phoebe flinched in disgust. "Fuck, no! I said no! You know how many witches are in that house? He wasn't ready to start a battle. That's all."

"Why didn't you tell?" Giselle asked.

Phoebe waved off the question. "Our family is in enough trouble. I didn't want to invite more."

Giselle asked, "Mother?"

Phoebe sighed. "Okay, I'll disclose it at the next meeting."

Phoebe approached Hayden and cupped her hands around his cheeks. "I love you, my beautiful son. I won't see you again until the trial, but I'll make sure Ty lets your father in to see you." Then to Ruby she said, "Thank you for bringing him home."

Phoebe left, but Giselle stayed and had candy with Ruby while Hayden had a drink and listened to them talk. He lounged in an armchair and was close to falling asleep. Hearing Ruby and Giselle talk made him feel like he was home, and he pondered how much he missed being home.

The girls giggled and threw pillows at each other, getting louder. Forgetting their cares was easy when they were hanging out together, and they reveled in childish behavior whenever possible. One of the pillows accidentally bumped into a wooden box that sat on a table by the bed, and their chatter stopped.

Giselle sat up with a start. "What's in that box? I thought I heard something."

Hayden opened his eyes and leaned forward in the chair. "Eros."

Giselle approached the box and felt around the intricate woodwork at the top, looking for a way to open it. Finding two buttons inset on either side, she pushed them. There was a click, and the lid separated from the box by only a tiny gap. She moved slowly while lifting the lid and saw two tiny black eyes staring back at her. She hesitated. When the creature inside told her it was okay, she completely opened the box. It was a red weasel with a white belly. The inside of the box was quite impressive. It was like a tiny apartment with a separate bathroom and a place to eat. She especially liked the silk sofa and all the tiny toys.

Giselle giggled and smiled. "Where did you get a Maltese weasel?"

"Malta," Hayden answered, and they all laughed.

Then Giselle gasped. "Eros says he belongs to Robin?"

Ruby said, "Elle, this is Hayden's plan to help us and maybe avoid punishment."

When Giselle looked confused, Hayden explained, "Robin's second home is a secret underground fortress beneath the hypogeum in Malta. He also has hidden places for magical artifacts only the fae know about . . . But Eros knows, too."

Giselle put her hand into the box and Eros ran up her arm to sit on her shoulder. "Okay, I'll see what I can find out once we get to know each other better."

"I was going to introduce you to him tomorrow," Hayden said, "but since you seem to be bonding, why don't you stay here tonight?"

"Yes," Ruby said. "I can get Ty to order another bed, and you can tell Jeremy you're staying with me."

Giselle was smitten with the friendly little weasel, so she happily played with him and fed him while waiting for the Dust housekeeping staff to bring her a bed.

Hayden finally fell asleep in his chair, so Ruby slipped away to meet Adam and share with him her magical vision of the drowned fairy.

"I've received some potentially useful information from the spellcasters in Calais, Normandy," Leilani explained to the assembled cabal members.

Adam didn't understand spellcasters. Edenian magic was difficult to document and trace over a thousand generations, but he kept eyes on his descendants, magical and non-magical alike. Spellcasters were something different though. Whereas witches shared one rare blood type, spellcasters shared a different rare blood type because of their common ancestor's relation to Eve, but not Adam. They upheld a religion he couldn't pinpoint a history for, and some of them found ways to leverage the Earth's magic through chants and prayer.

Even more rare were the spellcasters who used objects to focus and tune residual magic. They healed and protected their families with ordinary herbs. Good fortune manifested within their ranks through stone beacons and wooden talismans. Elders carried special wands or scepters in conjunction with verbal spells to direct the small remnants of magic they gleaned from the universe around them.

Although spellcasters were talented in their own ways, Adam and the cabal had no use for them due to their religious cultish nature. They didn't trust any global companies, including Dust, and their communities were sequestered except for necessary economic considerations. Society at large had no modern examples of religious cults and thought spellcasters were simply farmers who preferred nature to modernity. The world called their communes "Archaic Islands," and called them "Archaics." Only the Children of Eden knew what they really were. In addition to the spellcaster commune in Calais, there were two more smaller groups near Salem, Massachusetts and Varna, Bulgaria.

"They've never been eager to give me any information," Ty said. "How did you get them to cooperate? You were gone for, what? A day?"

Leilani and Danielle both laughed at him, and Danielle said, "You're all business when researching. Leilani and I showed up armed with food, libations, and small talk."

Leilani added, "Turns out, they were very interested to hear of Eve and her death, but they became completely cooperative when I dropped Robin's name."

The round table was abuzz with chatter about how the spellcasters could know about the fae. Questions were exchanged in excitement. How did the spellcasters know about Eve's existence in the first place? How did they know about Robin? Most of the witches didn't know about either of them before Eve's escape, so how did farmers with almost no outside social connections know first?

The time was prime for Phoebe to mention her unplanned rendezvous with Robin. She glanced across the table at Giselle. Her daughter was staring her down, prodding her with an aggressive nod.

Addressing Ty, Phoebe's voice rose above the uncontrolled conversations. "Ty, I wish to enter a statement into the record."

Chatter dissolved to sporadic whispers, and Ty replied, "Go ahead, Phoebe."

"While I was walking my dog on the beach two nights ago," she said, pausing to breathe and collect her thoughts, "Robin approached me and offered to spare Hayden's life if I would defect to him. I refused, and I thought he would kill me, but luckily for me, most of you were nearby, and he was not prepared for a battle."

"Danielle, Bastion, Leilani," Adam commanded with a controlled, assertive tone.

Bastion spoke first. "It's been too long. I wouldn't be able to—"

"Try anyway!" Adam interrupted.

Bastion approached Phoebe, his eyes telling her he was sorry for invading her personal space. He thought smelling her clothing would be useless, so he leaned over her shoulder and smelled her hair. Expecting to be backhanded across the face, he flinched when she shifted in her chair, but she only turned her body away from him. Floral shampoo overpowered his magical senses.

"Nothing," Bastion firmly declared.

Leilani didn't need to move around the table to exercise her power, so she was already studying Phoebe's subtle mood shifts as Bastion made his assessment. The other witch's eyes met hers and lingered. Her aura turned purple. Phoebe was balanced.

Leilani smiled and said, "Nothing."

Danielle removed a cotton glove from her right hand. The room was too still and quiet. She didn't like how her footsteps pierced the silence or how the space between her and Phoebe seemed like an ocean. She didn't want to find proof of betrayal but feared she might. Danielle searched Phoebe even though they both knew the best object to read was her communications bracelet. She searched for anything less intimate, but there was nothing. Phoebe wore no jewelry and carried no handbag.

Phoebe's eyes closed as she held out her wrist.

Danielle's breath faltered when Phoebe wouldn't meet her eyes, but she wrapped her graceful ebony fingers around the dainty wrist held steady before her. Every soul in the room focused on them. The reading went well for several moments, but then a gasp sprang from Danielle faster than she could control it.

"She told the truth," Danielle said, letting go of Phoebe and facing the table. "She refused to betray us."

Danielle began walking back to her seat but stopped when Leilani said, "There's something else."

Sliding her glove over her hand and buttoning it, Danielle didn't raise her eyes toward the table. "Nothing relevant. She stayed loyal."

Ty didn't want to see Danielle incite Adam's anger. "Dani?" he asked softly. "We all saw your reaction. Finish the read."

Danielle looked at Ty, focusing only on him. His support calmed her nerves. The details they wanted her to recount were disturbing, personal, and embarrassingly intimate.

"She . . ." Danielle breathed and started again. "She engaged in intercourse with him on the beach . . . Then she . . ."

"She what?" Adam demanded.

Danielle's eyes shifted to Adam.

"Look at me, Dani," Ty said. "You're almost finished. Then we can move on."

Danielle focused on Ty, took a deep breath, and blurted, "She stabbed him in the chest with a stick and walked away."

Bastion laughed openly.

Trent's mouth curved into a subtle smile.

Adam shook his head.

Ty looked at Phoebe quizzically, and Phoebe responded, "Oh, please! Like you've never met me? May we move on now?"

"How was it?" Bastion grinned peevishly.

"Wait, is he dead?" Jeremy asked.

"Moving on!" Adam declared. "But, no, he's not dead. Ty, keep control of the meeting please . . . Leilani, you were briefing everyone on the Calais spellcasters?"

Yes," Leilani said. "They are partially descended from the Daughters of Selene, which is an extinct moon cult. Eve exterminated most of them sometime during the First Dark Ages, and Robin took certain valuable artifacts from them. The spellcasters preserve the Daughters' sacred texts." Her fingers slid quickly across her tablet, and she continued, "I've sent everyone images to review."

The witches studied pictures of three crystals: a skull, an

obelisk, and a sphere. Crude drawings and handwriting on brittle parchment described them as keys to the universe gifted to them from the moon goddess for their dedication to her. The Daughters of Selene alleged Robin stole the keys to keep anyone from opening a portal to the fae realm. According to the spellcasters, the keys hadn't been seen since the First Dark Ages.

"Our focus now is to find these keys," Adam declared. "We must find them and decipher how they work."

"If these are the keys," Giselle said, "then there must be a door."

Adam nodded. "We're working on that."

Giselle smiled, knowing what information she intended to glean from little Eros. Ideally, she wanted the information prior to Hayden's trial the next day to help his case. She felt a bit guilty keeping the weasel a secret from Jeremy and the others, but she didn't want them to interfere or take him away from her and scare him before she could bond and communicate with him properly. Before Leilani went around collecting the meeting tablets, Giselle studied every image.

She'd sat idle, waiting while her mother, brother, and partner had fought Eve. Her determination to make a difference in the next fight was like a flame burning steady and true within her heart.

THE MALTESE WEASEL

Adam couldn't disguise his horror from Leilani. He appeared at ease to everyone else, but she knew his feelings were in turmoil. Ruby, his most trusted spiritual advisor—his recently deceased favorite's daughter—chose to sit with the accused, and Leilani knew Adam wouldn't get through the rest of the trial without her help. As she altered his mood, he sensed it and directed a nod in her direction.

The evidence against Hayden hadn't been nearly as damning as his full confession. Still, his apparent contrition and his professed ignorance and miscalculation of Robin's plan were swaying some of the jury members in his favor. He'd helped save their lives during the battle with Eve, so their votes would be difficult to declare.

Before the vote, Hayden was entitled to have the floor and invite others to speak in his defense.

"I have the means to correct my error," Hayden asserted, watching his mother send him an encouraging nod from her seat next to Ty. "I can pay for my crimes with information crucial to the cabal's victory over the fae."

"Do you have someone to speak on your behalf?" Ty asked.

As Giselle appeared through a door at the back of the room, Hayden said, "Camilla Giselle Cohen Rosemont will champion my plea bargain request."

Giselle approached the room's center and stood in front of the voting jury. Eros was perched on her right shoulder, and six jury members were immediately focused on the weasel. Trent was still looking down at his tablet, so Jeremy nudged him in the side.

Trent was clearly the most prejudiced jury member. He

wasn't consciously giving Hayden a difficult time, but his feelings about seeing Ruby hand in hand with her new lover were apparent in his attitude. He showed real interest in the proceedings for the first time when he looked up and saw Giselle's confident expression. She had something important to share, and he knew it.

"This is Eros, Robin's Maltese weasel," she said. "We've been communicating since yesterday. Those crystal keys? Well, they don't go to a door."

Giselle paused for effect; such was her dramatic nature. Eros leaned into her hand while she stroked his white belly fur and hummed softly to him. She saw Adam on the edge of his seat and prolonged the moment even more.

"Giselle!" Phoebe chided. "Get to the point!"

Giselle smiled weakly. "Yes, Mother . . . It's an archway. I know where it is. I propose Danielle and I go there, and she can use her touch to divine the keys' locations."

"The stoat can't tell you where the keys are?" Ty asked a little awkwardly.

"Um, he's—he is a Maltese weasel, Mr. Alexander," Giselle argued, pointing to the animal on her shoulder. "Eros."

Phoebe wanted to rip out her own hair. "Answer the question, Giselle."

"The keys have been hidden since the Second Dark Ages. I've gathered that's why Robin attacked then. He needed a big enough diversion to retrieve and hide valuable items without being noticed . . . I think because Eve knew where they were originally."

"I said answer him." Phoebe glared at her daughter.

"I did!" Giselle spoke with conviction. "Eros is five years old, so how could he have seen keys hidden since 2125?" She took a breath and moved closer to the jury. "He's been close to Robin. He's seen the arch, and he's heard Robin talk about the keys. We can find them if we start at the arch, I'm sure of it! This puts us much farther ahead than we were yesterday and is worth your mercy for my brother!"

Trent asked his first question all morning. "Where is the arch?"

"It's in a treasure room hidden inside Malta's hypogeum. Robin has a secret home there, but Hayden killed the home's caretaker when he took Eros. It's unguarded now," Giselle said.

"How do you know it's unguarded?" Trent asked.

"Robin's required to hold court from the equinox to the solstice. He shouldn't be in residence in Malta until midsummer," she explained. "We'd obviously still need to case the joint before barging in, but—"

Ty interrupted, "You got all that from a stoat?"

"No, I got it from this weasel, Eros." She pointed to her shoulder again.

Ty turned to Adam and said, "We need to see how much more information she can get."

Adam considered Ty's suggestion and asked, "Does Robin know we have his pet?"

Hayden said, "Yes, he knows I took his pet and killed his cousin to escape."

"Does he know we have an animal whisperer?" Adam asked.

Hayden shook his head. "No. I think it's best if we keep Eros until after we find the arch because if he's looking for me and looking for his pet, and also performing duties in the fae realm, he won't think to find any of us at the scene of my crimes against him."

"Still, he must think you had a reason to take him," Adam said. "He'll discover the reason soon enough, I wager."

"We use everyone we can and act fast, then," Ty suggested.

Leilani added, "Carefully, of course."

"Of course," Ty agreed.

The jury agreed that Giselle and Hayden had provided a solid plan forward. The problem was coming to an agreement about Hayden's fate. They adjourned for lunch and to deliberate behind closed doors.

Hayden and Ruby wanted a quiet lunch in Hayden's room. She went ahead to the elevator to get a head start on ordering their food while he stopped at the closest men's room. Nausea overcame him just as he made it to the toilet. Struggling to get a grip, he washed out his mouth at the sink and then splashed cold water on his face.

The door made a squeaky sound, and Hayden looked into the mirror to see Bastion entering the bathroom and approaching the adjacent sink. Hayden kept washing his face and then took a long time washing his hands, too. He didn't want to acknowledge Bastion. His bandwidth for social interaction was spent, especially while waiting for judgement.

"Did you tell them you saw me in Malta?" Bastion asked plainly.

Hayden didn't turn to him directly but looked at him through the mirror. "Our trials are open to everyone. You could have been there and found out."

"It won't go well for you if you did." Bastion turned and leaned against the sink.

Hayden dabbed his face with a towel before walking toward the door. He had no plans to mention Bastion at all. His presence in

Malta seemed shady, but it would be Hayden's word against Bastion's if he said anything to the cabal. It was essentially a problem for later, whereas his trial was an immediate problem.

⁓ ⁓ ⁓

Despite Hayden's anxiety, lunchtime passed quickly. As he and Ruby took their seats before the jury, his mother's face was unreadable. He noticed Adam and Trent were focused on Ruby. The others didn't seem to be looking at anything specific.

Ty read from his tablet. "Carolus Hayden Rosemont. You will spend a year in confinement between this Dust office and Camilla Rosemont House unless the cabal requests your presence at an official function, or you are required for field work. You will report your movements between approved locations to Trent Pinkerton. You will wear your emergency bracelet, and it will actively track your location."

Hayden felt arms embrace him from behind and looked down at his chest to recognize his sister's hands clasped there. Her chin rested on top of his head, which would have annoyed him at any other time. He placed his hands over Giselle's, and then Ruby placed her hands over his. Hayden noticed Jeremy watching them like he wished to stand by Giselle and join their group hug. The thought crossed his mind that Jeremy had always worried they wouldn't include him as kids because he was the youngest, yet he grew to hold more prominent positions in Dust and the cabal than any of them.

They continued listening to Ty read. "You will not continue your position within Dust at this time and will not have access to the network. You will work on cabal missions as needed. You will receive half your Dust salary until your sentence expires. Do you understand? Will you comply with these terms?"

"Yes, thank you." Hayden's relief washed over him like a warm shower.

Trent approached the trio to remove the restraining belt from Hayden's waist and lock a bracelet onto his wrist. "Excuse me, ladies. I'm sure he'll survive without you both touching him for two minutes while I do this."

"Jealous, I guess," Giselle commented under her breath.

Hayden whispered, "Behave, Giselle."

Butterflies aflutter in Ruby's stomach prompted her to reach for Giselle's support. Partially hidden behind her best friend's embrace, she spied Trent and Hayden interact. It was surprisingly difficult for her to face Trent. Maybe thinking about her soulmate's relationship with him made her uneasy.

The jury dispersed. Jeremy and Phoebe joined Hayden, Ruby, and Giselle. Phoebe embraced her children. She embraced Faustina's children, too. They visited together and watched the housekeeping staff replace the oblong trial table with the cabal's round table. The afternoon would be dedicated to planning what was essentially a heist in Malta, and Hayden was expected to sit at that round table with his kindred and act like he was okay.

Dust's formal event room once again provided an optimal training space. Five lifeless Companions were stacked near the piano, and five more of them were stacked in the room's opposite corner. The game's object was to swap their locations within one second, and winning became Jeremy's sole obsession.

Trent watched Jeremy pull five Companions through a rip in space and deposit them on the opposite side of the room before repeating the action for the second pile of Companions.

Jeremy then appeared, panting in front of Trent and said, "That was only forty seconds."

Trent cracked a taunting grin while strutting to the piano. He picked up a single finger from the floor in front of the Companions and dangled it in the air before Jeremy's widening eyes. Trent tossed the finger and Jeremy caught it.

Jeremy inspected the appendage that looked like it was precision cut away from its hand and said, "Okay, I almost did it in forty seconds then."

"Almost?" Trent laughed. "Your sister might kill you if you lost her finger somewhere across spacetime."

Jeremy rubbed his neck and sighed. "Yeah."

"Ready to try again?" Trent asked.

"Absolutely." Jeremy went to the far corner and reset his stopwatch.

"Remember, it's about making the portal big enough and having it open long enough for all matter to get through safely, so even though you need to be fast, you also cannot rush," Trent explained.

"That doesn't make sense, Trent, but I'll work on it."

Even though it took considerable energy, moving a person instantaneously through two points in space was easy work for Jeremy, but he needed to move a small team in one trip. Learning to do it rapidly was as essential as adjusting location on the fly for security concerns. In the event the team arrived at a point of interest to find an enemy waiting, he'd need to take them to a backup location immediately. If it took Jeremy longer than forty-eight hours to learn how to get a whole team to a location with all of their appendages still attached, he wouldn't be able to ensure their success in Malta.

DAUGHTERS OF SELENE

Dover, England, Blue Earth, 973 A.D.

Opaque white crystals formed a protective circle around the women while they danced in praise of the moon goddess, Selene, who had gifted them the great gateway shining at the circle's center. The goddess had granted them access to every dimension bordering the Blue Earth to open their minds and give them knowledge they prayed to receive. In return, they continued loyal devotion to her upon the fruition of each moon cycle.

On a rocky plateau overlooking the beach, they moved gracefully in pale moonlight. The night of the full moon belonged solely to Selene, their favorite among a pantheon of gods they revered. They joined hands to form another circle within the circle of stones. Facing the gateway, they chanted.

It was a stone arch that looked impossibly made. Crystals of various type and shape were seamlessly fused into a structure about the width of two standard doors. It reached six meters high at the topmost central point, on which the skull key perched. A crevice on the right side held the sphere key while an identical crevice on the left side held the obelisk key. The entire structure glowed brighter as the women's voices crescendoed.

Oberon and Robin appeared in a snap. Their bare feet almost touched the white crystals that lined the circle, but they couldn't step any closer. Their magic couldn't penetrate the circle either. For the second time, they were sensing the gateway's energy lifting the veil between the fae realm and the Blue Earth, exposing their kingdom to humans.

The women hadn't attempted to walk into the realm's boundaries the first time they'd opened the gateway. They were still learning through observation and appreciating the universe's beauty, so they'd only watched. They'd watched two other dimensions since receiving the gateway as well.

The fae had also been watching and waiting, and they would not abide further threats to their borders. During the five months since their borders were first disturbed, they'd appealed to an ally for help. Oberon studied the Daughters of Selene closely while waiting at the circle's edge with his son. It infuriated him that none of the women acknowledged him. He understood they feared nothing while Selene's protective crystals sounded them, but his secret weapon was on her way. The Daughters of Selene would soon fear.

"You were right, Oberon," Eve said, appearing between the two royals. "I've never seen anything else on the Blue Earth this beautiful."

Looking at her, Robin said, "I have."

Eve favored Robin with a mischievous smile while Oberon pulled her against him to establish authority over his son. She lost interest in the exchange and watched her bastard descendants worship a foreign deity.

Eve scoffed, "Pathetic fools. They don't even have sense enough to know they're in danger."

"They're not paying attention to us," Oberon said. "They haven't seen you yet."

"They wouldn't know me anyway," Eve replied. "I abandoned them generations ago."

"Go on." Oberon waved toward the circle. "Get it over with."

Eve smirked and stepped over the crystals. Energy popped around her bare feet, and she giggled from the tickling sensation. A young girl heard the noise, looked back at Eve, and gasped. Then, every woman was watching Eve. With a flick of her wrist, Eve's energy knocked the skull from the gateway's summit. The crystal structure dimmed and flickered until it became dull.

An elderly woman, who was clearly the group's leader, stepped forward and prayed, "Maiden, Mother, Crone! Remove this enemy from our sacred place!"

Eve cackled so loudly her petite body shook. Her hands were on her hips, and she looked around at every woman. "What kind of nonsense is that? I am your mother," she stated loudly while pointing hard at her own chest. "Strange gods cannot save you from me."

"Selene will hear our cries and deliver us from harm," the crone said.

Eve's movement was so quick that nobody realized she had plucked an eye from the old woman until she held it up to the moonlight. There was one scream of agony from her victim before many screams of terror from the others erupted.

Throwing the eyeball on the ground and squishing it between her toes, Eve said, "There's no magic in your eyes. You're all useless to me."

Another anonymous cry rang from within the crowd. "Help us!"

"Do you not see me within your circle?" Eve answered. "Did you not witness me maim your priestess? Selene will not save you from your true mother. You belong to me . . . You belong to Eden."

Oberon called to Eve from beyond the circle. "Finish it, Eve! I grow impatient!"

Eve opened her arms and announced, "Daughters of Selene, your deaths will not be in vain. I sacrifice you to strengthen my alliance with the fae. May your souls find peace beyond the Gaia Tree."

She clapped her arms together, and the circle of crystals shattered from all directions. The energy blast also knocked every woman and girl to the ground. She stepped forward amongst mostly lifeless, mangled bodies. Stepping around carnage, she searched for survivors. Each time she saw movement or a face watching her from the ground, she destroyed another life until still, quiet corpses littered the ground around her.

Eve picked up the skull key and studied it. She felt its energy and walked under the archway in awe at the perfectly carved structure. Oberon and Robin joined her for a moment of silence and amazement, each fairy taking the key and holding it carefully in their hands.

A whimper spoiled their moment. Robin followed the sound and discovered the old priestess on her back struggling to calm her breathing. One eye watched him blankly while he inspected the empty eye socket that was raw and bloody from Eve's attack. Placing a hand over the wound, he rubbed it until her flesh healed. The old woman stopped whimpering and closed her eye, taking a final deep breath as she died.

Between corpses' shadows, a small dirty face observed Robin. Estoile held her breath and remained as still as possible, even while her grandmother died under Robin's watch. She had no choice but to breathe, though it was a dangerous task. With every shallow breath escaping her nose, she braced for discovery and death.

"Robin!" Oberon shouted. "Take Eve with you back to the keep. I must move the gateway."

As Robin retreated, Estoile took a full breath and blinked hair away from her eyes. Hope tingled in the back of her mind. She heard two snapping noises ringing into the night and then nothing. She squinted. The silhouettes were gone. Where the center of the circle had been, there were no longer two fairies and a witch. Her people's gateway was gone. The one they'd called "Robin" and their lost matriarch, Eve, had slaughtered every woman in her clan and stolen their most sacred possession.

Estoile, alone, was left to carry the history and the magic of her people. The men were not pure enough to share the knowledge, and the children were not old enough. She walked from the hill with that heavy burden and prayed for Selene to give her strength to fulfill her duties honorably until more girls came of age.

Ty, Danielle, Jeremy, Giselle, and Eros had taken a private flight directly to Malta from New York. They'd needed Adam's connections to obtain special customs allowances for Eros and expedited arrival and departure timelines for the entire team. Jeremy shoved a few water bottles into his backpack along with some supplies he thought might be useful for an underground trek. Most of their other possessions remained on the plane when they transferred to the car. They were having snacks and shaking off jetlag on the short drive to the hypogeum.

Ty was where he needed, and wanted, to be. After realizing the cabal needed Danielle to do field work that required walking right into the enemy's house, Ty had volunteered himself to be the team's protection. Besides Adam, Phoebe and Duncan were the only other witches capable of directing energy as a defensive measure, and Ty believed he was a better choice to protect his longtime friend along with two youths. Phoebe was a loose cannon and Duncan was too old, in his opinion. After the Companion fiasco, Adam wanted Ty to shift positions within the company and defer to Leilani. Focusing his energy on cabal business was Ty's preference anyway.

Danielle felt safe with Ty. It felt just like when they were teenagers; he used to support her when bullies made fun of her gloves. She'd manifested strong powers earlier than some witches and going through that change before adulthood had been rough for her. They'd started as early childhood friends before growing apart over the decades, especially after Ty's partnership with a socialite

Adam had approved for him. When his partner had later committed suicide, Danielle hadn't been sure how to treat him anymore. The Children of Eden's recent reformation had rekindled their relationship, and just like when they were young, his support calmed her nerves and made her feel better about herself.

Jeremy was disappointed his strength and skill didn't yet allow him to take them all to Malta and back in a flash, but at least he could quickly move two people at a time once they arrived, especially since he was saving his energy in case they got into a pinch. He felt good about having Ty on the team, and the vampires had spies all over Malta and Gozo to feed them any information that could affect how safely and successfully they might infiltrate the hypogeum.

Giselle was more comfortable in her skin than she'd ever been. Her power had helped save her brother, and it was helping the cabal find tools needed to triumph over their enemies. Having her partner on the team helped calm her nerves. She loved Malta, and she thought back to when she and Jeremy had vacationed there together. Reminiscing about it kept her mind from imagining all the ways they could run into trouble. She pushed away unpleasant thoughts.

She remembered taking Jeremy for a drink and a casual bite to eat at The Artful Dodger before dancing in the streets among a group mixed with locals and tourists. It had been the most colorful and low-key night out they'd ever experienced together. She didn't love the idea of having to disappear from Malta quickly or the possibility of Ty having to fight, but she was determined to remain calm and focused no matter what. Giselle was also slightly conflicted about leaving Eros behind once he was home.

Eros loved food, cuddles, and anyone who'd give him food and cuddles. His new friend gave him extras of both and let him sleep on her shoulder against a warm neck and soft hair. He didn't know where he was or where they were taking him, but his life was going exceptionally well.

"Ozana and Dragos have had both islands under surveillance for two days," said Ty, "and they've not seen or heard anything suspicious."

The team got out of the car and moved to an alley to stand unseen while Giselle figured out the best way to enter the underground temple.

Digging into her bag, she pulled out a tiny harness and leash. "I can't get a good image from him right now."

"I didn't know they made harnesses for stoats," Ty said.

Giselle sighed. "Eros is not a stoat, Ty."

"You know he knows that." Danielle laughed. "You look ridiculous putting that thing on him."

"Let's see how ridiculous I look when it works," Giselle whispered.

Giselle gave Eros a snack and then placed him on the cobblestone path. Rather than lead them from the alley, he turned and scurried deeper into it.

"Are you really going to let your partner lead us into a dark alley?" Danielle asked Jeremy.

Jeremy shrugged and followed Giselle.

Ty favored Danielle with one of his rare subtle smiles. "Come on. This is far from the weirdest thing we've done."

When they caught up to Giselle, she was still holding a leash, but Eros was gone. The leash seemed to be protruding from a solid wall. She moved it up and down a bit, and they understood it wasn't stuck in solid stone as it appeared to be. She looked back at Jeremy, but he was deep in thought and cautiously reaching his hand toward the wall.

There was a tug against the leash from beyond the wall, and everyone paused to look down at it. Eros reemerged from the other side and moved next to Giselle's feet before turning and running back at the wall, an action he repeated three times.

"Well, I don't have to be an animal whisperer to know he wants us to follow," Ty stated.

"Is it safe?" Danielle asked Giselle.

Giselle lifted Eros until their eyes met. After about a minute, she rubbed under his chin and placed him back on the ground.

"I think the wall is solid unless you know it's a passageway," Giselle explained. "Since we all know that now, everyone should be able to walk through."

"I'll go first," Ty said.

Ty walked through quickly with confidence. A second after he disappeared, his face reappeared, looking to Danielle. Then his right arm sprang from the wall and beckoned her to take his hand. As soon as she had a tight grip on him, he pulled her through with a force that left her breathless as she crashed against his chest on the other side.

Giselle placed Eros on her shoulder and grasped Jeremy's hand. The three of them promptly followed Ty and Danielle through the passageway.

The team found themselves in a limestone corridor. An unidentified glow from above lit the way. With a sense of urgency, Giselle moved past everyone and continued walking. Eros jumped to the floor and scurried ahead of her. She moved faster when he reached the end of his leash, and everyone's pace accelerated to a slow jog.

Eros veered left through an open wooden door and took them through a series of intricately painted and tiled rooms before arriving at a dark stairwell leading down. He tugged at his leash. Giselle started to indulge him and stepped down the first step.

"Wait," Jeremy said and fished two small headlamps out of his cargo pocket, handing one to Giselle and one to Ty. "Put these on. I'll stay close to Giselle, and you can lead Danielle, Ty."

"Cheers," Ty said and donned the headlamp as they descended into cold darkness.

The stairs seemed to descend indefinitely, but nobody complained or gave up. Each witch understood they had specific skills needed for the mission, and that was too important for any one of them to lose focus. The enemy could be lurking anywhere, so they watched and listened while the stairs took them lower beneath ancient tombs and temples.

A glow gradually waxed brighter from above. It was exactly like the light in the first corridor they'd entered. Eros kept walking, so the witches kept following.

"Are those some sort of ancient magical motion lights, do you think?" Danielle asked Ty.

"That would be my guess, too," he whispered. "I don't trust it, though."

She gripped his hand tighter. "Agreed. I hope we find what we're looking for quickly and get out of here."

On cue, the stairway curved and then ended abruptly at double wooden doors. The wood was smooth, and detailed carvings lined the edges. The carvings looked like a cross between hieroglyphics and floral motifs. A gargantuan lock joined chains that were wrapped around the doors' handles.

Eros turned to the witches and sat up on his hind legs, looking directly at Ty.

"Giselle, does—does he know I can open that door?" Ty

asked.

She shrugged. "Maybe . . . He's smart."

"Yeah, a little too smart," Jeremy said.

Giselle sighed. "He's fine. Look at that cute little face."

"Yeah, a little too cute." Jeremy tried to approach Eros, but he ran to Giselle.

Scooping up the little weasel, Giselle laughed and said, "Don't be silly."

"Let's open that door. Ty?" Danielle asked.

Ty approached the chains and blasted them with his magical energy. The squeal of metal on metal echoed in the chamber followed by a sound of creaking wood. The door crept ajar. Ty pushed against one door, and Danielle pushed against the other one. As the doors swung open, the familiar overhead glow flared to life within the room.

It was a stone chamber made into a stately sitting room and adorned with Greek tapestries on the walls and Persian carpets across the floors. A consistent breeze flowed through that was comforting and surprising to everyone since they were underground and estimated they were somewhere far beneath all the known hypogeum levels.

Jeremy surveyed all the heavy antique furniture and said, "The fae must be able to transport objects instantaneously through the fabric of space sort of like I do. Look at all this huge furniture and sculpture."

"Speaking of your magic," Giselle said while staring into a far corner of the chamber. "I think we're going to have a slight problem."

Every head in the room turned in the direction of Giselle's gaze to notice the archway against a wall bathed in shadow. It was bigger than she'd estimated. They all approached it in awe.

"Oh, my stars," Danielle whispered. "It's enormous . . . and beautiful."

Jeremy clapped his hands together and rubbed them. "I can do it."

"But what if you can't?" Giselle asked.

"It's just crystal and stone. It's not like I'll kill it."

"You could damage it beyond repair," Danielle suggested. "What do you think, Ty?"

"I think you should go ahead and read it," he answered. "Then we'll see."

Danielle removed her glove and touched the smooth crystal. Magic met her fingertips, radiating from the structure. Taking a deep breath, she closed her eyes.

Images hit her stronger than she'd ever experienced before, and she spoke as if in a trance. "Skull key. La Calavera Bonita. United Mexican States. Mission Santa Elena, Tenochtitlan. Obelisk key. London. Cleopatra's Needle. Sphere key. Dowager Empress. Carnegie Museum. Pittsburgh."

Giselle's fingertips moved nimbly across her bracelet to record Danielle's words. "It's perfect—more than we could have hoped for. We have all the locations!"

Danielle jumped back from the arch and held her hand against her chest while panting heavily. The archway hadn't wanted to let her go, and when she'd resisted and broken free, she'd felt an electric shock to her hand.

Ty retrieved her glove from the floor and asked, "Are you okay, Dani?"

She nodded and took the glove from him, placing it over her aching hand. "I'll be fine. There's no burn or wound, but it felt like a very painful shock . . . Jeremy, you should be careful if you're going to move it."

"I am going to move it," Jeremy said while positioning himself under the arch. "There's no reason I can't use all the energy I can stand at once to get it home. If you all leave now, you'll make it back to the plane. We haven't seen any fairies or danger. There's no need for me to save energy to return."

Ty mulled over that plan for a minute and then said, "I don't see a problem with trying that. Whenever you're ready . . ."

Jeremy closed his eyes and imagined power pushing out from his body and enveloping the archway from the base to the pointed top. He concentrated on that image and took three deep breaths. On the third exhale, he pictured himself in the Dust event room.

He disappeared.

The archway disappeared.

Giselle breathed. "He did it!"

She removed Eros' harness and settled him onto a sofa. "You're home now." She smiled and scratched his chin.

"Come on, Giselle. We have a mountain of stairs to climb," Ty said.

Giselle followed Ty and Danielle from the room, and they started up the stairs. She felt something on the back of her leg and gasped. Eros had jumped onto her from behind, and he was crawling up the length of her body.

She let him perch on her shoulder and said, "Okay, you can stay with me as long as you want to."

Ty looked back at her. "I thought our plan was to ditch the stoat."

"It was, but it looks like Eros has other ideas." Giselle smirked.

The team continued their ascent. Ty's fitness and Giselle's youth served them well for the long climb, but they had to stop twice for Danielle to catch her breath and rest. Ty then carried her until they reached the top to avoid stopping a third time. Once they emerged from the stairs and got through the series of rooms, they moved quickly down the corridor.

They halted at the hidden exit, and Ty stepped through the passageway with caution to ensure the outside was safe before signaling for the women to step through.

Giselle and Danielle emerged into the alley, both squinting into the daytime light. They followed Ty to the street as he sent a message for their car to meet them and drive them straight to the airport. He messaged Adam to ensure he arranged for their private flight to depart within the hour. Ty reached behind him for Danielle's hand and felt it grasp his tightly. Looking back, he saw Giselle following closely behind Danielle.

Giselle glanced across the street as they approached their car and saw Dragos watching them. He gave her a slight nod, and she returned it before ducking into the car's back seat.

"That vampire across the street . . . Was that Dragos?" Giselle asked.

"Yes," Ty said, leaning back into the seat and exhaling an exaggerated breath of relief. "He and his partner are making sure we arrive to the airport and board the plane without any surprises."

THE SKULL KEY

Adam stood under the archway and admired its beauty and craftsmanship. His scientists and engineers had told him they couldn't identify some of the crystal stones. They'd told him they couldn't build another one, nor did they understand how it was built. A dedicated team continued studying it in a special room underneath Dust headquarters' basement, but Adam was sure they needed the keys before making any significant discoveries.

He noticed Leilani escort Sorina into the room and leave her just inside the door to wait for him. Sorina stood still and observed the archway until Adam locked eyes with her. Her blatant stare stayed with him while he crossed the room toward her. Because he wanted to savor her beauty, he walked slowly. Nearby employees asked him questions as they conducted tests on the archway, but he didn't acknowledge them. He walked past everyone, leaving them all behind and focusing solely on her.

Extending his hand to her in greeting, he said, "Welcome back, Sorina."

"Thank you." She clasped his hand, expecting a short handshake.

When he held her hand in his for a bit too long, she reciprocated by brushing her thumb across the back of his hand and holding his gaze. His response was to initiate his signature move; he brought her hand to his lips and kissed it softly, holding it there while admiring her silver eyes.

Adam never got enough of her eyes.

Sorina felt a desire stir deep within her. She'd also felt it at their last meeting, when he'd touched her back. She craved that feeling, having missed it for hundreds of years. The unexpected sexual awakening excited her. To know she was still capable of desire made her dare to flirt with Adam, showing him subtle attention. His green eyes were so piercing that she wondered if he could see into her soul.

She couldn't get enough of his eyes.

Adam's moment with Sorina had arrived. He could see it in the way she stared, the way she massaged his hand with her thumb, and the way she took a small step closer to him while his lips rested on her hand.

He moved her hand to his shoulder and trailed his fingers up her arm as he closed the distance between them and slid his other hand around her waist. He paused to make sure she was comfortable with the intimate moment, but she didn't retreat. Breaking eye contact, he admired her smooth neck then let his eyes travel down farther. The rise and fall of her chest told him her excitement was building.

Sorina kept looking at his face even when he looked away. It excited her even more to see him admiring her body while holding her waist and absently stroking her arm. She watched him raise his eyes up to her lips. She moved her lips closer to his but stopped and waited for him to take them. When his lips touched hers, she stopped holding back. She ran her other hand up his back and pressed him firmly against her body while deepening their kiss. Their intimacy consumed her mind and enthralled her senses.

It wasn't until Adam tried to pull down the neckline of her catsuit and kiss her breast that she gently pushed him back and got a grip on reality. "Adam, we are not alone."

Adam glanced at his employees going about their business across the room and sighed. "Would you let me kiss you again if we were?"

Sorina looked away. "I cannot promise you another moment, especially not alone."

"Very well," Adam said, coolly. "You're here to see the spoils of our Malta heist, so let me show you."

She walked completely around the archway twice before approaching it. She placed her hand against it. After some time, she pressed her ear against it and closed her eyes. Moving to the other side, she repeated the same actions.

"All of these different crystals . . . Does it work like an antenna, or a transmitter?" she asked.

"Well, we know it's what an ancient tribe called their 'gateway.' Our guess is if we can get it to oscillate at the frequency of another universe or realm, it will lift the veil between that universe and our own . . . Presumably, however it works, we can walk right through the archway into another world."

"And Jeremy Cohen was able to transport it here?" she asked. "If he'd accidentally activated it, he could be stuck in another dimension, or worse."

"It requires keys for activation," Adam explained. "I have drawings I'd like to share with you when we're done here, but to your point . . . Jeremy had trouble letting go of the archway once he got here, and he said a similar thing happened to Danielle when she touched it and used her powers."

"But we can touch it without powers." Sorina pressed her palm against it again.

"It seems so," Adam agreed. "Perhaps it was attempting to fuse to their powers, like the way its pieces are seamlessly connected. We may never know."

Sorina rubbed her hands over it. "It is truly unique and wonderful."

"Just like you." Adam made eye contact with her.

"I am flattered, Adam. I really am, but—"

"Stay with me tonight."

"It is forbidden."

Adam sucked in a breath then let it out slowly. "You shouldn't have told me that."

"Why?" Sorina asked, confused. "Don't you deserve to know why I will not stay with you?"

"Knowing it's forbidden only makes me want you more, obviously . . . You could have lied and said you aren't interested."

She laughed. "You really have a thing for forbidden fruit?"

"Doesn't everyone?"

"Maybe your kind, but not vampires."

"Sorina, you're a vampire. I'm not. You want me. It is forbidden fruit. Don't pretend to be above it all."

"I will do and pretend as I wish . . . Let us go look at some drawings and talk about those keys."

"Of course. Back to business," Adam said in a pleasant tone.

※   ※   ※

Mission Santa Elena was among the most famous ancient historical sites in the United Mexican States. Located near Tenochtitlan, it housed a museum, a botanical garden, and a restaurant. The museum was the home of a crystal skull called La Calavera Bonita, which had been in the building for centuries. The popular story was that nuns had discovered the skull beneath the altar on the same morning the Second Dark Ages swept across the world. They'd declared it a sign from God and had kept it locked inside a secret reliquary where it had stayed until discovered during twenty-third century renovations to convert the church ruins into a museum. As the most unique and mysterious artifact associated with Mission Santa Elena, it was always on exhibition within a locked and well-guarded glass case.

Jeremy, Phoebe, Ty, and Danielle stood in front of the crystal skull contemplating another heist, but instead of stealing from their enemies, they were going to steal a priceless artifact from a foreign government. Whispering to each other as inconspicuously as possible, they tried to solidify a plan.

"Why didn't Adam just try to buy it?" Phoebe asked.

Ty started listing obvious reasons. "Time, publicity, opportunity—"

"Shut up, Ty," Phoebe said.

"Can the vampires do anything?" Jeremy asked.

"They're working surveillance outside," Ty said. "Besides speed and strength, they can read minds, but you know that."

"Can't they fly?" Danielle asked.

Ty shrugged. "Possibly."

"You want them to fly it out of here, Dani?" Phoebe asked.

Danielle chuckled. "I'm just trying to think of anything."

"It's too crowded to use most of our advantages," said Jeremy.

"Not if we create a diversion first." Phoebe shifted her eyes around the room.

Her idea was unsophisticated, but it would be effective without question. With two people able to weaponize their magical energy, they would incite a panic. Ty and Phoebe would work from opposite ends of the museum and act like regular people exploring the exhibits, but they would make casual movements to direct their energy at random objects. With objects exploding all over the museum for no apparent reason, it would be chaotic enough for Jeremy to take the skull and vanish.

"I like it," Jeremy said, "but how certain are you the exploding objects won't hurt anyone?"

Ty answered, "We both have enough control to ensure we don't directly hurt anyone by choosing the right targets and distances, but we can't guarantee they won't hurt each other trying to get out. Although, I think the probability for that is low."

"Is this the best plan?" Danielle asked.

"It's the only plan we can think of that doesn't get one or more of us identified or arrested," Ty said.

"Dani, you and Jeremy stay close to the skull. Phoebe and I will start," Ty said and turned to Phoebe. "There's a stone gargoyle at the other end I'm going to collapse. When you hear it, start a ruckus on your end. Take out the surveillance equipment as you walk through."

Phoebe smiled mischievously. "Got it."

Phoebe and Ty struck out in opposite directions. Phoebe noted several ugly items she couldn't wait to destroy on her way back toward the team. When Phoebe heard the first series of crashes and bangs echoing through the museum, she looked around and realized there were plenty of windows at the end of the great room. No people stood between her and the glass, so she balled up her fists by her sides and stomped her feet. All the windows shattered outward at once. Through the chorus of screams, both close by and in the distance, Phoebe continued her wrecking campaign. Security cameras crumbled to pieces. An elephant-sized vase toppled from its corner pedestal. She looked overhead at a garish cloud sculpture made of feathers, and it burst, sending feathers raining down as the last few tourists and museum employees fled.

An alarm was blaring. Ty crushed it. Through the flurry of feathers and dust, he saw Phoebe approaching Jeremy and Danielle. He focused his magic on the crystal skull, and its glass display case shattered.

Jeremy grabbed the skull and disappeared.

With a loud pop, Robin appeared between Phoebe and Danielle and blocked an attack from Ty with a snap of his fingers and then spun around on Phoebe. He caught Phoebe distracted with trying to shield Danielle and stabbed her with the same stick she'd used against him on the beach. While she screamed, he pulled her to him to shield himself against Ty. Kissing her lips, he bit her bottom lip hard and threw her at Ty.

Horror gripped Ty as he caught Phoebe and witnessed Robin lay hands on Danielle. The witch appeared paralyzed under the fairy's clawlike grip. Ty quickly guided Phoebe to the floor.

Phoebe held her chest and croaked, "Get Dani!"

As Ty stalked toward Robin and Danielle, he saw Jeremy reappear behind them. The fairy didn't seem to sense an enemy at his back as he faced a frontal attack from both a witch and a vampire when Dragos appeared beside Ty.

Jeremy saw Danielle had a free arm and reached for it, hoping to take her home. A pop pierced the air at the exact moment he touched her arm, and Jeremy disappeared along with Robin and Danielle.

Ozana lifted Phoebe into her arms and carried her toward the nearest exit. "Dragos, bring Mr. Alexander. We must leave before the police get in."

Ty dropped to his knees where Danielle had been. He

frantically tried to message Jeremy. He felt dizzy and nauseous, not knowing if Robin had taken Danielle or if Jeremy had taken her first.

Jeremy didn't respond, and Ty raged. "Fuck! Fuck! Fuck!"

"Mr. Alexander, we need to move," Dragos said while looking around and listening for other humans or fae.

Ty didn't acknowledge Dragos because he didn't hear him. He repeatedly tried messaging Jeremy. His expression was vacant as he stared at his bracelet. His breaths were coming faster and more erratic by the second. Leaning forward and catching himself with his palms against the floor, he retched. Finally, he heard Dragos' voice.

"We're running out of time. You need to come with me."

"I'm not leaving without Dani!" Ty shouted at Dragos, hearing him for the first time.

Danielle was suddenly there. She was clinging to Jeremy, and Jeremy was struggling to steady them both. When she saw Ty, she fell into his arms while he reached for her and embraced her firmly. She squeezed him tightly in return and told him over and over that she was okay while he cried into her neck. It was the most emotion she'd ever seen Ty display, and it disturbed her.

The volume of Danielle's voice escalated as she tried to bring Ty to his senses. "I'm fine, Ty! We made it back . . . Where is Phoebe? She's hurt. Where is she?"

Dragos answered, "Ozana took her outside. We need to follow them now."

Danielle and Jeremy got Ty to his feet, and they followed Dragos. When they emerged behind the museum, they avoided contact with the crowd and headed straight for an unmarked van lurking behind an outbuilding. Sirens wailed in the distance, and they knew they'd evacuated just in time. Dragos escorted them into the van, then he left on foot.

Inside the van, Phoebe was bandaged up and smiling weakly at her team. She was pale but still the same feisty witch. Her sassy voice ordered the van to get them on the road and away from the mission.

Her arms reached for Danielle, and she said, "Hug me, but not too much. I have a hole in my chest. Although Robin's aim was shit, thank the stars."

Danielle laughed and embraced her gently. "I was so worried about you . . . Robin gave you a taste of your own medicine, didn't he?"

Phoebe grunted a soft agreement and said, "Maybe I'll kill him right one day."

Ty had recovered from the shock of seeing Danielle taken and asked, "Where did you go?"

"I tried to grab Danielle's arm and take her back home, but Robin's magic took us with him first," Jeremy explained. "He didn't realize I was hanging on, and so he was surprised when all three of us ended up—well . . . I don't know where we ended up."

"I think it was back in Malta. It was definitely a bedroom, but the stones looked like they did in the Malta stone chambers," Danielle said. "He must have discovered the archway missing and gone straight to the museum. Jeremy pushed Robin off me before I knew he was there. As soon as physical contact with Robin was broken, Jeremy took us away from there."

Jeremy said, "It seemed to take forever though. I suspect his magic tried to pull us back. I felt an odd sort of tug."

"Where is the skull?" Danielle asked.

"I took it straight to Adam. It's safe."

"Speaking of going straight to Adam," Phoebe said. "You think you could heal me up, Ty? Or does Jeremy need to take me to Adam? I am, in fact, hurt and can't heal myself. I tried."

Ty went to Phoebe and laid hands over her chest. "I'm sorry I didn't help you sooner . . . I couldn't think."

Phoebe placed her hand over his. "I understand. Thank you for healing me now . . . Why don't you and Danielle stay here in the U.M.S. for the night? Jeremy can blink me home with him."

Ty looked to Danielle, and she nodded. "We're overdue for a talk . . . It would be nice to spend some time with you."

"The van can take you to Acapulco," Phoebe said. "I'll make your excuses to Adam and tell him you're flying home tomorrow . . . Let's go, Jeremy."

Phoebe held out her arms to Jeremy, he pulled her to him, and they disappeared.

Ty ordered the van to take them to Acapulco before settling into the seat with Danielle and holding her. There would be time for talking later. They enjoyed a silent, comfortable ride in each other's company.

RECUERDA LA NOCHE

Danielle sat on the balcony of a beachfront condo she was sharing with Ty and thought about her life. She'd loved Ty since they were children. During their college years, Adam had encouraged him to partner with a non-magical wealthy heiress. Danielle had mourned her dreams of a partnership with him and moved on with her life, or had she? She'd never had a partner. She'd never been willing to give Adam the satisfaction of accepting any of the men he'd pushed into her life as romantic love interests. She had spent most of her life rebelling against Adam, which included avoiding partnership and never producing children for him to control long after her death.

She watched waves crash upon the shore and enjoyed the sounds they made. The salty air was cool and fresh against her face. Wind blew across the balcony, bringing with it the scent of Ty's cologne. She turned to find him standing in the doorway with a blanket in his hands.

"I thought you might feel a bit cold in the wind," he said while approaching her and wrapping the blanket around her shoulders.

"I love you," she said to him. "I always have, and I always will . . . You should know that."

He sat in a chair beside her and watched the horizon. "You ignored me for years, Dani."

"I couldn't handle seeing you in a partnership," she whispered. "Then when she died . . . I didn't want to say or do the wrong thing. I didn't want you to think I was waiting in line for you. Especially when you were mourning."

He reached for her hand and brought it to his face. He rubbed it along his cheek and kissed it. Her fingernails grazed his lips as she brought her hand down to cup his chin. He looked up at her, and she brought her face closer to his and kissed him gently.

"Be my partner," he said.

"I think we should fuck first to make sure we're compatible," she said.

"I'm serious, Dani."

"So am I, Ty."

"You've loved me your whole life, but you think a moment in bed will make a difference?"

"If it only lasts a moment, I'll definitely pass on the partnership."

"Touché."

"Besides, I'm not sure I can still have children the natural way."

"Do you want children?" Ty asked. "If you do, I'm sure we can try unconventional methods."

"No, I meant if you want them . . ."

"Dani, all I want is you. If we can't have children, it wasn't meant to be . . . We're not young." He laughed under his breath.

"What about your reaction today?" she asked. "You need to be able to function if something happens to me."

"I didn't expect to have such . . . an extreme reaction . . . I would never wish to interfere with your work. Today I discovered another of my many flaws I must work to improve."

"We all have flaws, Ty."

"But your flaws are beautiful. I don't want you to change

them," he said.

She laughed. "You're apparently blind to my real flaws."

"Be my partner, Dani."

"Take me to bed, and I'll give you my answer in the morning."

Vlad and Sorina followed Adam and Jeremy to the archway. The vampires wanted to examine the skull key, and Adam was happy to have Sorina in his domain for as long as she wanted to be there. Adam approached the archway and removed the skull key from a crevice on the right side. He handed it to Vlad.

"I thought it would be heavier," Vlad observed, holding the skull up to the light and looking into the eye sockets. "The detail is extraordinary."

"Does the key do anything when applied to the archway?" Sorina asked.

"The oscillating frequency of the entire structure shifts a bit," Adam said, "and what's most interesting is the numbers are different depending on where the skull key is placed."

Jeremy took the skull key from Vlad and placed it back into the archway. "The key sits perfectly at all three locks."

"Locks?" Vlad asked, his face showing a growing interest.

Adam pointed to the crevices on either side of the archway and to the summit. "We're referring to the alcoves on each side and the indention above the peak as the locks. Because this key sits securely in all three, we hypothesize it works in each lock in combination with the other keys to open different gateways."

Vlad looked closer. "It's glowing."

Adam and Jeremy both snapped their attention to the

archway and then back to Vlad. The vampire was squinting at the archway, studying it intently. Adam cut his eyes to Sorina and saw her doing the same.

"Fascinating," Adam said, looking at Sorina. "Your visible spectrum is different than ours . . . My team has observed changes with infrared glasses."

Vlad observed Adam's attention to Sorina and said, "We are natural warriors and predators, Adam. Remember that."

Ignoring Vlad's warning, Adam said, "Once we have the other two keys, we can identify and manipulate resonant frequencies in relation to each Earth's universe and different harmonics . . . We're optimistic about opening a gateway to the fae realm."

"Why are you so optimistic?" Vlad asked.

During Sorina's last visit, Adam had showed her writings and drawings the cabal had collected from Calais. The writings described the archway and the keys in the most rudimentary terms and clearly claimed they opened gateways to other worlds. The vampires knew full well opening a portal to their enemy's world was the endgame goal for their current collaboration.

However, those ancient texts he shared with Sorina said nothing specifically about the fae realm. There was an additional written history describing how the Calais spellcasters' ancestors observed the fae realm through the archway. It also described how they were massacred at the hands of Eve and a fairy king. Adam hadn't found that information relevant to share with the vampires though.

"The Daughters of Selene, the archway's original owners, were exterminated for their ability to use this as a gateway into the fae realm," Adam said and stepped closer to Vlad, closely studying his expression. "Surely your spies have uncovered some of this information?"

Vlad's expression remained blank, and his voice maintained an even, superior tone. "I've heard rumors. Myths . . . Were they really your late wife's bastard children?"

The question was asked pointedly with a touch of what Adam interpreted as malice, or perhaps it was thinly veiled jealousy that fueled the indelicate query. Adam smiled at the vampire leader and felt triumphant and grateful that neither vampire could read his mind. He was ready for a bit of a challenge after spending much of the day walking the diplomatic line.

"You mentioned warriors and predators," Adam said and turned to conspicuously admire Sorina before looking back to address Vlad. "You remember Eve was infamously both those things . . . I loved her despite her madness and the trail of carnage forever in her wake. I am like her in many ways, which is how I was able to stomach what we had to do to her. She was badly burned and broken when I last saw her, right before Jeremy—" He stopped and gestured to Jeremy, who silently turned his back to everyone. "Jeremy ripped the beating heart from her chest."

Ty had entered the room during Adam's subtle verbal attack. He saw Jeremy grow pale and turn from the conversation. Realizing he'd appeared in the middle of a parle to assert dominance, he approached Adam and cleared his throat loudly.

Shifting his gaze to Ty, Adam assumed he'd made his point about the cabal's lethality in comparison with Vlad's coven. He hoped it was also clear his interest in Sorina would not be deterred, nor did he want his relationship with Eve, or interest in Sorina, discussed in mixed company again.

Adam concluded his remarks. "But, yes. They were her bastard children, and she slaughtered them just as easily as she murdered our shared descendants over the years."

Sorina hoped to lighten the mood. "Good day, Mr. Alexander. Sylvia told me you entered a new partnership with Ms.

Cheshire this morning. Congratulations to you both."

"Thank you. That's very kind of you to say," Ty responded quietly.

Jeremy blurted, "Already? You two didn't waste any more time, did you? Congratulations!"

Ty resisted the urge to flinch at how hard Adam was staring him down. The moment was so intense he feared Adam might accidentally release harmful magical energy upon him. Still, Ty boldly faced Adam directly and waited for his response. He'd hoped to tell Adam the news himself, not counting on Danielle's correspondence with her girlfriends to reach home before he did. He'd been so close, too.

Adam managed to save face. "Yes, congratulations, Ty. Why don't we all share a celebratory drink in my office and continue our discussions there?"

"Yes," agreed Sorina. "We still haven't discussed the solstice celebration."

Sands Point, Blue Earth, 2279 A.D.

The summer solstice celebration was usually held on Adam's private island, but Adam and his entourage of sycophants had too much business in New York to depart for the Caribbean as scheduled.

It infuriated Danielle. It was her first year receiving an invitation to the party. The adults finally recognized her as one of them and included her in the most anticipated party of the summer, but she still didn't get to experience one of the legendary island celebrations they all gushed about every year.

Ty noticed Danielle leaning over a balcony overlooking the back garden. Her curvy figure was accentuated by the copper mermaid style dress she wore. The only thing he could think about was seeing it from the front as he crossed the room to be in her company.

"Hello, Dani. Having fun?" Ty asked, hoping she'd turn to face him.

She did turn. Her breasts were perfect. He'd known they would be. His desire stirred, and he buttoned his suit jacket.

Danielle faced Ty and waited while he openly admired her cleavage before answering, "I hate it here. I wanted to go to the Caribbean."

Ty shoved his hands in his pockets and shrugged. "At least we didn't end up in California. The parents were all working in the offices out there until last week, you know?"

"No, I don't give a damn what any of them do, you know that."

He tried to keep the conversation pleasant. "Have you been out here all night?"

"Yes," she said and held up her glass. "This is my fifth old fashioned."

He frowned. If she was drunk, he couldn't invite her to his room, and he really wanted to. Maybe she was still sober enough for a dance, at least.

"Well . . . Will you dance with me?" he asked, fidgeting a bit.

Danielle's face felt warm. She thanked the stars for low light and dark skin. She wondered if her breathing was betraying her and turned back to the garden to control it. She wanted him so badly but hadn't expected to see him in the main ballroom, nor had she expected him to approach her. They'd both just had breakups with lovers, and her attraction to him had been unrequited for two years. She'd also spied him involved in the boys' chess tournament hours ago and had assumed they'd be at it all night.

She gathered her courage, turned back around, and answered honestly. "I want to go to bed with you."

He stared at her in disbelief and then laughed nervously.

Her anger turned on like a switch. He was laughing at her. She threw her liquor in his face and stalked away.

After cleaning himself up, he looked for her all over the house before going back to the balcony where she'd been. He thought she might return since she'd apparently been perched there drinking all night. Finally thinking to look outside, he scanned the gardens below. It was quite a show. The late-night hours of debauchery had arrived. Looking past a couple openly fucking on a stone bench, he spied her among a bed of flowers. She was picking Adam's roses. He laughed. She was picking all of them.

Danielle's evening gloves were copper like her dress, and they were much thicker than her usual cotton gloves. They made it easy for her to avoid thorns while deflowering all of Adam's rosebushes. It was common knowledge that he tended them himself and enjoyed taking time with his roses to make them perfect.

"He might actually kill you for that, Dani," Ty said as he approached her.

She didn't acknowledge him.

He didn't give up. "I wasn't laughing at you earlier."

"What were you laughing at then?" Danielle asked with attitude. "There wasn't anything else happening."

"What I mean is, I wasn't making fun of you," Ty said. "I was surprised at your directness is all . . . I wanted to take you to bed tonight. I would have suggested it at some point if you weren't already drunk."

She looked at him but didn't respond.

Holding out his hand to her, he said, "Let's go sit somewhere less dangerous and talk." He noticed she had another drink sitting beside her. "Bring your whiskey if you want."

Hand in hand they walked down to the beach. In a desperate effort to recover the night and do something wild, Danielle placed her glass in the sand and unzipped her dress. As she peeled it off, her excitement escalated from the way Ty stared at her. Between the alcohol and her desire, she felt invincible.

"You going to stand there? Or you going to join me?" she asked and took a sip of from her glass before handing it to him.

He still didn't understand but took the glass and drank it empty. "What?"

She giggled and ran for the water.

"Oh, shit!" He stripped off his suit as quickly as possible, still unbuttoning his shirt and throwing it behind him as he waded into the water.

They splashed each other and swam around, playing like children. By the light of the moon, her skin glistened in the water. He reached for her, hungry for the feel of it. She went eagerly into his arms, straddling him under the water. Feeling his desire hard against her panties, she went for his mouth. The kiss was salty from the water but sweet from the whiskey's aftertaste. They both moaned and deepened the kiss, savoring their excitement.

"Danielle! Get out of the water this instant!" her mother was calling to her. "We're leaving!"

Ty and Danielle looked toward the shore. "I wonder what's got up her ass," Danielle said, and they laughed.

"Now!" her mother shouted.

"We better go," Ty said.

"Yeah, I sense old people drama," Danielle said. "Time for me to listen to music while they bitch all the way home."

As they walked across the sand and gathered their clothes, Ty said, "I'm going to stay out here for a while." He gave her a quick kiss goodbye. "Thank you, Dani. This was fun."

Danielle smiled. "Yeah, it was. Goodnight, Ty," she said before following her mother.

The solstice had started with a flop of a party on a night destined to be forgettable in every way, but it turned into something special. Danielle would always remember the night she kissed Ty for the first time.

SUMMER SOLSTICE

Ruby entered the room arm in arm with Hayden. She looked fierce and owed it all to Giselle, who had styled her for the celebration. Her red hair was loose and curled, covering her bare back. She wore a satin royal blue dress that dipped to her tailbone in the back but only showed a hint of décolletage in the front. It was floor-length but split three inches below her hip on the left side. A broach was pinned to the top of the split, and its center stone was a fifty-five-karat ruby surrounded by diamonds and sapphires. An identical broach was pinned to a velvet choker at her neck. The ruby broaches were the only jewelry she wore, but Giselle had painted Ruby's nails red to match them. The red ribbons of her satin ballet flats were crisscrossed all the way up to the middle of her thighs and sewed to matching garters. The left one was accented with a bow and visible between the dress' split as she walked.

As a member of the cabal, Hayden was required to attend. He didn't mind a night out with Ruby, and he had a new appreciation for Giselle's obsession with dressing him for special events. His designated prisons weren't uncomfortable, but they were still prisons. It felt invigorating to put on a silk suit and enjoy good food, music, and scotch. Even though he was rather reserved and boring at times, his friends were interesting enough to make up for that. He especially liked watching Ruby charm people while enjoying herself at parties.

Giselle's dress of emerald silk was only a strapless corseted bodice with a mini skirt attached. Her red hair was styled exactly like Ruby's, which they had planned, along with their matching nails. Giselle's stilettos were also red. She chose to make her mother proud by foregoing jewelry altogether. She and Jeremy waited close to the main entrance for Ruby and Hayden.

Jeremy always welcomed the opportunity to spend time with

everyone, and it felt like his family was finally starting to come back together. He wanted to see his sister and talk to her outside of Dust business or cabal duties. He wanted to know she was okay again, and he wanted to repair the distance between Ruby and their mother as well.

Jeremy saw his sister enter the room with Hayden. "There they are. Let's grab some drinks and meet them."

Ruby saw Jeremy and Giselle approaching. She liked her brother's suit. It had emerald lapels and trim, exactly matching the color of Giselle's dress. She never thought Giselle would be smitten enough to coordinate her outfits with a man. Giselle had always wanted to look different than everyone else, and she was usually so independent. Ruby was glad they were obviously happy together but surprised her brother had what it took to tame her best friend.

Giselle handed Ruby a gimlet while Jeremy handed Hayden a scotch.

"To family!" Giselle said, raising her glass.

"To family!" They all raised their glasses together and toasted.

"Did you arrange the party again this year, Giselle?" Hayden asked.

"How could you tell?" Giselle beamed. "Is it because of how perfectly I've done everything?"

Hayden laughed. "Well, I was going to compliment you, but I guess there's no need."

Vlad and Sorina arrived. Vlad was not wearing his leather pants and jacket, and Sorina was not wearing her catsuit. The vampires had traded in their usual clothing for formal attire, and it was quite a pleasant sight.

Sorina's gown was burgundy. It had a velvet halter top with

a plunging neckline. Although the A-line skirt was floor length, it was sheer. She wore velvet hotpants underneath. Her matching sandals were pretty, but less formal than the dress. They were clearly made for comfort and ease of movement.

"Oh, my stars," Ruby said quietly. "Adam is going to have a premature orgasm at the mere sight of her."

Jeremy whispered, "I wasn't imagining it then! Last time they came to see the archway, I kept thinking he was about to throw her against a wall."

Giselle rubbed Jeremy's arm. "It must be really, really obvious if you noticed it, Jer . . . Now I want to be in the room with them more often to witness this epic love."

Vlad wore a black and silver brocade waistcoat with a black shirt and gray trousers. The ensemble was tailored perfectly to accentuate his fit, muscular physique. Instead of his usual ponytail, his black hair was loose and smooth.

"Has anyone ever noticed how gorgeous Vlad is?" Giselle asked. "I'm surprised one of the elder witches isn't trying to jump in his lap already."

Jeremy whispered, "Apparently, it's against their laws to partner outside the coven . . . Also, they have ridiculously good hearing."

"I was wondering why you were whispering," Giselle said. "You could have warned me."

"How do you know that about their laws?" Ruby whispered.

Jeremy sipped his drink and whispered, "I've been around them a lot recently and paid attention."

— — —

The guest list was shorter than usual. Naturally, non-magical

129

spouses had to be invited to the celebration, but Adam didn't invite anyone who didn't know about his true identity and the cabal. However, he had sent an invitation to the Calais spellcasters. He'd arranged their transportation and prepared the best bungalows on the island to accommodate the thirty-six of them who'd accepted the invitation. He usually didn't associate with spellcasters, but it was necessary to express his gratitude for their assistance. The politicians and business partners usually in attendance at his soirees were not invited, which made room for spellcasters.

He was trying to attract Robin to the party and had planned a trap for him, so no outsiders could be permitted to witness it. He'd ensured Robin intercepted false information suggesting the skull key was on the island with them. There was a replica in the conservatory garden displayed in a locked case. Sylvia was actively listening for fae magic. Jinae and Youngae were prepared to use their magical gifts to subdue Robin if he arrived to take the bait. Leilani was keeping the key players calm, so they could enjoy the party while also focusing on the parts they had to play.

Adam presided over his domain, checking security and walking around the ballroom greeting guests. He embraced Jameson and acknowledged Phoebe. He stopped to have a drink and chat with Faustina. Ruby's dress caught his attention as it really brought out her natural beauty. He was glad to see her chatting with her brother. Bastion flagged him down, so he started toward him but stopped at the site of Sorina. His eyes worshipped her through a full dance with Vlad before he approached Bastion.

Faustina observed Jameson and Phoebe dance. Her lovers were beautiful, vibrant people with fascinating minds. She felt lucky to know them. They'd helped her through dark times between Joe's death and Ruby's estrangement. Jameson and Phoebe loved each other the way she loved Joe. Sometimes she found herself wondering if she wanted another love like that, or if she was content without a partner.

Faustina's daughter approached, dressed to kill. "You look fabulous, Ru."

"Thank you, Mother," Ruby said and glanced at Jameson and Phoebe. "Are you still living with them? I haven't seen any of you at Camilla Rosemont House. I've been staying there often with Hayden."

"We're staying at my house to give Hayden his own space. Phoebe chose not to tell him to avoid an argument over it," Faustina said. "I'm surprised Adam lets you stay away from Sands Point so often."

"He doesn't like it . . . He doesn't like Hayden either." Ruby noticed a black hair on Faustina's pink dress at the neckline, so she brushed it away.

"What was that?" Faustina asked.

Ruby sighed. "I assume it was one of Phoebe's hairs."

Faustina's blonde hair was neatly swept up into a French twist. "Oh, thanks . . . I like Hayden."

"I know you do." Ruby smiled.

"And I love you, Ruby."

"I love you, too, Mother . . . It's hard to see you without him." Ruby promised herself she wouldn't cry. One of the reasons she'd needed to wait before talking to her family was to prepare herself to hold back tears.

"Is that the real reason you didn't want to see me?" Faustina asked.

"Mostly."

"I hope we can move forward together now," Faustina said.

"Mother, Hayden is my lover, and my brother's partner is

Hayden's sister, and his parents are your lovers . . . Does that sound normal to you?"

"Your life wouldn't be normal even if I wasn't living with Jameson and Phoebe . . . I was patient with the way you handled your grief, so I hope you can be patient with me. Being with Jameson and Phoebe is good for me right now."

Jameson dipped Phoebe on the dancefloor then kissed her cheek as their song ended. He watched her saunter toward the bar before he looked back at Faustina, who smiled and waved at him with her index finger. That's when Ruby glanced his way, too, and his smile widened. His lover was finally reconnecting with her daughter.

"Dance with me, Ms. Cohen?" Jameson asked Ruby.

Ruby rolled her eyes. "Mr. Rosemont, you're the only person besides Adam to ever ask me to dance at these parties."

"Oh, good. Then you have plenty of time for me, yes?" Jameson offered her his hand.

She giggled and took his hand. "Sure."

Jameson led Ruby onto the dancefloor, and they waltzed as gracefully as Viennese nobility but looked much more attractive while doing it. He adored her almost as much as he adored Giselle, which was apparent in the way he looked at her. Although he knew Joe was irreplaceable, he hoped he could be a father figure to her if she ever needed one.

"It's charming the way you pretend not to know why I ask you to dance," Jameson whispered.

She blushed and repressed a giggle. "I guess I never expected you to keep your word indefinitely."

"I always keep my promises . . . How is my son handling life these days?" he asked.

Ruby sighed. "He's better. I think he's currently obsessed with restoring every piece of worn antique furniture in the house . . . Haven't you asked him about it yourself?"

"I have," he said, "but I wanted an honest answer. He wouldn't tell me if he was having a difficult time. He's so proud."

"It's not that he's proud, Mr. Rosemont. I mean, he is proud, but that's not the point . . . You're charismatic, charming. Everyone loves you. You're the governor of New York for fuck's sake, and he's messed up badly and lost his job."

The music ended before Ruby was finished speaking, so she wordlessly let Jameson know they weren't finished. Squeezing his hand, she kept his body close to hers as she slowed their dancing to match the next song's tempo.

She continued, "It's not pride, per se. He just wants you to think he's good enough. He wants you to think he's strong enough to face his failures and fix them. It's hard for him to live in the shadow of a great man . . . Mother told me you moved out to give him space, and I think that was a good move."

Jameson remained silent for a moment before he pulled her slightly closer to speak quietly beside her ear. "I'm glad he has you. You understand him more than I do . . . He will always be good enough in my eyes. I love him, like your mother loves you." He pulled back and looked her in the eye. "It's good you're here reuniting with her tonight."

Phoebe held two martinis, giving one to Faustina with a mischievous smile. They enjoyed a few sips and watched people. Phoebe growled salaciously when the vampires walked by, and Faustina gave her a little tickle, so she'd stop.

"Being a wallflower tonight?" Phoebe asked.

"Ruby stole my turn to dance, and now she's locked Jameson in an intense discussion of some sort that's lasted two dances." Faustina nodded in Ruby's direction.

"Ugh, that does look intense. She needs a drink. Or a candy . . . At least she's here with us though." Phoebe winked at Faustina and blew her a kiss.

Faustina squinted across the room, looking at the Cavendishes in the company of spellcasters. "Sylvia and Duncan seem to prefer the company of anyone except other witches." She laughed.

Phoebe took a sip of her cocktail and said, "I don't blame them."

Duncan and Sylvia Cavendish thought it was Adam's best solstice celebration in at least a century. They passed an especially pleasant evening chatting up a few spellcasters. Duncan described his herb garden to them, opening a fascinating discussion about healing herbs. Sylvia explained the art of scrying and they explained how they used different minerals and crystals.

Sylvia abruptly stopped speaking and sent a message to the Lee sisters. Making their apologies, she and Duncan headed to the conservatory. She'd heard fae magic and estimated Robin was about a half mile away.

GARDEN SNARE

Robin popped into one of the island's guest bungalows and found his spy waiting for him at the kitchen table.

"You took your time getting here," Bastion said while finishing a plate of food he'd saved from dinner at the big house. "I trust the coordinates weren't difficult to follow.

"I had business at court, not that it's any of your business," Robin sneered and looked around. "You're living here?"

"Yes. This is one of Adam's guest houses. I'm staying here for a few days."

"It's repulsive." Robin made a face like he smelled something foul. "Let's get on with it. Show me how to get the skull."

"Follow me," Bastion said and walked outside, sat on the porch railing, and pointed. "You can see the big house on the hill from here. There's a large conservatory on this side, and the skull is on display there for his guests."

"Are you sure they're all distracted with his little party right now?" Robin asked.

"There hasn't been anyone in the conservatory all night. It's set up for a brunch scheduled to be there in the morning. That's when they plan to view the skull."

Robin surveyed the house in the distance and observed the stars and night air. "Are you sure none of them can detect my magic from here?"

Bastion looked Robin in the eyes and said, "You're too far away. They don't know you're here. That's why I had you come here."

"I can't see the conservatory from here. I could pop into the wrong room."

Bastion sighed. "The second set of coordinates I gave you are specifically for the room, not the house."

"Of course . . . How long will I have once I'm close to the house?"

"Not long."

Without another word, Robin popped from the bungalow's porch and reappeared inside his enemy's home. The glass ceiling and walls let in enough celestial light to refract in the crystal skull displayed a few meters in front of him in a clear case. It caught his eye before anything else in the still, quiet room.

He advanced forward a few steps, but then his feet felt solid as stone. He was frozen in place. Before he could snap his fingers, his hands became paralyzed. The botanical garden behind him seemed to awaken. Leaves made whispering noises, rubbing together in a supernatural breeze that crept between the florae. Snakelike vines twisted slowly along the fertile earth until they reached the Mesopotamian mosaic tiles. Sliding effortlessly across the tiles, vines attacked Robin from two sides of the botanical garden. They were like living ropes as they tied his legs together and knotted themselves around his feet. They climbed to his arms and hands and tied knots between his fingers. His hands looked clad in green and brown mittens until a vine snapped around and tied his wrists together behind his back. A vine slipped up the back of his neck and over the top of his head. Leaves grew from the vine to act as a blindfold, and a piece branched off to gag Robin. He couldn't move, see, or talk.

In a white wrought iron garden chair, sat Jinae. Youngae stood behind the chair with her hands draped over Jinae's shoulders. It was a picturesque scene, the Asian beauties posed together beneath a purple crape myrtle tree. Their sleek black hair was loose and framing their faces, and their green eyes stared at Robin. The sisters' powers were apparent in their regal posture and confident expressions.

Jinae's telekinesis allowed her to freeze him in place before he even realized she and her sister were hunting him. Resting her body in the chair helped to direct all her strength to keep Robin from moving until Youngae could restrain him permanently.

Youngae's ability to manipulate plants was surprisingly useful against enemies. Nobody ever saw her coming for them. Once she had Robin entirely restrained with vines, she gave her sister's shoulders a gentle squeeze to signal Jinae she could stop using telekinesis.

Robin couldn't see or speak, but he could hear. Footsteps approached him and walked around him. He then recognized Adam's smell and growled.

"I'm lucky I decided to place guards here," Adam said. "While nobody knew about the guards, everyone in my household knows the skull is here." He walked to Robin's side and spoke close to his ear. "One of them has betrayed me tonight . . . Who?"

Adam slipped the gag away from Robin's mouth, "Tell me who helped you."

Robin remained silent.

Adam said, "Very well. I'll take you to the basement and put you in more permanent restraints . . . It won't be comfortable for you. Maybe you'll feel like talking to me later."

As Adam moved to replace the gag, Robin said, "Eve was mine in the end, not yours. You took what was mine, and your entire tribe will pay."

Adam shoved the vine back into Robin's mouth, but his expression remained neutral. "Big, powerful words from a small, powerless fairy."

Metal gloves kept Robin's hands perfectly still. He couldn't snap or channel his magic with his fingers and hands at all. He was gagged with a metal bit attached to a muzzle over his head, and a cotton bag was placed over that in lieu of a blindfold. His cloak and emerald crown had been taken.

He heard the door open and waited to hear someone or something. A small animal ran up his leg, and he wondered briefly if they were going to let rats eat him. When the animal perched on his shoulder and he inhaled its scent, he knew it was Eros.

Footsteps approached. "I'm still alive and free, so I'm assuming you didn't tell anyone I'm a spy," Bastion said.

Bastion removed the bag from Robin's head and looked into his eyes. He didn't see anger there, but he didn't see complete trust either. He could work with that. The muzzle was tricky to remove, but he finally got it open and carefully pulled it away from Robin's mouth and face.

Robin cleared his throat and roared, "You sent me into a guarded room, Roth!"

"The guards were Adam's secret," said Bastion, "but I'm here to get you out."

"Are you not afraid of being caught down here?" Robin challenged him.

Bastion held up the muzzle and the bag. "You want I should gag and blindfold you, then leave?"

Robin studied him, clearly analyzing the situation.

Bastion continued, "Adam's distracted at the party with the rest of them. He thinks you're secured down here, and you're the only reason he had guards in the first place, so they're also at the party now."

"But he knows there's a spy," Robin said.

"Does he?" Bastion raised an eyebrow. "He's specifically said something to you about a spy?"

"Yes. He knows someone is helping me but appeared to not know who it is."

Bastion sighed and nodded his head in thought. "We'll have to make this count then. In the event I get discovered and need to make an escape soon . . . They're going to get the sphere next, so you can get there first."

"What about the third key?" Robin asked.

Bastion dropped a backpack from his shoulders, and Eros jumped from Robin's shoulder into the bag. Bastion and Robin watched the weasel burrow into Robin's cloak, which was inside.

"They haven't found it yet . . . Look, I've got your crown and your cloak, and your weasel here for you . . . Just let me break you out of here, and you should just leave. There are a lot of powerful people upstairs."

"And what do you want in return?" Robin asked slowly, carefully.

"To see the fae realm."

"No."

Robin's answer came fast. It was as Bastion expected, but he would be remiss not to try. Bastion smelled Robin's magic rising and knew he needed to seal a deal. It was unclear how much influence he had over his magic verbally or visually even though his hands were clearly its main conduit.

Bastion stated, "I need something."

"Clearly . . . The bargain is this: My freedom and my belongings in that bag are returned to me. You are returned access to my Malta home. It has been fortified against my enemies, but you will still have access. Indeed, you have your own apartment should Adam discover your disloyalty."

"Done." Bastion removed the rest of Robin's restraints, freeing his hands and feet.

Robin snapped his fingers, and bones snapped in Bastion's arms. "That is for failing me."

"Dammit, Goodfellow!" Bastion screamed in pain and anger. "How am I going to explain magically broken bones?"

Robin laughed maniacally. "I don't care. The force was magical, but there's no magic in the bone. Sort it out on your own. You're the spy. If you can't, go to Malta."

"Then I won't be useful to you!"

"A witch is always useful to me, Roth!" Robin announced, exuding amusement from his expression.

Robin placed the emerald crown upon his head in a triumphant gesture. He looked at the backpack and snapped, making it disappear. Without another glance at Bastion, he snapped himself from the basement.

A pop echoed throughout the cut stone chamber followed by Bastion's heavy sigh of relief. He leaned against the wall and tried to control his breathing, but his pain was becoming intolerable as his fear and adrenaline subsided. He hauled his sluggish body up the stairs and called for help.

Adam returned to the ballroom invigorated and thought it

was time to ask Sorina to dance. A breeze whispered past him from the open French doors that lined the far side of the room. Several of his descendants stood in the open doorway enjoying the feel of the night. A handful of spellcasters and the vampires joined them. He worked his way into the group and stood beside Sorina. His fingers brushed her hand, so she dragged her nails against his open palm.

Vlad stepped between Adam and Sorina, glaring at Sorina.

Duncan watched the entire exchange with an amused grin before he and Sylvia excused themselves for the night and went along with some of the spellcasters to their bungalow to have a more relaxed, intimate afterparty and watch the stars.

Jeremy, Giselle, Ruby, and Hayden decided to wind down the night in the library with a chess game and a few doses of candy. They said their goodbyes to the parents and departed the ballroom in a gaggle of laughter and chatter.

A pop of fae magic announced Robin's arrival. He perched on the balcony railing for a split second, which was just enough time to grab Phoebe before she realized he was there. Trying to take her down with him, he fell backwards. His sharp nails ripped her silk gown across the waist as she resisted falling with him. She failed to keep herself upright, and they were airborne.

He knew he should have left when Bastion freed him. It would have been a clean escape, but his anger with Phoebe overpowered his ability to reason. Her continued existence made him livid. He had to kill her for trying to kill him.

Screams rang out from Phoebe's friends and family above as she realized it was Robin who had her, and they were going to hit the ground harder than her body could endure if she didn't use her magic. She positioned her hands facing down and expelled a hefty dose of destructive magic in hopes of dampening the impact of their bodies with the ground.

The impact knocked the wind from her, and she struggled

hard to breathe. Convulsions rocked her body. Powerless to stop him, she felt Robin roll over on top of her.

She managed to croak, "Fuck off!"

He pushed up her dress and ripped at her panties. "Yes, I'm going to be fucking. Then I'm going to be killing you for leaving me on that beach, you treacherous cunt!"

Catching her breath, she said, "You loved it!" Then she coughed up blood and spit it in his face.

A crazed laugh burst from his mouth. "Yes, you're a deliciously evil little witch, but draining your life is my rightful revenge and will be the ultimate pleasure."

Phoebe smiled a bloody, toothy smile even while Robin ripped the clothing from her body, but she wasn't smiling at him. She was smiling at the sight of Adam flying down from the balcony and quietly approaching Robin from behind.

Adam masterfully coalesced a full magical assault upon Robin. The fairy was blasted into the air and away from Phoebe as the bones in his hands were crushed, and his eyes filled with blood. Adam blasted him once more while he was down, and Robin stumbled and struggled to limp away.

Phoebe closed her eyes in exhausted relief as Adam placed his hands on her and sent healing magic into her. Then she felt two more hands, one on her belly and one smoothing down her dress. Opening her eyes, she saw Ty with Adam. Jameson and Faustina were there and waiting until she was healed enough to carry inside.

"Thank you," Phoebe whispered breathlessly.

Adam felt sick from seeing Robin's brutal assault against her and roared, "Shut up! You brought this on yourself."

"Be careful, Adam," Ty said. "Positive thoughts."

Phoebe drew in a labored breath. "You know I can't help myself . . . I'm sorry."

"Don't speak," Ty said.

Robin was healing faster than Phoebe, but not fast enough to use his magic to get off the island. He stumbled and faltered then ran for cover, which was a grove of trees between the house and the beach. He tried to snap himself away from Adam and the others several times, but each time he only reappeared a few hundred meters ahead.

Sorina sprinted from the balcony and landed solidly on her feet. She ran after Robin. Vlad followed.

Ty became aware that Robin was still running at the same time he noticed the vampires run past him. "Robin's running. Sorina and Vlad are chasing," he told Adam.

The trees absorbed three silhouettes as Adam managed to look away from Phoebe for long enough to shout at them. "Sorina, let him go! Come back!"

"Go help them," Ty said. "She's healed enough for us to get her inside. I'll take care of it from here."

With Ty's support, Adam wasted no time. He ascended into the night air to search higher over a vast island terrain. The sandy beach below looked calm until two dark humanoid shapes emerged from the tree line. After observing them for a moment, their interactions indicated a skirmish, so he knew it was one of the vampires and Robin. His sharp descent made his ears pop and sent a chill over his skin, but Adam's adrenaline was running too high for him to notice or slow his speed. His only thoughts were of Sorina. Panic sent a shiver through him when one of the silhouettes he approached disappeared.

Adam increased the speed of his descent even more, hitting the beach hard. His body rolled once before he found his feet and quickly approached the still figure lying on the sand. The realization it was Sorina weakened his step, and he fell on his knees before her. A chunk was missing from her neck, and her wrists were slit.

Scooping her into his arms, he covered her wrists with his hands to begin healing her, but his strength was diminished from healing Phoebe moments before. The neck injury gushed blood even though he'd dampened the blood loss at the wrists. She looked like death, and he was desperate to think of a life-saving solution.

Adam realized what he needed to do. He propped her head on his shoulder with her lips against his neck. Shifting both her wrists under one of his healing palms, he used his free hand to gently grip the back of her head and guide her to his jugular vein.

She was barely conscious, so he was shaking her and pleading, "Sorina! Drink! Take my blood!"

A frail whimper escaped Sorina's mouth before she used the last of her strength to bite down on Adam's neck and start sucking away his crimson lifeforce. Her eyes drifted shut. Between consciousness and oblivion, she remained vaguely aware of tasting witch's blood in her mouth.

"Sorina," Adam murmured.

Adam didn't know if he was having an orgasm, or if he was dying. Her blood stained his hands and chest as she replaced it with his. Unfamiliar magical elements surged through him. His magic still focused on healing her, but it felt like he was absorbing her magic through the blood on his palms and then giving it back to her through the bite on his neck. It was a magical circle of life and the most intimate experience of his very long life.

Sorina's eyelids fluttered open. She regained her senses and knew she had to stop feeding on Adam's ancient Edenian blood, but he tasted heavenly. She'd stopped bleeding. The gaping wound at her neck had clotted and started to heal, but he held her so lovingly. It was a warm, comfortable embrace that was irresistible in conjunction with the way he tasted.

As her body awakened, she returned his embrace. As she returned his embrace, Adam's arms slipped away from her.

Sorina held Adam as he went limp and fell back onto the sand, taking her with him. She withdrew from his neck in horror and slapped her hands over the wound. Blood trickled through her hands, so she tore off a piece of her dress and tried to stuff it against the wound.

She sensed Vlad approaching from the trees behind her and screamed, "Help me! Please!"

Vlad watched her and did nothing. "Where is the fairy?"

Sorina answered, "He has escaped! He almost killed me! Adam saved me!"

"I saw you feeding on him, Sorina," Vlad said. "It is forbidden. What is happening between you is forbidden."

"No! He offered his blood to save me! I did not—" she cried. "I did not take it. It was given! Help me!"

Rustling leaves in the trees distracted them, and Ty came running to Adam. "What's happened?"

Sorina grabbed Ty's hand and slapped it over Adam's neck. "Heal him!"

"We've just finished healing Phoebe," Ty explained. "My magic might not heal him completely."

"Just make the bleeding stop. I'll call Duncan to help," Sorina said.

"What happened to you?" Vlad asked Sorina, looking at gnarled flesh marring her neck.

"When Robin touched my neck, it felt like a hot blast hit me,"

Sorina explained. "When I fell, he dug his nails into my wrists and ripped them apart. He must have used his magic for that too because I was not healing on my own. At least, I was not healing fast enough."

Ty concentrated his healing magic on Adam's neck. "What happened to Adam? Did Robin do this?"

"No." Vlad did not elaborate.

Sorina's eyes betrayed her. The truth was apparent in the way she stared at Adam in horror and regret. She reached for his hands and clasped them tightly.

Ty glanced at her and said, "I see."

"He offered himself to me," Sorina whispered to Ty. "I swear it!"

"Like you, we don't heal as fast when foreign magic infects our wounds," Ty said, "but he's no longer bleeding."

Sorina said, "Vampire magic is younger. Not as volatile. It simply flows with life and death in the blood. I had no malice for him in my blood. I am surprised he did not heal on his own."

"He's exhausted. He attacked Robin below the balcony with a destructive power exponentially more potent than the rest of us could have done, he healed Phoebe, and then flew out here," Ty said. "I suppose he could have been affected by the fae magic in your blood, too. It's difficult to know."

Jeremy appeared in front of them with Duncan in tow.

"What can I do?" Duncan asked.

"Just give him a bit of healing. He's almost there, but I can't give more right now," Ty explained.

Duncan took a knee opposite of Ty and Sorina and placed

his hands on Adam. "Jeremy, get ready to take Adam back to the house. The rest of us will walk back."

"Now?" Jeremy asked.

Duncan concentrated on Adam. "Almost."

Still holding Adam's hands, Sorina felt his finders begin to close around her hands. His grip tightened. She studied his face intently, waiting for his eyes to open, then they did.

"He's ready to go now," Duncan told Jeremy.

"Sorina?" Adam said.

"Yes . . . Jeremy is taking you back to your house now. I will check on you later . . . Thank you." Sorina smiled sadly and let go of him.

"Worth it," Adam mumbled.

Jeremy pulled Adam into his arms and vanished.

REBEL, REBEL

Wind swept down a busy Chicago street. Claudia Devereux popped up her trench coat's collar and hurried along the crowded sidewalk as rain started falling. It was chilly for a summer day, especially with the moist air. She ducked inside a cafe and took a seat near a window facing the alley.

Claudia smoothed water droplets from her black hair and tied it in a messy topknot. Other customers began filling tables all around her, but she only paid attention to her tablet. The chair provided comfort against her back, and the scent of coffee made her feel at peace.

Trent leaned against a brick wall in an alley opposite the cafe. Rain soaked his clothing and poured down his face, but he didn't care. He couldn't stop himself from following his soulmate's mother even after the rain started. He had her hair, nose, and lips. Her youthful look made him wonder if people would ever mistake her for his sister.

A waitress brought her a warm drink, and he enjoyed her grin as she accepted the steaming cup. She smelled the rising steam with the gentle smile still across her glossy lips. A vague memory rose to his mind's surface of his own mother enjoying cappuccino with a pinch of cinnamon, and he wondered if the woman on the other side of the glass liked it, too. If not, what was her drink of choice? His thoughts of her were warm and comforting but also consuming.

Claudia put down her work and studied rain trailing down the glass while sipping warm cappuccino. She glanced outside. Her cup almost slipped from her fingers when she saw a man watching her from across the alley, but she carefully placed the cup on her table and kept watching him. He didn't seem to realize she was seeing him there. His eyes were trancelike. She scooted her chair to the window and placed her palm on the glass to get his attention. She knew it was her son although he looked different somehow. Magic was a mystery to her, so she often worried for her boy.

Trent's heart skipped when he realized Claudia saw and recognized him. He turned to leave as a hooded figure brushed by him. A hand reached out and clasped his forearm like a vice. He and the figure were pulled through a rip in space before he could form words or resist.

A short high-pitched squeal escaped Claudia's mouth before she squashed it. She knew her son could disappear like that, but it was still unnerving to witness. She smiled apologetically at the people watching her and went back to minding her own business and finishing her drink.

Adam faced Ruby with his hand extended. "Simply take a bit of power and envision throwing it at me with malicious intent in your heart. I'll shield myself."

She hesitated to place her palm against his. "What if I hurt you?"

"Ruby, you're not going to hurt me."

"But you were hurt badly last night. What if you cannot shield."

"If my strength hasn't fully recovered, that is even better for your training," Adam explained. "You won't be able to syphon a lethal amount, much less direct it back at me."

It was essential for the cabal to weaponize all the powers they could to fight against their enemies. Ruby's magical abilities were strong, so she needed to learn to command them properly for any situation. She placed her palm against his and breathed in the salty air.

They were alone on the beach only meters away from where Adam had fallen the night before. He'd decided a vast plot of sand would be the softest impact available if Ruby managed to knock him off his feet. He felt her take magic from his palm, so he shielded himself and waited.

She paced away from him and listened to the ocean's mighty roar. It was encouraging. The magic needed to exit from her in a strong, flowing wave just like water upon the shore. She pictured it in her mind and spun to face Adam with both palms pushing in his direction. Her breathing became labored from the exertion, but she only noticed him take a single step back.

Adam smiled at Ruby. Her first magical attack had gone much better than her flying lessons, but she still needed practice. He discovered she wasn't a natural fighter, but he wasn't surprised due to her natural ability as a magical lover. However, he had faith she would improve. There was a thin line between love and hate, after all, and passionate magical manipulations required expert control. Ruby flourished in situations she could control, which was likely why she didn't excel at flying or animal whispering. Both nature and gravity often eluded human control.

Ruby approached Adam, looking disappointed. "You barely moved."

"But you succeeded. You hit me rather hard," he said and laughed. "Remember who I am. Others might have fallen under that attack."

Sunset approached, but they'd gotten a late start due to the previous evening's frivolities and dangers alike. She walked to the water's edge and let the waves wash over her foot. He followed and admired the horizon with her.

"You're thinking about your last vision, aren't you?" he asked.

"It must be important!" she stated passionately. "Why won't

it come back to me? I need to see more!"

"You've been concentrating on other matters. Meditate on it, and the vision will come."

She walked along the water, splashing it around playfully.

"You're right. I'll start a new meditation regimen to regain focus on my clairvoyancy, but first . . ." she said and held up her palm. "Let's get in a bit more practice before the sun slips below the horizon."

Adam nodded his approval and raised his palm to hers.

Trying a different approach, she waded into the ocean. She'd abandoned her t-shirt and shorts, and they floated on the water in front of him. He wadded them into a ball and thew them behind him onto the sand. He watched her with a mixture of interest and pride, knowing she had a plan to attack him harder than before.

Ruby prepared to leverage the tide to fight against Adam. She wasn't stronger than Adam, but the ocean was. A wave approached her, so she spun around and jumped to ride it forward. Focusing her magic's force behind the wave, she pushed her arms through the water and toward Adam. She cackled triumphant at witnessing Adam fall. His body washed onto the sand under the giant wave's magical force, and she followed.

Running up the beach, she called out, "How did I do that time?"

Adam chuckled loudly. He stayed flat on his back and looked into the sky. When Ruby plopped down next to him, he turned his head to face her. Her beaming face was worth the defeat she'd mercilessly dealt to him.

"Well done, my dear," he whispered, catching his breath. "Well done."

Ruby saw the stars emerging in the darkening sky. "Adam?"

"Yes?"

"You and Sorina . . . Vlad doesn't like it."

He let silence linger for a minute before changing the subject. "How are you settling into your new writing project? I worry about your happiness in your new role as our historian. You used to be passionate about journalism."

"I'm enjoying my new work, and don't change the subject, please."

He crossed his arms behind his head and got comfortable enough to start a long conversation. "You and Hayden . . . I don't like it."

She huffed.

"See how that feels?" he asked playfully.

She looked at him. "The difference is, I don't get the impression you'd hurt me over my choices. However, I've come to understand vampires have a strict rule about romantic entanglements outside their coven, and I get a violent vibe from Vlad, so to speak."

"That's impressive alliteration, Ruby. Do write that in your journal for posterity."

"I'm serious," Ruby said.

Adam felt beside him for Ruby's hand and held it. "I wish to confide in you as my spiritual advisor right now."

"Oh, my stars . . . You love her . . . Adam, we barely know her!"

"I feel like I've known her since Eden, especially after we exchanged blood last night. She's like oxygen to me."

"I understand."

"Do you, really?" he rolled to his side and stared at her.

"Only a few weeks ago, I'd have sworn that feeling would never happen to me, but I'm now positive I can't live without Hayden."

"But you stayed here an extra night?" he asked.

"I'm in love, not codependent!" Ruby announced to the stars above.

Adam tightened his grip on her hand. "You must be prepared for whatever happens. We need you both in battle."

"I know . . . What about you? You and Sorina will both fight the fae."

"Sorina and I both possess envito. I'm sure we will survive emotionally. Between that and the losses of thousands of years."

Ruby whispered, "I envy you. Your experience. Witnessing the rise and fall of so many empires. It's fascinating . . . I pray we all live to see this enemy defeated and experience a generation of peace."

"About that," Adam said. "I've thought we might weaponize Giselle. Bring a pride of lions through the archway at her command, or something similar. What would she think of that?"

"I'm not sure what I think of that," Ruby stated firmly. "Innocent creatures would suffer and die for us."

"My father made the beasts of this Earth for my use, Ruby."

"It's barbaric."

"It's natural."

"Your dominion over the land's beasts doesn't absolve you from the responsibility of caring for them."

"I care for them," Adam said with conviction. "However, I care more for my people. Animals can be used as tools to ensure our survival . . . I want you to discuss it with Giselle and see what her ideas are."

"Okay . . . I still worry Vlad could break our alliance over Sorina."

"I don't think that will happen as long as we're not sleeping together."

"You're not?" Ruby asked in clear surprise.

"No, and recently I've come to the same conclusion as you. Mind you, I still intend to pursue her, but it can wait until after we've dealt with the fae."

Ruby argued, "It would be nice to maintain the alliance after that."

"True, but it won't be an immediate necessity. She and I would have time to repair the damage."

"Adam . . ." Ruby paused and touched her forehead to his. "If you love her, I want you to have her. I only meant to . . . I worry about your discretion. You're so used to doing whatever you want and being in charge, but Vlad rules her and her people. Based on what you've told me, I think you're on the right path though."

"Good," he said. "You keep me grounded. Thank you."

"Stay here and watch the stars with me?" she asked.

Adam pulled her closer and watched the sky. "That was my plan all along."

Ruby admired the sparkling clear night sky and contemplated their experiences with Adonai and Lilith. She somehow felt like Adam's father hadn't left them. His presence radiated throughout the Blue Earth. His image was reflected in

Adam's eyes. Ruby was at peace with living a life without seeing him again, but she did sometimes miss Lilith's unique presence.

"Do you think we'll see them again?" Ruby asked.

Adam knew she was talking about the Edenians, but he still asked, "Who?"

"Adonai and Lilith."

"I think it'd be hubris for me to presume."

"Yes, but I hope to."

"As do I."

Adam took Ruby's index finger in his hand like a pencil and raked her nail down his forearm. Horrified, she tried to yank it away from him, but he held her firmly and pressed down hard into his skin. The jagged cut dripped blood down Adam's arm and into the sand between them.

"Adam! What are you doing?"

"Heal me," he said.

She stuttered, "How—how?"

It was usually difficult to explain to someone how to use healing powers, but Ruby's abilities were different. "The same way you exchange magic when you make love, but when you take magic from my palm, focus it back on the wound only."

"But will that work?" Ruby asked in fear. "You usually can't heal yourself."

"I don't know," Adam admitted, "but I want to try it . . . Ruby, it's only a small cut. I'll still heal relatively fast; it'll be gone on its own by tomorrow. Your love for me is heightening your empathy and worry . . . If you can do this, it's a huge advantage for us."

She took three deep breaths and placed her hand against his palm. Her fingers locked down around his, and then she placed her other hand over his cut. On the dark beach, the golden glow between her hand and his wound was especially visible. Slowly, she released his hand and his arm. The cut was gone.

⚬⚬⚬ ⚬⚬⚬ ⚬⚬⚬

Trent stared into the eye of his soulmate.

His one eye.

"What's with the eye, man?"

Blue Earth's Trent lowered his hood and then raised the eye patch. "It's a trick I learned reading about ancient pirates. I move directly between distant points in space constantly, so the patch helps me to see immediately in a new place, so I can react to danger quickly. One eye is always adjusted to the dark."

"Well, that's fucking rad," Trent said.

His soulmate smiled. "Yeah, it is."

Trent took in his surroundings. It looked like they were in a cave but with modern conveniences. Under his feet, there was a hardwood floor. The electricity ran underneath the floor, which seemed to be raised a few feet above the ground. There was a bed, a sofa, a bar, and other furniture. There were no walls and no ceiling. Dark gray stone surrounded them.

"Does this pad include a bathroom?" Trent asked.

His soulmate approached a tapestry nailed to stone at the back of the cave and moved the material aside. Another stone chamber was revealed. They stepped into the bathroom. It didn't have a wooden floor. Instead, electricity from the bedroom was wired through a hole in the stone wall, and it was a much more spartan setup. There was one lightbulb and one outlet. A clear natural hot spring pooled in one corner of the chamber, and a series

156

of curtains in the opposite corner blocked off a toilette.

"Where the fuck are we?" Trent asked.

"Romania."

Trent chuckled heartily and covered his face with his hands. "Oh, this is perfect." He then shouted at his soulmate, "I hate vampires, friend! And now you've got me trapped in their nest!"

His soulmate remained calm. "Friend?"

"I don't know what else to call you. Feels weird calling you 'Trent.'"

"Nobody calls me 'Trent.'"

Trent waited for the other half of his soulmate's statement, looking at him in anticipation.

"They call me Pinky."

"Oh, absolutely not!" Trent was indignant. "They do not! Nope."

"What's wrong with Pinky?" asked Pinky. "It's short for 'Pinkerton.' Which is our surname."

Trent laughed again. "At least we're both smartasses . . . So, my soulmate goes by 'Pinky' and lives with bloodsuckers. Adonai surely has a sense of humor."

"Don't Green Earth witches suck blood, too?" asked Pinky.

"They mostly eat eyes, but sometimes they do," Trent said. "That's only because vampires started that nasty mess."

"I'd like to learn more about the Green Earth. Duncan explained to me your concept of soulmates, which seems to make sense, for the most part," Pinky said, "and I've heard all about the battle with Eve . . . He also explained why you don't trust vampires."

"Understatement of the century," mumbled Trent.

Pinky continued, "But look, you can't follow my mother anymore. My parents already get confused and scared about the supernatural world, and I don't really interact with them often. It's how I keep them safe, you got it?"

"Safe from what?" Trent asked in confusion. "This Earth isn't a giant battlefield, like mine."

Pinky explained, "Well, I'm a spy for vampires, so the list could be endless."

Trent studied Pinky's appearance. His hair was short, and his beard was long. Along with the eyepatch, Trent understood how Duncan and Sylvia might have dismissed him without really looking closely to see he was Pinky's soulmate.

Trent said, "As a spy, I'm sure you're a chameleon . . . So, how do we look with blonde hair? I've been thinking about a new look."

"Blonde hair attracts too much attention," Pinky said.

"Female attention?" Trent asked.

"Yes, actually."

"I'm sold!" Trent announced and started touching his bracelet. "Making an appointment with my barber for that."

"Honestly, I don't think you'll find a woman as gorgeous as Ruby Cohen. She's the ultimate smoke show."

"You spy on Ruby?" Trent asked.

"I spy on everyone."

"Creepy . . . Might want to keep that to yourself when you're talking to women, or you'll always live alone in a cave."

"It's a mountain," Pinky argued.

Trent glared at Pinky. Turning away from the conversation, he noticed a guitar sitting next to the sofa. He picked it up and sat down with it to play. The mountain's acoustics were fantastic, so he really got into the music and played one song after another.

Pinky went to the bar and poured two glasses of scotch and put one in front of Trent. He sat on the opposite end of the sofa from his guest and listened to him play. He'd never heard the songs, but it was a different kind of music from anything he'd ever heard. It appealed to him.

Trent finished playing and handed the guitar to his soulmate before enjoying the drink he'd been offered. He listened to his host play a familiar song and leaned his head back onto the cushions until the music eventually stopped. He then enjoyed a bit of silence mixed with scotch.

"I hate to ruin this deeply bromantic moment," Trent said, "but you belong with the cabal. Why don't you come with me to meet them?"

"I'm not ready for that." Pinky went back to the bar and refilled his glass.

Trent didn't get up but turned to face Pinky. "I can't keep this meeting a secret. I'm on the cabal's jury, and I'm a loyal member. They're the only family I have."

"Well, Duncan, Sylvia, and the vampires are the only family I have," Pinky argued.

Trent felt like he was talking to a child and wondered if that's what others thought when talking to him. "Firstly, Duncan and Sylvia are in the cabal. Secondly, they are my family, too . . . I can't promise Adam won't come here once he finds out."

"Vlad will protect me."

"You don't need protection from Adam, but put the shoe on the other foot, so to speak. Can you imagine what would happen if three vampires lived at Adam's house?" Trent shook his head and finished his drink before answering his own question. "Vlad doesn't approve of vampires mixing with others, and I doubt his reaction would be peaceful. I'm continuously in disbelief about him allowing Sorina to treat the Cavendishes like her children."

"My family is an exception to correct a wrong done to us," Pinky said. "Sorina loves me. Vlad is prejudiced, but he values me for the job I do for the coven."

"If you won't come with me now, you should contact Ruby directly. Meaning, don't creep up on her—"

"You mean like you did with my mother?" Pinky interrupted.

Trent continued, "Touché, but as I was saying, Ruby will help welcome you into the cabal. She has become Adam's spiritual advisor ever since Adonai chose to speak to her directly through her clairvoyancy gift."

"You still speak so respectfully of your former lover?" Pinky asked, genuinely interested.

Trent's expression betrayed sadness. "She's my late wife's soulmate."

Pinky was floored because nobody had mentioned the Green Earth's Ruby to him. "Well, that's a huge gap in my knowledge."

"Which part?" Trent asked. "The Green Earth still performing marriages, my involvement with Ruby's soulmate, or her death?" Trent thought for a second and waved his hands in the air in confusion. "Wait! My involvement with Ruby is how the cabal originally learned of soulmates. I told them."

Pinky patiently listened to Trent, still deeply interested in his

Ruby situation. "I'm sorry for your loss . . . So, Duncan said you don't like vampires because Green Earth Sorina killed your lover."

The unasked question lingered between them while Trent got up and refilled his own drink. He kept his distance, choosing to sit on a wooden trunk at the foot of Pinky's bed.

"It seems Duncan smoothed over a few details to make the story easier to tell," Trent said in a clipped tone but then made peace with having to explain the truth to his soulmate. "Sorina killed my Ruby. She was more than my lover, she was my wife, which is like a partner on the Blue Earth."

"Fuck," Pinky replied.

"Yeah," Trent agreed.

Although Pinky was every bit as cool as Trent, he had enough politeness to be contrite in the face of that new information. "I—I'm sorry I brought you here without your permission." He rubbed the back of his neck in discomfort. "I can take you anywhere you want to go."

Trent cracked a half smile. "Anywhere? Because this is my first full day off work in weeks."

A minute later, Pinky and Trent appeared shrouded in shadow beneath a stone walkover bridge. They emerged onto the San Antonio River Walk, moving with a lively crowd that sang along with a band playing from a passing river barge. Concerned they'd be seen, Pinky bought them two cheap cowboy hats from the first shop they passed. They ate puffy tacos and stopped to listen to some local music before spending the rest of the night talking over cocktails in a dark corner at one of the city's historic haunts, Bar 1919.

FAMILY LEGACY

Vlad entered his coven's sacred underground chamber intending to question Sorina about the witches' continued ability to close their minds to him. It infuriated him to discover Duncan, Sylvia, and Pinky were the only three witches he could still read. Years ago, he'd agreed not to read the witches living within his coven, but he'd needed to know if his powers had changed. Adam had found a way to shield his tribe's minds from him, and the cabal had gone so far as to exclude the Cavendishes to ensure the coven didn't know about it.

Vlad's eyes darted wildly from one vampire to another. Several of them gathered around the pool, including Sorina. He'd traveled all day and needed water. Thirst distracted him from his anger, so he scooped water from the pool and savored its nourishment.

Ozana's hair felt like silk gliding through Sorina's fingers as she carefully braided it in preparation for warrior training. After Sorina, Ozana was the next strongest female vampire, so they preferred to train together during one-on-one sparring. They especially preferred to oppose each other in team events, both enjoying leading squads for coven wargame nights.

Vlad's tongue scooped the last bit of moisture from his palm, and he was ready to confront Sorina. "I need the room. Leave," he announced to his coven.

Sorina followed the others toward the exit until she heard Vlad command, "Except for you, Sorina. You stay here with me."

She stopped and watched him silently until the other vampires were gone, and they were alone. She knew he'd been upset with her since Adam's party, but she tried to put it out of her mind until after training. Since the vampires were going to

Alexandria the next day to help the witches recover the obelisk key, mission focus had to be her priority.

"Are you still able to read the witches' thoughts?" he asked her.

"I don't know," she quietly replied. "I have not tried in weeks."

Vlad growled, "In weeks! Why?"

"They're our allies now," she calmly explained. "I saw no reason to violate their privacy."

"Call in your wards! Read their thoughts!" Vlad spat the words at her.

She stared at him in disbelief. "I will not!"

Vlad stopped shouting, and his voice became low but dangerous. "I am ordering you. For our coven's security. Call them here and read their minds, now."

"I. Will. Not." Her clipped tone crescendoed into a confident shout. "I don't blame them for finding a way to strengthen their minds! We would do the same!"

Vlad seethed. "Perhaps I will hold your eyes open and rip your thoughts from your head to ensure you have not betrayed me."

"It works both ways," Sorina hissed. "If you open that connection between us, I swear I will push into you mind and find every secret you've ever had."

Vlad threw back his head and roared. The sound echoed through the high dome ceiling. Powdery gravel fell around them as his voice continued to boom, and he stalked to a weapons rack and drew a pure silver sword.

Holding the sword to her throat, he said, "I am within my rights to kill you for insubordination."

Sorina held her chin high to avoid the blade's sting. She slowly took one step back and went to her knees in front of the vampire who was her coven's elder, priest, and general. Hair and shadow obscured her face when she bowed her head and locked her hands behind her back.

Her quiet voice said, "I am ready to die rather than break promises and embrace gray ethics simply because our advantages over the witches have dwindled. We still have leverage. We are still strong. We may even be stronger with them."

Vlad lowered the sword and turned his back to her. She was his oldest supporter and strongest warrior. He couldn't execute her so easily, but she'd never refused his orders before.

Sorina's words sizzled through the chamber, incendiary in their audacity and conviction. "You have made an unnecessary threat without the courage or desire to follow through with actions. Furthermore, the threat was not meant to sway me to the righteous path, rather the threat was to bully me onto a wicked path. This is not the action of a leader."

Vlad's eyes widened in disbelief. "How dare you?"

She stood and said, "I challenge you for coven command."

"Sorina." Vlad shook his head. "Remember what happened to Cyrus."

"Lilith wanted Cyrus punished," Sorina said, "but Lilith is not here. We are already exiled and left to make our own decisions. You will fight me here right now, or you will fight me before the coven's eyes. Decide."

"How can these words fall from your lips so easily after thousands of loyal years?" he asked.

"I do not make this decision lightly," she stated. "I will die before needlessly breaking a promise I made to my wards."

"They are not vampires. Their lives are not as valuable as our survival," Vlad argued.

Sorina said, "Foreign beings living within our coven should be treated better than our own people, not worse. Duncan, Sylvia, and Pinky are not a threat to us."

"I should not have let you treat them like your children. You are not their mother. You mistake them for family, but they can never be your family. The vampires of this coven are your only family, no matter how much you desire Adam Godwine!"

She gasped. "I knew it."

"Knew what?"

"This is not about coven safety or survival . . . This is jealousy."

"It is an abomination!" Vlad insisted.

Sorina looked miserable. "You've abused your power over me and lost my respect because of your jealousy."

"Have it your way!" Vlad snapped. "We shall engage in a trial by combat before training tonight. Only Dragos and Ozana will bear witness."

She nodded. "So, we shall."

October 30, 2130, A.D. Bran, Romania, Blue Earth

The ancient castle towered over a modern community dedicated to historic preservation and tourism during recovery from the Second Dark Ages. All Hallows' Eve in the Transylvanian Alps was the most internationally popular holiday celebration of the twenty-second century, much like New Orleans' Mardi Gras celebrations in past centuries. As Mardi Gras was the central holiday of Carnival, All Hallows' Eve was the principal holiday of

Allhallowtide Season. Three castles in the mountains northwest of Bucharest were the most popular tourist destinations during the three-day festivities, and Bran Castle was chief among them due to its dubious connection with an infamous fictional vampire.

Flour powdered the tip of Mina Cavendish's nose; it was in her hair and all over the kitchen, but she ignored the mess. She had to get a few more batches of pastries baked ahead of the next day's celebrations. Mina was pastry chef for the castle's restaurant, and her assistant had left for a family emergency.

Nathan Keleti was the castle museum's curator and Mina's lover. He was English, from Sheffield, and had moved to Romania to work at Bran Castle. The position was meant to be temporary, and he'd recently been offered a position back in England at London's Tate Vintage. He stepped into the kitchen and watched Mina work while she ignored him.

After a minute, he approached her and dusted the flour from her nose with his thumb. "You've got flour all over yourself and the kitchen."

She paused her work, leaned against the cabinets, and laughed. "I know! I'll take time to clean up after I get these last few pans in the ovens."

"Do you have a minute to talk to me now?" he asked.

She bowed her head in understanding. "I don't have an answer, Nathan."

"I want us to be a family," Nathan pleaded. "I want our baby to grow up in England with both of us and my sisters, my brothers, and my parents."

She argued, "My parents are here—"

He interrupted, "But they're English, too. Don't you think they'd like to move home, or at least visit often?"

166

She looked up at him with her sadness apparent in her eyes. "I've always lived in Romania."

"Do you love me?" he asked.

Quickly, she answered, "You know I love you! None of this is easy for me . . . I need to finish this. I'll see you tonight."

She kissed him.

He hesitated then whispered, "I can't wait."

Mina watched him leave then went back to her baking. Baking helped keep her mind from wondering about her life choices. Her work made her feel calm and soothed her nerves, and her work was in Bran. Where would she work in London? She silently cursed her mind for going full circle back to her dilemma.

She saw her mother's flaming red hair from the corner of her eye but didn't stop working. She'd already wasted enough time arguing with Nathan and needed to get the pastries into the ovens before entertaining anyone else, so she finished that task and then started vacuuming flour off the floor.

Sylvia Cavendish eyed her daughter and laughed. "I know you see me here, Mina."

Mina stopped the vacuum but kept her eyes on the floor. "I'm busy."

"You have time." Sylvia grabbed a towel and started cleaning the countertops. "Let's clean and talk."

"Mama," Mina said before tears dripped down her face.

Sylvia pulled Mina into her arms and held her. She waited while Mina sniffled and wiped away tears. As Sylvia used her hand to smooth down Mina's hair, she smiled at her beautiful daughter.

"I'm going to miss you," Sylvia said.

Mina's brow furrowed. "What?"

*"Sorina can hear two heartbeats when she's near you,"
Sylvia said. "When were you planning to tell us?"*

Mina said, "I'm scared."

"Why are you scared?" Sylvia asked.

*"When I was fourteen, I remember Vlad telling me I would
have to leave forever when I became an adult. You and Dad had a
similar discussion with me two years later. You mentioned it again
when I started working here, yet I'm still in Romania. Do you think
he'll make me leave now?"*

*Sylvia held Mina's hands tightly and replied, "I think you
should leave now with Nathan. You know your father and I have
been hiding you from dangerous people your whole life. It's been
hard work, and it needs to end. We've honestly been very lucky so
far."*

*"Every time the subject comes up, you make it sound like I'll
never see you again after I leave," Mina cried. "That's why I'm
scared."*

*"Your father and I will see you but not publicly," Sylvia
explained. "We won't interact with your new family or go on holidays
with you. We'll be able to see you in your home a few times a year."*

"But Sorina won't see me again, will she?" Mina asked.

*Sylvia closed her eyes and said, "No. You'll not see Sorina
or any of her family again."*

*Mina absently arranged dry ingredients on a shelf and
nervously asked, "Would it be different if I were special, like you?"*

"Yes, but not in a good way," Sylvia answered.

"Meaning?"

Sylvia put her hands on Mina's shoulders and gently turned her around to speak face to face. "If you had gifts like me or your father, your relationship with Nathan or anyone else would be much more difficult because you'd need to lie about who you really are. You'd have to choose between staying hidden here your whole life or being ruled by Adam."

"But you do it," Mina promptly argued.

"Mina, you don't belong in our world, and we don't want it for you. When the baby is born, you'll understand."

"No, I don't understand what's so bad about your world, other than the secrecy."

There was no easy way to reveal a terrible secret, so Sylvia just plainly stated it. "We live with Sorina because her brothers murdered our entire village."

Mina's eyes squinted and her brow furrowed at her mother's words as if she hadn't heard them correctly. "That—it doesn't make sense . . . Where was your village?"

"You know we're English."

"Mama! You know what I mean. Was it in the news that a whole community was murdered?"

Sylvia explained, "Vlad and Adam are both extremely powerful men. I can't stress that enough. But Vlad's position is superior. He made our village vanish overnight, and the outside world moved on . . . However, hiding the truth from Adam is Vlad's greatest power. Adam doesn't know where the vampires are or if they still exist, and he doesn't know my people disappeared because vampires slaughtered them."

"If that's true, I don't understand how you ended up in Adam's company."

"Sorina didn't plan to reveal us to Adam at all, but when our

gifts manifested, Vlad intervened. He bought us the house in Bristol. He still employs the household staff to act as if we're there all year . . . When we first moved to Bristol, we thought we'd never be allowed back here. We assumed Adam would discover us sooner or later, and he did."

Mina started loading dishes into the washer. She knew the rest of the story from there, and didn't want to just stand in the kitchen and fidget while trying to process her mother's revelations. Sylvia eagerly joined her daughter in the task, which provided them both a touch of comfort.

Duncan and Sylvia's first encounter with Adam hadn't been a surprise. They had been walking home from a friend's party when Sylvia had heard magic. The sound had met them in the street, getting louder the farther they'd walked. The couple had held hands as they'd walked into their front garden to confront Adam and two other witches, a seer and another witch with a magical sense of smell. Adam's strict, absolute leadership had been apparent from the start. Sylvia had already discovered her pregnancy and desperately wanted to shield her child's life from Adam and his company.

"Mama, there's another thing I don't understand. Why did you seek the vampires again? I think Vlad is just as ruthless as you describe Adam to be, perhaps even more so."

"Sorina brokered our deal with Vlad. She protects us. She gave us more freedoms than Adam does," Sylvia said. "She suggested to Vlad we'd be more loyal to him than to Adam if they hid you here. Of course, even though he agreed, he also suggested he'd execute us as traitors to the coven if we voluntarily told any witch about the coven."

"Seriously?"

"It was worth it. For you."

"Mama," Mina whispered and paused before gripping her

mother's arm and asking, "What if my baby has a gift? Could that happen even though I don't?"

"Sometimes gifts show up in childhood but not strong enough to gain Adam's notice. Most often gifts occur in early adulthood," Sylvia explained calmly, with the most comforting tone she could. "We shouldn't worry about that unless it happens."

Mina nodded, wiping down the countertop. "Tell me about your village."

Sylvia said, "We called it Cavendish, just like our name. Maybe there were about forty of us, if that many. We all took the same surname, as was tradition for ancient witch communes in Wessex. Adam's enforcers visited often from California. Sometimes they wanted to use our parents' gifts for Adam's gains. Sometimes they told them not to use their gifts. Duncan and I were children, so we were kept out of sight. Ours might have been the last traditional witch commune, actually."

Sylvia appeared lost in nostalgic thought. "I remember attending school but otherwise spending all my time with other Cavendish children. We played outdoors often."

Mina sighed and embraced her mother. "I'll miss you, Mama. Come to London when you can."

A buzzer sounded, ending their tender moment. Mina hurried to the ovens, tending to her pastries. She turned and tossed a pair of oven mittens to Sylvia, who smiled at the silent invite to spend more time with her daughter.

Dusk painted the sky beautifully above Dragos and Ozana. They kissed and held each other to enjoy the gorgeous moment alone together, yet they dreaded the darkness that would soon fall over the Carpathian Mountains. At nightfall, they knew their coven would change forever when Vlad and Sorina appeared on the hidden mesa they used as a fighting arena. The mesa's top was exceptionally flat and level. Because they often used it for training, there were stocked weapons racks on each side.

"Do you think one of them will die?" Ozana asked.

"Yes," Dragos muttered, "and we cannot afford to lose either of them."

"I agree," Ozana said and tightened their embrace for a moment before releasing it.

The partners walked to opposite sides of the arena and began sharpening blades and organizing weapons for their respective fighters. Warriors worked on the mesa where lovers had embraced moments before, and the sound of blades on sharpening stones echoed between them. Stars became bright against mounting darkness, signaling the time for battle.

The opponents arrived at the same time and reported to the arena's center, followed by their witnesses. Neither warrior spoke. They shook hands and held the grip. Ozana and Dragos placed their hands over Vlad and Sorina's joined hands.

Dragos and Ozana counted to three in unison and released their hands. The opponents sprinted in opposite directions to arm themselves as heavily as possible.

Sorina turned back to face the arena first and reached into a quiver that was hanging from the weapons rack, pulling out an arrow and raising her bow as Vlad spun on his feet to target her. The silver arrow sprang from the bow and flew at Vlad's eye. She followed it, dropping the bow and sprinting toward him. She pulled two weapons from sheaths across her back, holding a mace capped with a blade in one hand and a katana in her other hand.

Vlad swatted the arrow away with his longsword, and it fell within an inch of its target. He didn't sprint at her but stalked with a purpose. Two seconds later, he crossed blades with Sorina. Blow by blow, they blocked each other's attacks, but he felt himself struggling to keep up with her speed. Although she had speed, he had superior strength, so he knew he needed to start using it. When the moment finally presented itself, he gripped his sword with both hands and slashed.

Sorina raised the mace to block Vlad's longsword while thrusting her katana at him. As Vlad's sword sheared off the head of her mace and continued slicing toward her neck, she dodged it. The defensive redirect cost her when the katana missed its mark, barely slicing a shallow cut across Vlad's torso before he drew back and knocked it from her grip. Her recovery from the attack's force hindered her speed.

Vlad had another opportunity to strike. His opponent had dropped her weapon and didn't have time to recover it before he swung his sword. He was momentarily confused when she crouched and sprang at him, maneuvering under his sword. He realized too late her other hand still gripped the jagged hilt of the destroyed mace. As her body slammed against his, he felt a stab in his chest. Turning the sword in his grip, he was able to aim for her ribs.

Sorina stayed as flush with Vlad's body as possible while turning and digging the mace handle into his chest wildly. A searing pain erupted from her side right before she heard Vlad's sword fall to the ground, and they were both falling to their knees. Her katana was there by her knee, and she reached for it.

Vlad's sword was out of reach, but he couldn't let Sorina recover hers. He slipped a dagger from his boot and stabbed her hand as it gripped the katana. He tried to wrestle the weapon from her, but he felt himself go down with her as she threw herself over it to keep him from having access to it.

Vlad and Sorina were both on the ground and bleeding faster than they were healing. Vlad's chest was a mass of shredded meat where Sorina had frantically wounded him repeatedly, and Sorina had a gaping, bleeding hole in her side where she'd been run through with Vlad's longsword. Their strength and stamina dwindled as blood pooled around them.

Vlad switched from trying to move her off the katana to trying to rip her throat apart with his bare hands. Her hand came up to slap him away, and he leaned away from her. His dagger was still buried to the hilt in her hand with the blade protruding from her palm, and she was trying to slap the blade into his head.

Sorina had just enough wiggle room when Vlad leaned away from her. She kicked his chest, ripped out the dagger, and grabbed the katana as he fell back and spit blood. Her breathing was erratic, and she was dizzy, but the end was near. She straddled Vlad and held a blade to his throat.

Ozana went running into the arena. "Sorina, no! Please!"

Dragos made the only decision he could and ran to support his partner.

"Sorina," Dragos said. "Ozana and I acknowledge your right to Vlad's life but taking it will rip the coven apart."

"Spare him, please," Ozana begged. "Like you, he has fought well and with honor. Show him, and us, you are a better coven leader from the start."

Sorina stared down at Vlad and asked, "Will you yield? You must acknowledge my leadership, stay by my side as my strongest warrior, and join Dragos and Ozana to be one of my most trusted advisors."

Vlad's pride and anger were loud inside his head. However, the ability to experience envito meant he didn't have an inherent death wish, nor did he lack the ability to reason past the moment. He knew his rational mind would eventually work through the negative emotions, and perhaps he'd be the leader again one day. Fighting dizziness, he came back to his senses at the sound of Dragos' voice.

"Vlad," Dragos said. "It's best for the coven if you are with us."

"Yes, I yield," Vlad said firmly.

Sorina threw her weapon as far across the arena as her diminished strength would allow. She grasped Vlad's hand, and he grasped hers. Neither of them could stand, but they rested together against the cold ground as their bodies slowly healed.

"For the time being," said Sorina, "we will continue to present Vlad as the coven leader. Now is not the time for our enemies and allies to know we have had internal conflict. Agreed?"

Almost in unison, Vlad, Dragos, and Ozana answered, "Yes."

Dragos and Ozana looked at each other, sharing feelings of profound relief. They quickly carried Vlad and Sorina and headed to the pool deep under the mountain to accelerate their healing with the sacred water.

—————

Blue Earth, Chicago, 2309 A.D.

Claudia opened her front door to find three strangers standing under her dim porchlight. She hadn't been expecting visitors and hesitated a moment before reaching her hand out and latching the screen door that stood between her and possible danger.

"Hello?" she said in the form of a confused question.

"Hello," Sylvia said. "I'm Sylvia Cavendish, and this is Duncan and Sorina."

Claudia glanced over the old couple, but her gaze lingered on Sorina.

"Say something else, Sylvia," said Sorina. "She is thinking

about how odd I look, and she is scared."

As Claudia's eyes widened, Sylvia quickly said, "We're friends with your son, Trent. I believe he's expecting us."

Claudia rested her hands on her hips and leaned against the doorframe. The old couple were the most well-dressed people she'd ever seen on her porch, and the tall woman looked like an anime assassin. Since her son had just dropped out of trade school, she doubted his friendship with any of them.

"Nobody he knows well calls him 'Trent,' except for me," Claudia said. "Besides, you all look too old to be friends of his."

"Well, that's rather discriminatory," Duncan said, dramatically feigning offense. "Sorina is four thousand years older than us, but Sylvia and I still consider her a friend."

Claudia reached her hand behind the wall. She opened the drawer of an end table next to the door where she kept a .38 revolver. Her fingers rested on the walnut grip.

Sorina said, "Do not pick up the gun, Claudia."

"Maybe I'll just close the door and call the police then," Claudia said.

Sorina turned to Duncan. "I can hear his heartbeat. He is likely somewhere in the room listening to us."

Duncan sighed. "If that's the case," he said loudly, "he'll use his new ability to pop into the street and meet us. Let's go."

"Thank you, Claudia," Sylvia said sweetly. "It was a pleasure to finally meet you."

The three of them studied Claudia's blank expression as she silently closed the door. They heard two locks click into place before they turned and walked to the street. They turned a corner and continued onto a narrow sidewalk with Sorina in front and the

Cavendishes side-by-side behind her.

"I hear him," Sylvia whispered.

The trio stopped. Duncan shielded Sylvia. Sorina gauged their surroundings.

"I do not have time for this," Sorina mumbled. "Talk to your offspring. He will hear you."

"You don't have time?" Duncan laughed.

Sorina spoke in a slow, clipped tone. "Not. For. This."

"Well, you seem to have plenty of time for speaking slowly," Duncan mumbled.

"I do not like witch hunts," Sorina said. "I am also thirsty."

"Ah, you are hangry," Duncan said, rummaged through his backpack for her water bottle, and handed it to her with a smile. "Drink thy holy water and be filled with joy."

Glaring at him, Sorina took the bottle. The water soothed her nerves as she turned up the bottle. She drained it within seconds, handed it back to Duncan, and scanned the urban darkness surrounding them. A heartbeat sounded close by, and she turned to stare down an alley. It opened into a courtyard with a stone fountain in the center. The Cavendishes followed her down the path until they reached the green space's edge.

"He is behind that fountain," Sorina whispered.

"Trent Pinkerton?" Sylvia questioned sweetly. "Are you behind the fountain?"

Water trickled down stone in the silence that followed. Pinky was crouched behind the fountain listening to everything. He'd heard what they'd said from the moment they stood at his mother's door, and he was turning it over and over in his mind. The younger woman *could hear his heart beating, so he grappled with the idea she could attack him at any moment. He heard footsteps in his direction and moved.*

Pinky used his magic and appeared behind Sylvia on the sidewalk. "Who are you people, and how do you know my name?"

Duncan jumped in alarm and whipped his body around to face Pinky, who stumbled several steps back from Sylvia. The boy steadied himself and stared at his feet in confusion. Realization struck him a moment later, and he raised his head to scrutinize Duncan.

Pinky had successfully placed the older couple between himself and Sorina, having perceived her as the greater threat. However, the man had used an invisible force to push Pinky away from them, which suggested they could have already attacked him and his mother if they had wanted to hurt him. He wondered if the older woman had a power or an ability, too.

"My name is Sylvia, and this is Duncan. We're here because I can hear you when you use your magical gift. Magical hearing is my gift. We know your name because you're a distant relative of ours."

"Who's that one?" Pinky nodded his head toward Sorina.

Sorina observed the boy but didn't answer. She knew the others would wait for her to speak for herself. He was smart, she thought, and that was certainly a relief. His black combat boots looked surprisingly like hers, but he also wore jeans and a black fitted t-shirt. The only thing that really stood out about his appearance was his hair. His black hair was spiked and accented at the ends with hot pink dye.

"Your hair," Sorina stated. "Is that why they call you 'Pinky'?

"My last name is Pinkerton, genius. Like the old woman said a minute ago. My nickname is short for my last name."

Despite the sound of Duncan laughing at her, Sorina smiled mischievously. "You lie well, young one." She turned to Duncan and continued, "Perhaps Vlad would agree to protecting him if he were to spy for the coven."

"That wasn't a lie!" Pinky spat at her.

Sorina took the challenge. "My name is Sorina, and I am a vampire. Apart from my skills as a warrior, and my keen senses, I can read thoughts . . . You lost a bet to the wrong sort of friend when you were in middle school. He bet you would not assault a girl in the school corridor, and he was right . . . How am I doing so far? Should I finish the story? It is so close to the surface of your mind."

Pinky remained silent, but he nodded. The Cavendishes looked enthralled by the story. Sylvia wore a frown, but Duncan had cracked a subtle smile.

Sorina continued, knowing he was consciously letting her read the rest of the memory in detail. "His name was Kyle. You protected the girl, staying between her and Kyle. The girl, Amber, never knew. He broke your pinky finger in front of a group of boys who all laughed and started calling you 'Pinky.' By the end of the week, the whole school had adopted it as your nickname. It bothered you—embarrassed you. Then, one of those boys let slip to his sister the reason Kyle had broken your finger. Everyone found out you'd done a good thing. The nickname stuck, but you embraced it rather spectacularly," she said, looking at his hair again.

Pinky was amazed. "That's a badass trick. Almost as badass as mine . . . What do you mean about being a vampire?"

"We've rented a house not far from here. If you'll accompany us there, we can explain everything in detail," Sylvia explained. "Only, it's best if we don't use magic—our gifts, or abilities as you think of them. We should walk."

Sylvia started walking back to the sidewalk as she spoke. Duncan and Sorina moved with her around Pinky, wordlessly *encouraging him to follow. After she spoke, the group walked without speaking but listened to their harmonious footsteps against concrete. They approached the house, and it was apparent to everyone Pinky thought it was quite nice. It wasn't until they were inside that Pinky asked his next question.*

"You said something about me becoming a spy?" Pinky asked. "Because I could use a good job."

THE OBELISK KEY

Place de la Bastille was busier than usual, but Trent had still been able to get an outdoor table and a decent cup of coffee. Paris cafes were not generally among his favorite haunts for hot beverages due to their inconsistencies in service and cleanliness, but he was enjoying himself in the moment.

Trent glanced into the square and saw Giselle walking among purple and red flowers. Her hair was tucked into a black wig, but he still recognized her quickly because the hair made her look almost exactly like her mother. To complete the disguise, she carried a parasol and wore sunshades. He watched her sit on a bench. Snoopie was on a leash at her side, and she reached down to scratch him behind his ears.

Several witches and vampires were lurking about the square, sporadically taking turns inspecting the Cleopatra's Needle, an obelisk which stood in the middle of the square on a site the Bastille Prison had once occupied.

Trent marveled at the ancient artifact. In his world, the Green Earth, the Bastille Prison still existed, one of the Cleopatra's Needles had been destroyed, and one was still in London. On the Blue Earth, two Cleopatra's Needles still stood as magnificent remnants of an ancient civilization. Some days he still couldn't wrap his mind around the differences between the worlds, and it was a special kind of mindfuck to be sitting in the middle of Paris next to a needle that stood where his brain told him a prison should be.

When Danielle had read the arch, she'd said the obelisk key was in London at the Cleopatra's Needle. On the Blue Earth, the London needle had been repatriated to Alexandria after the Second Dark Ages, so most of the witches and their allies were in Alexandria. The consensus among the allies was the Alexandria needle was where they'd find the obelisk key, but they couldn't afford to neglect possible alternate courses of action, which was why a contingency team had been sent to France.

It was also why Pinky sat down across from Trent. He devoured a croissant and washed it down with a bottle of sparkling water.

Trent looked up from his coffee and glared at Pinky. "Are you lost, or do you really think it's a swell idea for both of us to be sitting together in public?"

Without acknowledging the question, Pinky said, "So, your object reader said the obelisk key is in London at the Cleopatra's Needle, and you said there's a Cleopatra's Needle still in London on the Green Earth. Your power works on the Green Earth. My power works here. So, hear me out."

"No," Trent said.

Pinky continued explaining anyway. "I take us to the Green Earth. We check for the key. You bring us back."

"No," Trent said again.

"Why not?" Pinky asked. "It's possible the key is there."

"I don't think it is," said Trent. "If Robin could have taken them to another universe to keep them from Adam, we wouldn't have found the skull key or the archway."

"So, you don't think he'd scatter pieces across all universes?"

Trent finished his coffee. "I understand where you're coming from, but I don't think Robin would risk any of the pieces falling into our hands if he could take them across universes. The magic in them must be primal and difficult to control."

Pinky seemed to agree with Trent, or at least he accepted

his assessment. "I see . . . But I know you've thought of us working together to cross between the worlds."

"I have," Trent admitted. "We'd be a prefect team."

"But?"

"Adonai told me I don't belong on the Green Earth anymore. I feel like I'd be disregarding his warning."

"And what if a dire need arises?"

"Then I guess I'll discuss it with Adam, you, and the others at a formal cabal meeting, assuming you ever join us . . . Now, leave before you're seen by someone who doesn't know there's two of me."

"Two of me, you mean," Pinky mumbled as he stood and walked into the crowd.

Trent saw Ozana and Dragos running across the top of an adjacent building and disappear behind it. He looked back at the square, and Giselle's parasol was blowing across the garden. She was nowhere in sight, but Leilani was forcing her way through the crowd in the direction of another cafe where he'd seen Ruby and Sylvia earlier. As a feeling of alarm shocked his system and he stood to follow Leilani, his bracelet pulsed against his wrist. A wave of nausea erupted from his belly at the news from Alexandria.

—— ≈≈ ≈≈ ≈≈ ——

The Lighthouse of Alexandria had been among the Seven Wonders of the Ancient world until an earthquake had rocked it to the ground in antiquity. The Cleopatra's Needle stood in its place with the sparkling blue Mediterranean for a backdrop. Cabal members and allies were posted up and down the shore and in the city. There was no sign of fae activity. They were in a race to get the keys and seemed to be ahead. Although Adam did not expect to see Robin or his subjects at the site, he had come to personally oversee the mission.

Sorina and Vlad watched from high upon a nearby citadel's ramparts and kept the witches on the ground informed when groups of tourists headed to the needle. The citadel had been a museum in the past but was no longer open to the public. The city still took care of the building, but it was kept locked and empty. Vlad and Sorina had easily disabled its security and opened a back door. The two vampires were working well together considering she'd almost killed him the night before. It was apparent to them both they needed each other, and the coven needed them.

Danielle poked around the needle's base. She was one of the few people in the world proficient in translating Egyptian hieroglyphics and ancient script. It looked like there could be a hidden compartment within the stone, so she was running her gloved hands along the seams. Ty and Duncan stood close to her on each side of the monument for her protection.

An ankh was carved into the stone deeper than the rest of the symbols. Its location was several inches lower than anything else etched into the stone. It was larger and didn't fit with the narrative. When she ran her fingers over it, she thought she saw symbols surrounding it in the shape of a square. Her eyes blinked, and the square around the ankh was gone.

"Key of life," she whispered to herself and traced it again. "It's a key. A key."

Again, symbols shimmered around the ankh and faded away in an instant. She traced her fingers around where she'd seen the square and pushed against it. Stone crumbled to dust from around the ankh, leaving symbols she could see and read clearly. She pushed at the corners, and the ankh protruded from the stone. She turned it, and the box separated from the stone base by a tiny fissure. It was like a stone drawer. She pulled on the ankh like a handle, but it didn't budge. Realizing she needed to twist it until it opened completely, she used both hands to open it faster.

As the compartment slid open, the obelisk key was visible

within. "I see it! I see it!" Danielle chanted and continued to work.

"As soon as you can, grab it and we'll retreat behind the citadel," Ty said. "Vlad will let us inside, so you can read the key in a private place to ensure we need nothing else from the needle before we leave."

A few more twists, and the stone wouldn't move any farther. She grabbed the obelisk key from the compartment and let Duncan take her to the citadel. Ty followed behind them. When they arrived at a small door behind the citadel, Vlad was waiting.

Ty looked at Duncan and said, "I'll guard the door until Adam gets here, then we'll come up and lock it behind us."

Vlad, Danielle, and Duncan walked down a skinny dark corridor. It wasn't very long, and soon they were in a well-lit room where Sorina was waiting.

Danielle held the obelisk key up to the light and examined it for markings. It was made of flawless, clear crystal. Colors refracted through it as Danielle turned each side to the light.

Danielle said, "It's beautiful. I'll go ahead and read it."

"Give it to me," Duncan said and held out his hands. "I'll hold it while you remove your gloves."

Danielle placed it in Duncan's waiting hands and started pulling at the fingers of her gloves.

"Duncan?" Sorina asked quietly.

Hearing Sorina's voice, Danielle looked up from her hands at Duncan. He was still standing right in front of her, but he looked dead. His eyes were unseeing, his skin was drained of color, and his features were frozen in mild surprise. She released a guttural scream as he collapsed hard. Danielle dropped to her knees and reached for him, continuing to scream his name while shaking him.

Ty and Adam raced into the room and froze, trying to understand the scene before them. Ty then dropped to his knees behind Danielle and supported her.

The obelisk key rolled away from Duncan's body and toward Danielle, but Vlad kicked it aside and said, "Don't touch the key with your bare hands!"

Ty saw Danielle's gloves on the floor and picked them up. She'd stopped screaming, but she sat in front of Duncan's body crying in muted moans. Ty took each of her hands and worked the gloves back over her fingers and hands. He pulled her against him and kissed her forehead.

Sorina hadn't moved or spoken since she'd uttered Duncan's name, but she finally walked to him. Her gaze fixed on him, she crouched to the floor and sat down next to Danielle. She pulled his body into her lap and hugged him close to her chest. As she started rocking him like a mother to a child, her unnaturally iridescent tears flowed. Still, she made no sound and her expression was blank.

Danielle mumbled, "I—I kill—killed him."

Adam stood next to Vlad and asked him, "What happened?"

"He died instantly when Danielle handed him the key," Vlad said.

As soon as the words left Vlad's mouth, Danielle wailed again, and Ty comforted her until she quieted and buried her face in his neck. He started sending messages to the cabal and planning their return to New York.

Adam looked at the obelisk key that had rolled into a corner before snapping his attention back to Sorina on the floor with three of his descendants. He'd lost another valuable Child of Eden, and although Duncan was very old, he wasn't prepared to lose him. Mourning him would be difficult, and he thought of how devastated

Sylvia would be.

"Why do her tears look like that?" Adam asked Vlad, referring to Sorina.

"Our tears are full of our magic. You're seeing the essence of what makes us immortal, heightens our senses, enables mindreading. A vampire should never cry," Vlad said. "She's being rather foolish, crying over her pet witch. It's weakening her."

Adam stared at Vlad. "Vampire tears have healing powers, don't they?"

Vlad stared back at him, but didn't answer.

Adam nodded. The degree of Vlad's coldness in Sorina's moment of turmoil surprised him. He left the vampire standing alone to join his people and the woman he loved on the floor. He closed Duncan's eyes and held Sorina's hand.

"Sorina," Adam said, but she didn't acknowledge him.

He tried again, squeezing her hand. "Sorina . . . Love, look at me."

Adam was vaguely aware of Vlad exhaling a groan.

Her head turned in his direction, and her eyes focused.

Knowing he had her attention, Adam said, "You must stop crying. You cannot help Duncan now. Your tears are helping no one, and they're hurting you."

"Give me this moment," she whispered. "Hold me while I hold him a few minutes longer."

He sat behind her and slid an arm around her waist. He used his other arm to help her support Duncan's body. He glanced at Ty, who nodded to him then returned his attention to Danielle.

"We need to leave soon," Ty said to Adam after a few

minutes. "The area is secure for now, but there's no reason to risk any other complications."

"Until we discover exactly what happened, Danielle should carry the obelisk key," Adam said and shrugged off his jacket, tossing it to Ty. "Have her wrap it in this for extra protection."

Ty and Danielle got up and prepared the obelisk key to travel. They were ready to leave but waited patiently for Adam to care for Sorina. Ty had a car waiting nearby for the three of them.

Sorina stirred in front of Adam. "I am ready to stand now," she said firmly. "Thank you, Adam."

Adam helped Sorina rise to her feet. She wanted to carry Duncan's body, so Adam placed him in her arms. He noted her tears had run dry, leaving a sheen on her cheeks, but her strength seemed to be fine enough. Sorina took a long last look at Adam before she and Vlad left, taking Duncan with them back to Romania.

Disorder ruled the round table in Leilani's absence. Adam was also late to the meeting, but Ruby sat in his place and shouted down the table at Ty to call the meeting to order. Her voice was lost among the bedlam.

Jeremy had been posted at the library in Alexandria at the time of Duncan's death, so he was trying to relay to Giselle and Trent a second-hand account of the tragic story he'd received from Ty.

Phoebe and Ty were holding Danielle's hands but carrying on separate conversations while Danielle remained the only silent witch at the table.

Danielle hadn't spoken since informing Ty and Phoebe she'd inadvertently read something from Duncan's body when she'd shook him in the citadel. She'd been in shock and hadn't thought about her gloves, which had fallen to the floor with her. She'd sensed a distinctly feminine energy, and it had been primal and violent.

Phoebe was in an active voice communication with the spellcasters in Calais, admonishing them in her signature abrasive tone. None of their ancient texts mentioned that only women could touch the obelisk key with their bare hands. The spellcasters hadn't been sure that was the case, but the information didn't surprise them. Historically, only women in their culture had wielded divine objects, so it hadn't occurred to them a warning should be issued on the subject.

Ty's conversation was with Dragos in Romania. Dragos was telling Ty information from the vampires' spies, who had been tracking a small band of fae royalty, including Robin, in Pittsburgh between the time Robin had crashed Adam's party and the time Duncan had died. All detected fae movements indicated they hadn't yet gone to Alexandria but were working to move the sphere key from the Carnegie Museum.

Sorina demanded answers from the cabal, and Ty struggled to provide as many details as he could to the vampires by listening to Phoebe's conversation with the spellcasters. Between Dragos' words, Ty could hear Sylvia and Sorina in the background frantically feeding Dragos more questions to ask him.

Adam entered the room flanked by Leilani and Bastion. Adam nodded to Leilani, and the room's intense atmosphere waned as her energy radiated around the table.

Bastion and Leilani were seated. Phoebe and Ty wrapped up their conversations as tactfully as possible. The other witches grew quiet. Ruby rose from Adam's chair, but he stepped behind her and placed his hands on her shoulders to gently encourage her to remain seated.

Adam addressed the cabal while standing behind his chair. It appeared more than his hands rested upon his young spiritual advisor's shoulders. His eyes and voice were heavy with emotion, and her presence was clearly a mental crutch.

Adam cleared his throat and searched for words, but didn't find them until Ruby reached up with her right hand and placed it over his left hand. "We have much to accomplish today, so please remain cordial and speak calmly. Firstly, we must discuss the obelisk key and plan to retrieve the sphere key. Then, we'll address steps to dissolve Dust, reorganize other interests and investments, and retain our most valuable employees for the cabal's research and development capabilities."

He paused, hesitating before delivering news he expected to rouse a vehement response from Trent and Phoebe. "Lastly, we must aid the coven for Duncan's funeral rites. Sorina wishes to conduct the ceremony in Romania. I have given my blessing, so they will proceed in the coven's tradition. We will travel there when preparations are complete."

To Adam's surprise, Trent kept his peace, but Phoebe said, "I worry your obvious attraction to Sorina clouds your judgement. But I admit your willingness to accommodate her makes sense in this instance."

"Understand, Phoebe, this decision wasn't directly about business or the alliance, although it could have potentially affected the alliance," Adam said. "It was about family. I am the Cavendishes most senior blood relative, and that holds weight within the coven . . . But to your point about Sorina, I've promised Ruby I won't consummate that relationship until the fae battle is won, not that it's anyone's business."

"But it is our business," Phoebe argued. "It affects the cabal."

Adam sighed. "You have my word already."

"Of course, any decisions directly concerning the alliance will be made here at this table," Ty added, addressing Phoebe.

"On that note, may we begin with identifying the obelisk key's curse?" Adam asked. "I have reason to believe it wasn't fae magic."

"Impeccable intuition, Adam," Phoebe commented. "Or perhaps you still keep a few secrets?"

Adam's face was unreadable. "What is it you've discovered?"

"Based on a feeling Danielle received when she touched Duncan, I've interfaced with the spellcasters," Phoebe explained. "I'm almost certain the obelisk key has been magically warded against men since its creation. Only women can touch it directly. Likely to ensure balance between the sexes regarding the archway's use, or maybe because the Daughters of Selene were women . . . It's not clear."

"And the spellcasters knew this?" Adam asked, his tone accented with indignance.

Phoebe bowed her head and shook it in muted disappointment. "It was overlooked as a type of magical stipulation that's common sense in their culture."

Danielle finally spoke. "We'd be nowhere without them. We should all remember that."

Danielle's words resonated around the table.

Adam sat next to Ruby and prepared to advance the discussion to the sphere key. He referenced notes on his tablet and noticed the others following suit. A meeting had never been so quiet, but he didn't know if he was grateful for the lack of bickering or if the quiet obedience unsettled him even more. It felt more like an awkward family moment rather than an orderly meeting of professionals.

Adam addressed Leilani, "Are you doing this?"

Everyone looked up from their notes, wondering where he meant to direct his question. Leilani met his eyes and slowly shook her head while the others returned to their reading. Adam glanced around at Jeremy and Giselle, who were reading from the same tablet. He observed Danielle between Ty and Phoebe, the three of them forming a picture of serenity. Something about Trent gave him pause, and he contemplated breaking the peace. Adam didn't usually take pleasure in destroying beautiful things, but he was starting to think their usual chaos was where their real beauty flourished.

"Trent," Adam said. "You look like you have something on your mind."

Trent looked up and donned his apathy mask. "I do, but it's unrelated to the keys. I was going to mention it at the end."

"Mention it now," Adam insisted.

"So, the Cavendishes . . . The, um," Trent stammered. "The Cavendishes are—they're my soulmate's fourth great grandparents." He took a deep breath through his nose, trying to manifest coolness.

"I fuckin' knew it wasn't you!" Bastion declared, smiling mischievously. "And you gave me that bogus story about having eye surgery!"

"You assumed it was me, man," Trent argued, throwing his hands up. "That's not my fault. Pinky wears that eye patch to see better when he moves instantly from daylight to darkness."

"Dang, that's fucking rad," Bastion said. "Wait . . .Pinky?"

Trent enthusiastically pointed his hand at Bastion, feeling validated. "That's exactly what I said! About both things!"

Adam leaned back from the table and crossed his arms over his chest. Listening to two of his most rebellious descendants argue over something both had apparently kept secret would have usually upset him, but in that moment all he wanted was for Phoebe to join their conversation. He felt like listening to her input would make him feel happy, like he was home. Adam smiled at seeing her mouth twitch.

"You guys want to keep up this verbal jerk-off, or can Trent enlighten the rest of us?" Phoebe asked.

"He's the first of their descendants to manifest a gift," Trent explained. "The vampires helped them keep their daughter a secret generations ago. They sent her off to live a normal life without them, but eventually Pinky came along, and they brought him into the coven . . . He's a spy for Vlad."

"How long have you known?" Adam asked.

"Not long. Duncan told me about him, but the cabal hasn't had a formal meeting since I met him in person. I told him I was going to report his existence to you, and I know Duncan wanted to tell you, too . . . I think the Cavendishes wanted him to contact you on his own."

"I think we should honor their wishes," Phoebe said. "For Duncan . . . I think we should vote on it."

"If you all vote to uphold Duncan's wishes, I think you should also consider discretion until he makes himself known," Bastion suggested. "As a spy, he could be in danger if everyone starts making a fuss over him."

"Right," Ty stated. "All voting members are present, so let's do it. Who votes to let . . . Pinky . . . come to us when he's ready to be known?"

Once again, Adam's descendants surprised him. Leilani, Jeremy, Ty, Phoebe, Danielle, and Trent raised their hands. There were no dissenters.

"Adam?" Ty questioned.

Adam raised his hand and turned to watch Ruby record possibly the easiest vote they'd ever decided. He thought Duncan would be proud. For that matter, he thought Joe would be proud.

Ty said, "I think we can get back to the sphere key now."

"Right," agreed Adam. "What do we know?"

"It's been moved," Ty said. "That's all we've got."

"I'm incredibly disappointed we don't get to do another museum heist," Trent said.

"I second that." Bastion raised his hand.

Phoebe laughed and raised her hand. "I third that!"

"I fourth that!" Jeremy said. "But I'm also hopeful it's been moved to another museum for us to heist."

"Never lose that hope, brother," Ruby said.

Laughter rippled across the table. When it died down, the chatter stopped, too. They were thinking through possible plans.

"Our only choice is to send a team to Pittsburgh for clues," Danielle said. "It'll obviously have to be me . . . Sylvia should go, but she may not agree right now."

"She might be more motivated to go," Phoebe whispered.

Adam listened to the cabal continue to pick a team and plan an intelligence collection mission to the Carnegie Museum the next day. They'd need his help to contact Vlad and Sorina to negotiate Sylvia's participation along with a few vampires for security, but he was content to watch them plan the rest of the mission without him. He picked up his tablet and started going over an asset liquidation plan for Dust. The group would soon be ready to transition from discussing cabal activities, and their Dust business meeting would start. After the meeting, he'd have Jeremy take him to Romania to negotiate the coven's involvement in person.

HUMAN TOUCH

Faustina sat at the foot of her bed lost in a memory. It wasn't the bed she shared with Phoebe and Jameson, but it was the bed where she slept alone on nights her lovers were gone. It was also the bed she had shared with Joe. Faustina and Joe had shared the bedroom for two decades. Since his death, she'd been content to be alone in it. More and more often, she thought about the last night they'd spent in their bedroom together.

She yearned for another love like that. She needed someone who needed her, or people who needed her. Phoebe and Jameson were amazing people and fantastic lovers, but they didn't need her. She wasn't an equal member in their threesome. They were committed partners, and she was their dear friend they enjoyed inviting into their bed. It was their bed they shared with her. No part of it was hers. She laid back on her bed and thought of Joe.

Although Jameson and Phoebe didn't always co-sleep, they spent a great deal of time together in Fairuza's old room. After that first night when Faustina had explained her sister's painting on the ceiling, they'd preferred that room. Faustina heard them speaking softly as she approached the open door, and she realized Phoebe had finally returned from her meeting in New York. Leaning against the door jamb, Faustina watched Jameson brush Phoebe's hair.

Jameson noticed Faustina first. "Good evening, Tina. How was your day?"

Faustina sighed. "It was productive . . . I'm glad you're both home."

Phoebe reached back to still the brush in Jameson's hand, then she turned to face Faustina. "I know that tone. We have outstayed our welcome, haven't we?"

"Oh, Fe," Faustina breathed with a sad smile. "Not exactly .

. . You're always welcome here. I love you both."

"But?" Jameson asked.

"Fe just said it herself. 'We' is the two of you. I'm ready to move on and find my own 'we.' You're both so wonderful, especially to me. And I needed what you gave me, but now I feel healed. When I think about our threesome now, your partnership and your commitment to each other is beautiful to me, but it doesn't include me . . . That was perfect for me when I was mourning Joe, but now I need to find something more."

By the end of Faustina's passionate explanation, Phoebe had tears in her eyes, which surprised her more than it did her lovers. Jameson wiped his partner's eyes and kissed her. Faustina sat next to Phoebe and embraced her.

"You're welcome to stay as long as you want to be here," Faustina said. "You're my best friends."

"Thank you, dear," Phoebe said, "but it's best if we give you space to find your true partner . . . or partners?"

Faustina laughed. "Yes, possibly partners. Although I imagine it will be one partner."

"So, ladies," Jameson purred. "Everyone down for one more romp tonight?"

Phoebe and Faustina looked at each other, both grinning seductively. "Yes!"

———— ———— ————

Ruby was in that blank, dark space between consciousness and a vision. She'd meditated in preparation for the next time the buried fairy came to her, hoping for more control to minimize her physical pain. The last vision had been so sudden and violent that she stilled her mind in the void and braced herself for what might come after the darkness.

She started falling, but not through air. Dark air turned to black water as she fell deeper into an abyss. Like her first vision, she breathed in water, but the water didn't burn in her chest. She breathed it as comfortably as she breathed air. She didn't feel daunting pressure. She wasn't unbearably cold. She felt like her physical being was protected from the dreamscape.

Glowing light became visible from below as she approached the familiar bioluminescent flora at the ocean's bottom. Hitting the stone sarcophagus, she bounced then found her feet. She stood on top of the sarcophagus to look around, but the wreckage in the distance was just as unfamiliar as it had been before.

She jumped to the sandy ocean floor and pushed the heavy lid away from the watery tomb. The gorgeous fairy was there, but her eyes remained closed. Ruby brushed her hand against the fairy's face and touched her flowing hair. The fairy continued to sleep.

Reaching both hands into the box, Ruby shook the fairy by her shoulders and shouted, "Una!"

Una's eyes popped open, and she sat up. Her delicate hands lifted the orb that had been resting on her abdomen and extended it toward Ruby. That's when Ruby realized what the orb was and why she was having the vision. Una held the sphere key.

"Find me. Take it," Una pleaded.

Ruby asked, "Where are you?"

Una repeated, "Take it."

Ruby reached for the sphere and grasped it in both hands. It glowed beneath her fingers like a lantern in the darkness. She smiled and knew that's why Una had given it to her.

"Una, why do you wear a crown? Who are you?"

The fairy frowned and lowered her eyes. "I am the true heir.

The true queen. The realm was taken from me."

Ruby became wary of the ethereal fairy. Not only did Una belong to an enemy race, but she claimed to be its rightful ruler. That could make her a threat to the alliance. It could also mean she'd make a good ally if she opposed the current fae regime. There were too many unknowns for Ruby's comfort.

"Can you tell me where we are?" Ruby asked.

Una shook her head and pointed to the distant wreckage. She then fell back into her coffin and closed her eyes. Again, she looked asleep rather than dead. Ruby was tempted to shake the fairy awake again for more answers but turned to go in the direction the vision was trying to take her.

Ruby walked by the sphere's guiding light. The wreckage seemed far away by foot, and she hoped to reach it before waking. She wondered how she was able to see the wreckage at all. Light shone from behind the shapes in the distance, forming dim silhouettes. Perhaps the light was manmade as well, like an underwater research facility. Something identifiable like that would be a vital clue.

The ocean faded, the sphere disappeared, and Ruby floated in nothing. She was waking. Hayden's voice penetrated the veil, and she knew he was talking to her. She fought valiantly against his voice, keeping herself in the darkness. But when his physical touch started dragging her into reality, she let go. Resistance was useless.

Faustina's unbridled moan announced her ecstasy. Jameson's tongue game was the most pleasurable foreplay she'd ever experienced, and she shuddered at a new sensation she'd never felt with him before. The thought crossed her mind that he was trying to get her to change her decision about ending their threesome, but her mind quickly went blank when he began sucking on her.

Phoebe wrapped her lips around Jameson's erection and glanced up to watch him pleasuring her friend. The sight of them enhanced her enjoyment of fellatio, and it fed her determination to increase Jameson's enjoyment, too. She savored his taste until she heard the particular high-pitched moan Faustina always made during orgasm. Phoebe switched places with her partner then, kissing Faustina hard while their bodies settled against each other, and Faustina rubbed her thighs against Phoebe's hips.

Jameson enjoyed the sight of Phoebe and Faustina kissing and grinding against each other. He then leaned over Phoebe, thrusting into her. He felt Faustina's legs come up and wrap around him. He pushed harder against Phoebe and watched Phoebe grinding harder against Faustina in rhythm with him. He knew one of Phoebe's hands had found its way between Faustina's legs when she started crying out. The sound drove him wild, and he went deeper into Phoebe and felt her come undone around him. He let go and chased her release with his own.

They rested together, appreciating their last moments sharing a bed. Jameson wrapped an arm around each woman and held them both, listening to them chat.

Phoebe's bracelet pulsed against her wrist, and she sighed when she checked the message. "I've got to go back to the city." She looked at Faustina. "I really wish I didn't have to right now."

"You just got home a few hours ago," Jameson protested.

"I know," Phoebe said and hesitated. "There's something I need to tell you both, but I didn't want to deal with it when I first got home. I just wanted a minute to relax, and then one thing led to another."

"I already know," Jameson whispered. "Adam sent me a message."

"Well, I don't know," said Faustina, "so you still have to say whatever it is."

"Duncan is dead, and we're one mission away from a full attack against the fae, so the next few days will be crucial . . . They'll be a bit intense."

"I should send Sylvia a message," Faustina said. "I definitely know what she's going through."

"If a battle is imminent, I should have our things picked up and moved back to Albany in the morning," Jameson said. "We'll need to spend time with Hayden at the house."

Despite Jameson and Faustina both issuing groans of protest, Phoebe left the bed and dressed. She'd already told them too much, but it felt wrong not to prepare them for possible additional deaths. They especially needed to understand the children were at risk. She pulled on her boots and kissed them both before leaving to meet the car.

Jameson and Faustina reluctantly watched Phoebe leave. They snuggled under the covers and held each other. Neither of them spoke. As they passed time in comfortable silence, Faustina fell asleep. Instead of carrying her to her own bed like he usually did, Jameson held her and slept well through the night.

<hr />

"Ruby!" Hayden tried to wake the woman snoring next to him.

He'd received a message from Giselle, stating Ruby had slept through multiple messages from Ty and Adam to come back to New York City. Giselle was waiting on a message back from him. He was supposed to confirm Ruby was awake, okay, and headed to the city forthwith. When Ruby didn't respond to her name, he was happy to take drastic measures.

Ruby twitched and kicked as she woke up with an angry roar, which dissolved into shrieking giggles. Hayden was tickling her, and she couldn't stand it. Rolling away from him in a fetal position didn't help her situation. She repeatedly screamed for him to stop between uncontrollable belly laughs. Tears of laughter dampened her red face. The sensations were overwhelming her, and she needed to pee.

Her hand walloped him across the face as she screamed, "You're going to make me pee myself! Fucking stop, you treacherous cunt!"

Hayden stopped and rubbed his face while laughing. "Strong language, Ru! Also, a strong hit."

"I was in an important vision! Why did you wake me?" Ruby asked, exasperated.

Hayden's face was a mixture of confusion and disappointment. "But you were snoring. It only looked like a deep sleep. I think you were even drooling a bit . . . It was nothing like before."

She got up and stomped to the bathroom but yelled, "It's not always the same, especially when I've been meditating on certain visions!"

"I'm sorry, but you slept through a lot of messages, and now Giselle won't leave me alone!" he yelled back at her while messaging his sister.

Ruby caught up on messages while sitting on the toilet. Her heart sank to think of leaving Hayden less than twelve hours after coming home to him. She washed her hands and splashed water on her face. Walking back into the bedroom, she noticed the sadness in Hayden's eyes.

She smiled and embraced him. "I love you, Hay."

He pulled away from her in surprise and studied her face. "Really?"

She giggled until his lips crashed down upon hers, and he

pulled her against him tightly. He reluctantly let her go, but he followed her every movement while she dressed in a hurry.

"I wish we had more time," she said and kissed him, "but even if they hadn't summoned me, I need to hurry back and share my vision with Adam."

Hayden brushed his hands through her hair and let her go. "I know . . . I'll have something special planned for us by the time you get back."

IF YOU COULD READ MY MIND

Adam wondered what the sky looked like though Sorina's vampire eyes. How did the air smell to her? How did it feel against her skin? Had a vampire ever bewitched a witch? He contemplated the last question at length but felt no danger or shame for the way he felt about her. He saw her as a blessing from Eden. Maybe he was meant to have another chance at love. Wind blew through the mountains, and he stood in the shadows and watched it play with her hair. From so far away, she looked small and delicate. She sat in the lotus position and seemed to be gazing at stars on the horizon. The arena was deserted save for her.

Sorina meditated in the middle of the arena. She'd smelled Adam's scent on the wind but let him linger unacknowledged while her mind rested. Knowing he was there aided her mental recovery from recent discord, tragedy, and change. His presence was like medicine for her soul. He wasn't close enough for her to hear his heartbeat yet, but she hoped he'd stay and eventually wander closer. Taking a deep breath as the wind blew his scent toward her again, she knew he was still somewhere behind her on the mountain.

She looked to be enjoying the quiet landscape. Wanting to move closer without disturbing her right away, Adam removed his shoes and socks. Pebbles stuck to his bare feet as he treaded lightly in her direction. The pain was worth her continued peace. As he drew close to her, he understood she was in deep reflection, perhaps even meditating. He stopped.

His beating heart became her white noise. The thought of falling asleep against his chest consumed her mind's eye. Negativity faded and retreated into her mind's depths. Weariness seeped from her heart as hope replaced it with every beat of her heart in harmony with his. Then the sound of his grew softer.

"Do not go," she breathed.

In a few agile movements, he was in a lotus position beside her. Her eyes were closed, and she breathed deeply but slowly. He simply watched.

Moments later, her eyes fluttered open and she turned to face him. "Thank you for staying."

"I'll always do anything you ask."

"I am a vampire, Adam. Be careful of vows you speak."

"Sorina," he said and reached for her hand. "You are my angel."

She moved swiftly, crushing the distance between them. His back hit solid rock beneath him, and her chest moved sensually against his. They were kissing each other deeply. In a bold, passionate move, Adam bit his own tongue and slipped it further into her mouth.

She drew back, gasping and searching his eyes for the consent she craved.

He understood. "Yes," he said. "Kiss me."

She reciprocated, biting her own tongue before pressing her mouth against his. Just like the night he'd saved her on the beach, the blood exchange was like an orgasm in heaven. The feeling was rendered even more pure given a pleasant night as opposed to a violent one. Together, their tongues healed within seconds, and the ecstasy dimmed. A desire to heighten their pleasure again drove Sorina.

Adam felt her hand slide into his trousers, and he silently cursed himself for having to stop her.

Adam's hand gripped Sorina's wrist tightly as he said, "I can't go further tonight."

"I have only just warned you," she replied, breathing erratically. "You will always do anything I ask?"

"I made a promise to the cabal not to consummate a relationship with you until after the fae war," Adam admitted. "So, there is the conflict."

She pulled back and stood. He followed suit.

"This has been a topic of discussion with your tribe?" Sorina asked loudly in annoyance.

"They fear what Vlad would do if he knew. They'll likely disown me if I ruin the alliance," Adam said and pulled her into an embrace she didn't resist. "What would Vlad do if he found you in my bed?"

Sorina ignored the question. "I still don't understand why you announced it to the entire cabal."

"I didn't have to. It was obvious to a few of them I was falling in love with you, so they brought it to the table."

"Love?" she asked. "Is this love? It feels like everything I have never felt before . . . But it also feels like being with you is the only natural, normal way to live now."

"There are many types of love, as I'm sure you know," Adam said, brushing his hand through her hair.

"Yes, of course, but this type," she said, rubbing his chest. "It is a surprise to me. A pleasant one, but also frightening sometimes in that it is . . . unique?"

"I feel the same way, but I promise you we are in this together, Sorina."

He kissed her, and she threw her arms around his neck. Pulling her against him tightly, he started levitating. He took them far above the mountains where they could enjoy the view. When Sorina finally drew back from the kiss and opened her eyes, she gasped and clung to Adam.

With her face buried in his shoulder, she declared, "Adam, I cannot comfortably or safely fall from this altitude!"

Realizing she was scared, Adam said, "It's okay. I've got you . . . Can you enjoy the view with me, or do you want me to take us down?"

She repositioned her arms to feel more secure and looked around. "I will stay up here with you."

"My apologies," he whispered. "I thought you could fly."

She laughed. "I am not actually an angel."

"Yes, you are," Adam purred. "However, everyone in the cabal thinks vampires can fly, and I am a bit confused now."

"We can leap from tall buildings and the like, and we can jump and propel ourselves through the air with our strength, so it often looks like we can fly," she explained.

She threw her head back and looked at the stars. "It is wonderful up here. Thank you, Adam."

"It is wonderful, especially with you. I would prefer to stay up here all night," he said, "but we must meet with Vlad."

"Adam?"

"Hmm?"

"Where are your shoes?"

He chuckled quietly against her ear. "Well, we'll get my shoes, then we'll go to Vlad . . . I removed them as to not disturb your meditation earlier."

"Clever. So, that is how you *almost* took me by surprise."

Kissing her neck, he whispered, "Don't I always take you by surprise?"

—

"How do you not get lost in here?" Adam asked.

Sorina's amused tone echoed down the corridor. "I have lived here hundreds of years."

She was leading him through a series of passageways within a mountain. They were almost like corridors in an old house in aesthetic but palatial in size. Hardwood floors creaked beneath their feet, and stark-naked light fixtures glowed high above their heads. Pastoral artwork graced the walls. Although the paintings looked masterful and familiar, Adam couldn't identify the artist.

"These are all by the same artist," Adam said, and it wasn't quite a question.

"Ananda paints them," Sorina explained. "Paintings in this corridor are from the period she was obsessed with the style of Millais."

"Yes!" Adam realized. "The detail is remarkable."

"Heightened senses and unlimited time are useful tools in art as well as war," Sorina quipped. "I prefer her Hieronymus Bosch period, which decorates one of our bedroom corridors, but she transitioned into her own style a few centuries ago . . . It is interesting, to say the least."

"I hope to get a full tour sometime," Adam said playfully.

Sorina glanced at him, but her tone was impersonal. "When this battle is won, you will."

The mountain was the vampires' castle, which was also known as the House of Ardelean in reference to the surname the vampires had adopted in the eighteenth century. Although some balconies, ramparts, and towers were cut into the mountain's stones and visible from the exterior, most of the architecture was internal to the mountain. They owned land surrounding and including three peaks along the southern Carpathians with their castle occupying the center mountain.

They entered a spacious chamber that reminded Adam of a medieval throne room. Instead of a throne, a long stone bench built like a church pew occupied the dais. Similar stone seating formed a semi-circle at the floor level facing the dais.

Vlad, Dragos, and Ozana sat on the high bench and observed Sorina and Adam approach. Sorina took her space next to Vlad while Adam was invited to sit at the floor level on the first row facing them. Sylvia entered and sat next to Adam.

Adam offered Sylvia his hand, and when she accepted it, he whispered, "I'm so sorry for your loss."

"Thank you, Adam," Sylvia said, squeezing his hand and then letting go.

Sylvia turned her attention back to the vampires watching over them.

He studied her for a second and noticed extra wrinkles around her eyes and mouth. She appeared to be aging rapidly.

Turning to the vampires, he got the point. "I need Sylvia in Pittsburgh tomorrow if she'll agree to it."

Vlad answered, "Of course—"

"No!" Sorina passionately interrupted but then regained an impassive demeanor.

Vlad looked at Sorina, who remained silent, then he turned to Adam and said, "Perhaps not Sylvia, but we will provide . . ."

Vlad exchanged awkward glances with Sorina before he

continued, "We will provide six vampires for security."

Adam had expected Sorina to protest Sylvia's involvement but hadn't expected Vlad to yield so easily and publicly to her protest. Adam noted Dragos and Ozana were as still as stone, their faces devoid of expression. Studying all four vampires, he felt odd.

Adam explained, "As of now, we don't have a location for the sphere key. Sylvia's magical gift could make the difference between failure and success in Pittsburgh."

Sylvia stood and said, "I will go. I must help finish this."

Vlad didn't respond. Sylvia retook her seat and patiently waited. Adam tried to make eye contact with Sorina, but she seemed to be avoiding his gaze on purpose. Then he noticed her hand, which was clutching Vlad's forearm.

"Very well," Vlad announced. "Sylvia is granted permission to go."

Something wasn't right. Adam had a feeling he was the only one in the room who didn't know something important. Vlad's arm was dripping blood. Sorina had dug her nails into his skin as he continued to speak.

Vlad looked at Sorina and continued, "After all, the main advantage of this alliance is to have all skills and gifts between the witches and the vampires available when needed."

Sorina released Vlad's arm and closed her eyes for a moment. Her stoic bearing was in place when she opened her eyes again. She looked directly at Adam and Sylvia and offered them a faint smile.

"I have one condition," Vlad said suddenly. "You must give Sylvia the ability to block her thoughts from us if she wants it."

Adam was unsure if he wanted Sylvia to know how the witches blocked their thoughts from vampires. He imagined a future battle in which vampires ripped the tech from witches' bodies. It was a convenient secret for his people to keep, so he quickly thought of a way to advance negotiations.

"Return Pinky to my tribe," Adam stated slowly but firmly, "and I will bring your request before the cabal. As it personally and physically affects them all, it must be put to a vote."

Sorina watched Sylvia for a reaction.

Sylvia leaned into Adam and whispered, "Please don't do this . . . Please. I will renounce the coven and leave with you now. You needn't trade a secret for me if you leave Pinky to come to you when he's ready."

Adam remained impassive. He couldn't look Sylvia in the eyes, so he focused on Sorina, who turned to Vlad. The two vampires were staring at each other, their eyes unnaturally wide open. He realized they must be communicating, and he felt even more suspicious and wondered if his love for Sorina blinded him. She was scheming with Vlad right in front of him, demanding his tribe reveal a weakness. He knew it was Sylvia's proposal—her sacrifice—causing friction between them, so there was a chance he was about to win the negotiations.

"No," Vlad finally answered. "You keep your mind blocking secret, and we keep Pinky for as long as he desires . . . Sylvia will be on our team in Pittsburgh. She and the others will meet your team there."

"Good," Adam said and stood. "Sylvia, do you mind showing me outside?"

Adam didn't want to be alone with Sorina again until he could sort out his anger and distrust. She was like oxygen to him; he needed her to live. Love was something new since she'd come into his world, but he couldn't risk his people and their fight against the fae. Eve had taught him how dangerous love could be for him, so he would be careful not to repeat his past mistakes.

Sylvia started walking. "Follow me," she turned back to Adam and spoke.

When they entered the corridor, Adam said, "I didn't want you to be forced to leave the coven, but I don't know Vlad's motives. If I tell him how I block his mind reading, he'll have information that can harm me and the others."

Sylvia spun around and asked, "How do you know about Pinky?"

"I know because Trent knows," he explained. "Apparently they've met."

"You leave him alone!" Sylvia ordered. "He's Duncan's legacy!"

"Sylvia, I'm sorry . . . I'm fighting the fae and closing Dust. When would I have time to bring him in?" he asked. "I had to leverage my knowledge of him today to protect the witches. Surely you understand that."

"I understand you think you needed to." Sylvia turned away from him and continued through the corridor maze.

Adam followed her in silence. There was nothing he could say to make her feel better, and he knew that. When they turned a corner, Sylvia stopped.

She pointed straight ahead and said, "Keep going that way, and you'll exit to a terrace."

She turned and walked away, leaving him standing there. He waited for a bit and felt guilt for the pain she was enduring. Cool air blew down the corridor, reminding him he was close. Outside he could fly hard and fast into the night to blow off steam and breathe easier under the starry sky.

Adam circled the mountain and landed on an adjacent hilltop. There was a flat stone that seemed to be made just for him to relax and stare at the sky. He was tired from excessive flying, and his eyes drifted shut. Thoughts of Duncan and his tribe turned to thoughts of Sorina within moments. Love, or something like it, consumed him.

Finally, he got up and prepared to fly down closer to the village where Jeremy could meet him. Small stones rolled down the hill behind him, and he turned to confront the sound. Sorina was there.

"I cannot explain what happened at the meeting," she stated.

Adam's expression and tone were bland. "I didn't ask you to . . . In fact, I left without asking anything of you."

"Why is a man always so predictable?" she asked, her voice smooth with only a slight tremble on the last word. "Two hours ago, I was your angel, but now I am just another vampire, is that it? And Vlad wonders why I have not felt anything for years and years."

"Two hours ago, Sorina, you weren't wordlessly speaking to another man with your eyes and plotting against my tribe."

"Another man?" Sorina laughed despite herself. "You really believe that is what happened? That I was plotting against you? Or are you more like Vlad that you think, and this conversation is more the result of jealousy?"

"Why do you think I'd be jealous of Vlad?"

He ignored her first two questions, and she smirked. Even without her ability to literally read his thoughts, she found him quite easy to read. She assumed his distrust of the coven was genuine. Vlad had seen to that by mentioning their mind reading defense. However, she was certain that distrust was multiplied beyond reason due to jealousy.

"Vlad and I can share our deepest thoughts if we so choose."

"I am not a simpleton," Adam spat. "Something was not right in there. All four of you were behaving . . . strangely."

"You have made certain promises to your cabal, and I have made certain promises to my coven," Sorina replied, her manner intentionally soft and serene to calm the air between them. "As I told you, I cannot explain."

Adam's eyes were downcast as he thought about the night, the meeting, and Sorina. He could admit to himself the intensity of their bond had heightened his emotions in a way he'd been unprepared to handle. Although his relationship with Eve had been toxic and had caused him to make wrong decisions from the beginning, he'd hardened his heart and kept his cool with her ever since their fall from grace. He'd owned his emotions for thousands of years and needed to be mindful, considering Sorina's effect on him.

"I see your point," Adam looked up and said to her directly. "What will you offer me in lieu of an explanation?"

Sorina maintained eye contact with him and declared, "Adam, I have given my blood to you. There is nothing more precious—more sacred—to a vampire. I have never shared that gift outside the coven until you . . . You have given me your blood, through which you gave me my life. You are my savior in more ways than one."

Sorina tucked her thumbs under two platinum chains hanging around her neck and pulled them, revealing smoky crystal pendants that had been tucked between her breasts underneath her catsuit. The crystals were small vials, but they were empty. She unclasped one of the chains and unscrewed the vial's stopper. Raising her index finger to her teeth, she punctured her skin and squeezed several drops of blood into the vial. She stoppered it and met Adam's eyes.

Adam stood still while Sorina placed a chain around his neck. The metal was still warm from her body heat, and the feeling comforted him. He released a breath he didn't know he'd been holding and gently wrapped his hand around the vial.

Sorina opened the vial she still wore around her own neck and held her hand out to Adam, asking, "May I?"

He raised his hand halfway to hers and hesitated. "Is— Sorina, is this your partnership ritual?"

"Yes."

Her simple answer prompted him to slowly place his hand into hers. Her eyes remained locked onto his while she bit into his finger. She then turned her attention to filling the vial, but he continued staring in awe.

"Sorina, you made this decision very fast."

"So did you."

"Because I know I don't want to live without you."

"I feel the same way about you, Adam . . . If I cannot have you physically, I will have you spiritually before we face battle."

Sorina dropped his hand and stoppered her vial. She tucked it into her catsuit between her breasts and noticed Adam was holding both his hands out to her, so she clasped them in hers.

In his tradition, he said, "We take each other as partners, to share joys and sorrows, to provide each other strength in times of weakness, and to share unconditional love."

In her tradition, Sorina replied, "With our blood, we bind our hearts and minds together, promising to honor, cherish, and love each other in all seasons."

They fell into each other's embrace.

Sorina then stayed while Adam flew down the mountain to meet Jeremy in the village. When she lost sight of him in the darkness, she walked home alone.

THE SPHERE KEY

Only witches needed for the museum mission gathered around the table in the morning's small hours. Coffee and tea filled the quiet air with a pleasant scent. Adam, Ty, Phoebe, Bastion, and Danielle were already seated when Ruby, Giselle, and Jeremy showed up late. Giselle and Jeremy had waited outside for Ruby to make sure of her arrival.

"Okay, kids," Phoebe said with a yawn. "Is there a reason I'm sitting here with my second cup of coffee waiting on you?"

The looks on the rest of the older witches' faces told Ruby they agreed with Phoebe's sentiment. She took her seat next to Adam, and he slid a cup of coffee in her direction. Jeremy had told her they'd decided on an early start to get in and out of the museum before it opened.

The plan was for Jeremy to take two witches at a time straight into the gem gallery. The vampires had confirmed they could bypass the museum's security system. Sylvia and a vampire team were ready to meet them on site.

"We've got a good reason for being late, Mother," Giselle explained. "Ruby was having a vision."

"So, Ruby has a good reason, but you and Jeremy are just late," Bastion stated and high-fived Phoebe.

"When are we leaving?" Ruby asked.

"We have a little over an hour left," Adam answered.

"Good," Ruby said. "I have time to tell you about my vision."

She described Una's underwater grave to them with as much detail as she could recall, including the noble fairy's appearance. She told them the sphere key was in the coffin. Then, she recounted the conversations she had with Una and explained she had been trying to discover the location when Hayden had roused her from sleep.

Ty pulled up a photo of the Dowager Empress crystal ball on his tablet and showed it to Ruby. "Are you sure this is what you saw?"

"I'm sure. Why would I be seeing a different crystal sphere?" she asked, exasperated.

Bastion said, "So, we know it's in the ocean, which narrows it down to roughly three quarters of the world. Very helpful."

"Actually, it is helpful," Jeremy snapped. "A minute ago, we had it narrowed down to the entire world, so this is something."

"Besides," Giselle added, "we can hopefully narrow it down further at the museum."

Danielle said, "I agree. This is a good start."

"Ruby should stay here and meditate," Phoebe suggested. "We have enough people on the mission. Her vision is more valuable than her syphoning powers in this case."

Adam reached for Ruby's hand and squeezed it. "I agree . . . What do you think, Ruby?"

Ruby looked disappointed. "I wanted to help today."

"You will be helping either way, Ru. Maybe staying is a good plan," Giselle said while Jeremy nodded.

"Does everyone else think I should stay and meditate?" Ruby asked.

Ty and Danielle looked at each other, and Ty said, "We think that's best."

"Yeah," Bastion agreed.

"When am I supposed to test my other skills?" Ruby asked Adam.

"There's at least one more mission to find the sphere key before we breach the fae realm," Adam said. "You'll go with us then."

"Okay," Ruby whispered. "This room will be empty and quiet when you're gone. I'll meditate here."

The others disappeared two by two until Ruby was alone at the round table. She slid onto the table and spread her body out like a starfish, looking up at the backlit stained-glass dome above her. She wondered how she'd never noticed the patterns in it before. It was their constellation. Staring at the colorful artwork, Ruby relaxed her mind.

Fae Realm, 1431 A.D.

Iron made the ruby crown heavier, but it still fit perfectly upon Eve's fair brow. She admired herself wearing it though a mirror Robin had placed above his bed. Red was her favorite color, so she loved rubies. Her naked body quaked, and Robin looked up from between her legs and smiled.

Laying his cheek against Eve's thigh, Robin asked, "What if she discovers it's poisoned before she puts in on?"

It's only lined with iron on the inside," she explained. "Then, I've put a layer of the red salt you have in this world over that, see?"

Eve held up the crown. It was impossible to see where the precious gemstone ended, and the poisonous minerals began. She studied its deadly beauty and placed it on her abdomen. When

218

Robin recoiled, she smirked and placed it back on her head.

"Salt and iron really repel you so completely?" she asked.

Robin rolled over onto his back and embraced her leg. "They render us powerless."

"Why do you have them in your realm then?"

"Don't be a fool. Why are things on the Blue Earth harmful to you?"

"If you're so intelligent, explain to me why I couldn't simply put the minerals into her food for you," Eve said, watching him through the mirror.

"I could feed her salt," he said, "but it would only paralyze her until the mineral runs its course through her body."

"What about iron?" she asked.

"That is not an option."

"Why?"

"If taken internally, she would die."

"You always keep secrets from me." Eve sat up and stared at him. "Why is her death a problem?"

"Several reasons," he stated cryptically.

Eve hissed, "Tell me!"

"You'll make a bargain with me?" Robin asked and reached for her hand. "I tell you one secret, and you only use that secret to help me. You never harm me with the knowledge."

"You'll tell me about the most important secret between you and Una, and I will not harm you with the knowledge," Eve countered.

Robin proposed yet another change to the bargain. "You will use the secret to actively help me if I tell you about the most important secret between me and Una."

Eve groaned but agreed to his terms anyway. She'd become familiar with the subtle feel of a fae bargain working its magic between her and Robin. It was so easy to overlook that she'd not felt it the first two times they'd struck bargains. It was only a slight itch burying itself into her palm.

Robin told his secret, saying, "Most importantly, Titania bound my magic together with Una's, so that we will protect each other and not do harm to each other . . . If one of us dies, we both lose our magic. I must keep her alive. Her magic must stay locked inside her living body."

Eve stood and paced the floor, deep in thought about Robin's plan. Robin meant to replace the crown in Una's boudoir before dawn and wait for her to dress for court. When the crown paralyzed her, Eve and her loyal witches would move Una somewhere Oberon and Titania wouldn't think to search for their daughter. Eve's plan was to pay humans to bury her in one of their villages on vampire land, but after listening to Robin's secret, she had a better solution.

"The oceans are saltwater!"

Robin eyed her strangely. "Well spotted, Evita."

She slapped him hard across the face. "Don't talk to me like I'm stupid."

"Will you keep slapping me around if I do?" Robin purred and dropped to his knees in front of her.

She grabbed his face between her hands and forced him to look up at her. "The oceans, you cannot go into them?"

He thought and answered, "Well, I wouldn't swim in them,

but we're near them quite often . . . We have a home on Malta. Sometimes I quite like the smell of a bit of sea salt on the air."

"Is it a fault in your brain—some sort of diminished intelligence—that causes you to answer every question with indirect answers?" she asked, her voice sickly sweet.

Robin laughed. "You're dangerously close to asking me to reveal another secret, so of course I'll give you a vague answer."

She sighed. "How about this? I'll be specific . . . If I placed Una at the bottom of an ocean, would your parents be able to endure that much saltwater to find her? Furthermore, would it kill her, or would it simply ensure she stays asleep?"

Robin cackled maniacally and wrapped his arms around her, his face warm against her navel.

A placard under the empty pedestal read, "The Dowager Empress."

"Ah, we're lucky they haven't moved the display case yet!" Bastion said, excited.

Giselle giggled. "This is Pennsylvania, not New York."

"What does that even mean?" Bastion asked.

"It means we're not dealing with the 'A Team,'" Ty explained.

Phoebe and Danielle laughed.

"Well, I don't think it matters. I adore this museum. It's got character," Phoebe declared.

"Did your mother just say something delightfully positive?" Jeremy whispered to Giselle.

"Anyone want to do their jobs, or do we keep standing

around chatting?" Adam asked.

Bastion shrugged. "I'm doing both."

"Really?" Phoebe snapped.

Bastion argued, "Absolutely. I smell saltwater, like the ocean. It's all over this area."

"Oh, bullshit!" Danielle chimed in. "We already know it's in the ocean—"

In an instant, Danielle stopped talking and froze. Her bare hand rested on the empty pedestal, and she was staring at it like she was repulsed. Her face morphed into a fully horrified expression. Her breathing was erratic at first, but then she started gasping for air. Ty wrapped his arms around her body and removed her hand from the pedestal. She leaned on him, coughing and trying desperately to catch her breath. He was rubbing her back and telling her she was safe, and she began taking long, deep breaths.

"I was in the ocean," she mumbled.

Bastion threw up his hands. "I told you."

"Shut up, Bastion. Dani's trying to talk," Phoebe whispered.

Danielle continued, "My hand transformed. It was grotesque, like it was webbed with scales. Then the scales went up my arm. Before long, I felt like I was breathing water."

"Ruby said she felt like she was breathing water during her first vision under the ocean," Giselle said.

"It must be a sea creature with magic," Sylvia called out from the back of the gallery. She and Ozana had just entered though a back corridor.

Everyone's attention turned to Sylvia. "In the service corridor, I heard faint traces of a strange magical frequency. It was coming from this," she said, holding up something too small for anyone to understand what it was.

"It's a fish scale," Ozana explained, noticing all the witches squinting.

"A sea creature who walks on land?" Bastion asked.

"I saw a hand change shape . . . I think it's a shapeshifter," Danielle said.

"But not a witch, like Nick Bishop? Sylvia said it's a different magical frequency?" Phoebe asked.

"That's not possible, is it?" Ty asked Adam.

Adam looked at Ozana for confirmation when he said, "Merpeople went extinct in the fifteenth century."

Ozana agreed, "Yes, the coven is not aware of any other humanoid sea creatures."

Ty stayed close to Danielle as she tried to read a few more objects and surfaces around the gallery. Because of the historical significance of everything on display, she wanted to read as many interesting historical artifacts as possible for personal enjoyment before it was time for them to leave.

"Okay, everyone," Adam said, looking around. "Finish checking the gallery for clues. We still need to leave before the museum staff arrives. And, Jeremy, bag that fish scale and take it to the lab when we get back."

Bastion cased the joint with Phoebe. They quietly joked together about which gems they would steal if Adam let them do another museum heist. When they made it up to the front of the gallery, they saw Jeremy and Giselle looking at one of the exhibits and whispering to each other. Phoebe approached the couple and stood next to her daughter. Giselle was studying a five-hundred-year-old piece of high jewelry called "The Garden Necklace."

"Giselle, what has gotten into you?" Phoebe whispered. "There's a diamond the size of an apple back there, and you're over here plotting for an aquamarine necklace that's probably worth less than several of the necklaces you have at home?"

"We weren't discussing heisting it," Giselle said.

"It's moments like this I'm glad I don't have kids." Bastion shook his head in feigned disappointment.

Jeremy laughed. "Giselle was telling me how much Ruby loves this necklace. Apparently, they've been here several times together, and Ruby always stops to look at it."

"Yeah, we picked out something to heist earlier," Giselle whispered. "We like the life-sized peacock carved out of amber."

Bastion scoffed, "That is ridiculous."

"That's why we like it," said Jeremy.

"Why were you even asked to be on this mission, Giselle?" Bastion asked.

"There's hardly any risk involved with us being in the museum, especially with the sphere key already taken," she said. "Why not bring me along in case there was an animal I could communicate with for a clue?"

Everyone in the conversation knew Giselle's real reason for being there was to stick close to Jeremy because she could. Especially since Ruby had also been on the list to go, Giselle had wanted to be included. Phoebe and Bastion started to walk away but hesitated as Sylvia and Ozana approached their group.

"I found this hair, too," Sylvia said, handing a golden strand to Jeremy. "Put it in the bag with the scale."

Jeremy held it up, and everyone examined the shiny strand. It almost looked like real gold instead of hair. Bastion took it, smelled it, and handed it back to Jeremy.

"What did Danielle see when she read it?" Bastion asked.

"I asked her to read it," Sylvia said, "but since she thinks it'll disturb her, she wants to do it at headquarters . . . I'm leaving now. Be safe getting back home."

Phoebe embraced Sylvia.

After the vampires left, the witches quickly regrouped with Adam, and Jeremy began transporting them back to New York. As Jeremy disappeared from the gallery with the last two witches in tow, exhibit designers arrived to remove the empty case and pedestal where the sphere had been.

Point Oubliette, Pacific Ocean, Blue Earth, 1431 A.D.

The last two surviving mermen struggled against chains Eve had wrapped around them while the last mermaid collapsed unconscious before her and the two witches flanking her. Their ship floated along the most remote location on the Blue Earth.

Wilda and Moira were Eve's ruthless disciples. She'd collected them from the Battle of Hastings' aftermath, and they'd survived centuries with her through massacres, power grabs, and bouts with Adam. Their witch commune had been war-torn. She'd sensed their power and offered them places by her side in exchange for more power and prolonged life. Together, they'd slaughtered the few surviving witches in their commune, feasting upon their blood and eyes until all three of them had been drunk with enough power to bring them to the brink of madness.

Wilda's knife hovered above the mermaid's shimmering scales. Wedging the blade under one of the scales, she pried it off and lifted it to the sunlight. Her eyes glowed with greed at the scale's sparkling beauty, and she started picking more of them from the mermaid's tail.

"Wilda! What are you doing?" Eve asked, looking between Wilda and the mermen, who struggled and fought while glaring at Wilda.

"I'm going to make jewelry from her scales," Wilda said while continuing to pick them off one by one.

"Stop it!" Eve waived her hand, and Wilda was knocked flat onto the deck. "You're killing her. How are we supposed to get the mermen to help us if she's dead?"

"Yes, Eve," Wilda agreed and scrambled to her feet.

"Moira!" Eve snapped. "Don't let the blood go to waste!"

Moira licked and sucked the mermaid's blood until her tail stopped bleeding. Moira's loose, auburn curls soaked up blood from the deck, making her look like a ravenous animal as she licked blood from her clawlike fingernails. She had two powers, teleportation and animal whispering. Both powers experienced surges when she ingested magical blood. She'd transported the entire ship to its remote location after draining blood from a vampire. Robin had been holding the vampire prisoner for trespassing too close to the realm's stone circle entrance and had offered the prisoner to Eve.

Eve approached the bound and gagged mermen. Kneeling in front of them, she picked one to tease. She preferred the younger one. His hair looked like it was spun from gold, and his scales were like shining aquamarines. She ran her fingers down his chest and onto his scales where a man's groin would be. His body stilled beneath her touch, and she could see terror in his eyes. She looked from him to his older brother, who looked furious.

Addressing the brother, she said, "I've never seen one. Would you like to take his place? Show me yours instead?"

The older merman nodded vigorously. Eve withdrew her hand from the young merman and stood. She looked at Wilda and then back to the merman. She didn't find him attractive in the least.

"Wilda," Eve said. "Come arouse him. I want to see a merman's prick before they're all dead."

Wilda's power was telekinesis, and it was always violently potent. Without physically touching him, she stimulated him. His eyes widened, and his breathing grew erratic. Her effect on him became obvious when the object of Eve's curiosity emerged from a slit about a hand's length below his navel.

Eve's eyes widened. "Fascinating." She turned away. "That will be all, Wilda."

"Wait," Moira commanded Wilda before addressing Eve. "Although they are weak and stupid, merpeople are immortal."

"And?" Eve looked at Moira in annoyed confusion, impatience penetrated her tone.

Standing her ground, Moira said, "Wilda's fertile days are upon her. We may produce a valuable crossbreed. One we could trade to your immortal allies."

Nonplussed, Eve said, "Ah . . ."

A crazed smile spread across Wilda's face. "Yes!" she cried and begged, "Please, may I?"

Eve nodded and walked away in disgust. If Moira's plan came to fruition, Eve liked the possibility of Wilda producing an asset they could use or barter. However, the thought of a witch with a merman made her stomach turn.

Eve heard Moira warn Wilda, shouting, "Don't kill him!"

Ignoring the sounds of her deranged disciples reveling and torturing in the background, Eve ordered the human crew to prepare Una's stone sarcophagus to be lowered into the water. They covered it in netting and hoisted it over the railing. They lowered the ropes until it hovered just above the surface.

Then, Eve approached the unconscious mermaid and checked her breathing. Thankfully, she was alive. Wilda was no longer screaming behind her, so she knew the debauchery was finished. She dragged the mermaid by the tail, placing her immediately in front of the mermen.

"I'm going to throw you both overboard, and you will guide that stone box safely to the ocean floor," Eve commanded the mermen. "Trust me, I will know if you've failed. But if you succeed, I will let your female live. I will give her back to you as soon as the task is complete. Do you agree to this trade?"

They nodded, so the witches plugged their ears against merpeople song. Wilda removed the mermen's gags and levitated them over the water before breaking their chains and dropping them into the ocean. The crew lowered Una into the water, and Eve watched the mermen hold the box at both ends as it began sinking. Moira opened a nearby barrel and lifted a squid from the dark water within. She communed wordlessly with the animal and thew it into the water. The witches watched it follow the mermen into the deep.

The crew threw buckets of water onto the mermaid until she awakened and curled into a tight ball out of fright.

Wilda stayed close to the prisoner and waited for her moment to do more damage. She was riding the euphoria of sex and blood.

Eve held Moira's shoulders and kissed her cheek. "It's time for you to dive in."

"Are you sure we ought to annihilate all of them?" Moira asked.

Eve said, "They'll not survive on their own, either way. This way, we benefit. If we leave them for someone else, they benefit."

"As you wish," Moira said and dove overboard.

"Wilda, kill the female," Eve commanded. *"Take what you want but give me the eyes."*

Wilda slit the mermaid's throat and lapped up the blood. She plucked out the eyeballs and ran to Eve, handing the eyes to her and watching her devour them whole. Excited for the opportunity to finish scaling the mermaid, Wilda returned to her kill.

Eve watched the water.

In the ocean, Moira rallied her great white sharks and waited. She spotted the squid swimming just ahead of the mermen. It reached her and wrapped its tentacles around her arm and neck, telling her the news she wanted to hear. She let it go with her thanks. Seeing the mermen had surfaced, she called the sharks to dinner.

Eve looked down on the mermen as they waited for her to throw their female overboard. "Wilda, toss what's left of her over!"

By the time the mermen realized it was a dead, mutilated body falling toward them, it was too late to retaliate. It was too late to retreat. In their moment of terror and distraction at seeing the last mermaid's dead body, sharks attacked them from below.

Moira recovered the mermen's eyes and teleported onto the ship's deck. She offered the eyes to Eve, who only took one.

"Three? For me?" Moira smiled.

"You've earned them," Eve said. "Now, take us home."

"The whole ship, or just us?" Moira asked.

Eve laughed. "Don't be ridiculous. We don't need this ship or its crew anymore. Why waste power, or life?"

The witches vanished.

THIRD FLOOR ROMANCE

Hayden led Ruby up the familiar spiral staircase at Camilla Rosemont House. During its stint as a museum, the home's third floor had been used for storage, but Jameson had remodeled it twice since then. First, he'd made it an adult party room. Later, he'd made it an open space for Giselle to use as she wished. Ruby knew it contained at least four secret doors leading to unfinished attic spaces, private corridors, and secret staircases throughout the house. However, the third floor's great room was finely finished and decorated in Giselle's ostentatious style. It had been one of Ruby's favorite hangout spots as a teen because she and Giselle had been able to play loud music and take candy without anyone bothering them.

Ruby concealed her surprise at Hayden having a key to Giselle's private space. The third floor belonged solely to her best friend. Giselle and Ruby had never allowed Hayden up there when they were teenagers. Moreover, they'd never even told Jeremy about it at all, and Ruby was almost certain Hayden hadn't told Jeremy because he had been embarrassed about how his parents had used the third floor for years.

Before Jameson and Phoebe had decided to gift the space to Giselle for her sixteenth birthday to encourage her to spend time at home, they'd used it for sex parties at least twice a month for three years. But, of course, Adam had gifted the entire property to Giselle as a birthday gift when she was eleven, so she'd had a skeleton key for every door in the house from the very beginning. Adam had presented the key to her with a red velvet bow tied to it. While most curious teens sneaked pornography, Giselle and Ruby had received quite an education from sneaking into the attic space and watching the adults' revelry through an old ventilation grate.

Camilla Rosemont House, Albany, New York, Blue Earth, 2311 A.D.

Giselle and Ruby entered the attic through a hatch in the floor they'd accessed through the ceiling in Giselle's closet. Giselle carried a small electric lantern and led the way to a skinny corridor not wide enough for them to carry their bags of wine and chocolates at their sides. Carrying the snacks and libations in front of them, the lantern's glow guided them into a larger attic space. An old wooden ladder leaned against a twenty-foot platform that ran along the far wall. Earlier in the week, the girls had erected nylon netting behind the platform and filled it with pillows and blankets. Giselle climbed the ladder first, and Ruby passed their bags to her before climbing up behind her. Giselle dimmed the lantern to a faint glow and sat it beside their treats.

Mountains of pillows and blankets supported their backs while they drank wine from bottles and watched through a large grate as Giselle's parents' guests arrived at the party. From where they nested, they were looking down into the room from a high wall. On the other side of the wall, the party room was bathed in a mixture of moonlight from the skylight and flickering candlelight from wall sconces and standing candelabras.

Guests arrived at the party wearing Venetian masks and long velvet cloaks. Shoes and handbags were removed at the door and placed into cubbies. No food was served, but two men and two women carried serving trays laden only with small cordial glasses. The four waiters wore La Catrina face paint and silver body paint with no clothing or shoes. The girls couldn't tell what was in the cordial glasses, but everyone knocked back a glass like a shot when they entered the party room. Some of the guests helped themselves to more drinks as they mingled.

After thirty minutes passed, a gong sounded. All the guests removed their cloaks to reveal naked bodies. Giselle smiled while Ruby choked on a sip of wine.

"Shhh!" Giselle chided. "They might be able to hear us before the music starts."

Ruby cleared her throat and tried not to laugh. "Sorry," she whispered.

Giselle had spied the party on her own twice, but she'd been dying to get her best friend to the house on a party night. Her mother had finally consented to let her have a sleepover with Ruby during the party on the condition the girls had to stay in Giselle's room after ten.

Music started, and dancing commenced along with foreplay. Ruby watched the hedonistic masterpiece in awe. She noticed a man with an incredibly hot body dancing with a tall blonde woman, who looked like a cross between a ballerina and a supermodel.

Ruby pointed and said, "That man is brutally handsome."

Giselle spit wine down her chin, wiped it with a blanket and giggled uncontrollably. "That's Father."

Ruby hid her flushed face in her hands. "Oh, my stars. I can't believe that's Mr. Rosemont . . . Who's he dancing with?"

"That's Josie Baker."

"Shut up! It. Is. Not."

"Oh, it is," Giselle purred.

"How do you recognize any of them? Aside from your parents, that is."

"It's not that difficult if you observe them for a bit . . . Plus, I know who my parents know."

"This is absolutely mesmerizing," Ruby said.

Giselle took another sip of wine. "Wait until the sex starts . . . You don't recognize anyone?"

Horrified, Ruby looked at Giselle. "Please don't tell me my mother is here."

"No, I don't think so. Your mother doesn't usually mix with my parents unless Mr. Godwine is hosting . . . But you really assume your mother and not your father? Your father is quite friendly with mine . . . and he's a catch. I'm sure he'd be popular."

"Gross." Ruby sighed. "Anyway, you know my father didn't come up in society."

"Neither did my mother," Giselle blurted, and pointed down at a svelte black-haired woman, "but there she is."

"I don't understand how your parents are fine with seeing each other party like this," Ruby said, watching Phoebe touch a strange man.

"Oh," Giselle said. "They have an open relationship."

"Elle, I might actually die if I ever saw one of your parents with someone else."

Giselle giggled. "But you're seeing it right now."

"You know what I mean," Ruby argued. "Like, in the real world. No masks."

"They don't advertise it," Giselle explained as if speaking to an ignorant child. "I'd be surprised if you ever saw them in public being indiscreet with others."

"Wait . . ." Ruby hesitated, looking at someone. "You mentioned Mr. Godwine a moment ago . . ."

"Yes, that's him, but I've only seen him watch."

"Looking at him makes me want to eat some chocolate . . . slowly . . . savoring it," Ruby mused aloud.

Giselle snorted and handed Ruby a bar of chocolate. Giselle pointed, and Ruby's eyes shifted to a woman bent over with her hands against a wall. She was getting thoroughly railed.

Ruby looked around and noticed Ms. Astor riding some redheaded bodybuilder in a chair. She averted her eyes and glanced nervously at Giselle.

"Yes, I see my mother having sex," said Giselle tersely. "No, I don't like it. However, I love watching the others."

"Does—does Mr. Rosemont . . ." Ruby couldn't get the question out of her mouth.

"Yes," Giselle answered. "I'm sure he's still with Josie Baker somewhere down there, but I'm obviously not looking for them. I don't desire a good vomit just now . . . I'm looking for the president's son. He's fucking gorgeous."

"Which one?" Ruby asked, looking around.

Giselle smiled lasciviously. "Norbert."

Footsteps approached across the floor behind the girls. They both ducked down behind the pillows and peeped through them. They watched Hayden approach below them and begin climbing the ladder.

Giselle's head popped up. "Don't come up here!" she hissed.

"Too late," he said, sitting on the ladder's top rung. "What are you two doing up here?"

"None of your business," Giselle said. "I'm going to tell Father you went into my room."

"The door was wide open, Giselle," he protested. "The closet was also open with the attic ladder down, so here I am."

Hayden noticed the music and looked past Ruby at the grate. "You're watching the party from here? That's disgusting."

"So, you've watched it before?" Ruby asked him.

"No!" His face looked like he'd eaten a whole lemon.

Giselle sighed. "Then how do you know it's disgusting?"

Hayden didn't answer.

Ruby noticed he tried to sneak a look at her but looked away when their eyes met. Even though it was almost dark in the attic, he seemed to be blushing. She could tell he was embarrassed about her seeing his parents' party or possibly seeing his parents in flagrante delicto. He climbed down the ladder and turned to look at Ruby again before leaving the attic.

Ruby and Hayden reached the top of the stairs, and he smiled at her while opening the door. The first things Ruby noticed as the door opened were two antique bicycles staged in the room's center. One was a beach cruiser, and one was a penny-farthing. Both were perfectly restored, and Ruby squealed in excitement. She ran her fingers along the penny-farthing's leather hand grips.

"I was hoping you still like bikes as much as you used to," Hayden said. "I thought we could ride them around up here."

"Yes! Which one do you want to ride?"

"Ruby, look around." Hayden pointed around the room. "This is all for you. You pick the one you want."

Ruby looked around the room and noticed Hayden had given her much more than bikes. He'd also arranged dinner, snacks, and entertainment. She walked toward the nearest corner where he'd built a blanket and pillow fort just like they used to make when they were kids. It had mixed sheets for a canopy and string lights lining the cloth ceiling. Inside, there was an overstuffed sofa with plenty of soft blankets and a cocktail table.

Her favorite foods, strawberries and popcorn, were each in giant bowls on the cocktail table along with assorted drinks. Next to the snacks, a chessboard and a scrabble board were both set. She turned to express her excitement but noticed candles burning on a table across the room.

On the opposite end of the great room, there was a formal dinner table set for two under the skylight. She hopped on the penny-farthing and rode over to see what he'd made for dinner. The bike went fast enough to generate a breeze through her hair, and she smiled. Seeing the entrée, she giggled. Instead of an intricate, fancy dinner, there was a deep-dish pizza. She loved pizza, especially Chicago style, and she was speechless at realizing Hayden had remembered so many of her favorite things.

Hayden rode over on the beach cruiser and leaned it against his chair.

"Hayden, this is . . . I love you," she breathed, dismounting the bike and admiring the details in its handlebars. "Where did you get this?"

He approached her from behind and wrapped his arms around her waist. "I've had nothing but time here . . . I restored them both myself."

She spun in his arms to face him. "That's amazing!"

"Are you hungry?" he asked.

She shook her head. "Let's ride around first. Race me!"

"If you win, it's because I let you!" He hopped onto his bike and followed her across the floor.

They raced around for almost an hour, crashing against walls and running into furniture. By the time Ruby was ready to eat, they were both ravenous. Hayden insisted the pizza tasted better cold, especially chased with chianti. They eventually ended up in the blanket and pillow fort playing board games and snuggling together.

"Ruby, will you be my partner?" he asked, surprising himself in the heat of the moment.

She realized that's exactly what she wanted, and it surprised her. After being so resistant to Trent's proposals and wanting so many other life experiences above wanting a partnership, she wondered when her mind had changed. After all, she and Hayden had only been together for about two months. It didn't make logical sense to her, but she felt different with him. Hayden was her home. Maybe it was because they'd always been close, she thought.

Hayden watched Ruby lost in thought and said, "I hope your silence is a good thing."

Snapping out of her daydream, she cried, "Yes! I'm just—it's an odd feeling."

Unsure how to receive her last statement, Hayden said, "If you're not feeling it, I understand."

"No!" She held his hand and squeezed it. "That's not what I meant . . . I mean, it's an odd feeling to for me to want a partnership. Because I'm usually quite turned off by the idea. But with you, it feels like the natural thing to do."

Joy spread across Hayden's face in the form of a toothy smile and intense eyes.

He hugged her to his chest and kissed her forehead before she leaned her head back and offered him her lips. They shared a tender kiss that deepened until Hayden broke away and brushed her hair away from his mouth. She laughed and smoothed her hair, tying it into a ponytail.

"I know you usually like to plan things and do them right," she said, "but I think we should make it official in the morning . . . I actually can't believe you asked me here in the fort. Asking over our candlelight dinner would have been more your style."

"I knew I wanted to ask you tonight, but I missed the opportunity earlier," he admitted. "I'm also surprised I blurted the question while snuggling in a blanket fort and playing Scrabble."

She slid into his lap, wrapped her arms around his neck, and whispered, "I'm surprised about two more things as well . . . Firstly, that you have a key to the third floor. Secondly, that you'd even want to come up here."

Hayden sighed. "Well, Giselle gave me her master key since I'm on house arrest . . . And I guess I'm tired of being the only person in the family who hasn't had sex up here."

Ruby nibbled his ear and whispered, "I've been fantasizing about it for years."

He looked at her inquisitively. "You didn't do it that night?"

She feigned ignorance. "What night?"

Hayden threw back his head and chuckled wholeheartedly.

She pushed him playfully and repeated, "What night?"

"Ru, you and Giselle are responsible for abruptly putting an end to my parents' parties up here. Your antics with Giselle prompted them to give this space to her."

"Oh, I know," she admitted. "I'm surprised you know though . . . To answer your question, tonight will be a first for both of us. I got caught at the party well before I could find a lover. Not that I would have anyway."

— ❀ — ❀ — ❀ —

Camilla Rosemont House, Albany, New York, Blue Earth, 2311 A.D.

It had been six weeks since the attic voyeurism

238

extravaganza and watching wasn't enough for Giselle anymore. Again, the night's guest list included Norbert Moon. Since starting university at Cornell, he'd been traveling from Ithaca to Albany for her parents' special soirees without missing a single invitation. She'd met him at a dinner party when she was thirteen and had been obsessed with his handsome face since then until she'd recently seen him naked. After noticing him at the parties, his fit body replaced his face in her daily thoughts and became the object of her nightly self-pleasure. She'd sent him a message to meet her by the swinging chairs after the gong sounded.

Ruby helped Giselle prepare to seduce her crush. She'd tried to talk her best friend into watching from the attic again or moving their sleepover weekend down to her house in Connecticut, but Giselle wouldn't be talked out of a rebellious weekend. The only other option Giselle would agree on was an adult-free house party in the Catskills. Ruby's cousin had invited her to attend and bring a friend, but Ruby didn't feel like spending the night with a house full of other highschoolers. She really just wanted a low-key weekend, although the danger of sneaking into the party appealed to her more than she wanted Giselle to know.

Ruby fitted a platinum blonde wig over Giselle's fiery red curls. Red hair was so incredibly difficult to hide, and she had to fuss with it for ages to get the hairline perfectly into place. She did smokey cat-eye makeup to hide Giselle's unique eyes as much as possible. She'd already applied her own eye makeup with the same techniques and added extra lashes. With the masks they'd chosen to wear, the only other makeup they needed to help their disguises was lip liner with lipstick, which they used to shape their lips in the Cupid's bow style.

In contrast to Giselle's new hair, Ruby's wig was so black it was almost indigo. She left it loose and flowing over her breasts and back to maintain a bit of modesty and warmth. She always got cold in Giselle's house, so being nude wouldn't help that. Ruby finished pinning Giselle's hair into a French twist with loose ringlets carefully arranged around her face and down her neck.

They both donned their masks and cloaks and headed to the guest wing to enter a secret corridor through a linen closet. Once they were in the corridor, they walked carefully to the end and up narrow stairs. The door at the stairs' landing opened into the third floor's great room near a dark corner. Giselle cracked the door open. There was a tapestry hanging in front of the door, so she was able to prop it open enough to peep through without anyone noticing. She looked past the tapestry's edge to see if the adults were distracted enough for them to walk into the room unnoticed.

The gong gave way to loud music, but Giselle still whispered, "The drugs they drank earlier should have fully kicked in by now."

"Wait until they're all fucking," Ruby said. "Then there's less of a chance they'll notice us slip in."

Giselle pouted. "But Norbert is waiting on me."

Ruby thought for a second and replied, "You go first then. It'll be less noticeable if I wait a few minutes and slip though after."

Giselle eyed Ruby suspiciously. "Ru! You're not going stay back here the whole time if I go—"

"No!" Ruby interrupted, impulsively stroking her fake hair. "I'll be out soon."

Giselle hugged Ruby, dropped her cloak, and slipped into the great room. After a few seconds, Ruby couldn't see her anymore.

Ruby balled her hands into fists at her sides and took deep breaths, trying to stop fidgeting. After a few minutes, she felt ready but waited until the people closest to the door were fully engaged in intimacy before she slipped into the room. The air smelled like sex and incense as Ruby confidently strutted through it. There was an empty settee nearby, so Ruby quickened her step to claim it. Wishing it was leatherette instead of brocade, she wondered how well the housekeepers had been able to disinfect it since the last party. She slowly took a seat but her back remained rigidly upright. Apparent tension ruled her body from the hands resting perfectly on her knees to her eyes staring straight ahead. She suddenly remembered to act cool and leaned back while crossing her legs.

Jameson didn't recognize the woman sitting alone across the room from him. Something about her body language was familiar, but he grasped for a thought as to why. Josie grabbed him from behind, so he pulled her against him and thoroughly tongue-fucked her mouth. He enjoyed playing with her, but he thought she was getting too attached to him. She tried to lead him somewhere to get more intimate, but he politely declined. As a celebrity, she could have her pick of men at the party. The way Josie pranced away from him reminded him of how young she was. With her youth in mind, he glanced back at the black-haired woman he didn't know and noticed her eyes darting around the room while she impulsively stroked the hair covering her left breast.

"Shit!" Jameson whispered to himself, realizing her identity.

Ruby watched Mr. Rosemont strutting right for her. The hand stroking her hair stilled, and she dropped it to her side. To play it cool, she slid to one side of the settee to make room for him. Her eyes devoured his body's every part and detail. Fear gripped her, but so did desire. Her gaze slipped down to his lap when he sat down beside her. When her wandering eyes finally made it back to his face, she knew he'd recognized her from the way he glared. It was time for her to put on her big girl panties, so to speak, and pretend she wasn't scared and dying from embarrassment.

"It's not fair how hot you are," Ruby said with a slight tremble. "It makes me sick."

"What a wildly inappropriate observation, Ms. Cohen. I know how attractive I am. I don't need a fifteen-year-old child to tell me."

"Your statement is comical considering how naked and close

to me you are," Ruby snapped at him, not believing her own audacity in the face of being caught.

He ignored the jibe and said, "Ms. Cohen, I can usually count on you to keep Giselle out of trouble." Jameson glanced around. "Where is she?"

"She wanted to go to a house party in the Catskills, and I tried to get her to come to my house instead," Ruby explained. "Crashing your party was the compromise."

"Where is she?" Jameson asked again in a softer tone.

Ruby didn't speak.

"If Phoebe notices either of you, this is going to get a thousand times worse," Jameson stated. "Where is Giselle?"

Ruby tilted her head and looked down at his body again. "She was looking for someone."

Jameson placed his palm under her chin and lifted her head, forcing her to look at his face. "Who?"

Ruby looked past his shoulder and noticed Ms. Astor busy with an orgy across the room but knew that could change within moments. Still, she needed to give Giselle time to finish what Ruby suspected was already started against a dark wall somewhere.

"If I tell you, it'll be awkward." Ruby gently pushed away his hand, leaned close to his ear, and whispered, "They're already together. You don't want to see that or make a scene. Better to punish us both later."

Jameson's guest list was thoroughly vetted, so he willed himself not to panic or make a scene. He was torn between a desire to slap the smirk off Ruby's face and a guilty feeling from failing to keep the children sheltered from the party. Even though there were no known predators of any kind admitted to his home, Giselle and Ruby looked like adult women. He knew Giselle had been sexually *active since starting high school in the Fall, but her boyfriends at school—that was different.*

His voice was barely audible against her ear. "This could ruin my family and Giselle's reputation. Underage girls at my sex party? Don't be a complete child . . . Ruby. At least understand me."

Ruby couldn't let Giselle get caught. "I'm sorry—but . . . He's only a few years older than us. Still a teenager. And you and Ms. Astor are the only people who could possibly recognize her."

Jameson guessed who Giselle was with. "Mr. Moon?"

Ruby's silence told him he was correct.

"Please go find her, and both of you leave," he commanded.

"That was already my plan before I saw you," Ruby said, matching his authoritative tone. "Now I require a dance before I go."

"Ms. Cohen, I will dance with you at every other event we attend together for the rest of our lives if you get the fuck out of this room and take my daughter with you right now."

Ruby knew it was time to bow out gracefully, so she nodded and said, "We have an accord."

Jameson's headache intensified while watching Ruby's hips sway away from him. He leaned his head back against the wall and looked up at the skylight. Guests gathered near him, but he didn't acknowledge them. His eyes closed, and he massaged his temples. When the settee's springs dipped next to him, he silently prayed it wasn't Josie. A familiar scent revived his good humor. His eyes opened, and he pulled Phoebe onto his lap. Her hair was one of his favorite smells, and he brushed his face against it as he inhaled the intoxicating mix of shampoo, sweat, and perfume that was unique to his partner. She poured a glass of special tonic into his mouth and leaned down to kiss his neck and chest. That's when he looked over her shoulder and saw Ruby traversing the crowd with a woman in a

*platinum blonde wig. The two girls held hands and made their way
out the main door.*

— — —

Connecticut was a new experience for Pinky. It wasn't his
vibe, but that was only his initial opinion. He'd only been in the state
a few hours, and he'd never spent time there before. Wealth wasn't
new to him, having grown up with the coven, but the people and the
estates he'd observed all afternoon represented a culture
completely foreign to him. The Rothschild home was no exception.
Its manicured, white exterior towered over him. His finger almost
touched the doorbell, but he hesitated and dropped his arm to his
side. It was his fifth failure to initiate contact with the home's
residents. He was turning to leave when the door opened to reveal
Faustina. She leaned her forearm on the doorframe and sighed.

"Trent, the housekeeper says you've been standing here
for—" Faustina stopped speaking mid-sentence and tilted her head
to the side as if trying to understand something.

"You're not Trent," she declared in surprise, and then she
paused. "Come in, please. Welcome to my home."

Pinky waited for her to open the door wider and step aside
for him to walk through the doorway. He thought her smile was
polite, yet genuine. Two small steps put him inside Ruby Cohen's
childhood home. It still shook him to think his soulmate had been so
connected to Ruby and her family on the Green Earth. The woman
standing in front of him was a stranger, and the house was strange.
The air smelled like cinnamon and apples, and it reminded Pinky of
his mother's baking. That put him somewhat at ease.

He glanced around and said, "Thank you for inviting me
inside. You have a beautiful home, Ms. Rothschild."

She smiled at him in approval. "Delightful. You're much more
polite than Trent . . . And of course I'm inviting you. You belong with
my family and friends." She extended her hand, and he shook it.

"Call me Faustina. It's lovely to meet you."

"Please, call me Pinky. I'm honored to meet you."

"Honored?" Faustina sauntered ahead and beckoned him to follow with an elegant hand gesture. "I'm flattered. We can get to know each other in the family's hobby room. It's less formal."

"Less formal than what?" he asked.

"All of it . . . Well, everything on the first floor. I'm not quite ready to invite you upstairs yet."

Her last few words rendered him speechless. They weren't provocative words at face value, but her tone seemed suggestive. Coffee, tea, sandwiches, and baked goods were already waiting on a table when they walked into the room, which was a better trick than some magical gifts he'd seen. Candles were lit, which also made it seem more like home to him. Faustina sat on a sofa, and Pinky followed her and sat on the opposite end of it.

"Tea or coffee?" Faustina asked.

"Coffee."

"Sugar, cream, both?"

"No, thank you. Just black . . . I'm impressed you already had all this prepared. Are you sure you're not a witch?"

"No, I'm something even better; I'm obscenely wealthy," she explained with a coquettish grin. "My staff monitors security, which is how I knew you were here, and they keep fresh items prepared in the kitchen in case I have guests in need of refreshment. They only needed to bring the trays in here while I was answering the door."

Faustina poured two cups of coffee and handed one to him. She observed him for a moment. There wasn't an eyepatch in sight, although that had been the most mentioned aspect of his appearance when multiple sources had gossiped to her about

Pinky's existence. They'd also mentioned different types of hairstyles and colors, but the man sitting in front of her didn't look very disguised. He was sporting Trent's shaggy black hair, and his eyes were as green as ever—both eyes. She could see two.

Pinky thought his hostess was looking at his face in confusion, so he asked, "Do I have something on my face?"

"No," she said, shaking her head slightly. "That's rather the point. I was told you'd be wearing an eyepatch, and I'm a bit disappointed that rumor isn't true."

"I usually wear one—" he said but stopped suddenly when he processed her entire statement. "Disappointed?"

"I know it's a bit forward of me to say so, but ancient pirates are a fantasy of mine, if you know what I mean," she said in a hushed voice and winked.

"I—what?" Pinky spilled coffee on himself trying to put it down on the table.

Faustina watched him struggle to regain his composure and felt guilty for her aggressive remarks. Pinky was clearly less experienced with women than Trent. Furthermore, she had clearly spent too much time with Phoebe. The ability to better voice her wants and desires since befriending Phoebe wasn't a bad thing but balancing it with her polite sensibilities was sometimes tricky. At least she hadn't picked up Phoebe's foul language, she thought.

"My apologies," she said. "It's awkward for you to look like someone I know, yet you're not."

Pinky's eyes widened. "And you would have said that to Trent?"

Faustina snorted. "That's ridiculous . . . Trent doesn't wear an eyepatch, so why would I?" Her sly smile widened.

Pinky laughed, relaxing a bit. He found Faustina to be

charming and gorgeous, but her wealth and standing in Adam Godwine's tribe made him cautious. People didn't usually treat him as nicely as she did, but that was because he spent most his time with vampires and only interacted with people for information and spying. He decided he might really like her if he got to know her better.

"I do wear an eyepatch," he quietly admitted. "When I'm working or traveling for work. It'd look a bit conspicuous here in Greenwich."

"Why are you here?" she asked.

"Trent said I could trust Ruby," Pinky said. "I wanted to talk to her about what it's like to work for Adam Godwine. Sylvia is a wonderful person, but she has the views of a much older generation."

Faustina refilled his coffee. "I'm sure she would love to speak to you, but she's not here."

"I tracked her here earlier." He looked confused.

Faustina recoiled, then laughed at him. "Don't say it like that. You're not a creep . . . She came by earlier for a short visit, but her brother took her to Albany. You wouldn't have known they left if you were stalking around outside. He used his magic to take her."

To Faustina, Pinky didn't seem as old as Trent, and that wasn't merely because he lacked the sultry devil-may-care demeanor. Although Pinky was refreshingly polite, he was slightly awkward. She assumed his years with the coven affected his social skills. Trent also projected a hardened attitude that thinly concealed deep sorrows from a devastating past, but Pinky didn't have those kinds of scars. He wasn't innocent, but he wasn't damaged either. That made him especially attractive to a mature woman looking for a connection.

He'd helped himself to a sandwich while she was sipping her

coffee and contemplating him, and she realized he might appreciate a proper meal and a place to stay. She could use overnight company, too, even if they only talked, played music together, or whatever else they could find to pass the time. She wondered if he played guitar like his soulmate.

"You're welcome to stay. Neither side will look for you here," she stated. "You can take your time to decide what you want to do without their influence."

"I know they wouldn't even think to find me here. That's why I really hoped to catch Ruby here and speak with her . . . I can't go to Albany. Hayden Rosemont consorts with the fae. I don't trust him, and his mother is powerful enough to kill me. I think she's there as well."

"Hayden is Ruby's lover," she warned. "She's not often without him . . . He grew up with my children."

Without saying it directly, she was telling Pinky she was on Hayden's side. Hayden had been rebellious but so had Ruby and Giselle at one point. It was difficult to raise children with extreme privilege. Their families constantly endured unique pressures and publicity. With the onset of their magical powers came additional stressors and dangers, and Hayden had always been different. His mind worked differently, and change was difficult for him. Faustina understood that and believed he never meant to hurt anyone.

Faustina continued, "I also don't believe Phoebe would harm you unless you tried to harm Hayden first . . . But it seems like you need more time before you meet everyone."

"How do you find it so easy to trust me?" he asked.

"Who says I trust you?" she asked and took a sip of coffee to hide her expression behind the cup.

He released a single breathy chuckle. "Understood . . . But you don't fear me either."

She slid closer to him. "Tell me why I should."

"Well . . ." He hesitated and whispered, "I'm an ancient pirate."

"I knew it!" Faustina expressed exaggerated excitement. "You've sailed across time to ravish me."

"I—" Pinky swallowed and tried again to speak. "Well, you're a treasure, and I'm a pirate, so makes sense."

"Well done," she said, nodding her approval. "That's nice start."

"I'd like to stay," he blurted, then looked around nervously. "Looks like there's plenty to do in here while we get better acquainted."

A guitar across the room caught his attention, so he got up and took the premium instrument from its stand. Returning to the sofa, he sat in the middle closer to Faustina and began playing. She leaned back and listened, but she also watched his fingers move up and down frets and across strings to weave hand-made music out of thin air. It was immediately apparent his artistry matched that of his soulmate, and she became lost in a simple moment of idyllic delight.

SCENT OF A WITCH

Magical scents were like ordinary ones in that some were pleasant, and some were wretched. Bastion found witches' scents agreeable to varying degrees, like other people enjoyed the smells of good foods. Some smelled spicy, while others smelled sweet, and there were many scents in between.

Differentiating scents from foreign magic was tricker because he didn't find them pleasant, and they were also very similar to each other. For instance, all vampires produced a faint metallic smell that Bastion neither liked nor disliked, but he found males to be slightly bitter compared to females, who smelled a bit sickly sweet. The fae smelled of carrion, so it was difficult for him to hold conversations with Robin for the first few minutes. After a while, he could get used to the same magical scent filling the space around him, so it was like becoming nose blind to ordinary smells. The nuances were not there with any foreign scent like they were when he smelled a witch.

A witch's scent became stronger in times of excitement or nervousness. The scent was weaker in times of despair. A woman's scent pleased him more than a man's smell, and among the women in his tribe, Leilani possessed his favorite fragrance.

It was spice with a hint of fruity sweetness like warm nutmeg with pineapples. Unfortunately, he wasn't thrilled when a strong version of her scent overcame his senses while he was snooping around her office in the dark. Looking around, he wondered where she was and grew apprehensive about his precarious situation.

Seeing Bastion's mood shift, Leilani knew he'd sensed her presence. Stepping from behind heavy drapes, she stood in front of him. A thump echoed through the quiet room when he dropped the tablet he'd been holding back into the cabinet.

Bastion muttered, "I—"

"Don't even try to excuse yourself! I can see your guilt as plainly as I see the rest of you," Leilani said.

"It's not guilt," he argued. "It's surprise and apprehension from smelling you using your magic on me from behind a curtain. Why would you be hiding from me and doing that? You're the one who should feel guilty," he began to babble in a weak attempt to gaslight her.

She stared at him in disbelief at his audacity. "This is my office, Bastion!"

"Which makes it even more strange for you to be hiding in here." His alarmed expression was so exaggerated he looked like a caricature of himself.

She huffed a short laugh. "I heard you walking down the corridor," she stated. "I was about to leave for the day."

"What do you want from me, Leilani?"

She stared him down while stepping behind her desk to put distance between them. Her fingers hovered on the emergency bracelet around her wrist, but she kept her arms down. Her wrists and hands were partially hidden behind the desktop, and she hoped he couldn't see she was ready to call for help. Footsteps echoed down the corridor from far away, but she kept her attention on him and her trembling fingers.

"Don't do that," he begged, glancing at her wrist. "Let's talk . . . You know me, Leilani. We're friends."

"You wouldn't be stealing from my office if you were my friend," she said as her voice cracked. "I've had my eye on you for a few months now. Something was off, and then—then . . . You let Robin go." She paused and whispered, "I know you did."

Bastion knew she'd see if he lied to her outright. Words

mean things, so he needed to keep his wits sharp and evade direct answers as much as possible. His mind needed to be in line with his statements as well, focusing on the truths rather than the omissions.

"I swear to you, I'm not here to get information for the fae," he finally said.

She studied his mood. His aura was steady, so she asked, "What are you doing here, then?"

"I'm Adam's spy," he admitted. "I'm in here to do an audit, so to speak."

"In the dark?" she challenged.

"Yep." He struggled but kept it simple.

"Ridiculous . . . And if I ask Adam?"

"If you do," he pleaded, "please do it in private. He has very good reasons—life or death reasons—to keep my identity secret . . . I could die if you tell anyone else besides Adam."

His words were the stuff of bad fiction, but she found nothing amiss in his aura. His mood remained stable even though his anxiety had been heightened since he'd discovered she was there. Her fingers withdrew from the emergency bracelet, but she kept distance between them.

"Get out," she commanded. "I'll speak to Adam tonight."

"Leilani—"

"Leave!"

Bastion backed away a few steps but kept watching Leilani. He couldn't smell her anymore, likely from a combination of her emotions settling and his magical nose blindness in the small office. He desperately wished he could catch her scent before he walked out the door. The desire for her scent overcame him. It felt like a physical thirst needing to be quenched.

Leilani kept her eyes on Bastion while he stood in her office. She wondered why he defied her wishes so boldly. Surely the moment was as awkward for him as it was for her. His mood changed, and she audibly gasped. It was impossible, she thought. A man who could sneak into her office and steal from her under the cover of darkness could not have genuine feelings for her.

Bastion opened his mouth but shut it without uttering another word. He reached behind him and pulled another tablet from his jeans' waistband, throwing it to the floor in front of her desk. The gesture must have worked to heighten her emotions because he could smell her again. He savored two deep, perfect breaths before abruptly turning his back to her and leaving.

⚬⚬ ⚬⚬ ⚬⚬

Ruby remembered she had fallen asleep naked in Hayden's arms within the pillow fort's safety, and she was still naked and falling through freezing ocean water as the vision commenced. The vision came so fast that she'd not experienced darkness between sleep and the abyss, but at least it wasn't a violent experience. However, the cold was bitter and unyielding. She hoped Hayden was keeping her physical body warm because her spirit body felt pierced with ice.

Onto the familiar stone sarcophagus, she fell. She needed to make the vision count and thought carefully about her next actions. After analyzing what she already knew, she decided not to open the box. Una was inside and she held the sphere, but the location was paramount and still unknown. She needed the location before Hayden had time to awaken her. Instead of walking, she decided to swim in the same direction she went before. She wouldn't need to waste time getting Una to give her the sphere to light her path along the ocean floor if she stayed above it. Swimming would be faster. All she had to do was swim toward the wreckage silhouettes. There was light on the other side.

Floating in the water and propelling herself forward turned out to be much easier than swimming in the real world. The sensation was more like flying with Adam. The light was very distant, so she kept swimming toward her goal. The darkness below her and around her was disconcerting. Fear of the unknown crept into her thoughts, so she stared forward and focused her eyes solely on the light.

After swimming for ages, she was among the wreckage and approaching enough light to see details in her surroundings. Most of the junk around her wasn't from nautical shipwrecks. Gargantuan smooth pieces of metal littered the ocean floor, and she recognized the cylindrical shapes of older rockets and spacecraft. It was a space junk graveyard.

She was tiny and insignificant by comparison to the decaying technological remains. The biggest artifact in sight was a great rocket in the distance. Lights were shining on it and equipment surrounded it as if a crew had been salvaging its pieces. Writing along the side said "USSN," and Ruby marveled at the antique United States Space Navy wreckage.

Most of the lights came from a sea lab anchored to the ocean floor, and its purpose appeared to be ocean cleanup. She noticed markings on the space junk from Joseon, France, China, and Prussia. Looking around with escalating excitement, she was sure she knew the location.

She was floating at Point Oubliette, the most remote location on the Blue Earth. It was in the middle of the South Pacific and a famous space junk graveyard. It had recently been in the news, so she was sure of the location. The countries responsible for the junk were finally collaborating to salvage the wreckage and clean the last corner of the ocean, ridding it of such extensive man-made litter.

She felt the vision slipping away, and she went peacefully back to reality and her new partner with the knowledge she needed to secure victory for her people.

Sylvia was the only witch missing from the round table. Ty had called everyone else, including Hayden. The fish scale and the hair collected at the Carnegie Museum were in a glass box, and the congregation passed it between them like a fascinating esoteric trophy. Jeremy had received DNA results from their lab, and both specimens had shed from the same creature. More importantly, the creature was related to Adam and Eve. It was half witch and half something else, and the moniker "sea witch" was whispered across the table for lack of a known name. Based on the few words they'd heard spoken between Danielle, the vampires, and Adam at the museum, everyone assumed it was half mermaid. News about Ruby's last vision generated excitement and hope around the table.

It was time for solid understanding and honing strategy. They needed to make final plans to retrieve the sphere key and attack the fae. The meeting was for the cabal only, but a final meeting with the coven was scheduled take place the following night in Romania. The entire alliance was to assemble for Duncan's funeral, so it was convenient for the final planning to happen after the memorial ceremony.

Ty called the meeting to order, ensured Leilani had given everyone tablets, and received a thumbs up from Ruby that she was ready to take notes. "Adam, you have the floor."

"Before we get to business, I'd like to be the first to congratulate Hayden Rosemont and Ruby Rosemont Cohen," Adam said in a reserved tone, reaching for Ruby's hand and kissing it. "Blessings, my dear."

Jeremy, Giselle, and Phoebe lost their minds with excitement but also expressed irritation with Ruby and Hayden for not telling anyone. Meanwhile, Trent looked like he was going to explode but managed to keep his peace.

Adam continued, "Now, for our first item of business. Danielle has agreed to read the items in the glass box you've all been passing around . . . Danielle?"

Danielle nodded and said, "Yes, I wanted to wait until I had time to recuperate from the museum and also have everyone here to help me if touching the items causes injuries or surprises . . . Jeremy, is all lab testing complete?"

The specimens were fragile, and Danielle needed to hold them in her hands. She wanted to make sure the cabal had all needed lab results in case they were crushed or disintegrated during the reading process.

Jeremy nodded. "You're good to go."

Ty took great care in opening the box and placing the hair in Danielle's palm. He worried she'd have an extreme reaction like she had in the museum. His arm rested on the back of her chair in a good position to catch her if she fell.

Danielle closed her hand around the hair, and after a moment, she said, "Wilda of Hastings."

"Is that the sea witch's name?" Ty asked her gently when she didn't say anything else.

"No," Adam interjected. "Wilda of Hastings died many . . . many years ago."

"You knew her?" Danielle asked, still holding the hair and trying to get more from it.

Adam bowed his head and said, "I killed her. She was one of Eve's most violent disciples."

Danielle frowned and said, "I'm sensing Wilda is this creature's mother."

"Wilda used brutal tactics to gain long life, but the creature would have to be at least eight hundred years old. That's not probable," Adam explained, then he asked, "Do you see anything else? The father might have been immortal."

"No," Danielle said and opened her hand.

Ty plucked the hair out of her palm and placed it back in the box, saying, "Well, the DNA tells us it's half human and descended from Adam and Eve, so Wilda is the mother. The father is likely immortal."

"Could the father be a fairy?" Leilani asked.

Trent said, "I thought the evidence suggests a sea creature."

"A shapeshifter, yes," Ty stated, "but specifically a sea creature? Maybe."

Danielle held out her hand to Ty and said, "Give me the fish scale, and maybe we'll find out."

As soon as Danielle's hand closed around the scale, she stared blankly at the space in front of her. Unlike the hair, the scale took complete hold of her senses, which usually only happened with powerful magical objects.

"Merpeople. Family. Peaceful. Life. Others. War . . ."

Words came from her as if they were part of stream of consciousness thought. Ty braced himself to help her, realizing she'd had a similar reaction in Malta that turned almost dangerous.

". . . Murder. Death. None. Master. Pain. Alone. Alone. Alone! Alone!"

Danielle was screaming the same word repeatedly. Her fist was closed around the scale so tightly blood dripped from where her nails pierced skin. Ty reached for her hand to pry it loose, but he couldn't help. Her chest was rising and falling erratically with each labored breath she took.

"Adam, help!" Ty shouted. "She's stuck!"

Adam was already on his feet and moving to Danielle. "Leilani, try to calm her!"

Leilani's magic reached out and massaged Danielle's mood.

Hayden noticed sweat glistening on Leilani's face as her cheeks grew red, so he placed a hand on her forearm and sent cooling magic to her.

Calming Danielle's mood was a heavy lift, but Leilani could tell it was working.

Adam's hands were on Danielle's shoulders. He sent healing energy to her, which healed her hand and prompted her body to recover from shock. He also felt Leilani's magic helping to calm her. Danielle's muscles relaxed, and her breathing resumed its normal rhythm.

Ty opened Danielle's hand and took the scale away from her palm. Her eyes focused, seeing Phoebe staring back at her from across the table. She felt Ty holding her hand, and Adam's hands released her shoulders. Memories that were not her own replayed in her head.

"Are you okay?" Ty asked while rubbing her hand.

Danielle looked down at their hands and then up at his face before whispering, "I think so . . . I'm glad you pulled me away from it. I wouldn't have been able to take much more."

"What was happening to you?" Adam asked slowly, his demeanor stoic.

"Potent traces of immortal magic linger in that specimen," Danielle said. "I saw images, like memories spanning generations of merpeople's existence. I'm not sure how much more my mind could have processed . . . But most importantly, our sphere key thief is certainly the daughter of a witch and a merman."

The witches listened, transfixed. She described mermaids

and mermen in detail and explained their immortality and the lost society they'd ruled in peace under the oceans. Witches, vampires, and fae were among the apex predators responsible for mass genocide in merpeople cities. As a culture unfamiliar with deception or greed, they'd fallen easily to foes that had hunted them to steal their power.

A grotesque vignette of the species' final demise replayed in Danielle's mind, and she took a deep breath and prepared to share it. Getting the words into the air proved therapeutic for Danielle, but it was devastating for everyone else. The carnage and depravity she described sent a wave of nausea around the table before Leilani realized she'd failed to rein in her revulsion. Adam's passive expression cracked to reveal a hint of sorrow when she explained what Eve, Wilda, and Moira had done to the last merpeople.

When the tale was complete, no other words were spoken. Adam thought about his late wife and her disciples, and how much damage they'd done while he was on the other end of the known world gathering his own following and building an empire. He wondered if doing things differently would have made a positive difference. If he'd charged in and fought Eve earlier, perhaps he and his people would be extinct along with the merpeople.

"Why didn't you help them?" From a silent table, Trent's pointed question erupted.

Adam's eyes darted to meet Trent's judgmental gaze. Trent's voice attenuated, but the question's impact remained. It was on everyone's mind as they watched Adam for a response. Some didn't blame him for ancient suffering, but some did.

"The world was much bigger back then, even for us," Adam muttered, lost in thought. "Who knows exactly when that happened? I must have been consolidating my camp and our power on a new continent, or maybe I was still in China. Eve and I each had our strongholds in the Middle Ages. She'd taken Europe and dug in. I wondered for years how she did it. Now I know it was the fae. What happened is what happened . . . Danielle, can you tell us more about this sea witch?" Adam asked, shifting focus in a blink.

"I stopped seeing her history, and I got tangled in her raw emotions before you disconnected me," Danielle said.

"So, it's a woman!" Bastion barked.

"Yes," Danielle revealed. "I sensed she's tethered to Robin, but not by choice . . . She feels alone."

"Does she have a name?" Adam asked.

Danielle said, "I couldn't see it. It's like she identifies more with her heritage than with herself . . . I've seen nothing else useful, only images of things long gone."

"I believe Danielle's story is entwined with mine," Ruby interjected. "You mentioned Eve made the merpeople sink a stone box before she killed them?" she asked Danielle.

"You think it's the sarcophagus from your visions," Adam said to Ruby.

"Yes," Ruby confirmed without hesitation. "From what I've heard today, and from what I know from visions, Eve put Una at the bottom of the ocean. She must have done it for Robin. Two days ago, the sea witch put the sphere key with her, and I know why . . . It's the most remote location on the planet. I saw it last night. It's at Point Oubliette. It would be impossible to find—"

"If we didn't have the Cohens to see the truth and then transport us there!" Bastion cried and then laughed, interrupting Ruby.

Her face betrayed a hint of a smile. "Yes."

"Well, now we have another dilemma," Phoebe said. "Surely, we cannot kill her. She's all that's left of the merpeople. But what if she's guarding the key?"

Trent looked at the doorbell but chose to knock on Faustina's door. Anything to counter the system gave him a hint of joy and purpose. He waited for someone to answer the door, but they never came. He knocked again and waited a bit longer, staring into the sculpture he knew held a security camera. Cursing under his breath, he rang the doorbell. The lock immediately clicked, and the door swung open to reveal a petite and elderly housekeeper. The old lady was so adorable. Trent wanted to yell at her but couldn't.

"I know you saw me waiting here," he said a bit impatiently. "Why didn't you let me in?"

She smiled pleasantly. "Ms. Rothchild's instructions were to wait until you rang the bell."

He sighed. "I have urgent business with her. I don't have time to stand around."

She giggled like a young girl as she gestured for him to enter. "I guess you should have rung the bell sooner, then."

He followed her into the house and was surprised when she continued to lead him up the stairs.

Sylvia had messaged Trent to ask him if he knew where Pinky could be. Pinky hadn't checked in with the coven, and he was still evading the cabal. When Trent remembered he'd suggested that Pinky should contact Ruby, it had made sense to run down that lead. If Pinky was anything like Trent, and he was, he could be looking for Ruby, or he could be studying her movements for the right time to talk to her alone.

After Ruby confirmed she'd not yet had the pleasure to meet Pinky, Trent had checked in with the Dust security details assigned to both Jameson and Faustina. Other than her meetings at headquarters, Ruby's known locations over the last day had been between their two houses.

Adam's key non-magical associates were always under surveillance in public for their safety. Camilla Rosemont House and the Rothschild residence had agents monitoring from afar when the homes' non-magical residents were present without a witch to protect them from magical foes. Faustina's security detail had confirmed a man matching Pinky's description had entered the Rothchild property but had never left.

Although he fought admitting it to himself, Trent was slightly nervous to speak to Faustina. He'd glimpsed her briefly on the island, but their last conversation had been before he and Ruby had called it quits. Her genteel confidence intimidated him, but it also appealed to him in the same way he was attracted to physical danger. The housekeeper pointed him toward a guest bedroom door that stood slightly ajar. Somber string music spilled from within. She turned and left him in the corridor, so he approached the door and knocked.

Faustina's sweet voice called, "Come in!"

Whatever he expected to see when he pushed the door open, it wasn't the sight before his eyes as he stood stupefied inside the doorway. Faustina lounged in a bay window, playing an antique wooden harp. Her pink silk robe was tied loosely around her waist, but it had slipped away from her bare legs because she straddled the instrument. She was exposed almost up to her hips.

Averting his eyes to focus on his soulmate didn't help his shock. Pinky sat on the bed stark naked and held a glass of wine, but at least he had the decency to look slightly uncomfortable in front of Trent. As Trent quickly collected his wits, he blatantly studied Pinky's body. Pinky continued to sip wine, and Faustina finished the song she was playing.

When the music stopped, Pinky asked with attitude, "Did you get a good enough look at me?"

"Just making mental comparisons," Trent deadpanned, "but

you both knew I was coming up the stairs. You could have covered up."

"I needed to hear her finish the song," Pinky said as though it was obvious. "And I didn't know I was going to expose myself . . . to myself, today."

"What the fuck?" Trent realized Pinky was under the influence of some euphoric substance, so he helped him by throwing a pillow into his lap. "Okay, now you're a bit more covered."

"We had a dose of candy about thirty minutes ago," Faustina explained. "Then you showed up, and I figured I should invite you up."

"Why would you figure that?" Trent asked, distracted by her messy hair and smooth thighs.

"You must be here for a reason, and I thought it might be important," she said and stood to walk toward him. "Are you saying you had time to wait while we sobered and dressed?"

Trent thought it was so hot that she was right. He didn't know if he was jealous of Pinky or not. His soulmate had obviously just had sex with Faustina, but she was Ruby's mother. The conflict within him was significant.

"Yeah—yes," he mumbled, trying not to notice the small gap in the front of her robe where her bellybutton peeped through. "I need to take him with me . . . Or he needs to take me with him, rather. Duncan's funeral."

"I can't go, Trent," Pinky whispered. "I can't watch them eat his eyes."

"What?" Faustina asked in confusion and looked at Trent.

Trent explained, "It's part of the coven's funeral ritual. It'll only be symbolic for Duncan since most of our magic leaves the body minutes after we die, so his eyes would have needed to be eaten immediately . . ." Seeing Faustina's horrified face, he completed his thought less graphically. "But the vampires' magic stays within them. Eyes are powerful for us all."

She pulled her robe tight around herself and crossed her arms to hug her chest. "I'm too stoned for this, Trent."

"Why don't you get that adorable old bat to bring up some water, food, and supplements for you and Pinky?" he asked. "You can help me get him ready to take me to Romania."

Pinky started to protest. "I just don't—"

"You will be there for Sylvia!" Trent proclaimed a bit too loudly.

Faustina reached out and rubbed Trent's forearm. "Hush. No need to shout."

"I don't think I'm ready to meet the witches yet," Pinky said. "I haven't had a chance to talk to Ruby."

"You can either watch from somewhere they won't see you," Trent argued, "or you can stand with Sylvia and not speak to them . . . They won't approach you on the coven's land while you're standing with the coven." He turned to Faustina. "Faustina, Sylvia really needs him to go home for the funeral."

She nodded, thinking of how much she'd needed her children when Joe had died. "We'll get him ready."

"Faustina?" Pinky begged.

"You should go, Pinky. They're your family," she said.

"I'll go if you come with me," he argued.

"The vampires only invited witches, but I'll go as your guest if you insist," she said. "As long as you go. Sylvia deserves to have you there."

Trent helped Pinky get dressed while Faustina hovered over the food tray her housekeeper delivered.

Faustina gave Pinky supplements with water, then she sat a plate of food next to him on the nightstand. The robe slipped from her right shoulder while she bent over the tray to pour herself a glass of water, and she noticed Trent's gaze lingering on her skin. She smiled but retreated to her room to freshen up and get dressed appropriately for the funeral. She saw Trent and Pinky both following her movements with hungry eyes.

Tranquil weather greeted the witches in Romania. The clear sky and a cool, gentle breeze made the setting appropriate for Duncan's final goodbye. Lotus flowers were passed around to everyone in attendance to symbolize the immortal spirit. A pyre was erected in the outdoor arena's center. They were invited to gather on the east side, while the coven gathered on the west side in magical alignment with the occasion's emotional gravity.

Four vampires carried Duncan's body on a wooden litter decorated with flowers. Perfumed and decorated cotton shrouds were wrapped around his body, covering him from head to toes. Sylvia followed the body until it was placed upon the pyre, then she stood beside Sorina and waited. Vampires and witches alike approached the pyre and said their last words or prayers for Duncan and threw their lotus flowers onto the pyre.

Pinky appeared through his magic on the arena's southern edge. Faustina held his right hand, and Trent held his left hand. He held onto them both tightly and didn't look at the cabal or the pyre while crossing the distance quickly to meet Sylvia. His usual bravery and drive were there, but they felt held together by the people supporting him on each side.

Sylvia heard Pinky arrive and looked to the south with hope. While she'd expected him to arrive with Trent, seeing Faustina was a surprise. She turned to Sorina and silently expressed worry, but

Sorina smiled and nodded to assure Sylvia that Pinky's unexpected guest was welcome.

Sylvia and Pinky exchanged an embrace, and she said, "I'm so grateful you're here." Then, addressing Faustina, she said, "Thank you for coming."

"I'm honored Pinky invited me. Duncan was a great man, and both of you were so supportive of my family at Joe's memorial celebration," Faustina said confidently, grasping Sylvia's hands and giving them a supportive squeeze.

Sorina said, "Welcome to our home, Faustina Rothschild."

Faustina offered a demure smile. "Thank you, Sorina."

Ruby and Hayden approached the pyre together and placed their flowers. Hayden thought how blessed Duncan had been to live a long life beside the person he loved most in the world. He knew Sylvia was blessed as well, but he still felt sadness for her loss. Looking past the pyre to the other side, he noticed Pinky. Then he noticed Faustina.

"Ru?" he addressed his partner, who was looking down at the flowers.

She barely made a sound. "Hmm?"

"I'm not sure what to mention first, actually," he whispered. "I've just seen Pinky for the first time, but your mother is with him."

"What?" She jerked her head up and scanned the coven's gathering, trying to see what Hayden was seeing.

Her mother was there, speaking to Sorina. Ruby glanced from her mother to Pinky. He seemed so much like her former lover but nothing like him at the same time. Everyone on the other side seemed to be getting along fine, so Ruby relaxed and allowed her mind to imagine a myriad of scenarios about how her mother ended up standing between Trent and Pinky at a vampire funeral. As her mother's daughter, she reminded herself it would be inappropriate to ask until they were home. The ceremony was for Duncan. Moreso, it was for Sylvia.

Giselle shuffled up to Ruby, leaned to her ear, and asked, "What is your mother doing over there?"

Ruby turned to Giselle and stared into her eyes for emphasis as she replied, "I don't know, but we're not going to ask until we're home, are we?"

Giselle nodded slowly. "Right. No gossiping at funerals . . . But that Pinky is hot, isn't he?"

On the other side of Ruby, Hayden released a single chuckle.

"He looks like Trent, Elle," Ruby whispered in annoyance.

Giselle placed her flower on the pyre as Jeremy approached and did the same. The junior generation Cohens and Rosemonts continued to stand there together and watch friends and allies pay their respects to Duncan. When they saw Vlad step forward with an intricate golden vessel in his hands, they braced themselves for the imminent grotesque display.

The gathering watched Vlad present the vessel to Sorina, and she reached inside. She held the eyeball between her thumb and her index finger and waited for Vlad to say words.

"Sorina Ardelean, accept this last gift from your adopted son, Duncan, and let him bless you in return for the blessings you bestowed upon him during his long life. Eyes are the soul's gateway, keepers of magic. Consume it in remembrance of him that he may live forever within you."

Sorina tilted her head back and opened her mouth. She held the eye above her mouth and breathed deeply before dropping it down her throat and swallowing. Sylvia's arm wrapped around hers for support, and she looked down at the little witch she'd been protecting for over two centuries. Their eyes mirrored the same sadness.

Vlad presented the vessel to Sylvia, and she scooped up the remaining eyeball with her hand. Holding it in her palm, she waited for the ceremonial words.

"Sylvia Cavendish, accept this final gift from your faithful partner, Duncan, and let him bless you in return for the blessings you bestowed upon him during his long life. Eyes are the soul's gateway, keepers of magic. Consume it in remembrance of him that he may live for the rest of your days within you."

Sylvia slapped her palm against her mouth and closed her eyes. She chewed as few times as possible to be able to swallow. Her hand remained in place over her mouth while she breathed and resisted a fleeting wave of nausea.

Vlad handed the empty vessel to another vampire and retrieved an unlit torch from Dragos. He walked around the south side of the pyre and hesitated in front of Adam. He looked at the witch strangely for a moment and inhaled deeply.

Vlad eventually handed Adam the torch and returned to Sorina's side.

Adam held the torch high and nodded at Hayden. Flames erupted from it and then stabilized into a steady white glow. Adam approached closer to Duncan and waited.

"Tonight, we return Duncan to the stars!" Vlad shouted. "Tonight, we watch them burn bright with him! In his honor!"

In unison, the vampires sang, "In his honor!"

The vampires looked to the sky while Adam set the funeral pyre ablaze. He thought of Duncan's image over the years and words that had passed between them. Joe and Nick entered his thoughts, their memories still fresh in their families' hearts. The last year had brought more sudden, profound losses than he'd seen in a century, although the carnage had been mild compared to the battles of antiquity. He prayed the losses would not increase, but he prepared for the worst.

He thought of Eve and stared through the flames at Sorina, his new, true love.

POINT OUBLIETTE

The most remote place on the planet had been a space junk graveyard for hundreds of years. The oceans were almost purged of manmade trash after ninety years of work, but Point Oubliette was the last ongoing global cleanup effort. It had started in 2318 and was projected to take ten years to complete. In fact, Faustina Rothschild was heavily invested in the project.

After humanity started building, salvaging, and recycling while in space orbit, almost all spacecraft, stations, and other satellites stopped ending up space junk. Earthlings had consistently made small breakthroughs over decades with experimental terraforming as far out in the solar system as Jupiter's moons, where they had become comfortable traveling. However, the popular opinion was that humanity's most significant scientific breakthroughs were advancements at home. The planet was healing, and the quality of life among the global population had exponentially improved since they'd recovered from the Second Dark Ages. Point Oubliette had a pivotal role in that healing and improvement, and that was why Ruby had recognized it in her vision.

Seven alliance members were on the sphere recovery team. Ruby, Jeremy, Giselle, Phoebe, and Adam took a hired flight to the closest island to their destination and brought two vampires with them.

Anica and Sorin were the coven's most experienced divers. Vampire body composition and strength made them less vulnerable in ocean depths, but they were also extremely skilled in the water and brought the most high-quality diving equipment with them. Both were excited to work directly with the cabal for the first time.

Since Jeremy couldn't move an entire boat, he'd asked Faustina to call in a favor to her friends in in the South Pacific. With the ongoing cleanup work, boats went back and forth from the nearest landmasses almost daily to bring supplies and switch out crews for the sea lab. A small crew north of Point Oubliette, on Solo Island, sailed their catamaran toward the point while the alliance flew to the island from New York. Solo Island was approximately 1,450 miles from their target, but it was the closest landmass. It saved the team precious time to have a boat already headed south for them. When the alliance arrived on Solo Island, they transferred to a large seaplane to rendezvous with the boat and switch places with the crew. Once they were alone on the boat, they were eager for the mission to finally begin.

Ruby estimated the sphere to be about a mile south of the space junk. Since they had coordinates for the sea lab, they had an approximate heading. They weren't far from it, so the vampires prepared to dive while Phoebe and Giselle used the boat's advanced imaging equipment to scan the ocean floor.

"Why don't you use the nautilus to look around a bit?" Ruby asked Giselle. "Faustina had the crew bring the aquarium just for you."

"The water here isn't good for advanced marine life, Ru . . . I'd rather not throw him in unless I need to."

"If Danielle's story was accurate," Ruby argued, "Moira used sharks and a squid to help her."

Giselle was getting annoyed. She knew Ruby was still arguing because she didn't like being wrong. Giselle also knew more about the ocean and the site than Ruby did.

Giselle knew that didn't sit well with Ruby.

"Ru, you're doing that thing where you think you're smarter than me," Giselle snapped, "but I'll argue anyway . . . I'm sure Moira didn't give a shit about her animals, first of all. Secondly, that was almost a thousand years ago, so I really couldn't tell you what this place was like back then. What I *can* tell you is the space junk and the tides in *this* century make the water here inhospitable. Are you good now?"

"Witch, I might be," Ruby mumbled defensively, but then she cracked a playful smile. "I'm sorry, Elle."

Jeremy yelled at his sister from across the boat. "Ruby! Help me with the harpoons!"

Ruby joined her brother and helped him prepare tranquilizer harpoon guns to use in case the sea witch attacked them. She loaded two for each of the vampires and passed them to Sorin when he came below deck to grab the rest of their diving stuff. She took the four guns Jeremy loaded up to the bridge and hid them in a storage compartment in case they needed them. She looked up and saw Adam hovering in the sky above the boat.

Adam scanned the water's surface around the boat. The water was calm. The ocean air was pleasant, but the task at hand was disconcerting. Fear for his people kept his eyes and ears sharp. He heard Phoebe call out for Ruby and knew they'd found something.

"Ruby!" Phoebe shouted.

Ruby scurried to the monitors and pushed between Phoebe and Giselle to view the image. It was a square stone with familiar markings, and she gasped in excitement.

"Yes?" Phoebe prompted.

Ruby announced, "Yes! That's it!"

"Perfect," said Phoebe. "Go tell Anica and Sorin to come get a look at this before they dive in."

Within minutes, the vampires were in the water, fading from Adam's view and descending into Una's vast, watery grave.

Ruby and Jeremy peered over the boat's edge where the

vampires had entered the water. It was going to be a long waiting game, but they couldn't help but to stand there in anticipation.

Phoebe and Giselle stayed at the monitor and kept it focused over the sarcophagus. They watched the vampires' shadowy images approach the tomb.

All vampires had black hair and gray-silver eyes. They were almost like direct copies of Lilith. Due to their warrior training and specialized intelligent design, they were all fit, but their shapes and sizes still varied. Anica was far less voluptuous than the average vampire female, and she was one of the tallest. Her lean frame helped her maneuver easily and quickly through water where she had the advantage over more curvy females such as Sorina. While the thicker, shorter females could better stand their ground in the arena, Anica's skills were invaluable for amphibious warfare because she could swim circles around anyone else in the coven, except Sorin.

Sorin was Sorina's twin in the sense that Lilith had created and grown them at the exact same time with the same experimental techniques. They were three Edenian days younger than Vlad but among the most senior vampires left in the coven. They had been equals in strength and skill back on Eden, but the exile to Earth had affected Sorin differently than it had Sorina. Something about the planet diminished him slightly, and he often joked about being allergic to humans. However, he commanded water like Poseidon, outswimming everyone in the coven, to include Anica.

The ocean floor wasn't as dark through vampires' eyes, and they scanned their surroundings for the sea witch. There were no signs of advanced life other than themselves, so they pushed against the sarcophagus.

Sediment plumed up into the water when the lid fell, and Sorin noticed movement within the sediment that looked like the outline of a large fish. He blinked and saw the faint outline of a woman instead. His brain caught up with his vision, and he knew it was a camouflaged foe.

Realizing it must be the sea witch, he lifted the harpoon gun and pulled the trigger. Not trusting his aim, he reached for a second weapon.

Anica didn't see the enemy until her eyes followed the trajectory of Sorin's weapon to see an odd glob of moving sediment right before the harpoon grazed its target. The sea witch became visible, and Anica saw only a shallow scratch on her arm where a small amount of tranquilizer must have disoriented her power. Anica raised her gun while the sea witch tried to recover. In Anica's peripheral vision she saw Sorin prepare to launch his second harpoon.

The sea witch was fast. Her body rocketed up and away from them, evading their harpoons. Since they couldn't know how long she would be gone, they raced for the sphere. Anica gently pried Una's fingers from it before Sorin placed the sphere in a bag and strapped it across his back. Una was stiff as a board, so they both placed their hands under her, lifting her out of her coffin and bringing her toward the surface with them.

On the boat, Giselle and Phoebe tried to interpret what they saw on the monitor. It looked like the vampires had retrieved items and were coming back, but some of their other actions were difficult to interpret.

"They used their harpoon guns, but we couldn't see why!" Giselle shouted down to Ruby and Jeremy. "The sea witch might be down there, so watch out! Anica and Sorin are on their way back up!"

Ruby went up to the bridge and grabbed a gun for herself and one for Jeremy and waited for something to happen. Ruby paced along the deck's edge, but Jeremy stood in place and kept a tight grip on his weapon. The only thing in front of them was still water.

Gasping, the sea witch surfaced near the boat, and Adam saw her immediately. Jeremy and Ruby were on the boat's other side, so Adam dived toward the boat to warn them. He wanted to avoid attracting the sea witch's attention, so he didn't call out to them from the air.

Landing behind Ruby, Adam said, "The sea witch surfaced on the other side."

"Let me syphon some power," Ruby said to him.

Adam held out his hand to Ruby and she grasped it for a moment. "Thank you," she said, letting go.

Adam said, "You go high, I go low. In case she goes under."

Adam could disable the sea witch with his power, and he could also maneuver well below the surface. If Ruby's tranquilizer harpoon didn't strike true, he'd try to cut her off when she dived to avoid it. He donned goggles and a breathing apparatus before slipping into the water and stalking around the boat.

Ruby took to the air and spotted the sea witch. To her surprise, her target was swimming toward the boat. She'd be easier to hit outside the water, so Ruby waited to see if she'd try to climb aboard. Her heart raced with excitement, watching the witch's fish scales turn to skin as she flopped clumsily onto the deck and writhed around in pain. Ruby didn't think the sea witch looked like a threat in her condition, but she raised her gun anyway while landing on the deck. Looks could be deceiving, and the strange witch's full powers were unknown.

The sea witch's eyes grew wide at the sight of Ruby, and her voice sounded hysterical when she screamed, "Don't kill me! Don't kill me!"

Ruby kept her weapon aimed and shouted, "The harpoon tips are tranquilizer needles. It won't kill you, but it will knock you out!"

She started crying and wailing. "No! No! It's killing me! Look at my arm!"

On the other side of the boat, Jeremy had helped the vampires from the water. Jeremy and Sorin had just placed Una's body on the deck when they heard a stranger's voice screaming. Anica and Sorin froze and looked at each other.

"Keep the sphere safe," Anica said. "I will go see what is happening."

Sorin nodded, and Anica sprinted around to the other side to see the sea witch screaming. The scratch on her arm was festering and spreading at an alarming rate, and Anica realized they'd almost killed her.

"Ruby, don't shoot her!" Anica shouted as she approached them. "Sorin's harpoon did that to her arm!"

The sea witch screamed, "Yes! I'm allergic to it! Look what's happening to me!"

Ruby kept the gun pointed at her target. "I can't let her go. Someone has to restrain her."

Phoebe and Giselle came running toward her. "Why aren't you shooting her?" Phoebe asked.

"Look at her arm," Anica said to Phoebe. "Sorin's harpoon did that. Her body cannot tolerate the tranquilizer."

"Phoebe, help me," Ruby said.

Phoebe assessed the sea witch sitting naked on the deck, cradling her arm, and rocking back and forth. Approaching her from behind, Phoebe kneeled and placed her hands on both sides of the sea witch's head. There was no reaction from the injured stranger.

"I can kill you with a thought," Phoebe said calmly with authority, "so don't do anything foolish . . . Ruby, put the gun down, find Adam, and get some restraints. Hurry."

The prisoner seemed to be in too much pain to resist or to speak, but Anica and Giselle kept a keen watch over Phoebe and the sea witch. Without warning, she passed out just as Adam and Ruby returned.

"Phoebe, what did you do?" Adam asked.

Phoebe looked terrified. "Nothing! She fainted! I think we've poisoned her . . . Look at her fucking arm."

"I told him," Ruby said, "but it looked like you—"

"I know," Phoebe interrupted and looked at Adam. "Just do something."

Adam handed a tangled mass of handcuffs and shackles to Phoebe and said, "You and Giselle get her restrained while I heal her."

Jeremy and Sorin arrived to witness Adam putting his hands on the sea witch while Phoebe and Giselle shackled and chained her wrists and ankles. The women gagged and blindfolded her as Adam's healing power took away the last traces of damage to her arm.

Adam looked at Jeremy and asked, "Is it secured?"

"I took the sphere to New York . . . I took Una to Romania," Jeremy answered.

"You took Una's body to Romania?" Adam asked in irritation. "It was to go to the lab."

"Right, but she's alive. Sorin could hear her heartbeat, and—"

"Is she awake?" Adam asked, intrigued.

"No," Jeremy answered, "but I thought if she did wake up,

we wouldn't want her and the archway in the same place, same as the sea witch."

"Good, thank you, Jeremy," Adam said. "Take me, the vampires, and the sea witch to Romania as well. When you get back here, let Faustina know the boat will be abandoned here, so she can make arrangements. Then you'll take Phoebe, Giselle, and Ruby back to New York with you. I want you there to start working on the archway with Ty."

"My name is Adam Godwine. What's yours?"

The vampires had a dungeon, and it had five prisoner holding cells within it. The sea witch's cell had a large bed with a thick mattress. It had a toilet and a sink with a fresh water tap behind a privacy screen. Light shined into it from somewhere far above. It wasn't a luxury apartment, but it wasn't a filthy hole either. Adam stood outside the barred doors and watched her.

"I suppose I should thank you for saving my wretched life," she whispered.

Adam stepped up to the bars. "Look at me."

She didn't move.

"Please, look at me."

She slowly lifted her head and looked at him.

He saw despair in her face, and said, "You are my descendant, my blood, my family. I wanted to save you. I still want to save you."

"My name is Nixie."

"Nixie," Adam repeated. "That's pleasant, and appropriate . . . What is your surname?"

"I don't have one! I'm just Nixie," she snapped.

"Well, we'll have to change that," Adam stated gently. "Your mother was Wilda of Hastings, so you could be Nixie Hastings, if you'd like."

"No! She sold me to Robin when I was a child. I hate her," she moaned and vented. "All I've known is a life of service. My only home was a room smaller than this cell in the bowels of the Emerald Keep, and now I don't even have that. He'll never let me back in now. I have nothing."

"You've been a servant for a thousand years?" he asked.

She answered his question with a question. "Where is my mother?"

"Witches are not immortal," he said.

"Aren't you?" she asked in confusion.

"No. I age," he explained. "Although I am older than you, you have the potential to live much longer than I will."

Nixie wanted information about her mother, so she rephrased her previous question. "What happened to my mother?"

"I killed her," Adam admitted. "Hundreds of years ago in a battle between two factions of our kind."

"Would you kill me?"

"I wouldn't want to."

"But you would."

"Yes, I would kill you to protect my other descendants and our allies."

Nixie didn't respond. The plain cotton garment Sorina had given her to wear had short sleeves and a modest neckline. It covered her to the knees, but it was thin. She didn't have shoes, but she did have blankets on the bed. Shapeshifting would make her warmer, but that wouldn't be practical. She sighed and tugged at the bed's uppermost blanket. Wrapping herself in it against the mountain's chilled air, she stood from the bed and approached Adam.

Adam let silence linger between them while he studied her. She had his green eyes, but her hair was obviously not human. It was beautiful and looked like it was made from gold, but he wondered how she fared in public places. He knew since she didn't have a last name, she must not mix often with society.

She became tired of his scrutiny, and said, "See something you like?"

"Do people stare at you in public?" he whispered to her as she stood so close to him, he could hear her breathing.

In response to his question, her image faded into the surroundings. She was like a chameleon, and her camouflage was remarkable. If it weren't for her clothing still visible before him, it would be difficult to see her. Of course, he could see past her magic, but he was actively trying even though he didn't betray his ability to see her. He didn't look at her eyes but focused on the blanket, which then fell to the floor along with her gown. Her nude body reappeared, and she smiled mischievously.

Adam's eyes didn't wander except to quickly meet hers. "Was that supposed to shock me, or tempt me?"

From behind him, Sorina's voice said, "I believe she meant for me to catch you engaging in some sort of impropriety."

Adam kept his eyes on Nixie's, but he smiled slightly and addressed Sorina, whispering, "Hello, my angel."

She responded, "Hello, my treasure."

"Hmm." Adam contemplated the new term of endearment. "I like that."

Nixie's eyes showed a flicker of surprise before her expression became blank. She squatted down and pulled her gown and the blanket over herself. When she stood again, Sorina had crossed the room and was standing over Adam's shoulder, watching her closely.

"How long were you watching?" Adam asked Sorina.

Sorina replied, "A few moments. I heard you say you killed her mother . . . I knew Wilda of Hastings. She was a psychotic murderer. I was glad to hear you say she died in battle against you."

"Yes," Adam agreed. "We recently learned she killed the last mermaid . . . But I believe Nixie already knew that, which is why we know it."

"I am the last mermaid!" Nixie proclaimed. "Hundreds of great generations live in me! I hold the memories and the blood of my ancestors."

Reading Nixie's thoughts, Sorina said, "She expects you to refute her claim. She's been treated as an inferior species her whole life."

"Don't read my thoughts!" Nixie screeched.

Sorina grabbed her own head with both hands and whimpered softly. Adam spun around and held her firmly in his arms. He touched his forehead to hers and sent her healing magic. Sorina's nose dripped blood, and Adam could feel a force opposing his.

"Nixie, stop!" Adam growled at her, turning his face to look at her.

Nixie's body was pushed back with brutal force, and she fell onto the bed. She scrambled to get back on her feet and ran against

281

the door, gripping the bars with both hands and watching Adam and Sorina. She realized Adam's power was the source of half her own and feared what could happen to her in the hands of witches and vampires. So far, Sorina was the only vampire she'd seen since arriving to her unknown prison, but she knew there were more. She remembered seeing them on the boat before she'd fainted.

Adam started to wipe away the blood from Sorina's nose and lips, but Sorina said, "No, don't waste it . . . You told her you age, and you will. But I will share my youth with you for as long as I am able. Drink it."

Adam tenderly licked blood from between Sorina's nose and lips. Some of it trailed from her lips down her chin and neck, so he tilted her head back and licked from the base of her neck up to her lips. When he reached her lips, he kissed her as if consuming her mouth was his only worldly desire.

"Let me go," Nixie begged Adam, her voice loud but trembling. "They'll take my blood and my eyes if you leave me here. You've saved me for nothing, then."

"I am the only one allowed down here," Sorina said, "and you have hurt me more than I have hurt you."

"You are half witch," Adam explained. "We don't want to hurt you. Your place is in my family."

"Lies, all lies," Nixie cried. "Witches and vampires killed thousands of merpeople."

"Centuries ago," Sorina stated. "Those witches are gone, and my people no longer hunt magical blood. We are seeking universal peace. The fae are the only significant force opposing us."

"My child," Adam said gently. "Think logically. We could have killed you on the boat and taken your magic if that's what we wanted."

Sorina said to Adam, "Robin's influence cannot be undone overnight, but her attack on me is enough for me to know I cannot be her keeper."

Thus, Sorina and Adam began a psychological campaign against Nixie. Sorina's small brushes against Adam's palm with her thumb told him she was secretly supporting him even while voicing her refusal to keep his prisoner in her home. Unsure of the outcome, he played along while trying to read the room.

Adam looked at Nixie while answering Sorina to make a point. "She said it herself; she hasn't anywhere else to go." He made a quick decision. "Perhaps I should take her with me."

"I do not think that is a wise decision," Sorina argued. "Let her go. Surely Robin will not think we read her thoughts and discovered his kingdom's weaknesses. He would not torture such a rare creature to find out . . . But now that I think about it, what if we did read her completely? How many vampires can she fight at once? One of us will surely glimpse Robin's location and know his powers."

"I don't know anything, you blood whore!" Nixie wailed. "I don't even know how to get home!"

Leaving Sorina a few steps behind, Adam approached the door and placed his hand over one of Nixie's that was wrapped around a bar. "Explain why you can't get to your home."

Adam felt her shaking. She didn't say anything. He had empathy for her because she was so afraid, and he knew she felt alone. He noticed she was looking past him at Sorina.

"Sorina won't hurt you," Adam said. "You need to accept that . . . Please. Will you tell me what I want to know?"

"I'm his. My mother sold me to him in exchange for . . ." She looked at Sorina again.

"Look at me," Adam said. "Speak to me."

Nixie whispered, "The blood and eyes of ten vampires were traded for me. Eve said they were priceless, but Robin took me as payment."

"You don't belong to anyone, do you understand?" Adam asked sternly.

Nixie shook her head vigorously. "Where will I go? How will I live?"

"You have a family," Adam explained. "We will help you . . . but tell me plainly why you cannot go home?"

"I don't know how," she blurted. "He kept me in my room unless he told me to do things for him. Then he snapped his fingers, and we were somewhere else . . . All I know is, my witch magic didn't work in the Emerald Keep. Others said we were in another world."

"Do you want to know why?" Adam offered.

"I'm not stupid," she scoffed but also looked like she would cry. "I'm aware of how ignorant I am about the world, but I'm not stupid."

"Explain it to me like I'm stupid then," Adam said.

"I was separated from you," she barely mumbled. "You're the source."

"Exactly," Adam agreed. "Following that fact, you should logically come to the conclusion that you belong with me and my people."

"Is that vampire your mate?" Nixie asked, watching Sorina still lurking behind Adam.

"Witches don't have mates," Adam explained vaguely. "That is Sorina. We are allies."

"Kissing allies?" Nixie asked.

Sorina walked forward, and said, "Do not be ridiculous. Vampires do not kiss witches."

Adam nodded and said, "Sorina, let me formally introduce you to my descendant, Nixie."

"It is a pleasure to meet you, Nixie," Sorina said firmly.

Nixie nodded in understanding, then said, "You don't use contractions when you speak."

Adam laughed before he could stop himself. It was a completely random comment in context, but it was a very true observation, nonetheless. Nixie's awkwardness was going to be a big hit at the round table, he thought. If he weren't so nervous that Nixie would hurt herself or someone else, he'd be even more amused. He thought he was really going to like her, or he hoped he would.

Sorina looked from Adam to Nixie and said, "Sometimes I do. I am—I'm a bit behind on my conversational English. I get comfortable at home and forget to improve. Over the centuries we've tried to sound more conversational across all languages we speak . . . My mother speaks in a very strange manner, and all vampires started our lives speaking just as strangely as she does."

"You sound perfect, Sorina," Adam said in an amused tone. "Much better than your mother. Your language quirks are barely noticeable . . . Nixie is exceptionally observant."

"What was your mother's name?" Nixie asked.

"My mother's name is Lilith," Sorina answered. "She lives on Eden with Adam's father."

Nixie looked between Adam and Sorina. She remembered hearing about Eden when she was younger, but the only thing she remembered about it was some of the Blue Earth's magic and creatures came from there. She was too frightened for her future to abide more small talk. Hugging the blanket around herself, she waited for either of them to say something else. Sorina looked like she was waiting for Adam's judgment too, so Nixie focused on him, her eyes pleading for mercy.

Adam came to a decision but wanted Nixie's compliance. "My descendants and I exist together in a fellowship we call the 'Faithful Watchtower Cabal,' and I want you to join us after we battle the fae. You will be an equal member of our tribe with your own home, job, pay, and freedom to travel . . . However, it's dangerous for you until then if you leave . . . We would all truthfully mourn losing the last mermaid if something happened to you . . . I want you to stay here, and I can come here daily to attend to your needs. You won't have to be alone with Sorina or any other vampire. But it's your choice."

Nixie looked around her cell and contemplated his offer. The room seemed to be in a cave or a mountain, but it was impossible to know for sure. Wondering what country she was in, she shivered. If she ended up in Romania, she would be surrounded by ravenous vampires. She was afraid to be alone in the world with nobody to give her food and shelter. She'd been scared enough when Robin had left her to guard the sphere with only a three-day supply of food. Even if Adam was lying, the possibility of having a family was better than facing Robin's wrath.

Nixie looked at her cold, bare feet and asked, "If I stay, can I have a pair of socks?"

— ⚜ — ⚜ — ⚜ —

Una's body was on a stone slab softened with a mattress pad. Her head rested on a down pillow, and a fleece blanket was tucked over her. The vampires didn't know if a bed would be too soft for her after resting in a stone coffin. There had been much debate about fae anatomy before everyone had admitted they really didn't know anything about the subject, so they made her a soft shrine and let it be. The room had no electricity, but Ananda had lit candles in

286

the wall sconces to provide a soft light for keeping an eye on her. The fairy's skin looked healthy but still, like tawny porcelain. Her fingers rested naturally, but by all reports, it had taken them hours to relax after Anica had pried them from the sphere.

Adam and Vlad entered the room and examined the noble fairy. Adam carefully removed the ruby crown from her head to reveal damaged, charred skin on her forehead where the crown had rested. Around her head, just above her ears, her hair fell out, and some of it stuck to the crown. He froze with it in his hand.

"What's done is done, Adam," Vlad said. "Just place it beside her."

"I'll take it." Ananda lingered in the doorway and then reached for the crown. "I will clean it and bring it back."

Adam passed it to her before asking, "Isn't it odd her only wounds are under the crown?"

"She could have more," Vlad argued. "She's not been examined."

Adam removed the blanket from her and lifted her dress. Her legs were perfect, but he kept neatly folding the skirt higher and higher. He wanted to be respectful of her and her possessions even though he was going to carefully check every part of her for damage. Despite being a thousand years old, her clothing looked new and radiant.

"If we take any prisoners, I hope one of them is a fairy seamstress," Adam commented.

"I was thinking the same thing," Vlad agreed. "Our alliance may survive after all."

Sylvia had been summoned to join Vlad and Adam, but she entered the room a bit late to find Adam under Una's skirt. She visibly recoiled, slapping a hand to her chest with a deep gasp. She looked from Adam to Vlad, but the vampire didn't seem to mind the inappropriate display.

Vlad peered down his nose at Sylvia and scoffed, "Adam's checking her for wounds like these on her head." He pointed to her forehead.

Sylvia wanted to retort but held her tongue and watched Adam closely.

Una wasn't wearing undergarments, so Adam examined between the thighs as quickly as possible and smoothed the skirt back down to her bare feet. The dress' sleeves buttoned at her wrists, so he worked on one arm while, to his surprise, Vlad helped with her other arm. Both arms proved flawless, so Adam unlaced her bodice and examined her chest and abdomen. Pushing the material aside, he rolled her slightly to check her back on both sides. He found no other damage.

"Thoughts?" Adam asked while lacing Una's dress.

Vlad leaned over the body to look, listen, and smell carefully. He heard her weak heartbeat. Looking closely at her head, he paused and brought his eyes so close to her that his nose grazed her pointed ear.

"I think her hair is growing back," Vlad said and stood to face Adam as if having an epiphany. "We should examine the crown."

Adam looked closely at her forehead and thought Vlad was right. By his perception, it seemed like a tiny bit of skin had healed around the edges of her wounds. He ran his fingers through her hair, looking at the raw bald spots.

Vlad stalked through the door and called down the corridor, "Ananda!"

"I called you here to ask if you hear anything," Adam said to Sylvia.

Sylvia quickly said, "No, that's not possible. She's been sleeping for a millennium."

She could see he wanted to ask her something else, so she asked, "What is it, Adam?"

Her voice sounded tired, and it unexpectedly broke his heart. Losing his children was getting more difficult with every passing century, and he wondered if the envito was making it hurt more as if his feelings were amplified. The lines around her eyes and mouth had deepened considerably within days, but her eyes were still full of magic.

"You're letting yourself die, Sylvia," he said, his tone spiked with pain.

"I'm glad Duncan and I lived to see you like this," she said, "but he's gone, and that's my cue to stop letting Sorina keep me alive. I'm well past my natural time."

"How long do you have left?"

She said, "There's no precedent for this . . . The battle is imminent, and I haven't been assigned a task yet." She smiled.

"I was going to ask you to accompany me to New York," he said. "If possible, I want your help calculating the correct frequency for the archway before we lift the veil between this world and the fae realm."

"Of course. I'll tell Sorina now and get ready," she said and left the room.

Vlad came back with the crown. There was a red coating around the inside that was almost gone from being chipped and rubbed off in multiple places. Vlad sniffed and then flicked his tongue out and tasted it. His fingers picked and pressed against the crown.

"What are you doing?" Adam asked.

"I've lived in Europe since my fall," Vlad answered, "which gives me the advantage of hearing much more fairy folklore than you, I'm sure."

While Vlad loosened a metal lining inside the crown, Adam said, "Go on."

Vlad separated the pieces and examined the main ruby element. "This is the original crown," he said, holding it up. "This other piece was added later, and it's made of iron and some sort of hard, red salt that still hasn't fully dissolved after a thousand years . . . Iron alone might be a coincidence, but why would a crown have a salt coating?"

Adam knew what he was suggesting, but asked, "Legend says they can't tolerate salt or iron. Is that what I am to understand?"

"Exactly," Vlad said.

Vlad placed the ruby crown on Una's pillow. He kept the iron lining in his hand and lifted her hand, pressing the iron against her hand and holding it there for a minute. When he removed the iron, the marks on her hand looked like a cross between a sunburn and a bruise.

"The crown was her prison as was the ocean's saltwater," Vlad concluded.

Vlad dropped the iron lining back inside the crown and left it next to her. He invited Adam to walk with him back to the meeting room. On the way, they saw Ananda again, so Vlad ordered her to have Una bathed to help wash away the saltwater residue. He also ordered her to keep a closer eye on the fairy and to keep the door locked.

With the sphere key put into position, the archway was complete. Jeremy and Ty were able to confirm four different key and lock combinations. The original theory that all keys would fit into all locks had been incorrect because the sphere key would not sit at the apex. When all three keys were in locks, they referred to the archway as "unlocked." They wanted to test every combination of keys and locks by leaving the archway unlocked until they could prove it was working, but they had to be careful. It needed to be relocked before the fae knew they were testing it, so they could not allow the veil to lift between worlds.

They eagerly welcomed Adam and Sylvia back from Romania. Dust had specialized meters to gauge factors like frequency and power outputs, but Adam trusted Sylvia's magical gift and wanted her to be there for redundancy.

After she spent an hour watching the men experiment with the archway, Sylvia had an idea that had nothing to do with her powers.

Removing at least one of the keys quickly stopped the archway from activating, and Sylvia was able to hear the frequencies of each combination the same way she heard magic. She detected significant changes before the meters did, so they didn't need to leave the keys in for as long. With her help, there was less of a chance anyone on the other side could sense they were knocking on their door. The average time from unlocking the archway until initial portal activation was about a minute, and that's when a solid wall started forming within the arch. Sylvia noticed the space within it always turned opaque, but the interesting part was that each opaque barrier was a slightly different color.

"Gentlemen," she stated. "I think it's obvious we don't need to analyze frequencies anymore."

The three men looked at her, expecting more explanation, but she only sat in her chair and looked back at them as if her statement carried a clear meaning to everyone in the room. She had the aloof confidence that usually came with age. Adam didn't mind it since he often shared her attitude, but Ty and Jeremy were losing their minds in suspense.

"Well?" Jeremy asked a bit condescendingly. "We can see a wall, barrier, veil—whatever you want to call it, so the next logical step is to lift it, but we still need to know which world is on the other side of each barrier before we disturb the space between worlds."

"I understand that, boy," she replied. "Was I the only one looking at barriers? We know which one we want . . . Place the skull at the apex, the sphere on the right, and the obelisk on the left."

"Sylvia," Adam said gently. "Perhaps you wouldn't mind explaining to everyone how you know that?"

"It's color coded," she said simply, blinking at them.

Ty threw up his hands. "Oh, for fuck's—" he protested before catching himself and remembering he was talking to an elderly woman in mourning, so he gently added, "Sylvia, there's no way a magical machine from the heavens is color coded. You're not thinking clearly—"

"Don't gaslight me, Ty Alexander!" she said sternly, like a sassy grandmother. "There are clearly four colors for our world and the three neighboring worlds."

Ty argued passionately, "Why would there be a combination for the Blue Earth? The archway can't be taken from the Blue Earth."

"If it can't be taken from the Blue Earth, then where was it before it was here?" Sylvia asked as if explaining matter and the universe to a toddler. "It makes more sense that Selene, or other gods, can move it elsewhere, but lesser beings belonging to these four worlds cannot."

"Adam?" Ty asked for help.

Time was running short for Ty to get a specialized team to secure the archway and move it to a large museum they had earmarked as the site from which to mount their attack in Avebury, England. Spellcaster texts placed the fae realm's center near a stone circle in Avebury, so they'd have the best chance of reaching the Emerald Keep fast enough to take it by surprise if they entered near there. The museum was the closest secure place to hold the archway unseen overnight. Each key would stay with the witches and not travel at the same time.

"I agree with Sylvia," Adam said, trying to hide a grin. "We make machines with color codes, so why wouldn't the gods do it?"

"Oh, come on!" Ty said and turned to Jeremy for validation.

Jeremy looked slightly embarrassed and rubbed his neck while mumbling, "The simplest solution if often the right one, I guess. Otherwise, it would be quite coincidental the barriers were slightly green, red, blue . . . and a whiteish gray, which lends to the belief the fae realm is bordering the others equally."

"Congratulations, Jeremy," Ty scoffed. "You know the color wheel."

Sylvia cackled loudly, clearly enjoying a belly laugh at Ty's comment. He couldn't help but to chuckle at her outburst. He found it adorable, although he still wasn't sold on the color idea. Nonetheless, it was three against one, so it was time to move forward with final testing and planning.

SECRET WEAPON

The witches were universally glad to see Sylvia at the round table. Danielle and Phoebe took seats on each side of her. They'd both noticed the same changes Adam had, so they wanted to spend a bit of time with her. Danielle invited Sylvia and Phoebe to brunch and mimosas after the meeting.

Sylvia's spirits were as good as could be expected, and she felt joy in watching the younger generations thrive in fellowship.

Trent sat on the other side of Phoebe, so she leaned close to his ear and whispered, "I've been dying to ask why you brought Faustina with you to Romania. I wanted to ask her, but we've been nonstop here."

"Why don't you ask Ruby?" Trent asked, looking bothered.

Phoebe's smile was sly. "No, now that I see how much it bothers you, I surely want to ask you," she breathed, her lips grazing his earlobe.

"Be careful, Phoebe," he whispered. "I've been single for a bit and won't hesitate to give your sweet cunt a thorough fuck if you keep doing that."

"Language, Trent," Sylvia leaned around Phoebe and said, pointing a finger of shame at him. "I'm old, not deaf. Take it to the bedroom, not at the table."

He cleared his throat and politely answered, "My apologies, Sylvia."

Phoebe struggled to bite back a laugh, but Trent was looking past her at the sweet smile Sylvia gave him in response to his apology. When he felt Phoebe's hand slide onto his thigh, he returned his attention to her. She waited patiently for him to give her gossip.

Trent whispered, "Faustina wasn't there with me. She was Pinky's guest, and that's all I'm sharing here . . . You're welcome to get the rest of the story from me later."

"Lovely. I'll do that." Phoebe removed her hand from his thigh and read her tablet.

Everyone studied new information and plans while Adam and Ruby were the last to take their seats. The cabal had everything needed to battle the fae, so it was time for Adam to reveal secrets he'd kept from the others. He nodded to Leilani to assure her the announcement was imminent, and then he nodded for Ty to call the meeting to order.

Adam waited for Ty to finish opening remarks, and then he announced, "Kinsmen, as Vlad had Pinky, and Robin had Nixie as covert operatives, I also had one of you working in the shadows."

The older generations didn't look the least bit surprised, nor did Ruby. Their underwhelmed expressions weren't from knowing about the spy, but they knew Adam well enough to expect a dash of spycraft and secrecy to survive within the cabal as it had always been at Dust.

Leilani looked somewhat annoyed as did Giselle, Jeremy, and Hayden, but Trent looked like he wanted to say something inflammatory.

Adam continued, "Bastion has been spying on the fae for months. He helped me lure Robin to the solstice celebration . . . He also released him at my request."

Amid gasps and sucked in breaths around the table, Trent vented his frustration. "Phoebe almost died!" He paused and added, "Sorina almost died!"

Bastion interrupted, "I think Phoebe shares some blame for

that, to be honest. I had convinced him to leave, but his need for revenge temped him to return unbeknownst to me. If Phoebe hadn't fucked and stabbed him—"

"Shut up!" Trent barked.

Bastion held his arms wide open and called, "Come over here and have a go if your think you're tough enough!"

Trent jumped on the table, and he crossed it in two quick leaps. He came crashing down on top of Bastion, and the chair fell back while Trent punched down on Bastion's face. Bastion blocked the punch and kicked Trent off him. Suddenly both men were flat on the floor and gasping for air under Adam's magic.

"Adam, that's enough," Ruby said.

Bastion and Trent both inhaled and coughed and bit while lifting themselves from the floor. They could breathe normally again. Bastion turned his chair upright and sat. Trent walked around the table and took his seat.

"I wasn't finished," Trent stated.

Ty said, "You'll wait. Adam will finish speaking now."

"Thank you," Adam said. "As Bastion said, Robin was supposed to escape but risked a room full of witches and vampires to attempt killing Phoebe."

Trent growled beside Phoebe, but she leaned against him and whispered, "It's okay. Turning a man into a psycho killer is an artform, and I am a master artist."

Beside Phoebe, Sylvia cackled aloud, and when Adam paused, she said, "Get on with it, Adam. I'm dying here."

Adam sighed and continued, "We let Robin leave and fed him false information to make sure all the chessmen ended up where we wanted them, so to speak . . . Which brings us here and now.

We have all the tools we need, and we're ready to invade the fae realm."

"Adam is right," Ty said. "We have come this far together successfully, and only the final battle awaits. Now is not the time to fight each other."

"I understand your point of view, Ty," Trent said, having regained his composure, "but when the battle is won, and we come back here to resume our business, we will discuss the decisions that have been made without the voting jury and decide a course of action together."

Without waiting for Ty to acknowledge his statement or call it to a formal vote, Trent raised his hand and shifted his eyes at each of the voting jury member. Danielle, Phoebe, Jeremy, and Leilani raised their hands in solidarity with him. Ty nodded at Adam, and Adam returned Ty's nod.

"Ruby," Ty said. "Record that as a unanimous vote to call a meeting to discuss Adam's secret use of spies and revising our rules and procedures."

"Of course," she said. "And I think it's time to get to the crucial topics of the day. We have much to cover."

Perhaps the most important topic, and the original reason for seeking out the fae before Robin's attack on Dust, was the tapestry map. They consulted their tablets to study descriptions of the sacred magical object. They poured over drawings and diagrams. Bastion and Jinae discussed bringing tools to pry open and blast away locked vaults and trunks. Familiarizing everyone with the object and planning for multiple scenarios was essential to increasing their chances of recovering the map ahead of the vampires.

Vlad had requested their presence in Romania that night, expressing the need to meet with the witches one more time before the battle to share weapons. The cabal was pleasantly surprised that Pinky had offered to help Jeremy transport the witches. Not only would the rest of the witches finally meet Pinky, but it was likely he'd join them in battle the next day.

───── ───── ─────

Fae Realm, 1432 A.D.

Spring was upon the realm, and the equinox marked a royal celebration and the return to court. Oberon and Titania reveled. Drunk on mead, Titania rode Oberon on the dais floor in front of their thrones. Both royals wore only their crowns. Oberon's crown was emerald, and Titania's was amethyst. Their cloaks were draped over the thrones. Titania held her goblet high in the air and shook it, and a wine steward raced to refill it.

The king and queen ruled their kingdom with balance between light and darkness. That was the purpose they had carved out for themselves between three young Earths after their creator had left them in their gilded cage to fend for themselves. They valued both good and evil, each representing one of those values. Both monarchs passionately believed in the need for each other's contributions, and that belief was the cornerstone of their love for each other and their people's culture.

Titania represented light. Her influences over the universe were good deeds, pleasure, and joy throughout all earthly realms. Her noble minions influenced crops to grow and animals to reproduce in the human realms. Her common minions influenced flora and fauna in the fae realm. She encouraged generosity and compassion among her people.

Oberon represented darkness. He ruled destruction and evil deeds. His noble minions spread sickness and rot in the human realms. His common minions influenced discord among the fae. He encouraged sadistic desires and greed.

Because fae immortality was limited to flesh and blood, Oberon and Titania had produced two heirs to carry on their legacy. Robin's purpose was to serve darkness while Una was a bright light cherished throughout the realm. As the fairy prince and princess grew, it was clear to both Oberon and Titania that Robin did not embrace a natural bond with Una. Likewise, Una did not approve of Robin's role in the realm. To ensure they worked together to preserve fae culture as intended, Titania had forced a magical bond between them. Robin and Una would survive together or lose their magic.

Spring equinox was the only time of year nobility and common fae folk celebrated together as equals in the Emerald Keep. As the realm's favorite, Una was the object of many fairies' thoughts. They wanted to see her and drink with her. Many wanted her to bless them with sexual favors.

The hour grew late, and Una still did not appear at court. When noble fairies started asking after her, Titania scanned the throne room for the recognizable ruby crown, but she only spotted Robin's sapphire crown. She reached out with her feelings, searching the realm for her daughter's magical signature but felt nothing.

Oberon sat on his throne with an almost empty goblet of wine. While watching his subjects celebrate, he spotted a beautiful common maiden dancing in a circle with others. He watched her spin and laugh, admiring her physical beauty and her spirit. She looked up at the dais, and their eyes met. He pointed at her and then pointed at the floor in front of his throne. The young fairy scampered to the throne and dropped to her knees before him. He grasped a mass of her hair and pushed her face into his lap, then he moaned in pleasure from feeling her lips slide down his cock.

Titania came back to the throne room, having gone to Una's room to check for her. When she'd found the room empty and the bed unused, she'd asked the servants if they'd seen her. Titania could find no servant who'd seen her, and they'd said her bed had been untouched for months. It wasn't unusual for her children to leave for months at a time, but Una usually came home a week before the equinox celebration to meditate in her room.

Titania interrupted Robin's conversation with his cousins and asked, "Where is Una?"

"I haven't seen her since midsummer last," Robin said flippantly.

"Have you heard tell of her whereabouts?" Titania asked impatiently.

Robin sighed and drawled, "Mother, you know I don't care."

Titania stomped her way back up the dais and stood before Oberon. Without acknowledging the woman pleasuring him, she stepped around to be beside him and leaned on his shoulder.

"I think Robin has done something to Una," she whispered into his ear. "She's not here, not in the keep."

"Can't you see I'm enjoying myself?" he asked her.

"Finish it," Titania commanded. "I need to you question Robin and send your knights to find her. I cannot sense her in the realm."

Oberon did as his queen commanded. Fisting the common fairy's pointed ears in his hands, he thrusted vigorously against her mouth three times to achieve quick release. He then pulled her away from him by her hair and stepped past her down the dais to look for Robin.

Titania watched him stomp away and then looked down at the young fairy broken on the floor. The girl held bloody chunks of hair in her hands. She bowed her head to her queen, and that's when Titania noticed the point of her left ear was snapped. The fairy queen dropped to her knees in front of her subject, inhaled deeply, and then blew her breath over the other woman's body. All physical and emotional wounds were gone and forgotten. Titania's magic washed them away, and the common fairy smiled at Titania before rejoining the dance.

Oberon returned and confirmed Titania's fears. "I believe Robin is lying," he growled. "I have ordered my knights to begin searching."

"We cannot give up until we find her, or he tells us where she is," Titania said. "We must find a way to fix this. They must rule together."

As Robin approached the dais, Oberon replied to Titania, making sure his son heard his thinly veiled threat. "The solution is simple. We make more heirs."

Titania was wary of the dangerous flash in Robin's eyes at Oberon's remarks.

WATER OF LIFE

Two by Two Pinky and Jeremy transported witches to the coven's sacred cavern until every member of the alliance arrived safely. The underground lake captivated every new visitor, and as a group, they timidly stepped closer and closer to the sparkling water.

"It didn't always have those sparkling flecks in it," Vlad explained. "Those came when Gaia appeared during your battle with Eve."

"Avoid drinking them," added Dragos. "They'll put you to sleep."

"So, they're dangerous?" Adam asked.

"Not for us," Vlad replied. "They're powerful. Dragos awoke invigorated when he tasted one, so most of the coven has indulged. However, we don't know how they'll affect witches."

"But you know how the water affects us?" Adam challenged.

Vlad pointed his hand across the lake at Sylvia, who was sitting on a smooth stone. She smiled sadly at Adam before casting her eyes downward and staring at the calm water.

Adam glanced around him at the rest of his tribe and saw desire and excitement in their eyes. It was clear to them what Vlad was suggesting, but Adam wondered if Vlad was offering water to them. If so, Adam was wary of the price.

Adam said, "I assume it isn't free."

"You have already paid the price for a cup of water to each of your people," Vlad stated. "Drinking a cup tonight will not add centuries to your lives. Sylvia has been drinking three drops a month since she was twenty to slow her aging. You drink tonight to strengthen our combined forces for battle . . . And if your witches live, perhaps they gain an extra decade to live."

Gasps echoed in the quiet chamber. Adam looked at Sorina, conveying his concern and hesitation to her in his expression. She nodded to him and caressed the chain around her neck.

"Is Sylvia . . .," Adam glanced at Sylvia. "Is she aging that fast from not drinking?"

Sorina explained gently, "She's lived almost three human lifetimes. Without ingesting more magic, she may continue to age faster. We don't know."

"Convince her to drink," Adam said to Sorina.

"She is finished," Vlad said sternly. "She does not possess envito. Her desire to die is a sign of madness to come. Prolonging her life may worsen the condition."

"What a barbaric point of view," Phoebe interjected from beside Adam.

In a condescending manner, Vlad said, "It is common knowledge and our way."

Ananda appeared with a basket full of crystal chalices about the size of teacups. She handed one to every witch, favoring each of them with a polite smile. When she approached Giselle and handed her a cup, she paused with her arm stretched halfway. As Giselle reached for the cup, Ananda withdrew it quickly. The women peered at each other in confusion.

Giselle's voice was little more than a whisper. "Is something wrong?"

"Sorina!" Ananda called out, glancing around.

Sorina rushed to Ananda, and Ananda continued, "Her scent."

Giselle went from nervous to self-conscious and stepped back a pace. She reached beside her for Jeremy's hand, which he gave and held onto hers tightly. As Sorina's hand reached for her, she flinched.

"Don't be afraid," Sorina said. "I won't hurt you . . . May I examine you, please?"

Giselle held onto Jeremy for support, and he stepped closer to her side and kissed her cheek. She nodded. Sorina reached for Giselle's free hand and grasped it with the palm facing up. Holding out the witch's arm, Sorina moved two fingers gently over the veins down to the wrist. She held Giselle's wrist for several breaths and then brought the hand to her face to smell it. After gently placing Giselle's arm back at her side, Sorina went to her knees in front of her and placed her head against the witch's abdomen.

Pulling back and rising to her feet, Sorina said, "I am sorry, Giselle. You will not drink today, and you will not fight tomorrow."

"Why not?" Jeremy demanded. "What is wrong with her?"

Sorina knew enough about etiquette not to spoil a family surprise, but Adam stepped between Giselle and Sorina. After observing Sorina's actions, he understood. He placed a hand on Giselle's shoulder and concentrated for a moment. There was an abundance of magic at work inside her as was natural with pregnant witches.

He smiled at Giselle and glanced between her and Jeremy. "Congratulations to you both," he whispered.

Jeremy still looked baffled as Giselle threw her arms around him and cheered, "We're having a baby!"

Seconds later, Phoebe had her arms around them both as did Ruby. The witches huddled around to offer their blessings to the couple. Jeremy finally snapped out of shock and wore a grin, holding Giselle against him while his family and friends shared in his happiness.

Ananda resumed her task, making sure everyone had a cup. When she handed Jeremy his, she explained to him and Giselle the importance of abstaining from drinking the water while pregnant because the vampires didn't know how it would affect the mother or the child. She explained they didn't know what caused the Cavendish bloodline to be without magic for so many generations, and they couldn't rule out the fact that Sylvia had kept drinking it while pregnant. Giselle walked around the lake and sat next to Sylvia while everyone else prepared to drink.

With Vlad and Sorina's encouragement, the rest of the witches sat at the lake's edge and dipped their cups into the water. Sorina's gaze landed on Phoebe, who was staring into the water with her empty cup lingering above the surface. Phoebe then withdrew the empty cup and placed it on a nearby stone.

Sorina sat next to Phoebe and said, "You can trust us."

"Despite myself, I do," Phoebe answered. "I just—I can't do this without Jameson. It's too important. It's life."

Sorina left for a few minutes and came back with what looked like an empty glass medicine bottle. She dipped the bottle into the lake and then took great care to stopper it well. Phoebe was speechless when Sorina held the bottle out to her to take, but she reached for it.

"Now you have an equal gift for your partner . . . Your power is strong and lethal. We need you at your best. Now you will drink?" Sorina asked.

Phoebe was astonished and moved almost to tears from Sorina's generosity. "Yes . . . Thank you, Sorina."

Pinky was drinking water next to Trent. He still hadn't properly introduced himself to Adam, but he was working up the courage to do much more than that. It was important he bide his time until the witches had imbibed sacred water, and the two sides felt comfortable and less likely to break the alliance.

There were too many secrets between the allies. If he was going to fight with them, and he intended to do so, the two sides needed to be more honest with each other. After all, one side was his adopted family, and one side was his biological family. For the first time, they would be forced to handle their messy issues together in the same room instead of hatching plans in two separate rooms before coming together to carefully negotiate specified demands and trades. He was a better spy than any of them gave him credit for, which was rather the point of being a good spy. Secrets were about to spill one way or another. The alliance would be tested, and he had faith in its survival.

Pinky stood and announced, "I want nothing more than to stand in support of you all in battle . . . However, I believe it's important to fully trust the people fighting and possibly dying beside us. Yes, I'm a coven spy, but I hear and witness more than even they realize. Now is the time to tell your secrets, or I will."

Still seated, Trent looked up at him and said, "I don't understand how we're the same person, yet you're so damned naïve. Do you want to die tonight?"

"No," Pinky stated, gathering his courage. "I want to face the issues dividing us and fix it right now. We cannot be divided in battle."

"That is wise, Pinky," Sylvia said. "I'm proud of you."

"So am I," Sorina said, and after a pause, she added, "I will tell the first secret."

Adam tried to control his breathing and prayed his heartbeat wouldn't race enough to give away his nerves. He wondered if she was going to confess their partnership, or if she was hiding something else from him.

Sorina continued, "I am the coven leader."

Adam chuckled. His surprise was apparent, but he wasn't angry. Past interactions started to click and make sense in his mind, and he was relieved.

The first protest came from a source that surprised everyone but Pinky.

"What?" Bastion shouted but then quieted, clearly angry at something.

Pinky nodded and said, "Go on, Mr. Roth."

"No," Bastion said. "I should have kicked your meddling ass in Malta."

"Alright, then," Vlad said. "Let's get this done without dragging it out too much . . . Bastion started spying for me after we both realized Adam and Sorina are in a partnership."

In response to a few squabbling murmurs from the witches, Adam said, "Don't judge me. There have been two new recent partnerships among the witches that weren't mentioned to me until after they were done."

"They partnered with other witches, not a completely different species," Trent couldn't help commenting. "I mean, love is love, but I'm just pointing out the obvious."

Ruby chastised him in front of everyone. "You promised me—promised us—you'd not jeopardize the alliance before the battle!"

Vlad snickered at Adam allowing a such a young witch berate him. Other vampires watched her audacity with a mixture of awe and fear. Their regimented society allowed little room for them to question elders.

"His promise to you," Sorina said, her voice rose above the

whispers and side arguments, "was not about partnership. He promised not to take me as a lover, and he has kept that promise . . . Likewise, the coven has no rule against partnerships outside the coven, it is merely implied by the rule against lovers outside the coven, which I plan to change after the battle."

"You're lying!" Bastion accused Sorina. "Your smell is always on him."

Dragos growled at Bastion, and Bastion said, "Sorry, I meant no disrespect to your leader. My concern is for my kind. We are different and shouldn't mix with creatures who thirst for our blood."

"Look, man, I get it," Trent added his opinion. "I don't dig bloodsuckers either, but it's Adam's and Sorina's choices, and look at what the coven shared with us here. This water is . . . Well, it's a big deal . . . If you don't like vampire-witch relationships, don't be in one."

Adam reached under his shirt and pulled out the vial of Sorina's blood. "It's this crystal vial of her blood you smell, Bastion. It symbolizes our partnership."

"I wear one too," Sorina said. "Every vampire here can smell it if they're close to me, but no member of the coven has asked, not even Vlad . . . I do not know why."

"We respect you as our sister and our leader," Dragos said. "We trusted you would address it when the time was right."

"Excuse me," Phoebe said. "How is Bastion involved in all this?"

Trent quickly added, "Yeah, all this seems to imply he's a traitor, which wouldn't surprise—"

"Fuck off, Pinkerton," Bastion interrupted. "I was going to give Vlad information about how we prevent mindreading, but I didn't."

"Only because I caught you," Leilani snapped.

Bastion looked pained by her accusation and explained, "I was going to alter it, so it wouldn't be accurate and see if he would try to use it. I could have proved trusting them is a mistake."

"And how would we fight the fae then, genius?" Phoebe asked.

"Phoebe, you ignorant slut!" Bastion yelled. "Go suck off Pinkerton and let decent people talk."

"Enough!" Adam commanded. "Danielle, read his bracelet."

"Let Sorina read him!" Phoebe interjected.

Adam considered Phoebe's idea. He reached out to stop Danielle as she was about to remove her glove. She looked eager to retreat to Ty's side and not have to see Bastion's deeds and secrets. Adam didn't want to say anything in front of Vlad about the existence of their implants, but he knew Phoebe had honed her skills enough to discreetly destroy it.

"Phoebe," Adam said. "Can you do it?"

Phoebe stalked toward Bastion with a vengeance, but he stepped back. When she lunged to grab his shoulders, he drew back his fist to punch her, but Adam sent a burst of energy directly at his arm. A bone cracked loudly, and Bastion howled in pain while holding his arm. Phoebe's hands clamped down on his shoulders.

"Stop," Bastion pleaded. "You can't subject me to her without a vote!"

"I vote yes. Phoebe votes yes. Leilani, do you vote yes?" Adam asked, and Leilani nodded slowly. "How does the rest of the jury vote, concerning one of our own attempting to steal from us?"

"I vote yes," said Ty.

Jeremy said, "So do I."

"Me too," Danielle agreed.

The vampires watched the scene with great interest. Most of them didn't know the cabal had an elected jury and a voting process. They assumed Adam's leadership was absolute. Sorina, like Vlad before her, had absolute power unless challenged. Vampire leaders had advisors to help develop plans and implement them, but the leader did not need a vote to decide anything. Ananda and Sorin whispered together about how efficient the system would be if it weren't for the witches' endless internal bickering and insults.

Phoebe was done in a second. She had targeted the implant with her energy and destroyed it. Bastion looked at her like she had betrayed him, but she appeared apathetic. She released his shoulders and stepped back without a word.

"Phoebe?" Bastion asked, and when she looked back at him, he continued, "Will you heal my arm?

Rolling her eyes, she walked away from the man who had just slut shamed her and tried to punch her in the face. She'd let Ty or Adam heal him because she never wanted to touch him again.

Adam placed his hands on Bastion's arm, healed him, and said, "Sorina, you may read him now, if you're ready."

Sorina shuffled through Bastion's thoughts, looking for applicable information. He was easy to read, but the experience was still distasteful to her because she uncovered his extreme prejudice. She felt sadness for Adam because she knew he'd trusted Bastion with his life and the lives of his descendants. Bastion's love for Leilani was at the forefront of his mind as was his fear that she'd never trust him again or want him. It was clear Leilani was Bastion's anchor to the cabal. Sorina saw glimpses of their implants and pulled away from those thoughts. She'd never mention them or betray them. Vlad's complicity was apparent in the next thoughts she read, so her heart grew even heavier. She faced Vlad.

He saw the sorrow in her eyes, but his expression was blank.

"Vlad?" Sorina asked. "Would you hurt them against my orders?"

"Probably not," Vlad drawled. "Unless we become enemies again one day, I simply wanted to know how they did it."

Fearing for Vlad's life, Dragos whispered to Sorina, "Please. He doesn't have support from the coven, so he couldn't have harmed them."

Sorina didn't respond to Dragos. She didn't continue conversing with Vlad either. She considered what had occurred, and reached for Adam's hand, which he gave.

Finding Pinky's face among those watching her, she asked, "Are you content, Pinky? Or are there more secrets you cannot abide?"

He shook his head. "No, that is all."

"Hear me," Sorina announced. "Witches have an inherent right to their thoughts and minds. Therefore, not disclosing their means to protect those things is also a right we will not violate without official permission from the cabal jury."

She focused on Vlad and said, "Vlad, your collusion with Mr. Roth is an insult to my leadership, the generosity I have extended to you, and the coven. I wish for you to receive a fair punishment. Because I believe your actions were a personal vendetta against me, Dragos and Ozana will decide your punishment when we return from battle."

Sorina's eyes followed Vlad as he silently made his way to the chamber's exit. Before he disappeared into the mountain, he turned and sneered past her at Adam. She squeezed Adam's hand to show her support. She was there for whatever he needed to do to make sure his cabal was unified.

He asked, "Was Bastion truthful?"

"His extreme prejudice was at his mind's forefront, and he did wish to destroy the alliance," Sorina said. "However, he did not intend to share accurate information. For his private reasons I do not have the right to share, I believe he will remain devoted to your cabal."

Bastion had been staring at the ground, feeling his emotions torn in every direction. But when Sorina expressed respect for his private thoughts, he snapped his head up in surprise.

Sorina knew he hated her, but she chose to repay him with discretion rather than pettiness or cruelty.

Her qualifications and popularity as a leader became apparent to him in that one moment, but he struggled to see her as a witch's equal.

Following Sorina's example, Adam asked, "Who among my tribe has an appropriate punishment for Bastion?"

Ty stepped forward and said, "I think this public interrogation in front of our allies in conjunction with the removal of his ability to block their mindreading powers is sufficient punishment for the crime. Leave his mind unguarded among those he's prejudiced against and let us move on."

Adam found Ty's common-sense approach to life especially refreshing in that moment, but he could see Trent and Phoebe didn't feel the same way. They likely feared Bastion's thoughts would betray the secret of their implants and other information, but Adam trusted Sorina would keep that from happening. Besides, Adam would wait a few weeks and give Bastion another implant anyway.

He didn't necessarily need votes from Phoebe and Trent. If the vote was four or more in favor, the awkward episode would be over. Ty raised his hand to signal a vote was taking place, and Adam's hand went up quickly to agree with him. Beside Ty, Danielle slowly raised hers when she saw Leilani doing the same. Jeremy was the last to agree while Trent and Phoebe kept their arms crossed out of spite. Adam ensured Ruby recorded every decision and vote to be added to the rest of their official actions in the headquarters archive.

The coven hosted the cabal for another two hours while they discussed plans to meet in Avebury the following day. Trent accompanied Pinky to meet each witch individually while Adam and Sorina sat by the lake and witnessed their alliance thrive through the conversations and interactions happening all around them. The evening's interruption had been a surprise, but it was an essential turning point on their journey toward victory.

Una's eyes fluttered open to the sight of shadows dancing across a jagged stone ceiling from flickering candlelight. Sight was the first of her senses to awaken, yet her mind didn't comprehend the image. The shifting light lulled her, and she closed her eyes again.

A draft passed through the door's iron bars powerful enough to extinguish one of the candles. Lucidity forged a way through fog in her mind with the smoky scent as a guide. Her eyes popped open again, and she inhaled deeper, becoming aware that she was in a strange place and smelling smoke. Her joints and limbs were stiff, but she concentrated on her magic and moved slowly.

Her body felt like it hadn't moved for years, and she tried to recall her last memories. Finally summoning enough power to rise from her makeshift bed, she rolled onto her belly and slid her legs off the stone slab. She felt her feet touch the floor but didn't yet trust her legs to carry her. As she rested her upper body against the stone, she observed her surroundings.

Beyond the pillow sat her ruby crown. She reached for it, but when she picked it up, an iron lining fell from inside of it. The metal crashed to the floor. As the sound echoed around the room, she realized what it was and associated it with a memory.

Her brother and his witch mistress had poisoned her crown. They had watched her place it on her own head and laughed at her confusion as she had grown dizzy and collapsed. The last memories she recalled before she'd lost her ability to see and hear were the terrifying images and sounds of Robin and Eve placing her into a coffin. She recalled the horror and the sorrow she'd felt. Opening her mouth for the first time in almost a thousand years, she cried out in agony.

With renewed strength and resolve, her hands pushed down on the stone. She lifted herself and walked to the door, but the bars were iron. Using her blanket as gloves, she placed the iron lining back inside the ruby crown, then wrapped the blanket around it to take with her. Maybe she wasn't yet strong enough to transport herself home, but she could snap herself to the other side of the door and be free from the room.

Once in the corridor, she saw light coming from one direction, and the other path was dark. She chose to walk toward the light. Whoever lived there would have already hurt her if they had wanted to, she thought. They'd likely saved her from Robin and the coffin in which he'd buried her. The chamber at the corridor's end was vast and bright. It looked like a throne room, or a place to hold court. On the other side, there was another corridor, so she continued to search for help or a way outside. It didn't matter to her which she found first.

The path she took dead-ended at stairs that went down into a tunnel. She hesitated. The candles lighting the path were only halfway spent, so hoping she would finally meet someone, she descended the long, curved path. It ended at a thick wooden door with an ancient lock. It wouldn't open, so she peered through the keyhole to see an open space on the other side.

She snapped and appeared on the other side of the door. It was a dungeon, she realized. Her eyes scanned the cells lining the room's edges. In the last cell, there was a woman sitting on a bed and staring at her.

Nixie stood, shuffled closer to the bars, and breathed, "Una?"

Una tried to remember the girl but couldn't. "I'm sorry. I don't know you."

"No," Nixie agreed. "You don't know me. I was birthed seven months after Eve buried you at the bottom of the ocean."

Una's expression was curious. "But you're not a fairy."

"Well spotted, princess." Nixie laughed nervously, not wanting to think about placing the sphere in Una's coffin and leaving her to sleep. "Your portrait used to hang in the Emerald Keep's throne room in the days of Titania and Oberon." Her tone turned dull. "I was your brother's slave for centuries."

Una stumbled back, the words feeling like a punch to her belly. Many centuries had passed, and the strange prisoner had implied her parents' reign had ended. Her body went rigid at the thought her brother could be nearby.

"Did my brother lock you in there?" Una asked. "Is he here?"

"No," Nixie said, watching the fairy with interest. "I'm locked in here for protection from Robin and your people . . . Yet here you are anyway."

Una relaxed a bit, studied Nixie's hair, and asked, "What are you?"

Nixie curtsied and said, "I'm the last mermaid."

Una shook her head at the woman with human legs and mermaid hair. "Mermaids don't have legs."

Una witnessed magnificent magic wielded before her eyes

when Nixie transformed her lower body into a brilliantly scaled fishtail. Nixie held up her hands and webbing materialized between them. Una came as close as she dared to Nixie without touching the bars and noticed her witch's eyes.

"You're a shapeshifting witch," Una said. "Your power is beautiful."

"My mother was a witch, but I disowned her," Nixie spat. "She sold me to your brother . . . My father was the last merman. I'm immortal, like him."

Una thought again of her parents and asked, "Do you know where my parents are?"

"He killed them," Nixie said quietly. "Your mother really should have protected herself the way she protected you . . . Although, you're lucky you had a mother who cared about you . . . Perhaps you should go home and fight for your realm before the witches and the vampires destroy what's left of it."

"Explain!" Una commanded, but then remembered her situation, and asked, "Please?"

Nixie scoffed, "You don't have to hide your royal arrogance from me." She backed away from the bars and carefully explained, "Your brother has made enemies . . . Tipping the balance to darkness seems to come with consequences. He slaughtered most of Titania's devout followers, but perhaps the battle has evened the numbers by now. It would be a shame if another immortal race is destroyed."

"The battle is happening now?" Una asked urgently. "In my realm?"

"Yes," Nixie said, and looked around. "This place is the vampires' home. They've an alliance with the witches . . . That's how despicable your brother is. He's ended thousands of years of separation between witches and vampires." She shrugged and looked thoughtful. "Perhaps it was meant to be to bring us all together . . . Or perhaps it all means nothing."

Una said, "I must go to my faction's haven. If any have survived, I must return with them to the realm."

"Haven?" Nixie asked with interest. "There is a rumor some fairies of the light fled to safety. I always secretly hoped it was true and that they would return and free me." She laughed madly. "What a silly girl I was . . . But fate has freed me from Robin anyway."

"Help me, please," Una begged with a hint of impatience in her tone.

"A simple fairy bargain, then," Nixie said. "I want you to leave. I want you to leave me here unharmed. I want you to leave this place unharmed . . . What do you want in return?"

"I need fresh water," Una stated. "As much as I can drink. If you give me that, it's a bargain."

Nixie laughed. "What luck! You've chosen the only valuable thing I have in here to give. . . It's a bargain!"

FALL OF THE EMERALD KEEP

In the museum's spacious storeroom, the alliance gathered before the archway. Adam flew up to the apex and placed the skull key in its lock. Jeremy placed the sphere key, and Danielle remained on standby to place the obelisk key when the fighters were ready to walk through the veil.

Danielle's task was to activate the archway and stay behind to make sure it stayed open and guarded. Ananda's task was to stay behind and protect her if plans went sideways. She had a squad of vampires armed with rifles and iron bullets waiting around the room's perimeter.

Giselle was also staying with Danielle due to her pregnancy, but she'd brought guard dogs with her. She also held the controls to a special modified sprinkler system in the ceiling that would rain salt into the room if she pushed a button. Surrounded by lounging dogs, she rested on a chair behind everyone while they organized into their chosen battle formation.

Like birds in flight, the fighters formed four wedge formations. The first and last wedges were smaller squads and contained their strongest leaders. The second wedge was the vampire squad, and the witches formed the third squad. Along the right and left sides of the wedges, five paces separated each person from the person in front of them. Approximately ten paces separated each squad.

They had thirty-one fighters in all with Sorin leading fourteen vampires. Their numbers were based on spy intelligence from both Bastion and Pinky, estimating the fae population had dwindled to less than fifty fairies since Robin had seized the throne. It was believed half of Titania's followers were murdered before they could flee, and the rest had not been seen since the coup. Oberon's faction

had been split between Oberon and Robin. Those remaining loyal to Oberon had been killed. In the centuries since, others had been lost under Robin's chaotic rule. The alliance wanted to remove Robin and offer survivors a chance to live and make a deal with them, but they were also prepared to wipe out the fae to save themselves if necessary.

Danielle placed the obelisk key into the lock, and the archway was unlocked and starting to open. The barrier appeared and turned from gray to bright white. Its opacity then waned gradually until it disappeared. A touch of relief and excitement lessened Adam's anxiety when the Emerald Keep became visible against the fae realm's landscape.

Adam was the first wedge's point, leading the alliance into battle. Ozana and Vlad followed behind him on each side of him. With Adam crossing under the archway first, they ensured every witch could use their full powers immediately after crossing into the fae realm. With two of the most powerful vampires with him on each side, they were better prepared against immediate attacks.

The vampire squad followed. Sorin took lead at the front, and fourteen vampires formed the wedge behind him with seven on each side. Pinky occupied the wedge's center, so he could transport his entire squad to another location on the battlefield if they were overpowered or needed to help another squad.

Jeremy held the same center position in the third wedge. Phoebe was first. On her left side followed Hayden, Jinae, Leilani, and Trent. Leilani and Trent formed one unit, walking side by side at the end. Since neither of them had offensive powers, they protected each other. Like everyone else, they wore a thin layer of iron armor, but they also carried iron tipped weapons and salt spray. On Phoebe's right side, followed Youngae, who commanded a murder of crows. Most of the birds flew overhead, but four of them perched on her shoulders and arms. Behind Youngae, Bastion and Sylvia were the last two witches on the right. They stayed together, mirroring Leilani and Trent.

The fourth wedge secured the allies from the rear, ensuring the enemy would be met with strong opposition in the event they were attacked from behind. Sorina led them, and Ruby and Ty followed behind her on each side. Ruby had syphoned fire magic from Hayden and was holding it until needed. Once she used all the fire, she could borrow power from Ty, or anyone else in the thick of the fight.

Danielle and Ananda watched the last group walk through the archway and cranked down an iron chain-link overhead door from the ceiling to cover the entrance. The vampire guards then pieced together an iron cage to protect the archway, Danielle, and Giselle. The vampires sat around the cage's outer perimeter.

The alliance fighters marched fast, hoping to make it to their target before encountering enemies.

A rolling meadow was all that separated them from the castle, and there was not one fairy in sight. The vampires' senses were on alert for any deviation in sight, sound, or smell.

Vlad knew there was something amiss about the realm itself. They were marching through grass, but he only smelled dust. The day was bright, but there was no sun. There were no native animals as far as he could see, except for the murder of crows at their command.

"Adam, Ozana," he called as they kept advancing. "I think everything we're seeing is a glamour. Try to use your hearing and smell to confirm what your eyes see . . . It is off."

"I agree," Ozana said. "Can't you do something, Adam?"

"What do you propose?" Adam asked.

"You have the most powerful magical gift," Vlad said. "You can cast it in front of us to ensure the path is clear."

"We're almost to the castle's gate," Adam argued. "Using

that much power might alert them if they haven't already felt the archway."

Ozana said, "But what if we're not close to the castle? I see green meadows, but I smell dust and smoke."

Adam inhaled and said, "I'm starting to smell smoke, too." He held up his hand, and everyone stopped. "Ozana, bring Youngae up here."

With Ozana's vampire speed and stamina, it took only seconds for her to cross the formation and carry Youngae back to Adam.

"Send the crows toward the castle," Adam said to Youngae.

Youngae took a deep breath and exhaled slowly. Taking a knee, she put her hand on the ground and tried to listen to the grass and the flowers grow, but she heard nothing. It was then she understood Adam knew there was danger ahead they could not see. She lifted her arms toward the castle and commanded the birds to fly, but she warned them to be cautious and turn back if there was danger.

"In the third squad Bastion has just told us the smell of fae magic is overpowering," Youngae said, "as if they're actively using it everywhere."

"We agree," Ozana said. "We must keep all of our senses alert."

The alliance watched the crows soar overhead and continue across the meadow. As they approached the castle, something strange happened. To the witches, it seemed as though the birds had hit an invisible wall and turned around to fly back to Youngae. With their enhanced sight, the vampires saw a bit more. They noticed three birds quickly incinerated as the others abruptly turned.

"Did you see how fast those birds burned?" Ozana asked Vlad.

"There is a fire between us and the castle," Vlad said, "and it's not natural. It was put there to keep us out."

"They're in there waiting for us," Adam said. "We must plan and move quickly." To Youngae, he said, "Thank you. Return to your place behind Phoebe and send Hayden to me."

Vlad understood Adam meant for Hayden to cool the fire, and he said, "We should get as close as possible, then you and Hayden can both attack forward with maximum force. Then when we can see an open space on the other side, Pinky will transport the vampire squad forward past the fire, perhaps even past the gate."

"Yes," Ozana said. "While they're watching us push though from this side, Sorin's warriors will surprise them from inside their defenses."

Hayden took position in the lead squad's center with Adam, Ozana, and Vlad forming a protective triangle around him. Ozana relayed the plan to each squad's leaders, who informed their squads. Adam raised his hand and signaled for everyone to start moving.

The air was still, and the only sounds were their footsteps. Youngae's crows circled the air behind the alliance. Everyone was aware the quiet journey was coming to an end. Like a violent storm looming on the horizon, the enemy's power would soon clash with theirs, leaving behind death and destruction. Leilani reached deep into her soul and spread feelings of calm, focus, and resolve to everyone as they halted again.

They were much closer to the castle, and besides the burning smell, the air was physically warmer. Adam's wedge reformed into a line facing the castle. The witches stood in the middle, and the vampires flanked them. Together, Adam and Hayden blasted power forward at the invisible obstacle.

Adam's power tore a hole through the glamour wide enough to see a ring of fire surrounding the castle with magical blue flames climbing high into a sky that was dark and tumultuous. The ground was barren and scorched. A team of guards stood in a line between the fire and the gate.

Hayden's power froze an approximate sixty-meter stretch of the fire, giving them enough visibility to act. Hayden held his ice in place against the blue inferno while the alliance charged forward. At the same time, Pinky transported the vampire squad to attack the guards from behind. The alliance was successfully overrunning the guards, so Adam ordered Phoebe to advance the witch squad past the gate and open it. Her squad collapsed into a huddle around Jeremy, and he transported them.

Anticipating opposition on the other side, Jinae and Phoebe placed themselves on opposite sides of the huddle and faced outward to better provide shields for everyone. When they appeared beyond the gate, Jinae used her telekinesis to hurl stones and earth. Phoebe couldn't shield and attack at the same time, so she projected her destructive energy. Their initial attack kept them alive as fairies fought to surround them.

Once Jinae had enemies on whom to focus her power, she was able to send small balls of iron flying through the air like bullets. The fairies were fast, but she killed two while the others scattered. Leilani and Trent flanked her and assisted with their iron weapons. Trent plucked out the dead fairies' eyes and instructed Leilani and Jinae to eat. The women's fear and desire to survive overpowered their repulsion, and they swallowed two eyes each.

On the other side, Phoebe was knocking down enemies, but they were getting back up. She'd have to get closer and touch them to do real damage, so she knocked four of them down and picked the closest one to jump on while he was down. She put her hands on his head, and when blood started pouring from his nose, mouth, and ears, she let go.

Youngae, Bastion, and Sylvia flanked Phoebe and used salt spray to defend themselves and push fairies back into positions where Phoebe could attack them.

The witches had killed three enemies while managing to stay alive, but they were getting tired. At eight against ten, they were also outnumbered. As fairies started attacking from the ramparts, Phoebe knocked them down to keep them from having the advantage of position.

The alliance had won the field outside the gate, and vampires started scaling the walls and fighting fairies off the ramparts as well. Two of Sorin's squad had fallen in the fight, paying the price for victory. Twelve fairy guards had died, and their blood and eyes were divided between witches and vampires.

With renewed strength, the rest of the alliance joined Phoebe's squad. Ruby and Adam flew over the gate as Vlad and Sorina jumped onto the ramparts. Together, the two vampires ripped a fairy in half before jumping into the courtyard.

At the gate, Ty and Hayden waited to get in. Jeremy magically transported himself outside the gate and then transported them back inside. Jinae, Leilani, and Trent ran to assist the group when they saw fairies popping up around Jeremy to attack. It seemed the fairies had figured out Jeremy and Pinky could travel through space instantaneously, like fae nobility, so they wanted to eliminate them from the fight.

Since everyone was inside the gate, and Phoebe saw half of her squad defending Jeremy, she took the other half of her squad to Pinky as fairies advanced toward him. She, Youngae, Bastion, and Sylvia defended Pinky. Using a combination of crows and salt spray to push the fairies back, the team was holding steady while Phoebe made two kills. As they took on too many foes, Bastion and Sylvia ran out of salt spray and clutched their iron knives.

Phoebe and Youngae were defending against three fairies when another fairy ran straight at Pinky between Bastion and Sylvia. Bastion placed himself between Pinky and the fairy. The fairy's magic broke Bastion's hand, and he dropped his blade. As Bastion's defeat seemed imminent, Sylvia crossed behind the fairy and jabbed her blade through his neck. He whirled around and grabbed her neck in return. Magic flew from his fingers and snapped her neck before he fell dead on top of her.

"Jeremy, don't move," Ty said. "If you move through space, and they corner you somewhere else, they've won. Just let us fight them."

"Right," Jeremy said. "What if I move us all?"

"We have to fight them eventually anyway," Hayden shouted as he prepared to throw fire.

Five witches surrounded Jeremy. Ty threw back four fairies while Hayden burned three more, but they kept coming. An iron bullet from Jinae killed one, but they were still outnumbered by one. That's when Leilani, fueled with extra power from eating the fairy eyes, turned on her mood power. The fairies dropped to their knees overcome with love and desire. Moments later, Jinae's iron pierced the backs of their heads.

Ruby found unexpected success in the heat of battle. Fairies didn't seem to understand how she was making them fall under her hands. They kept grabbing her in close combat, trying to use their magic against her through their hands. All she had to do was put her hand on theirs to syphon the power and blast it back at them, and it came easier than any other magic.

During battle training, Ruby had discovered she possessed no natural defense against vampires unless another witch with useful powers was present to syphon from, and her defense against other witches was hit or miss depending on their defensive powers. It had bugged her to discover fighting was another thing she wasn't great at. So, it was a lifechanging revelation to discover that if she needed to fight, it best be against the fae.

Fairies were dead across the grounds. All of them were

militant. None of them surrendered.

The alliance moved fast to regroup and ingest blood and eyes. Trent and the vampires taught more of the witches how to harvest the eyes swiftly and efficiently. Although some witches were hesitant to partake, Trent convinced them it was the only way to quickly replenish their magic and strength for the next fight.

Sorina saw Pinky holding Sylvia's body and sprinted to them. She cradled her adopted daughter's body and closed her eyes.

Vlad approached and said, "Don't let them go to waste."

"It is too late!" Sorina snapped. "She's been dead too long."

"Her magic hasn't gone to waste," Bastion said. "She's not a vampire. Her magic has gone back to the source. I'm sure you'll take her eyes during your barbaric funeral ritual anyway."

Vlad read Bastion's thoughts and said, "She died protecting you."

Pinky saw wrath in Sorina's eyes as she looked at Bastion, so he interjected, "Sorina, Bastion was protecting me. He stood between a fairy and me. When he was overpowered, Sylvia killed the fairy from behind before it killed her . . . It's the death she would have wanted. You know that."

Sorina nodded and rose to her feet. She had just lost Sorin and three other warriors as well. She felt their losses, but she kept her focus for the sake of the others.

The alliance gathered by a wall that was out of sight from the main keep's windows to finish a quick plan.

"Pinky, we have seven dead," she announced. "Arrange them by the gate so we can take them home when this is finished . . . Dragos will now lead the vampire squad."

Dragos nodded solemnly. He usually led a squad, but Sorin had asked for the experience. Dragos knew Sorina blamed herself for allowing her brother to lead and sacrifice himself for his squad, but it was a just and honorable warrior's death. He started drawing a diagram of the Emerald Keep in the dirt.

Adam stepped beside Sorina and said, "It's time to take the keep. Dragos got the layout from a fairy's mind."

"If there's any fae nobility left, they'll be in there with Robin if they haven't fled to one of the Earths," Vlad said. "These fairies out here were common folk, but the nobility holds more power and can move through space, like Pinky can. We must be vigilant."

"The corridors will nullify our numbers anyway, so its best if we split up and use multiple means of ingress," Adam said. "Ruby and I can fly to the upper windows directly. I can carry someone with us."

"Take Ozana with you," Sorina said. "That leaves me, Vlad, and Ty from the small squads, so we will split between the large squads . . . Vlad and Ty will follow the vampire squad through the main corridor, and I will follow the witches through the servants' entrance."

The alliance moved, invading the keep from all sides.

Adam, Ozana, and Ruby hovered outside the high windows and looked inside. It appeared to be a long, open throne room, and it was empty. Adam and Ozana went inside first, and Adam immediately shielded them both and took a closer look around. Looking up, he realized where the keep got its name. The ceiling was sparkling with emeralds. He nodded to Ruby, and she landed on a ledge and stepped down into the room.

There was a pop. Faster than anyone could react, a fairy was behind Ruby. The short fairy stood on the window ledge. Ruby stood on the floor in front of the window. One of the fairy's arms was wrapped around Ruby's chest, pinning Ruby to against her. The same hand was on Ruby's throat. The other hand had already plucked out Ruby's right eye.

The horror on Adam's face amused the fairy. When she laughed, he donned a neutral expression and made sure his shield was still strong around himself and Ozana. He noticed Ruby's right hand slowly creeping up her body toward her throat to take the fairy's hand, but he was careful not to look directly and bring attention to it. He focused on the fairy's face, but he worried for Ruby. He thought if she wasn't in extreme pain yet, she would be after the adrenaline ran out and the shock abated.

"Should I eat this pretty witch's eye, like she ate them from my people?" the fairy asked in a shrill tone.

Adam softly answered, "If you're going to eat it, you best do it soon before the magic is gone."

The fairy gave him an odd look as if wondering why he would tell her that. She seemed to be disappointed in his calm reaction. Adam guessed she derived pleasure from taunting her victims.

Dangling the eye in front of Ruby's face, she said, "You must be just a tiny bit upset I ruined her pretty—"

Ruby's hand was waiting just below the fairy's hand, and when she started speaking again, Ruby snatched it with a tight grip and syphoned hard. She'd eaten four sets of fairy eyes. She felt like she was drunk on magic, and nothing could stop her. She brutally attacked the fairy with her own magic. To her audience, Ruby looked unhinged and livid. When the fairy became weak, Ruby walked forward, dragging the fairy out of the window and onto the floor. She put her knee on the fairy's chest and pinned her tight before grabbing her own eye from the floor by the fairy's hand and swallowing it.

"It's mine, you little bitch!" Ruby cried in sorrow tinged with pain. "Nobody gets it but me!"

Ruby then syphoned more power from the fairy. She

syphoned so much the fairy was barely awake.

"An eye for an eye," she moaned before plucking out the fairy's right eye and eating it while the fairy watched.

Ruby then killed the fairy, blasting her with the rest of her own power. She looked up at hearing footsteps coming from the room's main door. Her breath was ragged as she got up and stumbled away from the corpse.

The vampires entered and made a circular perimeter in the center of the room, so Adam dropped his shield from Ozana as she joined them. He then approached Ruby cautiously. She didn't notice him at first. He had to stand directly in front of her before her eye focused on him, but she still looked disoriented. He held out his hand to her, and something clicked in her mind. She ran into his arms and collapsed. He held her up while she moaned softly, hiding her face.

"Ruby, I need to heal the wound," he whispered. "It will feel better and won't bleed anymore."

She lifted her face and began rapidly whispering to him, breathlessly babbling, "It feels—it feels like half my face is gone. I can't think how much more it would hurt if I hadn't eaten those eyes. The pain. I—I felt . . . I think she used magic. It can't be fixed. I'll never have another normal eye."

"Try to stay still and let me heal it," he whispered. "We'll worry about the rest later. The battle isn't over."

Following close behind the main squad, Ty and Vlad appeared dragging another dead fairy between them. It was a male dressed in fine clothes and wearing a ridiculous number of jewels. When they saw the female, they left him next to her and started questioning if those were the only two nobles left in the realm.

Dragos glanced to the other corridor at the room's side and wondered if the witches had met with enemies along the way. He charged Ozana to lead a few vampires to meet them. He and Vlad made sure everyone stayed in a circle and close to each other.

Ty walked over to Adam and explained Vlad's plan. "I'm going to be on the other side of the circle, and you'll be on this side. If we hear a popping sound, that means one of those royal assholes is in here, so we'll both throw our shields around our halves of the circle, okay?"

Ty stopped and realized Adam was holding his hand over half of Ruby's face and there was a lot of blood. "Is she okay?"

"That female fairy on the floor took her eye," Adam said. "But I'm closing the wound. She will be okay."

"I'm sorry, Ruby," Ty said. "Do you need help healing it?" he asked Adam.

"No, it's important you stand on the other side in case one of them comes," Adam said.

The witch squad arrived through the side corridor, complete with Ozana's search party and Sorina. They were moving slower because they had a living prisoner in tow, and it took several witches to make sure they could hold her. Phoebe was behind her holding her head. The fairy's mouth was gagged, and her eyes blindfolded. Trent and Bastion flanked Phoebe, and each had a hand on one of the fairy's shoulders. Youngae and Jinae were holding her fingers apart and keeping balls of iron pressed against her palms.

"This one's powerful," Bastion announced. "Whoever reads her mind, don't get too close."

Sorina and Jeremy dragged another fairy body and placed it by the others. It was another noble male. The vampires' custom was to collect the enemy's leaders, even the dead ones, in case they needed to use them later for bargaining.

Vlad directed everyone around the circle where to stand, placing them according to their strengths. The prisoner was in the middle, still held by Phoebe, Jinae, and Youngae. Jeremy and Pinky were also placed in the middle.

Hayden looked for Ruby and growled to himself in anger when he saw her folded into Adam's arms. He watched Adam rest his lips on his partner's forehead and kiss it over and over. He observed Adam rocking her from side to side. He stayed where Vlad told him to stand, but he couldn't help watching Ruby. He wanted her to look at him and care that he had made it through the keep safely.

Sorina noticed Hayden's discomfort, but she assumed there was a reason her partner was holding another woman in a room full of people during a battle. She approached Adam. He smiled sadly when he saw her but kept a firm hold on Ruby.

"Is she alright?" Sorina said.

Adam nodded at Sorina but spoke to Ruby. "Everyone's back, Ruby," Adam said. "Hayden's here too."

Ruby lifted her face and asked, "Hayden?"

When Ruby looked around, Sorina saw her wound and understood Adam was comforting her and trying to heal her.

Sorina said, "Ruby, why don't you go stand with Hayden? He has been worried about you."

Sorina and Adam let Ruby run to Hayden, observing the young witches.

Hayden gathered Ruby into his arms, holding her in a tender embrace. When Ruby pulled back and looked at him, he caressed her face and kissed her.

"He doesn't like your relationship with her," Sorina said, lacing her arm though Adam's.

"And I don't like his relationship with her, so we're even,"

Adam replied. "I think I like it a bit more right now, seeing him treat her as he should even when she's disfigured."

"I've noticed she is your favorite," Sorina said.

He laughed. "I'd question those keen vampire senses if you didn't notice. . . She is my spiritual advisor. My father has come to her in visions to deliver messages, and she often has other visions in which she sees and interprets the future. Her abilities as a seer and oracle are beyond any I've ever seen in my people."

"It is time for me to read the fairy's mind," Sorina said. "If I do not get to tell you later, I love you."

"I love you, my angel," he whispered as she walked away.

Sorina moved to the circle's center and asked, "Do we know who this fairy is?"

"Not a clue," Phoebe said.

Sorina pulled down the fairy's blindfold and studied her golden eyes.

"Iris," Sorina said. "Her name is Iris."

Sorina shuffled through Iris' thoughts and found answers to their most important questions. Iris was from the oldest known fae generation, and she was Queen Titania's sister. Robin's location was in the castle. He'd locked himself in the dungeon. There were three more noble fairies. They'd taken their servants and fled to Malta.

"Phoebe," Sorina said in a dull even tone. "Help. I can't look away."

Phoebe slammed Iris' head back against her chest and slid her hands over the fairy's eyes. She applied a bit of magical pressure against Iris' brain.

"Are you good, Sorina?" Phoebe asked.

Sorina blinked her eyes and few times and rubbed her head. "Yes. Thank you . . . Robin is here. He is alone in the dungeon, and the tapestry is down there too. We need a team to go."

"How many others are here?" Adam asked.

"None," she answered. "There are three remaining alive, but they fled to Malta with a handful of servants."

"Why would they go there?" Bastion asked. "We already know where it is and how to get in."

"Perhaps they did not know where else to go," she said, "and perhaps they've fortified it."

"We'll take a team back there tomorrow and look around," said Adam. "Right now, we need a team to go downstairs . . . Sorina, I'd like to go."

"Then I'll stay here," she said. "Vlad and Ozana can go."

"Phoebe and I should stay here in case we need a shield," Ty said.

"No," Bastion said. "Phoebe should stay here so Robin doesn't go psycho."

"Shut up," Ty snapped.

Adam said, "I'll take Jinae, Hayden, and Ruby."

"I'll go with you," Pinky said. "You may need my skills, too."

Adam looked at Sorina, and she nodded.

"Welcome to the team, Pinky," Adam said. "Let's move."

"Wait a moment," Sorina said.

Sorina took Ruby's hand and guided her to the fae bodies.

She reached down to the fairy Ruby had killed and plucked out her other eye.

"We usually leave important bodies intact," Sorina explained to Ruby. "It makes them more valuable trades, but I assume you already took her other eye?"

"Yes," Ruby simply replied.

Sorina handed the eye to Ruby and explained, "Eat this one, too. Fae nobility have immortal power, like vampires have. That is why Eve's disciples used to eat our eyes. They give youth and regenerate tissue."

Ruby touched her wound and asked, "Will it . . .?"

"I do not know," Sorina said, "but it is powerful medicine nonetheless."

"Thank you," Ruby said and ate the eye.

Ruby returned to the others, and the team of two vampires and five witches descended below the keep. Each flight of stairs seemed more tedious than the last. All they heard was the clicking of their feet stepping on stones for minutes on end.

Pinky decided to break the silence and said, "So, Ruby. I really like Faustina."

"I hope that doesn't mean what I think it means," Ruby mumbled, "but knowing Phoebe's influence on my mother, it probably does."

Laughter echoed through the stairwell as Hayden vigorously expressed his amusement. "I guarantee you it means what you think it means," he said.

Ruby chuckled at Hayden. "I can't believe how mellow you've been about your parents' lifestyle lately."

"What's wrong with it?" Pinky asked.

Ruby sighed. "Nothing . . . Except for the fact it's our parents."

"But personally, I think Pinky is a better choice for Faustina," Hayden said.

"A better choice than your parents?" Ruby asked with an attitude. "Of course he is . . . That doesn't mean my former lover's soulmate is altogether ideal for everyone involved."

"Well, since Faustina and I are the only two involved, I respectfully disagree," Pinky stated.

It was Adam's turn to laugh, and his laughter was contagious. Jinae started giggling, and then Hayden and Ruby started laughing at her. They continued to chat more amicably as the stairs kept going. Ozana wore a small smile while listening to the witches' banter, but Vlad was clearly annoyed and kept to himself.

Finally, the stairs wrapped around a corner, and they could see the room at the end was too large to be another landing. All chatter stopped as they anxiously approached the room. As they searched the room, they realized it was full of empty cells. The only door left to check was made of solid wood, and it was alone at the room's far end. When they approached it, Adam pried it open to discover another stairwell. Everyone, including the vampires, audibly groaned but followed Adam down the steps.

At the landing, there was a small room with a metal door across from the stairs. Pinky approached it and ran his hand down the metal. Jinae did the same thing.

"This door is made of titanium," she whispered. "I think he must be in there."

Hayden pulled on it, expecting it to be locked. Metal screeched against the stone floor as it cracked open. He jerked his hands away like it was hot and looked at Ruby to validate what he'd done was okay. Vlad and Ozana slinked against both sides of the door and listened. Adam glared at Hayden, but Jinae and Pinky just froze and tried not to make even the slightest noises.

"I know you're there, Adam Godwine!" Robin called from the door's other side.

Adam's posture became rigid as he braced himself for confrontation. He placed his hand on the door handle and looked at Ruby. She nodded confidently.

"Everyone, keep close to me," Adam said. "I'm going to shield us."

He opened the door to find Robin sitting on a stack of ornate trunks, surrounded by piles of antiques. Gold, silver, and precious stones covered the mountainous horde of treasures. The magic in the room was palpable, and Adam recognized why. Robin was holding the tapestry.

"I know you came for this," Robin said, holding up a fistful of material while the rest of the tapestry cascaded across his lap and onto the floor.

"Then why didn't you move it elsewhere?" Adam asked.

"It won't leave!" Robin roared. "I brought the cursed thing into the realm, but I can't remove it."

Vlad drawled, "And you have not left without it because . . ."

"If Gaia wants her tapestry here in my home, then she must also want me here," Robin explained, sounding like a madman. "It still smells faintly of Evita." He smirked at Adam. "My Evita."

"*My* wife," Adam whispered, "is gone. Get over it."

Robin's smile grew even more sinister as he shifted his attention to Hayden. "Hayden Rosemont, you traitorous scoundrel .

. . Is your whore mother here, too?"

"I didn't think anything could be more annoying than listening to witches speak," Vlad stated, "but I was wrong."

Robin snapped his attention to Vlad. "I can't tell if I know you. What's truly annoying is how much all bloodsuckers look alike."

Jinae's attention was on the tapestry. They were so close to it. Wondering if she could move it by using her telekinesis from behind Adam's shield, she concentrated. A corner of the fabric was on the floor just past Robin's foot. As she willed it to move, it crept in her direction. Her already racing heart felt like it would burst from her chest. She balled her fists and focused, knowing she needed to put all her power behind one quick action. In a swift, fluid motion, she raised her fists and brought them to her chest as if she imagined herself physically pulling the tapestry from Robin's grasp. Her voice boomed, the battle cry forcing as much power as she could summon into the move. The tapestry flew toward the allies.

Vlad's reflexes were quicker than Robin's, and he grasped the tapestry's edge as it flew at him before Robin could jerk it away. Between Vlad and Jinae, there was a moment of tug-of-war with Robin before Adam reached for the tapestry. When he touched it, the powerful ancient artifact rapidly unraveled. The individual threads faded to dust. As the dust approached the floor, it faded to nothing before their eyes. The priceless map and universal star chart, touched by Gaia and woven from the fabric or reality, was gone.

Ruby's immediate fear was that Robin would disappear in a snap with the tapestry gone. She lunged at him just as he raged and tried to attack Adam. He was more than a head shorter than her, but he was strong. He threw himself behind her to shield his body from the others. He was then on her back with his arm around her throat. He was cackling wildly, believing he had the upper hand. However, Ruby was smiling even as her face turned red from his arm's pressure. She had his hand gripped in hers.

Robin abruptly stopped laughing and his face grew pale when he realized she was draining his power. With his other hand, he snapped. Ruby and Robin both vanished.

Hayden grabbed Adam and violently shook him, screaming, "This is your fault! Do something!"

Adam's power knocked Hayden backwards, and he fell against the stack of trunks, knocking them over. When Hayden scrambled back to his feet, he tried to use his fire gift. Adam shielded.

"I don't want to hurt you, Hayden," Adam said. "Ruby would never forgive me."

When Hayden swung his fist at Adam, Pinky grabbed Hayden from behind and they disappeared. They reappeared just outside the titanium door.

Another snap echoed through the treasure room, and Ruby and Robin reappeared. She was on top of him, pinning him down. He was fighting her, but his movements were sluggish. She was still draining power from him.

"Stop!" he howled. "Get off me, you Amazonian cyclops!"

"Stop fighting me, then!" Ruby roared.

Vlad and Adam reacted, making sure Robin's hands were restrained. Jinae gave them iron to tie to his palms, and they separated his fingers while tying his wrists behind his back. Ozana gagged and blindfolded him with strips of his own tunic.

"How did you get back?" Adam asked, amazed.

"It's his power," Ruby explained the obvious. "It works everywhere in the universes . . . I think he took us to a different Earth, but I used his power to bring us back."

Adam said, "We'll discuss that at length later."

Pinky and Hayden scurried back into the room. Hayden coaxed Ruby off the floor where she was kneeling next to Robin, but Pinky got distracted by an old wooden trunk that had busted open during the scuffle.

A wooden object sat inside on top of a purple silk pillow. Pinky wondered why something so plain would be protected with an ornate box and cushioned with silk. He picked up the object. It was round, like a wreath, but it was the size of a crown. Although, it would not make for a practical crown because it had thorns.

Ozana approached him, studying the object. "It smells like magical blood," she said.

With Robin secured, everyone snooped around the treasure room. Adam and the vampires studied the trunks and piles of treasure closely, but they were not interested in gold or precious stones. Magical relics were their side quest, and they weren't going to leave without collecting any they could find.

Adam found a leather satchel against one of the trunks, so he picked it up and placed a few objects inside as he looked around. Pinky gave him the wooden thorny object to place in the bag. Adam collected bones, vessels, textiles, and other curiosities.

"Why are we stealing these things from the fae?" Hayden asked.

Vlad answered, "Because they stole them first. None of these are fae relics."

"Pinky, do you mind transporting us back to the throne room?" Adam asked.

Adam's team appeared by the throne room's side entrance and carried Robin to the throne. They tied him to it and removed his gag.

Sorina ordered the alliance to shift their defensive circle

around the dais and place Iris on the floor next to Robin's throne.

Sorina, Adam, Ruby, and Vlad stood next to Robin and prepared to interrogate him and solicit his surrender. Vlad had an iron dagger ready for the tyrant monarch's execution. Sorina was ready to read his thoughts. Ruby took almost all of Robin's power and held it within herself before Adam removed his blindfold.

"Will you order your remaining subjects to surrender to us?" Adam asked.

"If you let me live," Robin said, "I promise I will wipe out your tribe. I will do the same to the vampire coven."

"It is what he truly desires," Sorina confirmed. "We cannot reason with him."

"So be it," Vlad said and held the iron blade close to Robin's throat. "Take a deeper look into his thoughts. Find his secrets before I execute him."

There was a snap and Una held her hands toward the alliance and yelled, "Stop!"

Wind strong enough to blast them away from Robin flew from Una's fingertips, but Adam shielded them. He and the others stood firmly around Robin's throne and watched Una, who had arrived surrounded by fairies. She walked with regal patience, approaching the room's center and stopping closer to the dais.

"Una!" Ruby called out before stepping down from the dais and approaching the fairy princess.

"I dreamed of you," Una whispered, studying Ruby's face. "Ruby."

Ruby said, "I dreamed of you, too . . . I found you, and we saved you. You were entombed in the ocean."

"Do you lead this army?" Una asked Ruby.

"Adam Godwine and Sorina Ardelean lead this witch-vampire alliance against Robin Goodfellow," Ruby explained and pointed her hand to Adam and Sorina standing together by the throne. "Adam stands with his people to shield them from your power. Sorina, his partner, stands with her people."

"You are not shielded," Una observed.

"No," Ruby agreed.

"My subjects and I will move closer," Una announced, "and I will step up to the throne to speak with your leaders and confront my brother. Walk with me, Ruby."

Una approached the throne and stood in front of Robin. Ruby took her place by Adam on one side of the throne while Sorina and Vlad remained on the other side. Two of Una's noble fairies stepped forward and flanked her while the rest remained a few steps behind them.

Una reached for her brother and touched his face. "I can barely feel your magic, brother."

"The redhead cyclops took it!" he raved. "Touch her and leave me be!"

Una looked to Ruby, who explained, "I syphoned a significant amount of magic from him. I could return it, but I won't return it to him. He has vowed to kill all my people . . . I can return it to you if you want it."

"The time has come to strike a bargain," Una said, "but I must do something first."

Una reached for Robin's crown. He tried to move his head around to dodge her hands. He snarled and struggled against her, but she patiently worked the carved emerald from his head and raised it high above her head in both hands. Facing her people, she brought it down upon her head and settled it into place. The fairies fell to their knees. She held out her hand, and the fairy beside her placed a velvet bag into her hands. Reaching carefully into the bag, she removed the ruby crown and handed the bag back to the other fairy. She held the crown delicately around the outside as to not touch the iron lining.

As Una raised the ruby crown above Robin's head, he screamed, "No! You useless quim! Get that away from me!"

Una kept a confident posture and serene expression as she faced insults from her own brother and thought of all he'd done to her. She thought of their parents as she placed the crown snugly upon his head and watched him faint. His head nodded forward, but the restraints kept him sitting upright on the throne.

"I may keep him here, sitting on the throne he killed our parents to take, forever," she said.

"We must execute him," Vlad said. "He has vowed to destroy us if we don't."

Una considered Vlad's words and addressed Sorina. "My brother's life is the one item of value I absolutely must gain from our bargain. If I cannot have him, we will not strike a bargain, and I doubt you will survive a battle against this many noble fairies . . . What do you want?"

Sorina held up her hand, signaling to Adam she had something to say before he made demands from Una. She glanced over the fairies standing with Una. Twenty-seven fairies stood against them should negotiations fail. Less than half were fae nobility, but that was still too many to take lightly.

"I am not sure yet," Sorina answered. "First I need to know why he buried you but killed your parents."

"Our mother bound our magic to make it impossible for us to kill each other, so Robin buried me alive," Una explained vaguely. "When we were young, I loved him, and he hated me. As we grew older, those feelings didn't change, but we both wanted to rule alone. I wanted the realm ruled in the light, and he wanted it ruled in darkness."

"Were you meant to rule together?" Adam asked.

"Yes," Una answered. "Oberon and Titania had a religious devotion to the concept of universal balance. The scales of power are clearly tipped to evil now, and I desire to tip them to peace and goodness. However, our parents valued both equally and obsessed over keeping them even. My father and his faction performed terrible deeds throughout the universe with my mother's approval even though her faction, which is now my faction, spread goodness—light . . . They made heirs to replace them if anything should happen to them, and they groomed us to carry on their culture and beliefs . . . We had other ideas."

Sorina nodded to Adam.

"We want you to attend an alliance meeting with us at my home in New York," Adam said. "You need not agree to join the alliance right now, but we want you at a meeting next week for further discussion. We want you to consider a witch-vampire-fae alliance."

"I would require a promise from you," Sorina said to Una. "You may never awaken your brother, and you must also control Robin's subjects hiding in Malta."

"Although I do not know where 'New York' is, I may accept those conditions," Una said. "If we strike a bargain, I will also let Ruby keep my brother's magic for as long as her human body manages to hold it. It is a gift in exchange for freeing me . . . What were you planning to do with Aunt Iris?"

Sorina joined Adam on the other side of Robin's throne where Iris sat on the floor with her back against the chair. Iris' eyes and mouth were covered, and she was still restrained with iron. Sorina forced Iris to face Una and removed her blindfold and gag.

"She has committed no crime against us except refusal to surrender," Sorina said. "She is your family. It is your decision."

"Iris," Una said. "Will you now enter a bargain with me? You may keep your life for as long as you are loyal to me?"

"I am bound to Robin by the same bargain," Iris admitted, sorrow in her voice and expression. "Regretfully, I cannot . . . It is a blessing to see you again, Niece Una. Please, make my death swift and painless."

Una placed her hand on Iris' forehead. A moment later, the older fairy collapsed to the floor. Her eyes were closed, and the hint of a smile graced her lips as if she slept in peaceful dreams. Una snapped, and the body was gone from the dais. She pointed to the other dead fairies, and one of her advisors inspected the bodies before disappearing them.

"If you agree, our bargain will be as follows, and all witnesses here in the realm on both sides will be bound to it," Una announced, returning her attention to Adam and Sorina. "Immediately after your departure, I will go to Malta and disband Robin's faction. I will always keep my brother imprisoned here under the ruby crown. I will appear before your alliance on a date you set with two of my advisors. We will enter peace negotiations at that time . . . You will leave here immediately without harming any living fairies unless they attack you first. You will take your dead with you along with your current possessions. You will not take any additional lives or property apart from what you've already taken. You will never enter the fae realm without my permission . . . We are all magically bound by this bargain for as long as Sorina, Adam, and I shall live . . . Do you both accept this bargain?"

Adam reached for Sorina's hand, and she gripped his tightly, looking at him. He nodded at her, and she faced Una.

Realizing they were about to accept the bargain, Vlad argued, "Sorina, he will kill us if he is ever free!"

Knowing the bargain was the only way to ensure the witch and vampire races survived, Sorina ignored Vlad's protest and said, "We accept this bargain."

Vlad snarled in anger with determination lighting his eyes. He drew back the iron dagger and brought it slamming down toward Robin's neck. At the exact moment before the blade's tip would have pierced skin, Vlad's body froze. A muted grunt escaped his mouth as if he were trying to speak or resist an invisible force. He slowly retracted his arm and stumbled back before dropping dead in front of the throne.

Dragos announced, "Our leaders have made a bargain! Nobody else move against the fae!"

Sorina's breathing turned labored and erratic as she watched Vlad's violent end. Adam pulled her against his chest and pressed her forehead to his. When she heard the unmistakable sound of Ozana's cries, a moan escaped her mouth before she could stop it.

"Not here, my angel," Adam whispered. "We must leave. Take him home and mourn there."

Sorina focused and gently pushed away from Adam. She glared at Una.

"Was it necessary to execute him?" Adam asked Una.

"I did nothing other than create a strong bargain forged from my realm's magic. He was bound to the bargain," Una explained. "The magic has answered crime with consequence."

Sorina scooped Vlad's body into her arms, and Dragos rushed to her aid. He reached for Vlad's body, and she willingly surrendered it to him as Vlad's most trusted disciple.

"Pinky," Sorina said. "Take the rest of our dead to where we started and wait for us."

"Do you think you have power to take the cabal and wait with Pinky?" Adam asked Ruby.

"I think I have much more than that," she whispered. "I will take them and wait for you."

Adam ordered the cabal to go with Ruby. He ordered Jeremy to take the vampires. As he and Sorina stood watch, Pinky vanished from the throne room, followed by the cabal before the vampires vanished. Adam and Sorina stood alone before Una and her people.

Una had been observing Adam and Sorina together, and she glanced between them for a moment then said, "Your alliance is bonded with love . . . I admire that."

"How shall I deliver your invitation to my home?" Adam asked.

"You were careful not to mention Selene's gate," Una said, "but I sense its power humming close by. We will discuss it later. For now, keep it safe. Nothing breaches the realm without my knowledge as ruler and protector . . . Opening Selene's gate will not defile our bargain if you don't step through. When you want to call, open it and wait there. I will come."

"Until next time, your majesty," Adam said. "Be blessed."

"Blessed be," Una replied.

Adam pulled Sorina against his body, and she locked her arms around his neck. The fairies let them fly across the room and out the window. Sorina closed her eyes and buried her face in Adam's neck as he soared high above the realm toward the gate where the alliance waited in safety, eager to return home.

MATERIAL RELIGION

Adam had a house full of battle-weary witches. Vampires were on the way, and a fairy queen was scheduled to arrive after lunch. After millennia of maintaining steady control while separated from the divine and other supernatural beings, the year 2320 had triggered a change explosion. His old standpoint had burned to ashes in less than two years, and he felt like a phoenix rising from the ashes with a new life and another chance to serve his father and his people.

He stood at the window behind his desk and watched the sun rise across his garden, attempting to cultivate a peaceful mindset to begin the busy and complicated day. He hadn't bothered to get dressed after taking a shower to throw off lethargy. A breeze passed through the open window, blowing through his robe. It felt good on his skin. His back was to the office door, but he heard it open and close, and he heard the lock engage.

As he gathered his open robe and began tying it at the waist, he said, "You're up early. How does your eye feel today?"

"I am not Ruby," Sorina said. "No need to cover yourself . . . It is time I finally see my partner, completely revealed."

He spun around to face his partner, surprised at her presence ahead of schedule. They hadn't seen each other in days and hadn't been alone together since before the battle. Their people had needed them in the battle's aftermath, and they'd both had too many important responsibilities to ignore for long enough to spend time together. Her simple cotton dress inflamed his desire.

Sorina's trademark catsuit and combat boots suited her and drove Adam wild, but he loved seeing her in a dress. She truly looked like the angel he believed her to be, standing before him covered in thin white material and wearing a playful smile. The morning light shone through the dress, accentuating her body's curves.

She purposefully walked slowly to meet him. Her hungry eyes took their time devouring the sight of his naked skin and his hardening manhood. Starting at his chest, she slid one hand around the back of his neck and ran her other hand down his body. Her fingers lightly brushed down the length of his cock before she wrapped her hand firmly around it.

He gripped her wrist gently and said, "Are you sure we're not rushing the moment? I have a special night planned tonight for our first time together."

"We're thousands of years old, Adam," she whispered. "We're beyond grand romantic gestures and setting up perfect moments . . . This moment, in the morning calm together, belongs to us."

As his hand slipped away from her wrist, Sorina dropped to her knees before him, and he wove his fingers through her silky black hair. She teased him with a few firm strokes of her hand before sliding her lips down his length.

Adam inhaled deeply at the feel of her sharp vampire teeth barely sliding along his shaft's sensitive skin. He tightened his grip on her hair. As his grip grew tighter, he felt her mouth lock onto him. He moaned, feeling her suck him slowly, passionately from base to tip. After the first taste, both the speed and intensity of her fellations crescendoed until Adam's legs were too shaky for him to stand.

As he leaned back against his desk for support, Sorina felt him tugging her hair, guiding her to move with him. She slid her knees forward a pace, his apparent pleasure provoking her desire to feel him come undone in her mouth. She relaxed her throat as he held her head still and thrusted once. When she tasted his release, she held him in her mouth and savored it while he let go of her hair and watched her.

Even though Adam could feel her throat constrict around him as she swallowed, he still didn't feel close enough to her. His desire to know every part of her mind, body, and soul was intoxicating. He reached behind his neck and hit his implant with enough magic to disable it.

Sorina heard a noise she couldn't place and looked up at him.

Adam saw the question in her eyes and said, "I want you to read my thoughts and know me as deeply as possible."

She shook her head. "I should not—it is impossible for me to reciprocate."

He lifted her from the floor and held her against his body. "I will give you every piece of me possible, and you will do the same for me."

"I want nothing more than that," she breathed. "If you could read thoughts, mine would already be laid bare for you, I swear it."

Cupping her chin, he lifted her face to his and begged, "Please, look at me. See all of me and understand what you mean to me."

Sorina let go and felt as if her consciousness was falling into Adam's green hypnotic gaze. She recognized his love, compassion, and envito, but she also experienced his fear, anger, and jealousy. She understood he wanted her to see his every truth but couldn't recall them all.

He opened his most important memories to her, and she read all the wonderful, terrible, shameful, and prideful thoughts he associated with those memories. He wanted her to know he'd killed hundreds of his own descendants. She saw he'd also sacrificed and provided for thousands of them. He wanted her to know he'd slept with Ruby to control her parents, which wasn't even his most recent regret.

His most recent regret was making decisions that had resulted in her injuries at the solstice celebration. She saw his love for Eve and how much it paled in comparison to his absolute devotion to her from the moment he'd saved her life.

Stepping back from Adam, Sorina kicked off her sandals then gathered her dress and lifted it over her head. She took his hands, pulled him off the desk, and traded places with him. Sliding the robe off his shoulders, she kissed him before sitting on the desk and reclining back. She bit her finger and squeezed it until a drop of blood formed on the fingertip before spreading her legs and rubbing the blood around her labia.

Adam went to his knees and lifted her legs over his shoulders as he fervently shoved his face between her legs to lick the precious blood gift from her delicious cunt. From the moment his tongue tasted her immortal magic, he felt like he'd orgasm again without even a touch from her. The blood magic's taste, mixed with her womanly taste, unhinged his desire. All he could think about was an intense hunger for her, which drove his stamina to nibble and lick her for his own pleasure.

Sorina's cries filled the air as her pleasure reached a fever pitch. Her rational mind knew the other vampires in the house could hear her, and maybe the witches could too, but her rational mind was not in charge. Her mind was lost to physical ecstasy and deep emotion, so she continued to scream freely as her body quaked at climax.

Adam stood between her legs and watched her breathing heavily. "I've never seen you so beautiful as you are right now," he whispered.

Coming to her senses, she said, "I think I was too loud."

"We'll fix that," he said, sliding his cock into her and placing one hand on her shoulder. "Open your mouth."

She obeyed, and he gagged her with the edge of his other

hand. The crevice between his index finger and thumb was in her mouth. He pushed down with his hand and gripped her face while also tightening his grip on her shoulder as he started thrusting into her.

"Sorina, bite into my hand," he said breathlessly, increasing the rhythm of the fuck. "Drink from me."

Her eyes grew wide and wild as she pierced his skin and sucked at the bleeding flesh. The harder he gripped her face, the deeper she sank her teeth. When she heard him hiss in pain, she wrapped her legs around his waist and encouraged him to fuck harder. Between the blood, sex, and magic, she lingered on the edge of another orgasm.

Adam felt her body rock as she came all over him. Her sexual release prompted him to slide his hands down her body and grip her ass to thrust harder and deeper until he was spent.

He took his time admiring her body in the afterglow of lovemaking. She reached for him, and he pulled her up against his chest.

Sorina was again sitting on the desk's edge, and she kept her legs locked around Adam. She bit her tongue and kissed him, giving him another small gift to tenderly end their first encounter as lovers.

"Nixie Delmar?" Jeremy asked, repeating the full name Nixie had adopted. "No middle name?"

Nixie was in the pool at Adam's Sands Point home with Jeremy, Ruby, Giselle and Hayden. The entire cabal had been staying on the property for several days to decompress from battle. Adam was concerned for everyone's mental health following the brutality and loss they'd experienced, so they had been asked not to work or go to the office for a week.

Therapists, healers, yoga trainers, and other personnel hired to cultivate the witches' physical and mental health came and went from the house as well, but they'd left for the day.

Nixie was free to change into her mermaid form and splash around in the pool with her new friends. Even though she was almost a thousand years older than Ruby and Giselle, she felt comfortable around them. Since most of her life had been spent in solitude, there were many things they could teach her. Because of her long life, they found her stories fascinating.

She continued her conversation with Jeremy, explaining, "Since a middle name isn't required, I didn't see the point."

"You don't use a middle name, Jeremy," Giselle called to him from across the pool where she lounged alone in a giant inflatable unicorn.

"Yeah, but you and Hayden do," Jeremy argued.

From beside Nixie, Hayden replied, "Don't drag me into this."

Ruby swam up behind Jeremy and said, "Stop bugging her about her new name."

Jeremy looked back at her and jumped. "Shit!"

"What?" she said.

"Pull your sunshades down," Jeremy snapped and made a gesture at his eye, mirroring hers. "Your eye situation is really scary right now."

"Oh? You mean the evil twin I'm growing out of my face?" Ruby asked. "Should I rub it on you, so you get used to it? Come here, baby brother. Give Ru a hug!"

She chased after him, and he splashed her while swimming away and yelling, "Get away from me!"

Jeremy had been teasing her relentlessly about her wound because it was undergoing bizarre changes, but Ruby was in good spirits about it. Her eye was healing and growing, and she was being patient with the process. She was hopeful that she'd eventually have a new eye and be able to see with it. Because she'd ingested a noble fairy's eyes and absorbed large amounts of immortal power from Robin, Sorina and Adam thought Ruby had a good chance of regaining sight in the eye.

So far, all she had was a droopy red eyelid with a half-formed eyeball underneath. It looked like her eyelid was open about a centimeter with a solid white marble peeking out of her eye socket. Ruby thought she looked possessed by a demon, but she enjoyed terrorizing her brother with it, especially on days it leaked fluids. She was at peace with not knowing the outcome, but she had faith it would get better one way or another.

"Why don't you get a normal eye transplant?" Jeremy asked.

"There's too much magic in the wound, Dork," Ruby said. "The fairy and Adam both altered the tissue in it. The surgeon couldn't do it properly."

"I think my lovely partner can do much better than a *normal* eye anyway," Hayden argued. "I'm hopeful it will be a nice shade of purple and capable of firing lasers."

"If I can fire lasers," Ruby said, "Jeremy will be my first practice target."

Ruby cooly slid her sunshades down from her head to cover her eyes as Jeremy splashed her face again. She tried to splash him back, but he dodged the water and laughed at her.

While Jeremy was still laughing with his mouth wide open, Nixie flipped her fishtail out of the water and splashed him hard. Jeremy started coughing, and Ruby giggled uncontrollably while Nixie only smiled.

Nixie ducked below the surface and swam laps. The others observed her scales sparkling in the sunlight while her golden hair danced under the water. Even after standing in the presence of deities, riding in spaceships, and experiencing the fae realm, Nixie's mermaid form fascinated the witches in a different way. Her magic was beautiful in the same way Adam's magic was powerful. She was to beauty what Gaia was to enlightenment.

Nixie had accepted Adam's offer to live in the house until she decided what she wanted to do with her freedom. Because she'd never been to school, he planned to have her grade school documentation forged, hire tutors, and ensure she was prepared to take university entrance exams if she chose a future in academia. Otherwise, he would bankroll any other interest or profession she chose.

Nixie swam under Giselle's float and surfaced next to it, propping her arms on the float next to Giselle's head.

The others decided it was time to have a drink and gathered close to them. The float included a drink cooler compartment, and Giselle had filled it with beer, wine, and sparkling water for herself. Jeremy climbed into the float with Giselle while Hayden and Ruby draped their arms over the side opposite of Nixie.

"Have you thought about where you want to live or work?" Giselle asked Nixie, handing her and Ruby servings of wine.

"I was actually thinking of going back to Point Oubliette and helping with research and cleanup projects," Nixie explained. "Adam said he'd build me a house on Solo Island, and he said Faustina could help me get involved with the work out there."

Giselle pouted and moaned, "That's so far away."

Ruby said, "If she decides to go, Jeremy can bring her back to New York to visit sometimes."

"I know, but I'll still miss her," Giselle said.

"Let's change the subject to something fun," Nixie suggested. "Anyone else hear Sorina screaming this morning?"

"I'm happy for her," Giselle stated. "She deserved a good fuck."

Ruby and Jeremy cackled loudly while Nixie gave a little giggle.

Footsteps echoed from the house, and they turned their attention to the noise as Adam approached the pool with Una and two more fairies, Gyn and Bry. Adam had told everyone to expect the fae queen and her advisors, but they were surprised to see them so early in the afternoon since the alliance meeting wasn't until after dinner.

"Good afternoon, Cohens, Rosemonts, and Ms. Delmar," Adam said pleasantly. "I'm giving Una and her advisors an estate tour . . . Una, I believe you already know Nixie and Ruby by name. The other redhaired beauty is Giselle."

"Well met, Nixie, Ruby, Giselle," Una said, nodding to the women.

"Pleased to meet you, your majesty" Giselle said. "This is my partner, Jeremy. He's Ruby's brother."

Una nodded. "Well met, Jeremy."

"It's an honor to meet you properly," Jeremy said.

"And this is my partner, Hayden," Ruby said. "He's Giselle's brother."

"Welcome to New York, your majesty," Hayden said.

"Well met, Hayden, and thank you," Una said. "It is my pleasure to introduce my two most trusted advisors and friends, Gyn and Bry."

Not quite in unison, the witches enthusiastically greeted Una's friends and offered them smiles. The fairies kept blank expressions and only nodded. Their golden eyes watched the witches as if they were trying to see into their souls. Gyn was a female even shorter than Una, but Bry was tall for a fairy. He stood a head above Una, and as her most skilled warrior, he had a thick, muscular build.

After Adam led them away to tour the stables, Giselle said, "Are all fairies that intense?"

"For the most part," Nixie said, "but most of them have been alive longer than anyone else on the Blue Earth, so it makes them different."

Once again, Adam had the round table brought to Sands Point and placed in the ballroom because he wanted to send a strong message to the fairy queen that everyone was equal at his table. Meeting invitees arrived and congregated around the table. Dragos and Ozana flanked Sorina. Gyn and Bry flanked Una. Ruby and Ty flanked Adam. Since the entire cabal was present, they filled in the rest of the space. Nixie had joined the cabal, but had yet to attend an internal meeting, so the alliance meeting was her first time at the round table.

Ty called the meeting to order and then announced, "On behalf of the alliance between the Faithful Watchtower Cabal and the Ardelean Coven, I welcome Queen Una and her advisors to the round table." The fairies nodded and Ty continued, "The agenda this evening includes funeral arrangements for Sylvia and the departed vampires, an addition to the magical object catalogue, and the Daughters of Selene's archway."

It didn't take long for the alliance to discuss funeral arrangements since all the deceased had lived in Romania with Sorina. The decision to observe vampire funeral rites for Sylvia seemed like a natural decision to the witches after Duncan's funeral.

The vampires wanted to conduct all the rites together in one ceremony. Again, the witches readily agreed because one trip to Romania was easier to plan than several, especially with most of the witches involved in liquidating Dust.

Fairies didn't have funerals for their dead. When a fairy died, a noble's touch dispersed the fairy's essence throughout the universe. Their magical energy went into all things. They had observed many funerals in their lives, spanning cultures, universes, and time. Because the concept was born of Eden, they didn't fully understand its significance.

"I understand Eve is recently deceased," Una said. "Did she receive funeral rites?"

Nobody answered. Ruby's right hand was busy documenting the meeting on her tablet, but she nonchalantly slid her left hand along the table, placed it over Adam's, and gently held it.

Adam realized everyone waited for him to answer, but it took him a moment to collect his thoughts. The way Eve had to die and then unceremoniously leave the world still bothered him.

"Our creator, my father, took her body to Eden," Adam stated. "There was no funeral."

"Eve first arrived in the fae realm with my brother," Una explained. "When my father made her his concubine, the rift between father and son widened. Over hundreds of years, she, my father, and my brother conspired to commit countless crimes in the name of evil. However, she and my brother committed high treason when they imprisoned me. It is the most egregious crime a witch has ever committed against the fae."

Adam was beginning to feel uncomfortable because Una clearly felt the wrongs done to her had yet to be righted. An unknown demand for justice from Una's lips was looming unstated, and it threatened to destroy the fragile peace. With one glance at Sorina, he could tell she already knew a hidden truth.

"Therefore," Una continued, "it is my solemn duty to inform you, the Green Earth's Eve has been executed for her crimes."

"That's not the way it works!" Ruby snapped. "On the Green Earth, Sorina's soulmate killed mine, yet here we sit at this table as allies."

A low roar of chatter in hushed tones spread around the table. Trent stumbled away from his chair and threw up on the floor. Giselle called the household staff to assist Trent and huddled close to Jeremy. Leilani was too shaken to calm anyone.

Sorina stared at Ruby, obviously shocked at her statement before regaining her wits and cutting her eyes to Una. "You did this before you came here because you knew we would not approve," she shouted above the chatter, which subsided at the sound of her booming voice. "This is why the fae cannot be trusted!"

"Sorina, please," Adam said holding up his hand.

Sorina argued, "No, Adam. This is unacceptable. She has effectively started a war with the Green Earth witches, and when they come for her, she will try to punish you for their perceived war crimes as well!"

"Why should they seek war?" Una asked.

The table fell silent in the wake of Sorina's statement and Una's question. Phoebe rubbed Trent's back while he drank water and tried to calm his nerves. Bastion looked livid while the other witches looked terrified. The vampires and the fairies waited for Adam to speak again.

"Adam," Ruby whispered, her voice trembling. "Say something."

"Una, you have crossed a line you can't come back from," Adam explained, speaking to her directly. "When our souls were split, both halves were given free will. Green Eve was not responsible for Blue Eve's crimes. The alliance's goal is universal peace, but that is near impossible now . . . My hope is to keep peace with you, but we can no longer offer you alliance membership if you do not accept responsibility for murder and wrongdoing."

"I have done what I judged right," Una answered. "I have lived longer than anyone here, and I know what is good and right." She addressed Sorina, saying, "I executed Eve before I arrived here because it needed to be done, and I don't answer to you."

"How is executing Eve good and right if it leads to my people's extinction?" Adam asked. "You do not know everything, especially not everything about the Children of Eden. You are correct that you don't answer to us, but a righteous leader would have consulted us. Your decision was wrong because of your lack of information . . . Green Eve's death makes the road to peace exponentially harder."

"Your hubris is astounding," Nixie interjected, surprising everyone. "It reminds me of your brother . . . In terms I think you can understand, it comes down to recognizing and respecting the leadership of other races represented here as they recognize your sovereignty."

Una whispered to Gyn, who addressed Nixie. "As a half-breed former slave, Queen Una will not negotiate directly with you. Though you have no right to judge my queen, we will consider your argument."

"I am the last mermaid and represent my entire race," Nixie announced. "My right to parle with the queen is equal to that of Adam and Sorina . . . Furthermore, Una wouldn't have made it back to the fae realm from Romania without my help."

"We acknowledge your help," Bry said. "That is why we will consider your argument."

"I will consider everything said here today," Una said. "I accept Adam's decision to withhold an alliance offer to my people, but I share his desire for peace and wish to continue this meeting if that is acceptable to our host?"

Sorina was hesitant to agree but nodded to Adam, and he said, "To be clear, this table is round to symbolize everyone's equal rights to be here and to contribute for the greater good. I lead my people, so I speak to you on their behalf, but they have rights to speak and to question us."

"When you make decisions in a vacuum without the people's input, mistakes are made," Sorina interrupted. "Adam has explained as much already . . . My apologies for interrupting, Adam."

Adam continued without acknowledging the apology, "Trent, are you well? We require your input."

"I'm very fucking far from well, Adam," Trent answered. "What do you want to know?"

"I've been remiss in not inquiring until now," Adam said gently. "Tell us about Green Eve."

Trent placed his elbows on the table and wiped his eyes with his palms. He met his soulmate's eyes across the table, and he found empathy in them. Realizing he'd not been so emotionally wrecked since his wife's death, he glanced at Ruby and sighed before closing his eyes to gather thoughts and words.

Leaning forward with crossed arms, he said, "She was every bit as brutally unhinged as Blue Eve, but she was loyal to her people and her Adam. To my knowledge, she only killed within the confines and the laws of war. She saved my life many, many times . . . Green Adam's tribe is hardened by years of war and fighting for survival. They will not rest until they find a way to retaliate. We must prepare . . . As a team, Pinky and I can move between the two Earths for negotiations, although I've not suggested it before because Adonai warned me to stay here."

Trent finished speaking and leaned back in his chair. He

reached inside his jacket and removed a silver case. When he opened it and took out a cigarette, nobody reprimanded him. His hands trembled as he tried and failed to strike a match twice. Hayden leaned around Phoebe and held out his finger to the cigarette, lighting it for him.

"Thank you, Trent," Adam said, "but I have other ideas for travel between Earths. They will be expounded shortly in relation to the relic, which we'll present now."

Jeremy slid the thorned wreath into the table's center and explained, "We took this from Robin, and it was in our possession when you arrived in the Emerald Keep. It has undergone scientific and magical analysis, and we know it is saturated with Edenian blood and DNA almost identical to Adam's."

The fairies nodded as Jeremy explained the magical object before them, but their faces remained expressionless.

Realizing the fairies wouldn't respond unless specifically asked, Adam added, "Tell me everything you know about it."

"It's a crown of torture belonging to one of your Children of Eden on the Red Earth," Una said. "A band of knights left it with us along with several other boxes of treasure not long before I was buried."

Adam had suspected it wasn't from the Blue Earth because an analysis showed the type of wood it was made of didn't exist. However, he expected it to be from the Green Earth. To his knowledge, there were no Children of Eden on the Red Earth.

"My father did not send witches to the Red Earth," Adam stated.

Una smiled knowingly and smoothly replied, "My father did."

"I smell a fairy bargain gone wrong," Dragos mumbled.

"Indeed, it did," Una said. "One must take care with any

bargain, but bargaining with evil fairies is especially dangerous . . . Although the witches didn't know my father was a fairy. They prayed to their god for help, and my father appeared and told them he was sent to help. The witches built a great boat during a flood but lost their way and almost died. Robin said they ran out of provisions and wouldn't slaughter the livestock. I don't know the bargain's details, but I know the witches expected to be taken to a part of the Blue Earth where floods had already subsided. My father and Robin laughed for centuries about transporting them to the Red Earth and leaving them there without ties to their family or their magic."

For thousands of years, Adam thought Noah and his family had perished in the great flood. The world remembered the flood because of stories others had told and retold about Noah's great boat. It had been a marvelous structure to behold at the time, and everyone told tales that got more and more outrageous as years passed. Some witches had even asked to sail with Noah, but he'd refused to take anyone but his immediate family. Most other witches had traveled east with Adam. In theory, it had been a good idea to build a boat for saving beasts of the land from drowning. In reality, Noah had been lost while others had found their ways through the catastrophe. Food had been scarce in the mountains during those years, but the tribe's magical gifts had ensured their survival.

"Why am I not even surprised Noah's great boat is a real story?" Phoebe asked aloud to herself.

"Because you met a robot-god-alien, then you went to a parallel dimension and fought fairies," Ty deadpanned.

Phoebe smiled and pointed her finger at him. "I think you're onto something."

Nixie giggled.

"Don't encourage them," Jinae said to Nixie.

"About this crown . . . Who wore it?" Adam asked.

"I don't know," Una admitted. "The knights valued it immeasurably, but I do not know why."

"Secure it, Jeremy," Adam commanded.

As Jeremy took the crown of thorns from the room, Adam contemplated what had taken place over the last week and what he had learned from the meeting. Between the trouble Una had made for him on the Green Earth and the trouble her family had made for part of his tribe on the Red Earth, Adam was even more committed to the cabal's plan to avoid relinquishing any part of the archway to the fae.

"We need control of the archway," Adam said. "It's the only way we can possibly search for any descendants left on the Red Earth. It's also the best way to attempt repairing relationships with Trent's people on the Green Earth."

"It must be safeguarded," Una stated.

Sorina argued, "It already is. We protect it. Additionally, we are bound by your bargain not to enter your realm. What else could you possibly want?"

"You cannot let anyone in," Una said. "If you will not surrender a key to us, I require a bargain explicitly keeping you from sending anyone from any Earth into my realm in exchange for keeping all the keys."

"Sorina?" Adam asked.

"It is a bargain," Sorina said.

Una smiled. As she stood from the table, her advisors followed suit. She nodded to Adam, then to Sorina. To everyone's surprise, she also nodded to Nixie.

"Thank you for your hospitality," Una said. "Although we do not leave here part of your alliance, we leave here in peace."

With a snap, the fairies were gone. The table erupted in a symphony of sighs. The room's tension dissipated, but dull anxiety remained. They had started the day hoping a peaceful future had already been fought and won. The cabal had been looking forward to a pleasant tomorrow along a smooth path, but the universe had other plans for them.

"Someone say something positive," Pinky said.

"I read some of their thoughts," Ozana said. "They do not intend to betray us."

"No," Phoebe agreed. "They're not purposefully problematic."

"They're more socially awkward than Hayden," Giselle said, "which is really saying something."

Nixie snorted.

"I told you not to encourage them," Jinae whispered. "They'll never shut up."

"I hope they don't," Nixie said with a smile. "I love having friends."

The cabal still faced a messy road to peace littered with risky missions and unknown foes, but their progress was an achievement to celebrate, not something to take for granted. Continuing the journey was a blessing not everyone received, and they honored the dead by embracing the future and maintaining good works. Friends, family, and lovers had been lost, but they were remembered. In the spaces between trials, new friendships blossomed, and roots grew deeper on the family tree.

EPILOGUE: COSMOGENESIS RELIC

Wiltshire, England, Red Earth, 1314 A.D.

English, French, and Spanish outlaw knights prowled through a frosty spring countryside, protected only by God and the darkness of an overcast night sky. Their white tunics adorned with red crosses were like targets for papal assassins' arrows, so they abandoned them before continuing across an open meadow. Once they were standing among the stones, they each took a knee. In a tight huddle around their treasure, they tried in vain to read their map in the pitch-black air.

Reeling from their grand master's death, a last remnant of the fallen Christian military order carried four wooden chests that housed what was left of their once unlimited wealth and power. After the church declared them heretics, the knights had worked quickly to protect their legacy. They had gifted a large property in Malta to the fae, making a bargain requiring the fae to hide as much Templar treasure as the knights could bring to them.

The Knights Templar and the fae had been allies since the Second Crusade, when Oberon had recognized their power and influence across Europe and their growing ties to the occult. Powerful magical objects had consistently found their ways into the knights' possession over a short time span of two centuries, which impressed and fascinated Oberon.

A stone glowed, casting light over their map. The knights slowly looked up to observe the light's intensity waxing around a humanoid silhouette.

She stepped out of the stone like an angel floating from a mausoleum, graceful yet powerful. They'd never seen a woman dressed in armor, and she was so tall. She couldn't be a fairy. Her body was covered in the ornate armor from head to toe. Only her fair face and contrasting black hair remained visible beneath her copper helmet adorned with silver and emeralds.

"Follow me," Sorina said.

ABOUT THE AUTHOR

Mrs. DeWillow, also known as the Wasted Wordsmith, leads a semi-vagabond, extra-marvelous life working for the Man. When she's not toiling for coin or occupied with family and her menagerie of evil pets, she enjoys writing and drinking gin.

www.ingramcontent.com/pod-product-compliance
Lightning Source LLC
Chambersburg PA
CBHW061923170626
46813CB00006B/2279